Then
COMES
THE FLOOD

Then
COMES
THE FLOOD

John Payne

XULON PRESS ELITE

Xulon Press Elite
2301 Lucien Way #415
Maitland, FL 32751
407.339.4217
www.xulonpress.com

Printed in the United States of America.

Paperback ISBN-13: 978-1-6312-9992-6
Hardcover ISBN-13: 978-1-6312-9993-3
eBook ISBN-13: 978-1-6312-9994-0

For Cher, who believes

March 2003

"I feel dirty."

Nurse Suzan Winders removed the blood pressure cuff and dropped it onto the table beside the monitor. "It's over, Megan."

"I don't remember anything. What was it?"

"It wasn't anything. It's nothing. Get over it."

Megan raised her head to get a better view of the nurse's face. *Why is she talking this way? Why is she so cold toward me? What did I do wrong?*

Nurse Winders pulled a pen from her side pocket and made a few final entries on the pad she held. Megan's vital signs were good, and the nurse walked Megan to the recovery room. She cried all the way. Nurse Winders didn't say a word.

Megan remembered seeing her baby during the ultrasound. Nurse Winders had the screen turned where Megan could see, but when Megan looked, the nurse turned it away. *She's taunting me,* Megan thought. Once she saw her baby, Megan wanted to change her mind, but she decided it was too late, so she let it happen. "I just wondered if it was a boy or a girl. I want to know so I won't have to wonder about it."

"Megan, the best thing to do is to forget about all this. Take my advice. You got yourself in trouble, and we fixed it. Believe me, you should be glad—we solved your problem. When you're a little older, you'll see we did you a favor."

***

On the drive home, Megan and her mom talked freely. "How do you feel?"

"It wasn't the worst pain I've experienced. I cramped up in the recovery room, but I cried so hard my body forgot about cramping. I wish I hadn't done it, Mom. That nurse, Ms. Winders, tried to make me feel guilty, and it worked. I've murdered my baby. She said it wasn't a baby, but I couldn't tell if she meant it or not. Either way, she acted like I had done something wrong. I know I did, but she didn't have to pass judgment on me."

"Who knows what makes people act the way they do, honey? I'm sure that nurse has had countless patients go through her hands—enough to develop an attitude of resentment. Let's try to forget it and move on with our lives."

Megan raised herself from the pad she put in the car seat to see if there was any sign of bleeding. Her belly pains were worse than she thought they would be. "I'm disgusted with my life right now, Mom. I made a mistake. This is not what I wanted to do, but I didn't see any other way. You and Dad were right. Murder is never the right thing to do."

"Megan, your dad and I didn't think you were deciding that. We weren't calling it that."

"I know. You didn't say it, but it's there all the same. I had a baby I didn't want, and now I don't have the baby I wanted."

"Megan, none of us asked for any of this to happen, but it did, and we can't change any of it. You know your dad and I love you, and we will do everything we can to support you. We will help you deal with this."

CHAPTER 1

February 2019

"Number 472," the loudspeaker announced. Megan stopped at McDonald's for a cup of coffee to go. It beat driving in the wrong direction to her regular coffee shop, and it saved time. *Need to save a little time,* she mused. She placed her order inside for the same reason—waiting in a long line at the drive-through was next to impossible. She exchanged her ticket for the coffee. *Number 472. How did they serve so many before seven o'clock?*

As usual, but this morning in particular, with snow-covered roads causing slower driving, she had allowed more time than necessary to make it to the prosecutor's office, so why the need to save time? The truth is she hated to wait, and waiting in line is a waste of time.

Saving time. Time is of the essence. That phrase punctuates every proposal Megan's company sends to customers. To Megan, essence is not just about time. It's more than just performing by the date specified. It means attention to detail—every act, large or small, demands attention, with no distractions, no waste of time anywhere in the process. Lose that focus, lose the essence.

That's what caused the accident in the first place. A simple distraction caused everything, she thought. *Now my days are filled with an ever-present memory of that tragedy. Time has lost its essence.*

On the day of the accident, Megan went to the library to scan some old clippings related to her current St. Jude project. She stopped at an ATM and put the cash in her handbag on the floorboard. Looking away for a split second, she felt a little jolt. An oncoming car tapped the front bumper on the passenger side of her car. "Where did that car come from?" she questioned aloud to no one.

Megan applied the brakes, but her car was motionless. She hadn't accelerated at all. In that split second, a driver swerved and lost control, sliding sideways into a steel light pole that crushed the side of the car behind the passenger-side door. Megan remembered a moment of dead silence before she understood what had happened.

She ran to the other car, which had traveled a couple of hundred feet before it crashed. It looked all banged up, and she saw a young woman with two kids in the car. She called 911.

Picturing events of that day gave Megan a sad, empty flush. Over the last few months since the accident, Megan developed a respect for Kayla Dean, the driver of that car. Kayla and her daughter were not severely injured, but her seven-month-old son, Danny, died a few days after the crash.

Another driver had pulled into the street and caught the back of Kayla's car as she passed. Kayla lost control and crossed into the oncoming lane, where she clipped Megan's front bumper.

If I had pulled out a second sooner, Kayla might have crashed into my car instead of that light pole. Her baby might still be alive. If I had not taken a second to open my handbag, that would have been enough. Split seconds. Infinitesimal events happening in nanoseconds create eternal results—the essence of time.

***

Snow, packed in mounds on both sides of the street, muffled the sounds of driving. Megan placed her coffee in the cup holder and her handbag in front of the passenger-side seat. She checked a text her dad had sent. He was asking about the weather—"That's my dad," she whispered. *He knows it's snowing and so cold. He's just checking to be sure I'm okay, as he does.*

She knew his real concern was her meeting with detective Williams, or Jack, as Megan had come to know him. Her dad asked why the detective wanted to meet in his office. Doesn't that seem a little unusual? Yes, but he has requested that I meet with him in his office a couple of times before. Doesn't that seem a bit curious? Yes, but—

Megan wondered the same thing. *Why does Jack want these one-on-one meetings? The questions he asks are about the case, and he makes the personal ones seem to be related to the case. Surely, he's not trying to establish an extra-court-case social relationship. Probably not, he's having office meetings with Kayla as well.*

She let the suspicious side of her mind wander. *Is Jack just being thorough, making sure he has all the available facts? Maybe he's looking for more evidence that might change the structure of the case, evidence that might point in a new direction, a direction leading toward Kayla or me? Does he suspect there's more to this story than what is on the table? Why does he require meetings with us one-on-one? Is he searching for incriminating evidence? Am I a suspect? Is Jack . . . wait . . . wait . . . that's silly. Why would he do that? Jack is on our side. Kayla is the victim here. Her kids are victims, but I'm not. I'm involved because my car was a part of the accident, even though it sat dead still while the crash happened all around me.*

The rear of her car experienced a slight swerve. "Whoa," she declared. *Driving this morning is more like sledding. Slow down and pay attention.*

She decided to confront Jack directly.

***

"So, what's going on, Jack? What's all this about? Why is Kayla not here?"

"I don't know what you're asking, Megan. I apologize for any confusion I may have caused. I'm just doing my job. There's no quick victory expected in this trial, and I owe it to the DA to prepare the best case for conviction."

"Have I withheld anything, any evidence? Has Kayla?"

"Of course not, but we believe the defense is up to no good. We don't know any of the details, but one thing we know for sure; Frank Zingeralli is as good as they come. He has a long history of successful defense in Judge McCain's court. He even appeared before her as a teenager when she was a Juvenile Court judge, and Frank was still a wayward youth. She might even accept a share of responsibility for straightening him out. The point is, they go way back. Judge McCain knows Frank is not going to waste the court's time, and she will allow whatever he presents. We've got to be ready."

"Isn't that a conflict of interest on her part?" Megan asked.

"Not at all. Sending a troubled kid down a road that leads him to become the best attorney around doesn't create prejudice. Just the opposite."

"What should we do?"

"That's what I want to discuss. Kayla and I will meet a little later. I'm meeting with the two of you separately because this is not a team strategy. I just want the facts, without any influence the two of you may have on one another. I need the view from both sides, not for inconsistencies that question guilt, but answering those inconsistencies to prevent any assumption of guilt."

"Shouldn't you talk with Mark Jones? He's the one who caused this. Who else have you interviewed?"

"I've spoken to the defendant and Zingeralli together. Jones is not telling the truth. I've been to the scene a dozen times, to discover what happened. If he fabricated this story about the homeless girl, why was he in the strip center parking lot? Had he stopped to purchase something at one of the shops—cigarettes, coffee, a snack? What? I talked with employees in every store in that center. A few of the stores closed that day, and people in the others don't recall Jones being there. It's an older center without cameras and no cameras on the street. I checked everything but came away with no clues. I know Zingeralli has checked everything too."

"I didn't even know Mark Jones was involved in the accident right away," Megan said. "I saw Kayla's car come past me and slam into that pole. I didn't see Mark until he came to check on Kayla after I called 911. And I never even saw his car, so I can't vouch for anything he says either way."

Jack ran his finger alongside the notes he kept of the investigation. "It doesn't add up," he said.

CHAPTER 2

Mark Jones stood near the full-length lancet windows framing one side of his attorney's cathedral-like office balanced atop a downtown Memphis skyscraper. Staring at the snowed-in city below, he could count the few blocks from the courthouse to the jailhouse. He pulled the cap off the twelve-ounce stadium cup he held, still filled with coffee now cold from inattention.

One side of a heated telephone conversation boomed from an adjacent office, with staccato proclamations jammed into the phone, like a referee calling out a boxer knocked to the canvass. The referee's hand goes down with each count.

"It will never work," he heard. "This idea of yours won't work. Not with this judge. In the most conservative town, in the most conservative state in the land, it's an impossibility."

The front office door opened. Mark's attorney, Frank Zingeralli, entered and apologized for being a little late. He asked his clerk if Mark was ready for the meeting, and addressed the claim hammered into the phone as he rode the elevator. "Don't say it won't work, Sam. It has to work. It's our only chance."

Mark took his seat at the conference room table, listening to the conversation without hearing, like low volume elevator music. His mind heard the fuss of people entering the room, files being taken out of computer cases and plopped onto the table, chairs pulled out, coffee cups placed where attendees sat—more elevator-music-talk communicating little to him, now a two-sided conversation in a language that spoke even less.

Sitting with his feet crossed and hands folded in his lap, Mark glanced at his cell phone—8:30 A.M. For the other people at the meeting, their day had just started. For Mark, time had lost any association with beginnings and much of its relevance. Time had been stopped, set aside for now.

Frank spoke first. "How are you holding up, Mark?" Mark ignored the question. "I know this legal process is difficult, but with a good defense, we can put this behind you. We're pleading not guilty."

Mark looked up after what seemed an eternal stare at the floor. "Put it behind me? Not guilty—why are you saying that?"

Mark saw his life as an imbalance of dreams and facts, with a just-below-the-surface fear that a fateful day would come when the illusion would disappear, forcing him to face the facts.

Now it seemed Frank considered Mark's frightful case a bump in the road, a minor problem, or a crooked picture on the wall that needs straightening a bit. "Fate is knocking at my door, Frank. What's the point of a not guilty plea? My life will never be the same. Kayla Dean and her family—their lives will never be the same either. It's no little thing, Frank. It's going to be the end of me."

"Don't be too hasty, Mark. Let's back up a bit. None of us knows what's around the corner, but we have to make sure this is far from over. We're not talking about the end here, and I don't see this case as a little thing, Mark, it's a big thing. This is your life."

Frank eyed his team—Sam, his law clerk, his paralegal, Clarence, and the two legal assistants at the table. He stared a straight line into Mark's eyes. "We are entering a not guilty plea because you're not guilty."

His uncrossed feet now under the chair, Mark grabbed the arms of the chair, as if preparing to stand in protest. "Nobody believes my story. Nobody believes anything I say. You think I'm guilty too."

"I don't think any such thing, Mark. I've considered this thoroughly, and I'm telling you the truth."

Sam, the law clerk, spoke with tones of sincere proclamation, spur-of-the-moment sentences that fit together like proverbs. "Mark, I was opposed to a not guilty plea until this moment, but I believe Frank when he says he believes this to be the right course of action, and I support him 100 percent."

Clarence, the paralegal, scooted forward, picked up his law book, and declared, "Yes. Yes." His endorsement of Sam's statement seemed sincere.

The legal assistants looked at one another with their eyebrows only slightly raised.

"It's impossible. How can that be?"

"I've heard that over and over, Mark, but I don't believe it's impossible. I've considered everything—the judge, the prosecutor, the jury—and I see it as the right way to go, but remember, Mark, this is still your decision."

Mark leaned forward, his eyes beginning to fill. "I caused the accident. It was my negligence. I should not have picked that girl up. She was a crazy person. It was my negligence. I killed that little boy."

"Let's go over this one more time, Mark. To date, we have no witnesses. No one saw anything. You picked up a homeless person who happened to be walking along the street. Why would a young girl, even a homeless one, get into a car with a strange man?"

"She wanted to get warm. She wasn't carrying a will-work-for-food sign or anything. She motioned for me to stop, so I pulled into the strip center parking lot. When I offered her a couple of bucks, she asked if she could get in. I sort of shrugged and unlocked the door. As soon as she got in the car, she said, 'Wow, instant warmth,' and unbuttoned her coat. She offered her hand and said, 'Hi, I'm Jill.'

"She talked about her family taking advantage of her, how they threw her out of the house because she couldn't handle her father's abuse, and on and on. She talked ninety miles a minute, nonstop—a typical hard-luck story."

"Then what happened?"

"I've told you a hundred times, Frank."

"Once more."

"I had turned around in the parking lot and stopped at the driveway, ready to enter the street once the traffic cleared. She kept talking, going on about how confused the world is. Right is wrong, wrong is right. 'I'm not a liar,' she said. 'Is that a lie? Truth—what is truth?' She was a psycho, and I wanted her out of the car. So, I took out the bills I had in my pocket. I carry my cash loose in my pocket, not in a billfold or a money clip, just loose. I've done it that way since I was a kid.

Anyway, I pulled the money out to pick off a few bills to give her and told her I needed to go. I had my wrists on top of the steering wheel to count off a few bills, $20 or so. She grabbed the whole wad. It wasn't much, maybe a hundred bucks at most. Anyway, she snatched it from my hand and yelled, 'I'll take it all. It's mine, anyway.' I took my hands off the wheel and reached for her. She was halfway out of the car.

In the commotion, my foot tapped the accelerator just enough to move into the traffic and hit near the rear of Kayla Dean's car, passing in front of me. It was awful."

"After your car struck Kayla Dean's car, you turned, pulled alongside the curb, and stopped?"

"Well, my front wheels turned to the right, and when I hit the Dean car, it pushed me into the curbside lane. I stopped the car and saw that Ms. Dean lost control and traveled into the oncoming lane of traffic. That's when she hit the other car."

"Megan Alladee's car?"

"Yes, she didn't hit that car full on, just tapped it. It had little damage. But Ms. Dean's car was out of control. Her car slid sideways into a steel light pole. Major damage. She wasn't hurt, but she had two kids in the car with her. One was okay, but her little boy, just a baby, was taken to the hospital. It all happened so fast."

"How did you determine what happened?"

"Well, the Dean car was on the other side of the street, a couple of hundred feet from my car. I saw Megan Alladee running toward Ms. Dean's car. I ran to Ms. Dean's car to see if she was okay, to see if I could do anything. Megan Alladee called 911. I didn't know what to do. I don't remember a time of feeling so helpless. I thought about the girl back in my car. She had caused the whole thing. I hurried back to be sure she was okay and to make sure she would stay there until the police came. She was gone."

"That's where we have a problem, Mark. No one saw this girl, and of course, no one saw her leave the scene. You say the door on her side of the car was left open?"

"Yes, I shut the door and went around to turn my flashers on. I looked around inside the car. The money was on the floor of the car on the passenger side. It was all there. The girl didn't take any of it."

"Saying this girl is crazy is an understatement," Frank said. "She split without taking the money. It makes no sense. Why would she do that?"

"I don't know. Maybe she was scared or confused by the commotion. I don't know, but she wanted out of there. I'm sure she didn't want to see the cops."

"The problem is we don't have any witnesses. This crazy person grabbed your money and ran away, but you still have your money. This girl left the car door open when she ran, but the police saw the door closed when they arrived. And nobody saw any of it. It's an accident caused by a phantom."

"Well, the door was closed because I closed it. And the money was there, so I told the police I had it. Both of those are the truth. If I wanted to make up a story, I would have told the police the money was gone, and I would have left the car door open."

"I know, but the police say if you had had time to plan a story, that's the story you would have told. It sounds like you're making it up as you go along, to cover for your mistake of accelerating into traffic, whether accidental or not, and we continue to have that problem—no witnesses."

"Yes, I know, no witnesses," Mark said, "But what can I do about it? That's why I'm saying we should plead guilty. The judge is going to believe I'm lying, just like everybody else does. At least by admitting I'm guilty and taking responsibility, the judge might go easier on me."

Frank reached for the law book Sam handed him. "That's one thing we have to change. You have been the toughest sell for this defense. But with your total buy-in, if you come to believe this is the right course, nothing is impossible."

Mark put his elbows on the table and cupped his hands around his face. His mind wandered through impossibilities. Using the impossible as a strategy had not occurred to him. "I don't know much about legal strategy, but I'm afraid they will laugh us out of the courtroom. What will the prosecutor say? 'Your Honor, this defendant is blaming his action on a ghost.'"

Frank pointed to the law book Sam had stuffed with notes. "Mark, the objection from the other side is what will work for us. Nothing is better than the truth. Sam and Clarence have completed the necessary discovery, and they have done it well. We will show—"

Mark interrupted, "Sam is the one who said whatever you're considering is impossible. Isn't that right, Sam? Isn't that what you said before Frank came into the office?"

"Yes, it is, Mark," offered Sam. "Forgive me, but let me say that my role here is, well, let's just say I play devil's advocate in cases involving unusual approaches to our defense. That's the way we work things in this office, and that's what I did. We're in Judge McCain's court. If anyone can make this work in her court, Mark, it's Frank."

"I'm not buying it. Are you guys for real, or are you just looking for ways to draw this out, creating billable hours? Why the need for two legal assistants in this meeting? Four people around me—overkill, billable hours. Don't you know I will have a tough time paying you in the first place? All this expensive stuff in this high-priced office. It's impossible—"

Frank interrupted. "Mark, I know what you're thinking. I don't blame you for believing we must be crazy. And don't worry about having these people involved. We'll work it out."

Mark remained incredulous. "Frank, explain to me again how this is going to work."

With that, Frank vocalized a legal discourse outlining his reason for this course of action, covering everything from his opening statement to what this particular judge will and will not allow. He included why he had been reluctant to involve Mark in the decision the legal team made today.

"I'm wondering who you want to persuade, Frank—me, or the team, maybe yourself. I guess I've got this single-minded devotion to doubt, and I know you're trying to soften me up."

"I'm trying to help you listen to reason."

Mark began to soften. "I hear what you're saying, and it makes sense to me, but you still haven't told me what you mean by saying I'm not guilty. I failed to control my car. Phantom or a real person, it doesn't matter. I hit the accelerator."

"All I'm asking you to do right now is to trust that I wouldn't recommend a fairytale defense to you, and I want you to believe we know what we are doing. We can cover the details later."

"Once you've made them up? Sorry, I'm trying to come along. I want to, but I'm scared of what all this means."

"None of us can be a hundred percent sure of what is going to happen. My job is to develop and ask questions. The jury's role is to answer those questions and draw the right conclusion from their answers. If I didn't believe in a reasonable chance of success, I wouldn't take this route.

"I've had success in Judge McCain's court. She is more tolerant of mitigating circumstances requiring different proceedings. We have much to gain with this defense in her court. But I should make one thing clear to you. Judge McCain's tolerance comes with a price. She tends to adjudicate maximum sentences with a guilty verdict, even if the defendant pleads guilty. As I see it, the way Judge McCain works, the risk is no greater with a not guilty plea."

"Shouldn't I have to pay for the suffering I've caused? I'm in such misery because of a stupid mistake I made. How can a simple reflex action lead to such immeasurable loss— loss of life?"

"*Mistake* is the operative word here, Mark. You must stop assuming guilt. You're in criminal court because of a mistake you made, yes, but more than that, because of a stupid choice your passenger made. I don't mean to minimize the loss of a little boy's life, but mistakes don't make you a bad person, Mark. You are not a criminal."

"I will be if this doesn't work."

At her home, less than four miles east of downtown, Kayla Dean pulled the last few dishes out of the dishwasher before placing them into the cupboard beside the sink. Trying to stay busy, she fidgeted with activity while waiting for a visit from Paul Moody Davidson, her pastor at Open Door Church. A slight, sweet, milky baby fragrance lingered in the air of her spacious home, more pronounced in the kitchen. It reminded Kayla of the many fulfilling hours her family had spent in the kitchen with her happy little son, Danny, lost to her for now.

She leaned against the countertop and bowed her back as she looked up, trying to stifle her tears. *God, how I want to believe that. Lost to me for now, but not forever.*

Opening the cupboard door, she saw a platoon of milk bottles organized on one shelf, lined in neat rows. They're standing at attention, awaiting orders to become the holder of another meal of baby formula, an assignment that will never come. Seeing the never-to-be-used baby bottles ripped at Kayla's heart. She closed her eyes and slammed the cupboard door—a way to shut the memory in and shut the calamity out.

Kayla stood motionless with her hands clenched into fists. She leaned a little forward over the sink in the rigid posture of one frozen in despair. Her heartbeats were cannons firing on the battleship of her mind.

It's been over two months now, she thought, *and I'm more bewildered than ever. Not much time, but it's an eternity without my baby, without feeling his fragile body, his warmth in my arms.*

She tried to settle herself and regain control. *Pastor will be here soon. Where is that pastor? He is usually not late without good reason. Maybe God won't move a snowbank in front of him. He could, but he won't. Or he's in a line of cars with other drivers who can't make it over the same hill.*

It's still early, eight o'clock—he's not late at all. She plodded toward the glass-paneled front door in the oversized foyer to wait for the sight of Pastor's car. Relief pushed against the pain throbbing in her chest from the anticipation of spending a little time with Pastor, who Kayla believed had direct communication with the Almighty.

And there he was, Pastor, now pulling into her driveway and getting out of his car. He was known as Pastor by everyone, not by his first name, Paul, or even Reverend Davidson, not Pastor Paul, not Brother Paul, not Pastor Davidson, just Pastor, used as a first name.

Kayla often smiled as Pastor combed his full head of more-white-than-grey hair with a symmetry that matched his outlook and his bearing. Pastor brought comfort, and he spoke with a consistent mix of authority and theology, putting all comers at ease.

"Hello, Kayla. God bless you," Pastor offered as he stepped inside her home, giving her a hug.

"Hi Pastor, thank you for coming; you're right on time."

"Now is the appointed time," Pastor responded with a smile, hanging his overcoat on the coat rack near the front door. They walked together toward the kitchen. "Congratulations on the work you've completed, Kayla, on your Apologetics thesis at Liberty. You've done an excellent job. How is Kim? Last week you were concerned with how she is dealing with the loss of her little brother."

"Daniel took her to Gramma's this morning because we want her to be free of hearing conversations about her brother. Daniel does a good job when talking with her. He sees a thin line between not talking enough and talking too much, and he has a way of letting Kim decide how much. He says if we don't give her the facts, she will fill in the details, and that won't be good. We led her away from thinking Danny is not here because of something she did."

***

Kayla held Kim in her arms tightly the day after Danny's funeral service. With her heart pounding in her ears, Kayla had practiced what she and Daniel believed the best approach to give Kim the facts about Danny's death.

"Grownups don't understand everything, Kim.

"It's not your fault.

"It's not God's fault either.

"We should help each other when we are sad."

Kim listened without moving, her face expressionless. In the middle of one of Kayla's pronouncements, Kim interrupted with, "Mommy, why didn't I die?"

"Honey, it was an accident. It wasn't your fault," Kayla assured her. "No one was supposed to die; it just happened. We all live with many unknowns, sweetheart, but one thing we know for sure. God loves us. He loves you, and we love you." Kayla considered her doubt. How can I convince her God loves her when I can't convince myself?

***

Kayla poured coffee for Pastor. They sat together at the kitchen table and traded stories about how Danny brought such happiness to everyone. For Kayla, it was like churning butter. She morphed from positive to negative, back and forth.

"Danny was smart," Kayla said. "He recognized his sister, and when she played with him, he would try to give Kim whatever toy belonged to her, as if he knew it was hers. He knew—what can I do, Pastor? I don't have your faith. Why Danny? Why not me? If it was one of your sons, what would you do?"

"I would cry the way you are crying, Kayla, but we can be comforted in knowing God is with us. He records every tear; they're all in his book. Yes, I remember how intelligent Danny seemed to be at only seven months of age."

"One morning, when Danny heard his daddy coming down the stairs, he knew Daniel would be going out the door. He had this expectant look on his face. He raised his little eyebrows, and his eyes widened as if saying, 'Here comes my daddy!' Daniel picked him up for a hug and told him to be a good boy today. A kiss for Danny, a kiss for Kim, a kiss for me, and out the front door he went.

"I nibbled the last bite of my morning toast, watching Danny's constant waggle on the little checkered play mat Gramma bought him over three months before he was born. After a bit, Kim and I were ready for our morning devotional. When I opened the little book we use for Bible study, Danny slapped his hands on the floor beside him, and his little chest bounced up and down. He had to know what was next. 'Time for Bible study,' I said to him. He became excited with that anticipatory look. I put him in my lap, and we read the Bible together. I couldn't imagine how much, if anything, he understood, but I hoped he would remember those happy times for the rest of his life. Those times are no more."

"Are you continuing to pray and study your Bible?"

"I've tried to find answers, hoping God would show me, tell me, communicate reasons to me. I've prayed, and I've begged God, please God, give me a reason; tell me why. But I get nothing." She bowed her head and would not let Pastor look into her eyes. She apologized for being somber and for choking up.

Pastor viewed her with eyes of great compassion and understanding, with love for her that wanted to share in the pain gripping her heart. "I can only imagine the emptiness of your heart right now, Kayla, but the Lord is close to the brokenhearted and those crushed in spirit."

"Why did he let this happen, Pastor? If he's a loving God, if he's true to his promises, none of this would have happened. He just lets us hurt," she moaned, turning to him now, her face streaming with God-recorded tears.

Pastor knew he had no answers. In his heart, he believed God has the privilege to conceal things, and as he has seen through a lifetime of experience, God rarely chooses to answer those questions in this life.

"God loves you, Kayla." Pastor rose from his seat and moved toward her, placing a comforting hand on her shoulder. "It's okay to hurt, feeling lonely and sad. Being angry is okay too. God's ways are so far above ours that you may never have a satisfactory answer as to why this has happened. But dear, sweet Kayla, God knows you're confused. He understands your anger and sadness."

"I know, Pastor. I remember those times when you told grieving parents how God understands. He lost his Son too, I know, but he is God. You've said, again and again, he has an incontestable understanding that we can't have. It's hard to

THEN COMES THE FLOOD

accept. With his super understanding, how can it hurt him as much as it does me?"

Pastor believed he saw an opportunity for Kayla to accept her faith and return to the truth she knew in her heart. "Kayla, listen. You know the answer. It's not a question of whether it hurts God when he sees your grief for Danny. He is God, and he wants you to give your hurt to him. Don't just offer it to him. Throw it on him. Thrust all your anxiety on him because he cares for you. He carries your burden daily, and he will sustain you, both for the same reason—he cares for you."

As Pastor spoke those words, Kayla struggled with the conflict of heart knowledge and head knowledge, a spiritual issue she had to deal with early in her studies. The apologetics program at Liberty put heart knowledge into her head, a mental witness to what she believed in her heart. Kayla sought to prove those beliefs, or modify them through verse-by-verse Bible study.

In heart and head, Kayla knew that, until now, God's testing of the sincere conviction of her heart had never happened. She had studied the historical details of her faith, and, when faced with being truthful to herself, she struggled, not with unbelief, but with the pragmatics of living out her faith. *I know the truth, and I can't blame God.*

"I know it, and I believe it, Pastor, but don't expect too much. The pain of losing my Danny is extreme, and I'm praying God will help me through it. I'm barely strong enough to grieve."

"I know, Kayla, but remember, Christ's power is made perfect in weakness. It's hard for you to hear this right now, but God knows the plan he has for you, to prosper you and not to harm you, to give you hope and a future. God knows what he is going to do. And he knows that what you believe will determine what you are going to do.

"You know painful and helpless feelings that will allow God's grace to strengthen you, like a promontory, a lighthouse of God's power. The waves break against you, but you will stand firm with God as he tames the waters about."

"That will make a great sermon, Pastor, and, yes, it is hard to hear right now. I know I should hear it, and it helps me. I'm going to talk with Daniel tonight. Most of my waves break against him. He and I want to be strong together, looking to the Lord, to get through this."

"Now you're talking, Kayla." Pastor squeezed and patted her hand. "As we discussed after church yesterday, I've asked Dr. Phillips to visit with us this morning. Since you've missed the Friday morning Bible study classes for the last couple of months, I wanted Jerry to stop by and bring you up to date.

"As you know, we began with the section Jerry calls *One Path among Many*, focusing on the self-refuting views of atheism. The study included the first class you missed after the accident, and I know you will have a great interest in this."

"Yes, I miss studying and fellowship. I've had discussions with members in the class and at snack time after class. I miss those sessions. You know the professor is also an attorney, right?"

"Yes, but he doesn't practice."

"Mark Jones's trial is coming up. Will Jerry answer some of the questions I have?"

"I'm sure Jerry would be delighted to help you with that." Pastor felt some relief since Kayla suggested on her own the possibility of talking with the professor. He had asked Jerry to fill Kayla in. He also believed the criminal trial would become a spiritual trial for Kayla and Daniel, and he wanted Kayla to have interaction with the professor as a Christian attorney.

Kayla smiled with anticipation. Jerry's enthusiastic belief in Christ, and his singular ability to reveal the deeper meaning of scripture, helped his students witness the real-life application of his teaching. His approach created a positive impact—he made the characters of the Bible real and approachable, people who could be your friends.

"I'm sure that's Jerry now," Pastor said when the doorbell rang. "I'll get it. You pour the coffee."

Kayla worked on a fresh pot of coffee, and she microwaved a package of sweet cinnamon rolls that brought to mind the snack time Bible study discussions from Jerry's class. Kayla smiled a greeting. "Hello Jerry, thanks for coming."

"Good morning, Kayla; you look well. We have missed having you in class for the last couple of months. Your out-of-the-box questions focus on the heart of the matter. That's been a big help for your classmates."

"You mean questions like if God is in control, why did I lose my child in an accident?"

"Yes, those are the questions to which I refer. However, that one didn't originate outside the box. It came from within the box if you follow my meaning."

"Here's another one. Why can I not put my belief into practice? Am I struggling with unbelief?"

"People struggle with the alternatives of right or wrong and having only two choices, good or bad. They can't reconcile awful things happening to good people who believe God is in control. If God is omnipotent, why does it seem he can't control events? If one is in control, letting terrible events take place is no different from causing those terrible events."

"Okay, tell me. Where is the reconciliation?" asked Kayla.

"God may have given us this incapacity for reconciliation to demonstrate our faith. It seems more probable that atheism is false than it does that Christianity is true. People accept proposition A without faith, while proposition B requires faith. God being in control is simple to accept. But faith is required to believe God can allow an event without being its cause."

"I'm glad faith doesn't require understanding, because I don't understand it."

"Faith means knowing God's judgments are unsearchable, and His understanding no one can fathom," Pastor said.

Kayla wanted to move the conversation in another direction. "I have a question about this trial with Mark Jones. He says he stopped in the parking lot driveway facing the street. A girl in his car grabbed the steering wheel, creating a distraction, causing him to accelerate and hit my car. Why haven't the investigators charged this passenger? She should be the one on trial."

"No passenger was in the car when the police arrived, making his story hard to believe," Jerry said.

Pastor noted that no witnesses had turned up to corroborate Mark Jones's story, and no one saw anyone leave the scene.

"He shows remorse, but he could be making up this story as a way to dismiss, or at least diminish, his guilt," continued Jerry. "If no passenger was involved, this story will nullify any remorse he has shown."

"He is responsible for my son's death." Kayla wiped a tear from her cheek. "The driver of that car had no intent. It was an accident on his part. But he should accept his responsibility and be willing to suffer the consequence of what he did."

"Well, as you know, he is being charged with vehicular homicide, a form of manslaughter, which doesn't require intent. The charge indicates he was negligent, criminally negligent, with no real intent."

"I can't believe we are referring to my precious baby's death as manslaughter. I don't know how I'll ever make it through a trial. The prosecutor refers to this as his latest case. I've seen enough to know that people view Danny as a statistic in a case. This is not a case. It's my life we're talking about here. It's my husband's life. It's our lives we have to live without our little boy's life."

"That is the truth of the matter, Kayla," Jerry said. "The court demands that the proceedings provide justice for you and your family. Prepare yourself, though, for a setting that may seem to have nothing to do with you. The courtroom procedure will, at times, appear cold and intolerant of your anguish."

"I accept and support innocent until proven guilty," Kayla said. "Most people's knowledge of the law, including mine, is what they've seen on TV. I've had one courtroom drama in my life, and I saw the court favor the accused over the victim. It's nothing more than a contest. Whoever makes the best argument wins. That doesn't seem fair."

"You are closer to the truth than you may realize, Kayla. It's a play with a cast of characters but without a script. In the court's eyes, the best argument uses the available evidence. Whoever creates the best script for the play makes the best argument and wins."

"It makes for good TV."

"Courtroom law doesn't come to us from on high," Jerry continued. "God wrote the Ten Commandments with his own hand, but the laws we live by were written by people who have a vision of justice, with the power to turn that vision into a legal system. Their view may, at times, seem contrary to reason, but, given that, conducting a legal system must still be seen as fair.

"Attorneys for both the prosecution and the defense are allowed—no, encouraged—to operate without emotion. That's how they create a powerful script, the best argument. What we have to do, what you have to do, is not take the bait, not yield to their argumentation."

"Their hot temper stirs up strife," offered Pastor. "But nothing presented in a courtroom will change the truth."

Kayla spoke to Pastor's statement without hesitation. "The truth can't win unless spoken. I can accept their suspension of emotion. Abandoning truth is what makes it tough for me. The state called me as a witness in the trial of Aaron A. Moore. Remember? He was the guy charged in the beating death of Beverly Pruitt. Beverly and I were classmates in high school, and the court called me as a material witness. By the time Moore's attorney was through with me, the jury saw me as the one who committed a crime. His honor, the judge, scorned my testimony. He sustained every objection made against me."

"Yes, I remember the trauma of your experience," Pastor said. "You testified with honor and were a witness for Christ on behalf of your friend Beverly."

Jerry expressed surprise. "I wasn't aware of your involvement in that proceeding, Kayla. How painful that experience must have been for you. Is the pressure you're feeling toward this upcoming trial influenced by your earlier testimony?"

"Jerry, look. How often in our class have you talked about logical fallacies in the Bible made by unbelievers? You know— the earth is flat, and it has corners."

Jerry hesitated, not sure of her intent. "I'm a little confused. Where are you going with this?"

"Well, the Bible refers to truthful lips, which indicates speaking. When a witness is speaking, is he telling the truth?"

"He has taken an oath. Truth in the courtroom consists of the facts presented," Jerry said. "That's the law. The problem for you is facts that are outside the context of spiritual truth. We have to come to terms with the court's mandate to separate church and state—even when the facts are spiritual truths."

"Truth is the word of God. Truth is nothing without Christ. If called as a witness, I will try to tell the truth, but I fear that I won't be allowed to speak the truth." Kayla saw a gauzy look on Jerry's face. *Did he not get it?*

Jerry continued, "To a witness, the truth is what he or she believes to be the truth, and the court recognizes that. In the court's view, what you and I would call 'real truth' is not what's important. The court is not after truth. The court seeks justice. I know that seems condescending, but it's true. The court can accept as truth only what it sees as facts substantiated by the evidence. If those facts agree with what the witness is saying, the witness is telling the truth."

"Unless the witness is a Christian," Kayla said. "A Christian witness swears on a Bible, to tell the truth, the whole truth and nothing but the truth. After the swear-in, a Christian witness can't speak the truth. It's not separation of church and state. It's the separation of truth and state."

"If called as a witness, you should be asked to state the facts, the physical events that led to the accident, and nothing more."

"What happened that day is unexplainable. It may be considered an accident by the court, but—"

"One second, Kayla." Jerry's cell phone rang. "It's Megan Alladee."

Taken aback, Kayla was unaware Jerry and Megan had been in contact. She had his phone number? "How does Jerry know Megan?" Kayla asked Pastor.

"Jerry has a business connection who knows Megan's father, and Jerry contacted Megan through that connection with her father. He wanted to hear the facts from her perspective,"

Jerry disconnected the call after a moment of conversation. "I intended to tell you that I spoke with Megan and asked her to call me back about the possibility of the two of you getting together. I know you have a connection with her through Jack Williams at the DA's office, but when I spoke with her, I learned the two of you had not been together outside the DA's office. You should meet with her outside the investigation. I didn't know she would be calling back this morning, but I'm glad she did. Would you be open to meeting with her?"

"Jack has kept us apart and meets us one-on-one. He wants to be sure we don't pollute each other's stories. To Jack, a consistent witness will come from our not being able to compare notes. I'm a little surprised you spoke with her."

"Why?"

"I'm a little jealous, not in a sinful way, of course, that you would talk with her without telling me first."

"I must have your permission?"

Kayla showed a slight grin. "Of course, what other reason would there be? I don't have a problem with a meeting, but we don't have much in common. She's single and doesn't have kids. She's a high-tech professional who works at St. Jude. I'm just a no-tech, full-time mother and wife."

"Megan's dad recommended a meeting that would be beneficial for both of you, not to discuss the trial, but to share a common experience and see where it leads. Megan is open to it."

"Text me her contact information, and I'll call her."

CHAPTER 4

The phone text from Dr. Rochelle Meyers caused a quick jump in Megan's heartbeat. MEET ME AT 902 TODAY. Between Megan and Rochelle, that phrase was code for *we may have a problem,* demanding immediate action, without overreaction.

The message, LET'S MEET IN ROOM 902 AT 10:00 A.M., whether scheduled for today or tomorrow or any date and time, for that matter, meant just what it implied. MEET ME AT 902 TODAY conveyed a specific meaning. It's an immediate call to discuss business, personal, or social issues that should not use text, email, telephone, or any other media. MEET ME AT 902 TODAY required one-on-one contact.

Room 902 is their usual meeting place, a ten-foot conference room on the ninth floor of the St. Jude Children's Hospital office tower in Memphis. Once together, they could move to a more convenient location.

Rochelle and Megan were best friends back in high school and planned to attend college together. Rochelle's interest in medicine led her to the University of Tennessee instead of Rhodes College, where Megan enrolled. Rochelle witnessed the dream of a lifetime when she became a member of the physician staff at St. Jude.

Megan took a position with Proton Beam Transportation Systems, or PBTS, the biotechnical company in England owned by her English family. This company accepts contracts to manufacture, install, and maintain cyclotron-related equipment for Proton Therapy centers. Her company's St. Jude contract includes the regulatory authority as the service provider of their proton system. The authority's job is to guarantee the necessary uptime for treatment configuration.

The onsite personnel required to ensure a continuous process comprises a team that dwarfs other hospital service and maintenance groups. St. Jude's proton therapy center was no exception. Megan's team reports on significant downtime events and corrective action taken to eliminate breaks in the process flow of the transport system, a minor step but a technologically advanced part of the overall process. Megan had been with St. Jude since her graduation from Rhodes. She got promoted to the site-manager position of her group in 2015.

She and Rochelle saw it as the ultimate irony. They planned to attend the same college, with no idea where their career paths would lead, only to study at different colleges and land together at St. Jude. They worked together to prepare proton system presentations to the staff team, with Megan as the primary point of contact for issues related to the transport system provided by her employer.

Was it fate or coincidence? Neither could decide, but whether fate, coincidence, or the plan of a higher power, being together provided mutual benefit.

***

Megan didn't want to delay Rochelle's call for a 902 meeting. She turned into the reserved parking lot of the Marlo Thomas office building at St. Jude on Danny Thomas Boulevard. She had been mindful of events in her life that led her to this place. Megan owed a lot to Rochelle's steadfast determination and judgment. She respected Rochelle's competence, above all.

For Rochelle's part, she marveled at Megan's technical expertise, which filled Megan with contradictory feelings of humility and pride.

Rochelle had not arrived. *I guess she's running a little late.* Her tardiness increased the anticipation.

Megan pulled into the designated parking space marked RESERVED FOR MEGAN ALLADEE, with an undeserving feeling that having her own parking space at St. Jude created within her. *Why should I have a parking space of my own while certain medical team members don't?*

At the same time, she felt entitled. *No, not entitled; that's the wrong word for it. I've earned it,* she decided.

She owed that idea to her dad. After the events in her life the year following 9/11, her dad told her she could accept her fate and allow that fate to control her life, or she could use those events to move on to greater things. Megan remembered those events of sixteen years ago, like a gunshot fired next to her ear, creating a pain she would never forget.

In November 2002, Rochelle took Megan to the annual Veteran's Day ceremony at Memphis National Cemetery. That year the program recognized the heroics of 9/11 first responders and honored those who died or were injured.

They met Ron Hicks at the event, who introduced himself by giving Megan and Rochelle red poppies to wear in their lapels as a remembrance during the ceremony. Ron told them he served in the Indiana National Guard, had volunteered for Task Force Eagle in Bosnia in 1997, and took part in Operation Joint Guard. Transferred stateside in mid-1998, he planned a move to Memphis after his release from the National Guard.

Megan and Ron were an ideal match. She blushed when their eyes met as Ron pinned the red poppy to her blouse. They spent the rest of the day together, and Megan stayed behind with Ron as Rochelle drove away at the end of the festivities.

Megan didn't know if Ron's obvious feelings toward her were real. Without question, the genuine emotion that pulsed in her was magical. They had a simple dinner of barbecue with slaw and home fries, after which Megan set aside the tinge of uncertainty she felt about going into his motel room. They intended to have a glass of wine to toast an eventful day.

She felt safe with Ron. It was only a room, after all, a place where they could top off the evening together with a glass of wine, becoming acquainted, and he could take her home. They could build a new friendship together, and who knows what opportunities lay ahead? Pretty naïve, she thought. Does unreality beget reality?

They sat at the little table in his room, recounting the day's events after Ron made a quick toast to new friends. Within minutes, he leaned toward her and took her hand. "You are beautiful," he said, in a voice that made her heart beat faster. "I want you."

She responded with a smile and a little chuckle, "I want to continue with you too." In an instant, before answering, she asked herself what he meant by saying those words. Does he mean he wants me physically, at this moment, or does he want this relationship to continue? He couldn't mean sex. Not even a hint of sex has happened today. He doesn't mean sex.

Asked and answered.

Suddenly standing, Ron squeezed her hand in his. He grabbed the upper part of her arm and jerked her into his arms. He held her in a full body grasp and kissed her neck and face. "I've got to have it."

"Have what? Ron, don't do this. This is wrong. I'm sorry if I made you think I wanted to do anything."

He backstepped to the bed and pulled her into a sitting position. "What do you expect? You knew this would happen." He put his hand under her blouse and pushed up her bra.

"Ron, stop! I don't want this. Not this way."

He pushed her down, forced her toward the head of the bed, and got on top of her. He tore at her clothes, pulling her blouse over her head. She saw the red poppy become unpinned from her blouse and fall to the floor beside the bed. A part of her slipped away, and she knew she would never get it back.

In a matter of minutes, it was over. Without even a word, Ron rolled over on his side, stood, and loafed toward the bathroom. A minute later, Megan ran out the door and headed to the motel office. She called Rochelle to come to the motel.

Standing in the motel lobby waiting for Rochelle, Megan cringed at the physical pain, the agony, and the guilt she couldn't dismiss. All she could remember saying at the time was, "I'm sorry, Dad."

Megan didn't see Ron again after that miserable night. Rochelle drove to the motel office after Megan's call within a matter of minutes. Saying the words "I was raped," even to Rochelle, created guilt. "If I hadn't gone into his room, none of this would have happened."

"If he weren't a rapist, none of this would have happened. You know this isn't your fault. Right now, we must get you to the ER. I want you to call the Rape Crisis Center, but you don't have to do that tonight. We should call the police."

"We can't call the police. My parents will become involved. We should get away from here. I'm afraid he will try to find me. I'm surprised he hasn't shown up in the motel lobby looking for me."

"He's long gone by now, Megan. He's a stranger. You were with him all day, but he's still a stranger. Strangers don't hang around after they rape someone. I doubt he even used his real name when he checked in. Even if he checked in under the name he gave us, Ron—"

"Hicks," Megan said. "Ron Hicks."

"Right, Ron Hicks. I doubt that's his real name. He's too smooth for that. He came across like a Greek god, a war hero who fought for you and me. He had a line of crap a mile long. He's out of here. Come on, let's get you to the hospital."

The ER people asked a million questions—what happened before, during, and after, but they seemed concerned with helping her. They didn't seem judgmental. Their attitude helped her deal with the trauma of the treatment.

Of course, the police showed up. Megan couldn't see how they even knew of it. She had told Rochelle she didn't want to call the police. She reasoned the hospital personnel had made a report, and the police came to take care of their part. They asked many of the same questions the hospital people asked but in what she saw as a more direct way, and from a different perspective.

The cops seemed interested in making sure a rape had occurred. They asked Rochelle to wait outside the room. They explained that Rochelle not being in the room during the interview would prevent her from having to be called as a witness.

Was there any alcohol or drugs involved? How long were you with him? Did you go willingly into his room? Describe exactly everything that happened during the *event*.

They didn't ask many questions about Ron or whoever he turned out to be. What make and model of car did he drive? "I don't know. I didn't see his car. We were together at the Veteran's Day event and the restaurant. After dinner, we went to his room." They wanted Megan to complete a written report at the station tomorrow, and view photographs of suspects. They agreed Rochelle could accompany her if Rochelle's presence would make her more comfortable.

They wanted to keep her clothes. They kept her blouse and undergarments. She kept her jeans and her jacket. Rochelle expressed resentment for the lack of concern shown by the police. She made a note of the names and badge numbers of the officers who talked with Megan, which they were glad to provide for the record.

Before the officers left, Rochelle asked if they planned to search the motel and check the registration. They told her not to worry; they knew how to do their job.

Rochelle took Megan to Megan's new apartment downtown and urged her to call her parents and tell them what had happened. Rochelle offered to spend the night with Megan, but Megan said no. She wanted to be brave. She wanted to go inside, take a shower, and put this behind her.

Megan felt lucky the guy didn't brutalize her, or worse. She had heard of cases where rape victims were beaten, kept for hours, and suffered multiple assaults. She accepted that it just happened, and she was grateful it happened in a matter of minutes. "Goodnight, Rochelle. I'll call Mom and Dad after I get some sleep."

Megan walked toward the high-rise apartment building. Rochelle didn't drive away until she saw Megan inside with the door closed behind her. Megan took the elevator to her floor in a daze, disappointed with herself for letting this happen.

Inside her apartment, she sat on the side of her bed and began to take off her clothes. When she realized she had no bra or panties to remove, it hit her. She slid from the bed to the floor in a ball of tears, with no comprehension of the feelings that had surfaced. Her world ended, with no way to get it back.

She was alone in a way she had never been before; an unknown emptiness filled her heart. It made her sick and drove her into the bathroom to throw up. She lingered over the commode for what seemed an hour and forced herself into the shower. She needed to scrub a layer of skin from her body to survive. A layer of life?

She knelt in the shower, slumped into a sitting position, and remained there until the water became too cold to tolerate. She dried herself off, got into bed, and cried until sleep overcame her.

***

Rochelle pulled into her space, three across from Megan's. Megan shook her head to release the negative memory of her past. Once together, they took the shortest route from the parking lot to Starbucks, now located in the new Marlo Thomas office building, and sat at an inconspicuous table.

"It's my little sister," Rochelle said.

"Cindy? What's happened? Is she okay?"

"Yes, nothing has happened, but she made a revelation yesterday that, in and of itself, though surprising, would have been okay in the long run, but she destroyed any hope of acceptance by—"

"Oh my God, she's pregnant!" guessed Megan. "In a way, I'm not surprised, the way she and Kevin have been carrying on."

"Yes, you guessed it. I'm not too surprised either, although I wish they had waited. Marriage is not that far away. One problem—Cindy is considering an abortion."

"She can't do that," Megan said, without hesitation.

"It's Kevin's idea. Cindy said when she revealed her pregnancy, the first words out of his mouth were, 'Abortion, right?' She doesn't want to do it, but I wouldn't rule it out."

"She can't do that. Have you talked with her? Haven't all the battles you've had—we've had—with Cobel Clinic had any effect on her?"

"Yes, you know she has been right there with us for at least the last two years. We have fought the good fight, and she has been a part of it. Now she's stepping back."

"This may create problems for Cindy's involvement in the SAVE program," Megan said. "Eliza Stokes is speaking at the meeting tomorrow night, and we're preparing material for the rally this weekend. Cindy should attend. Eliza's talk will address unplanned parenthood in a way Cindy probably hasn't considered. Will she come?"

"It's hard to say. You know Cindy hasn't changed what she believes, but she says it's different when it's your problem. When you become pregnant, abortion takes on a new life. I hope she comes. She should bring Kevin. He is the one who should hear Eliza's message. I know you'll be there."

"Yes, it's too important to miss. Cindy should not miss Eliza's remarks. It may drive a point that could influence a life-changing decision, and she must make the right decision."

"Will you talk to her?" Rochelle asked.

"Of course. Cindy knows the right thing to do. She knows abortion forsakes a vow—"

"Wait, Megan. You know what I mean. I'm asking you to, you know, talk to her."

"I can't do that. No one knows what I did, except for my parents and you. You know Cindy doesn't even know about the rape, much less the pregnancy and the abortion. None of the People at SAVE know. The people at work, the people at St. Jude, they don't know either. It's as if it never happened."

"But it did happen. And look at the result, your total commitment to anti-abortion activity. I remember the anxiety and depression you experienced. And you overcame it."

"That's because I was determined to put it behind me, again, like it never happened."

"Yes, that's what you intended, Megan. But that's not what you did. You didn't put it behind you. You put it in front of you, and you killed it. Look at you. You're a champion for unborn life. You've saved the lives of kids and changed the lives of their parents, and you got involved with the kids at St. Jude. How you dealt with what happened to you is what got me involved."

"What you say is true, even though you may exaggerate a bit. Whatever I've done on the anti-death front, I have done without telling my story. I've taken it from principle. No one knows, and I don't want anyone to know. I'm not ashamed of what I did, but it's private."

"I know you're not motivated by shame. I get that. I have been amazed at how victorious you have been through these years. You've clung to the truth and the decision you made. And you've dealt with it."

"I don't want to tell people, to reveal my story. I don't need a release. I'm not looking for closure. I have that. I'm through with it."

"I see what you're saying, and I'm not arguing with that. I don't disagree with you, but—"

"When you say, 'I don't disagree with you,' do you mean you agree with me?"

"Okay, that's a good one. You got me there. I guess it means I don't disagree a hundred percent, but I don't fully agree with you either. You live like a part of your life never happened. But it did, and you have come far enough to be objective."

"I don't disagree with you," Megan said.

"That's a start. We agree Cindy should not have an abortion. She should allow the life within her to survive. We must convince her she agrees with that too. Cindy needs rock-solid advice about her dilemma.

"Coming from me is too authoritative for Cindy. And Mom— Cindy hasn't told Mom yet. Mom will be so emotional, and, bless her heart, Mom can't be objective. Don't even mention my dad. He'll bring out the Torah, and he'll read it to her. Don't get me wrong. I don't have a problem with the Torah, but that won't help Cindy right now. She needs advice from someone who has been through what she is about to experience, someone she loves and who loves her."

"I don't disagree with you."

"Okay, enough said. Would you at least consider telling her?"

"I'll consider it, but I'm not as objective as you might think."

Rochelle paid the bill, as their tradition would have it. By agreement, whoever called a 902 meeting paid the bill. They agreed to meet later in the afternoon to prepare for the staff presentation.

Leaving the coffee shop, Rochelle crossed over to the Marlo Thomas Center. Megan turned south toward the patient care center to meet upstairs in the medicine room with Carla, a patient having her last round of chemotherapy. Carla's mom came from the parent's room adjacent to Carla's room, where she had caught a few minutes of naptime during Carla's chemo.

Megan had grown close to Carla and her mom during two years of Carla's chemotherapy for acute lymphoblastic leukemia, ALL. It did Megan's heart good to visit the patient care center. The walls of the chemo floor contain dozens of kids' artwork, all about the kids' lives, not their treatment. Hallways, filled with nurses and doctors in a playful atmosphere, are intentionally unlike a treatment center. Everyone seems happy.

A doctor held a young boy in his arms while discussing his treatment. Nurses cuddled and laughed with the kids, several of whom traveled in little red wagons pulled by their parents, leaving the floor headed back to their rooms.

Today is a momentous day for Carla, a celebration of her last chemo treatment. Her mom pulled a red wagon into the medicine room as Megan squeezed in with nurses, doctors, and technicians. As a nurse cranked up the head of Carla's bed, another blew a note on a little harmonica, and everyone in the room sang the off chemo song:

> *Our patients have the cutest s-m-i-1 -e.*
> *Our patients have the sweetest h-e-a-r-t.*
> *Oh, we love to see you every day.*
> *But now's the time we get to say,*
> *Pack up your bags, get out the door,*
> *You don't need chemo anymore!*

The nurse playing harmonica threw confetti over enchanted Carla's bed while her mom struggled to hold back joyful tears. Hugs and kisses all around and everyone moved out to serve another patient—precious moments in time.

CHAPTER 5

Organization for Women's Rights Conference,
Atlanta, Georgia

F our women at a table.
"We should be open-minded enough to hear what everyone has to say," the registered nurse said. "Tolerance should be required of all."

"Nobody knows the truth anyway, so I agree," the medical technician said.

"That would be a reason not to listen," the newspaper reporter said, as she and the teacher took their seats at the table. "Everyone has a right to state a position, but if no one tells the truth, what's the point?"

"That is the point," the registered nurse said. "For years and years, the scientific community argued the earth was the center of the universe. They were wrong, but without those arguments, we could not determine why they were wrong."

"They were right," the teacher said.

"See what I mean?" the registered nurse asked. "After all that effort, people can still be wrong."

"Wait a minute," the teacher said, "you can't impose your beliefs on me. That's intolerant."

"So, we have to tolerate intolerance?" the medical technician asked. "This is getting too complicated for me. It's over my head."

"We've haven't met. I'm Suzan Winders," the registered nurse said to the teacher, offering her hand in friendship, "This is Alice Beal. Alice is head of the medical tech department of Cobel Women's Health Clinic in Memphis. I work in the Women's Health Management division there. Alice and I were sent to the conference to hear about NOW's involvement with the latest development in legislation that will impact the services we offer our clients in Memphis."

"A pleasure to meet you, Suzan, and you too, Alice," the teacher said, offering her hand in return. "I'm Sarah Smith. I teach secondary level science at a local high school here in Atlanta. This is Brenda Wood. Brenda is with the Atlanta *Daily News*. We are attending the conference this week to glean the benefit of current legislation from an educational and political perspective."

"We're as interested in gleaning what damage the legislation will cause as much as what benefits, if any, it may provide," Brenda said.

"Yes," Suzan said. "The folks in Washington are determined to destroy what little is left of women's rights, particularly health care. We're interested in the Reproductive Rights Committee, who have done valuable work with community-based activism against idiotic legislation, and fighting the lunatics who support it."

"You're referring to abortion," Brenda said.

Alice answered defensively. "It's not just abortion, although abortion may be the focus. It concerns everything involved in women's health issues."

"So, you consider health care an individual right?" asked Brenda.

Suzan responded, "Let me answer without hesitation. Health care should be available to everyone, women included."

"That's an answer I hear a lot," Brenda said. "So, is abortion a part of women's health care?"

Suzan pushed her head back. "Who are you? You sound like one of those punks in Washington everyone at the convention is talking about this week."

"I just want to be sure we hear what everyone has to say," Brenda said.

"Touché," Suzan said. "Yes, as I said before, we should be open to hearing all positions, even if we believe most of them are wrong. Every woman's way is right in her own eyes. But I'm looking at the bigger picture here. Yes, Alice and I came this week to hear the Reproductive Rights Committee's primary position on anti-abortion agendas in the states and nationally. But we all spend so much time arguing about who is right and who is wrong, we let people be taken advantage of, especially minorities. That's the bigger picture. We should stop talking and start doing. Medical needs are widespread, and it's our responsibility to meet those needs. Simple as that."

Brenda rose from her chair, indicating she was ready to leave. "Yes, I'm a proponent of charity. I'm glad to meet the two of you. I hope we'll be together later this week. Sarah and I should round up our partners before the next breakout session."

Suzan offered her hand with a smile in a way that also spoke for Alice. "Goodbye. See you soon."

Sarah took a quick last sip of coffee, set the cup onto the table, and caught up with Brenda.

Alice questioned what had just happened. "That didn't take long. They were here for, what, two minutes?"

"She's a newspaper reporter, playing both sides, trying to be devil's advocate. When we're together later this week, she may argue an opposite point of view."

"I don't know. That girl, Brenda, seemed a little intolerant if you know what I mean. I saw the teacher, Sarah, nodding her agreement to Brenda's question about abortion."

"Mary Lou Hochman is moderating the Reproductive Rights Committee's breakout session this week. If Brenda takes a contrary view in that session, Mary Lou will set her straight."

"Are we going to stay for the full conference? I know you want to go back to Memphis to help your brother prepare for his trial. Isn't the trial scheduled soon?"

"I won't be attending the trial. I don't want anything to do with it."

"Don't you want to support your brother? He's facing severe charges."

"Vehicular homicide—trumped-up charge."

"All the more reason to be there. Poor Mark, he doesn't deserve having to face that. From what I hear, the criminal justice system in Memphis can make a tough case, no matter what the facts indicate."

"They don't want justice—and they don't want the facts. They just want to prosecute."

"It's a movie script. First, a simple ticket for causing a minor accident, then the little boy in the other car passes away, and all hell breaks loose. The police practically broke down Mark's door; they handcuffed him and took him away. Seems beyond reason, but that's the way they do it when a death is involved," Alice said.

"That's the real problem."

"What do you mean?"

"No one died as a result of that accident."

***

Alice wrestled with Suzan's statement about no one dying. She knew Suzan believed abortion doesn't involve a person, and therefore abortion is okay. Childbirth is nothing more than another step in becoming a person. In Suzan's view, that little boy who died in the accident wasn't a person.

Alice couldn't rationalize her mind and heart. She questioned how the unborn could be a group of human beings but not a group of people. She could understand why embryos were not a group of *people,* but she could not accept that no person is growing in the womb.

She struggled with the ever-present question if they're not persons or people in the womb, when do they become people? If one sees the unborn as not being persons beforehand, is it reasonable to accept the unborn achieving personhood at the moment of birth? To Suzan, human beings don't become persons until they have met the parameters required by people who follow Mary Anne Warren and Peter Singer, both of whom Mary Lou Hochman championed in the breakout session that day.

In Hochman's view, a human being is not synonymous with being a person. Even a three-month-old baby is not a person, according to Hochman, and Suzan agreed. A baby lacks self-motivated activity and the self-awareness required for personhood and is therefore not entitled to the rights of a real person.

Hochman agreed with Peter Singer. A dog has more personal characteristics than a baby, but if no one wants it, the dog is put to sleep. In the same way, if no one wants a baby, it should be okay to put a baby to sleep, a concept Alice found intolerable.

Suzan recommended dinner at a Mexican restaurant she had visited during an earlier trip to Atlanta and suggested they leave early to beat the traffic. "I'm completely frustrated about this, Suzan. Are we supposed to believe an unborn child has no form of personhood?"

"I favor the position my boss, Dr. Brent, holds regarding whether the unborn can feel pain," Suzan responded. "The fetus cannot feel pain until well into later embryonic stages, and therefore cannot be considered a person."

"What does feeling pain have to do with it?"

"You have a significant level of emotion when dealing with this issue, Alice. But to make good decisions, you should leave emotion out of it. To feel pain," Suzan declared, "one must have a level of awareness a fetus doesn't have."

"Suzan, you're an RN, and I know you can hold an objective view, but how can you refer to the pain of a child without emotion?"

"We're not talking about a child in pain. We're talking about a fetus with a lack of pain, so get over it."

Alice looked puzzled. "I still don't see the connection."

Suzan pulled into the restaurant parking lot and parked in a spot as close to the entrance as she could find. "When dealing with abortion law, court studies have shown that, even though reflex responses are observable in a fetus, the undeveloped cortex is not involved in the process. The thalamus and lower brain stem alone can't generate a perception of pain. Without the cortex, there can be no connection and, therefore, no functioning brain. No brain, no pain."

"So, you're saying the cortex is what makes us into living, reacting individuals. Without the cortex, the brain of a fetus is not functional enough to be aware of pain. Does that unawareness equate to not being human?"

"Correction—not being a person. They're human beings, yes, but not persons. When the cortex is finally, but not yet fully developed, the neural network is there. The fetus can feel pain, still with no presence of self-concept or self-awareness. The response to pain is a reflex action. My point is the lack of pain indicates the fetus is not a person, and the neural network doesn't indicate a person has developed either. Development of personhood doesn't take place until even a year or more after birth."

"Okay, I've had enough of this for one day. I hope this restaurant is as good as you claim."

"You'll love it."

As they walked together toward the entrance, Alice's spirit recovered a bit, anticipating a delicious meal. "Remember the Chinese restaurant in Memphis you recommended the day I took you home from the office? It was exceptional, and I'm still surprised at my not having been there before."

"It's a great place."

"I'm so glad you recommended that restaurant; otherwise, I wouldn't have Chinese to add to my list."

"Reservation for two, Winders," Suzan said to the maître d.'

"This is fabulous," Alice said. "Mexican food is my favorite."

CHAPTER 6

At age twenty, Scott Rider's two-year stint with Mark Jones had paid off. He took advantage of a lucky series of steps leading to a secure position, and the good fortune had worked both ways. Mark let Scott work adjusted hours while he attended the University of Memphis.

Scott blamed unexpected family problems for his having to drop out of the university. He expected Mark wouldn't look favorably on his continued employment, and his university departure might cost him his job. To his surprise, Mark gave him a break, saying Scott's family issues created difficulty. He hoped Scott would re-enroll once he got his personal life in order.

The top-notch deal Scott worked on the Verajen project impressed Mark. A national manufacturer of building components for the construction industry, Verajen has a large team of sales and service personnel throughout the United States, with multiple manufacturing centers. The company became a new subscriber to Manufacts, Mark's industry-specific, vertical customer relationship management program, a sales platform allowing all users to operate on a national level with real-time data.

Old Mac Jenison seemed incapable of operating in what he called the faketrician environment. "Everyone's an expert, but no one can tell me anything. I can break down and service every piece of equipment required for our manufacturing operation. I just can't operate those machines," he would say, referring to the latest personal technology now in the hands of his employees. He understood, however, what it meant to have a user-friendly software program to provide his entire sales and service network, "all the information all the time." CRM could be a lifesaver for his company and the industry.

Scott arrived at the office first thing, with editor Sally and code writer George for the final run of Manufacts 7.0, their current on-demand software upgrade with a go live date less than a week away. As a development team leader for the updated release, Scott steadfastly determined to find and work any last-minute bugs created in the program to minimize user problems. "Keeping the bugs out from the get-go is the one sure way to be bug-free in the end."

Without the need to attend classes, Scott could work longer hours. He took on the secondary role of design specialist. With the responsibility of design came the requirement to perform low-end user training outside the service center. He had a scheduled call with Mac Jenison at Verajen at 8:00 A.M. "I should leave the shop by a little after seven this morning, or I might be late, and I can't afford to be late."

"We're at a point where we can work in tandem without a third party," Sally assured him. "Mark will be in by nine, and we can use him as the third party if the two of us can't work it."

"Here comes Mark, now," George said. "Coming in early. He has been working crazy, long hours since this trial got scheduled. I can't believe he's in this fix. Mark wouldn't hurt a flea. Now he's in big trouble. I don't see a way out."

"Good morning, guys." Mark headed straight for the coffee maker. "Too bad none of you go for coffee. How can anyone work without coffee?"

"We didn't know you would be in this early, or you would have it. Sorry for having to come in and make coffee."

"It doesn't matter. I make a pretty mean cup. It's not Starbucks, but it's still good, maybe in some ways even better."

"How are preparations for the trial coming?" Sally asked. "Making you deal with this is unfair. I'm sorry for that lady who lost her baby, but it wasn't your fault. Did they ever figure out who that bitch is you picked up? She's the one who should be on trial. Will they take your word for it—the prosecutor and the judge, I mean? It should create reasonable doubt."

"From what I can see, they think I'm lying about the girl being in the car. They see it as a cover-up."

George tossed a pen-drive onto the work table. "She's a prostitute, not a homeless person. How can a young girl become homeless? I would take her in."

"I don't do prostitutes. She was a mixed-up person down on her luck. She needed help, and I had the time, so I stopped. She made a stupid mistake, compounding the mistake I made, as it turned out when I picked her up."

"Why are you defending her?" Sally asked. "Just like you, Mark—give everyone the benefit of the doubt."

"Circumstances are not necessarily the way they seem. Things can get off track in a hurry. This is not a conversation I want to have right now. Scott, how does it look for your meeting this morning with the Verajen group? Are they ready to commit? Do they know the full benefit of our complete package?"

"They'll come through once they use the 7.0 upgrade," said Scott. "Our upgraded import function will make the best use of Excel and Access to provide customer data. Mac Jenison sees his money coming back many times over. And they will have a value add no one else in their group has."

"It's called return on investment," Mark said. "Don't oversell them, Scott. This software has to sell itself, with a little

49

help from you, of course. Verajen shouldn't focus on return on investment. They should see the process improvement that 7.0 provides."

"Yeah, I know. I know the routine—uh, sorry, that's not what I meant to say," Scott added after seeing the expression on Mark's face. "I meant to say I know how to show them the real benefit of Manufacts for their system. I've told them the key is to trust the software and conduct business from inside the site and quit the practice of sending their data to it like a glorified filing system. This morning they will learn to make the program user friendly for their operation. Soon they'll question how they ever did business without it."

"Good answer, Scott," Sally said. "That's why we're sending you."

Sally and George returned to their duty stations, and Scott reviewed the software update with Mark. "Verajen's biggest concern is the security of their data. They're skeptical about whether an on-demand CRM is as secure as an onsite version. I've shown them how, with the backup redundancies and limitless storage capacity available on-demand, their data is more secure in the cloud. They don't have to worry about a breach of their in-house system."

"Security is a process, but don't sacrifice freedom when looking for security. Or you lose both."

"Yeah, that's good, Mark. Franklin, right? I see what you mean. On-demand gives them the best of both worlds. They have the highest level of security and unlimited ability to handle endless amounts of data in the quickest possible way, with the freedom to customize the software to fit their business process—well, got to go. Thanks for your help on this, Mark."

"Thanks for the good job you're doing, Scott. The upgrade exceeds my expectations, and I appreciate your working with our users in particular applications. It's one key to our success. And try not to worry. One way or another, we'll get through this trial."

CHAPTER 7

Kayla and Megan met at Kay Kafe, the new cafeteria Danny Thomas planned to be a central gathering place. Kay Kafe is a safe house, an oasis, where the patient's food is made to order and served the same as if at home. The focus of the cafeteria layout is the kids. It serves as a refuge where patient families, employees, researchers, clinicians, and guests can share a common understanding, where a look and a smile speak volumes about their collective endeavor.

They scheduled Wednesday at 9:00 A.M. to allow Megan enough time for the final preparation of the meeting with her team. Megan hoped Kayla wouldn't keep her waiting. She glanced at her phone. A long list of texts and emails awaited her response. She responded to one from Rochelle, confirming the catered lunch scheduled for noon sharp today. Megan kept most Wednesday schedules clear, allowing the team meeting activities to take full sway.

Megan saw Kayla at the door. She stood so Kayla could see her, and they waved, with grins, as their eyes met.

"Hi, Kayla."

"Hello, Megan. Hope I didn't keep you waiting. I know I'm a little late."

"Not at all. Are you doing okay?"

"Yes, considering everything. I guess I'm holding up. Today is my first visit to the campus. What an awesome care-giving place St. Jude has become. Thanks for arranging my pass to enter the gate."

"Yes, it's extraordinary. What a vision Danny Thomas had—and what a legacy he left. If he could see it now."

"He does see it."

"I hope so. Mr. Thomas would be pleased with the way his dream of service to kids and their families has been preserved, not to mention his dogmatic belief in a cure. It's inspiring."

Kayla's pulse increased with the drumbeat of her pounding heart. *Lord, please help me control my feelings,* she prayed. "Inspiring, yes, but St. Jude is a place taken for granted, even by people with children."

"Until they need it."

"Yeah, that's true. I'm thankful my family hasn't required St. Jude's treatment. At the same time, my lack of involvement makes me feel a little guilty. As I said, I have not even been on campus. We've contributed financially at times, and we sponsored a few events, but nothing more."

Megan identified with Kayla's emotion, and her sadness—kids everywhere, but none she knew as her own. Megan knew no right words were available. She had, on occasion, sat at this table to speak first words to a mother, a friend, who had lost a child at St. Jude. But more often, Kay Kafe had been a rallying point for first meetings with parents after successful surgery, or healing and discharge, or continuation of treatment of their child's condition. "I'm sorry for your loss."

"Thanks, Megan. Don't worry, I'm dealing with it, with waves of desperation—a yo-yo, up and down. But I'm getting there. I can't imagine coping with what I see here, what the parents in this room have to deal with every day of their lives. It helps to keep things in perspective."

"Well put. I become more thankful with each passing day, considering what I might have become had it not been for these children and their parents. If there is a God, St. Jude has been his gift to me."

If there is a God. Kayla repeated Megan's words to herself. *How can she not believe in God? How can anyone not believe in God?* "So, you don't believe in God?"

"My apologies, Kayla. I spoke metaphorically in saying, 'If there is a God' in the same way I might say, 'Yes, there is a God.' I didn't intend to be offensive."

Kayla felt naïve. "Oh, no, I should offer the apology. I didn't mean to come across as judging you."

They laughed together.

"Glad we got through that one," Megan said with a chuckle. She took Kayla's hand and lifted her coffee cup as a toast. "I don't have to ask if you believe in God. Jack Williams tells me you study the Bible at Liberty University. I'm sure the syllabus is compelling."

"Yes, I'm a Christian, and my main course of study is apologetics, which centers on knowing what you believe and why you believe it. It comes from a word that means "to give an answer." The idea is to have a ready answer for anyone who asks why you believe what you believe. For me right now, I'll admit, it's more about answering those questions for myself."

"The more you're able to answer your own questions, the better you're able to answer those questions for others. For myself, I've learned to live without the answers."

"It's tough when you can't answer the 'why' question."

"So, why bother?" Taken aback by Kayla's curious look, Megan added, "It's a blame game, Kayla. Every one of these kids has asked the question, 'why me?' and so far I've heard no satisfactory answer. But, unlike older folks, they don't get stuck on the question. It's more important to deal with the disease than to answer why it happened, so the kids bravely accept having no answers and conclude the matter.

"The kids' determination and hope lead the parents down the road to reality. Optimism relieves pain." After a brief hesitation, she added, "Forgive me. That was cold. I don't want to be insensitive to the pain I know you're experiencing. I'm oversensitive to my world, and I'm wrong to compare my world with yours."

"I'm not offended in any way, Megan. I know you didn't mean it negatively, and I can see it. These kids don't deserve their dilemma, and neither do their parents."

"It's often those parents who profess to have faith who begin by blaming God. Usually, the little boy or girl breaks the parent of the blame. You can't blame God. Even if I believed in God, I wouldn't blame him. What God would cause such suffering?"

Kayla was impressed. *She has more faith than I have.* "Your point is well taken. I can see how a reasonable unbeliever wouldn't blame God. It defies logic for any unbeliever to blame God. An atheist can't blame a God he or she doesn't believe exists. An atheist might say, 'If there is a god, he caused this by letting it happen.' It's a straw man argument. You can't have it both ways. You can't blame a God who doesn't exist.

"The tough part for a Christian—a true believer, if you will—is expecting God to prevent such a thing. He may not have instigated it, but by not preventing it, he becomes a cause. I'm not saying I believe God is a cause of our pain."

"No offense, Kayla, but I'll bet you do. Tell me, why does God allow suffering? Why would—"

A young voice from the other side of the cafeteria interrupted.

"Megan!" a little boy shouted as he ran to the table and wrapped his arms around Megan.

"Ethan, my little sweetheart, I'm so proud of you," Megan sang to him with a hug tighter than she should. "Are you ready to go up?" Megan held the boy at arm's length. "Let's dance!" She took his hands in hers and moved his arms up and down, swaying herself back and forth.

"Hello, Terrance," Megan smiled, as she gave the six-foot-six-inch man who followed the little boy, and who Kayla guessed was Ethan's father, a strong hug. "How is Kamala doing? Let me guess: she loves her new job at the Arts Center." Terrance smiled with affirmation.

Megan wrapped one arm around Ethan and outstretched the other toward Kayla as if presenting a celebrity. "Kayla, this is my good friend Ethan, and his dad, Terrance. Ethan is here today for his third round of chemo—correct, Dad? And the hope is he will have only one left. Kayla, you would never guess this little guy is sick—he's continually running and jumping around. Ethan loves Superman, and he loves dancing. You are my little Superman," she said with a cadence and another big hug.

"I'm Superboy," Ethan corrected her.

"You sure are. You're my brave little super boy, and you'll grow up to be a super man, just like your daddy. Terrance, I'm glad to see you today. Tell Kamala hello for me. I'm glad we don't have to hang together the way we used to, but I still miss her."

"She misses you too and will hate she wasn't able to be here today. Take care. Good to meet you, Kayla. Hang in there."

Ethan's dad walked away, carrying Ethan. "Bye, Megan, I love you."

"Love you too, Ethan. Bye. You'll do good."

"He seems to be a happy little boy," Kayla said, watching Ethan's dad walk toward the hospital.

"After he turned three, he had severe headaches. A CT scan revealed he had a tumor in his brain tissue called ependymoma, and he had chemo to shrink the tumor. After chemo, he survived surgery, followed by weeks of radiation. He's had three more rounds of chemo. It's been just under three years. He's here today for chemo, and the doctors hope one more round will do it."

"How can a six-year-old deal with what he's been through?"

"He accepts his life as it is. He's positive and doesn't see himself as sick. And he loves Superman. He draws Superman's picture in the playroom, but he draws it with lightning speed because he can't stop dancing for more than a couple of minutes. Ethan is another St. Jude hero. Sorry, where were we before Ethan came in?"

"You were asking me why God would allow Ethan's brain tumor. I don't know. The usual answer from the Christian perspective is we can't know. God is sovereign, meaning he can do whatever he wants, and only he knows why. He may allow certain things to happen, and in some sense, he is the cause. At other times an event happens, not because he causes it, but because he just doesn't prevent it." Kayla didn't know where that idea came from, but it made good sense to her. "Sorry Megan, I didn't intend such an *esoteric pronouncement.*"

"Don't apologize, Kayla. I'm interested in hearing how other people, particularly Christians, answer those questions. Ever wonder why we unbelievers are quick to blame God for suffering, but few of us, if any, blame the devil? 'If there is a devil, he caused this to happen.' Ever hear that expression?"

"'The devil made me do it.'" Kayla had a quick laugh. "That's an expression used to excuse a human activity, not to point to a divine cause."

"So true. Those *why* questions have plagued me. I didn't intend to accuse you of blaming God for your tragedy, Kayla. I was accusing myself. I struggled with deep, maybe even clinical, depression in my earlier life. But seeing Ethan and other young people who deal with these torturous diseases, and seeing the strength of their parents, changed me. I'm not saying I got the answers I wanted, but I quit asking the questions."

Pleased to hear Megan's forthrightness in voicing her opinion about the spiritual side of things, Kayla could feel at ease with Megan. "You've been helpful to me, Megan. I envy your strength. I may not attain such a position until I get to heaven."

Within fifteen minutes, they discussed more topics than anyone can cover in such a brief period. Megan touched on her role as manager/ambassador for SAVE and how they are dealing with the problem of unwanted pregnancy. She seemed a little surprised that Kayla could discuss pregnancy and abortion so early on.

Kayla wanted to attend the upcoming SAVE meeting. She also wanted to know more about St. Jude and what it would take to become involved in a supporting role. Megan invited Kayla to meet her friend Rochelle. Megan said apologetics would be an irresistible topic of discussion with Rochelle. Kayla asked Megan to visit her church.

CHAPTER 8

E ach biweekly team meeting, held on Wednesday, was planned with the absolute precision demanded by the St. Jude board. For Megan and Rochelle, the no-nonsense atmosphere required by the agenda reflected their preferred way of doing business. Neither of them expected anything less, ensuring that the robust and predictable proton delivery system remained a priority of hospital leadership and a focus of the ALSAC board.

Eliminating redundant activities was a process-driven endeavor. Megan believed elements of their cost-efficient success were the result of new testing procedures and resources designed to minimize redundancy, most of which she developed. Rochelle guaranteed staff and vendor attendance, bringing together a compelling mix of the right people, those who needed a message about efficiency and excellence in proton beam delivery. Megan and Rochelle together were seen as a picture of efficiency and excellence.

Where's the fun in that? Megan was a stalwart supporter of no-nonsense presentation of data when young lives were at stake. Still, she believes the facts, if presented accurately, are unencumbered, often enhanced, by livening things up a bit.

Rochelle concentrated on the physical environment, making sure delivery of the meal, expertly prepared by St. Jude chefs, was on time and accurate. She used Fit the Pace Catering, the new company founded by her sister Cindy, who concentrated on delivering the satisfaction of individual customer service to members of the group. Cindy created an artful, *Kids at St. Jude* setup, which could be modified between meetings, adding an atmosphere of freshness to a gathering of boring sameness.

Cindy personally supervised food preparation and delivery for team meetings, being in attendance at each serving. One enhancement was serving the meal in the first few minutes of the meeting but holding a special surprise dessert until the end. Cindy's staff researched the dessert most favored by each attendee, accommodating any who didn't fit the mold.

Megan began the meeting with an oral quiz, a six-minute list of five questions that she would answer during her presentation. She only used questions that she was sure no one could answer before her delivery. With few exceptions, all attendees scored zero or near zero. She also ended her presentation with a quiz, using the same five questions, and most scored 100 percent. As Cindy served desserts, Megan asked the group what they learned today. Most attendees could name at least five new facts they learned.

Megan arrived early to review her PowerPoint for the meeting. Cindy grabbed her immediately to express doubt about accurately providing for two respected visitors to the meeting today.

"Hi, Megan. The attendance list shows Doctors Hamm and Kohn in the group today. I'm concerned we were not able to accommodate Dr. Kohn's dessert specialty. We've got chocolate babka. I tried it, but I'm not sure if it tastes good or bad."

"Don't worry too much, Cindy. Dr. Kohn will not be harsh. He will appreciate the special effort you made for him. The setup today is beautiful. Rochelle will be pleased. I know I am."

"Thanks, Megan. Thanks for the opportunity to cater your events. The cafeteria staff at St. Jude is helpful beyond measure.

They are willing to take a back seat to let us handle everything. They're the best, and they make me look good."

"Yes, everything they do is an expression of their concern for the kids. It's their calling. Hey, listen, I know that you know that I know you have a difficult choice ahead of you. Have you and Kevin made any decisions?"

"It's all we talk about these days. Kevin has the same concerns I have. We're not ready for marriage, and we don't want to bring a baby into the world without a family bond. We wouldn't be ready for a baby even if we were married. Adoption is not even an issue. I can't accept the idea of someone else raising a child of mine. It's hypocrisy. We were stupid to let this happen in the first place. It's not what we wanted."

Megan dismissed the idea of revealing her abortion. *Now is not the time, even if I were ready.* "I know these decisions are difficult ones to make, Cindy, but consider that you may regret certain decisions for the rest of your life."

"You can't imagine how difficult. I don't know what I may regret more, having this child or not having this child.

"Stop, Tommy, hold on a second." Cindy turned back a food runner from entering the room. "Don't even bring out the dessert tray. We don't want anyone to know what they're gonna get. Sorry Megan, maybe we can talk later."

Megan wanted to begin a conversation with Cindy about her pregnancy and move to her decision to have an abortion. Neither had even spoken the word in their forty-five second encounter. Still, Megan noted that the conversation began with unspoken abortion. The pain of her deep-felt emotion surfaced when she considered her decision and the bouts of icy depression she has suffered through the passing years.

Rochelle entered the room at a quick pace. "Megan, it's time," she said, bringing Megan back to the present.

"Yes, I'm ready. Let's open the visual for the presentation. I want to check that the quick filter I've embedded in the dashboard displays my list of twenty points only two at a time, with a scroll bar. Viewers will jump ahead of me if I show the complete list." Megan moved to the dais, raised a step above the floor, to open the presentation platform.

"Andre is standing by to help if any problems surface."

"It looks good, a great setup and ready to go."

Cindy and her group positioned the nondescript red packages around the designated seating arrangement. Cindy personalized the drinks as well, the result of polling ahead of the meeting.

Cindy's attention to detail and her scrupulous organizational skill reminded Megan of Rochelle, and she decided it was a family talent acquired through generations. Cindy and Rochelle made it look easy.

The presentation went well. Questions ensued, and Megan considered the audience participation a good measure of the meeting's success. Megan chatted with attendees and addressed additional issues at the close of the session.

***

"Cindy, the meal was superb," Megan said, "another powerful addition to the meeting. I've not seen a more positive environment for the delivery of useful, even if tedious, facts. I don't know how you guys do it. Your setup and box-lunch presentation are what I call a book undercover."

"Yeah, don't judge a book by its cover. Right?"

"Something like that. It's more like a delightful book without a cover, at least nothing more than a red cover. You bring out these red bags, designed to announce a catered lunch, but prepared to deliver fine cuisine. It's a book undercover."

"Thanks, Megan. It's good of you to be complimentary. I got close enough to Dr. Kohn to hear a little moan of pleasure as he took his first bite of babka. He seemed to like it, although I don't know why. To each his own, as they say. I heard a number of them say, great meeting, great meal."

"To each his due. The meeting is so worthwhile, and we were able to deliver a message the team needed to hear. I'm delighted."

"Same here," Cindy said. "We'll clean up and be out before you know it."

"Can you let your guys drive the truck back? You and I should visit. I'm heading out, and we can talk in the car. I'll take you back to your shop."

"I came in my car, but I can take a few minutes. We can talk here if you want."

"Yes, I want to hear what's on your heart."

Rochelle anticipated Megan and Cindy were about to meet, and she walked with an attendee as an excuse to leave the room.

"I love you, Megan, and I know you and Rochelle are against even a hint of abortion."

"Don't beat around the bush."

"No, I won't. You are against it on principle. Your allegiance to SAVE motivates you to uphold certain principles. I've never viewed it from the perspective I'm seeing it now. I want to honor the message SAVE has preached, but now I'm one of those women who face that awful abortion decision." Cindy clenched her fists. "No one understands the position I'm in, having to make this decision. I don't want to be pregnant."

"But you are."

"I don't have many options."

63

"Adoption?"

"Out of the question. I'm certain if I had this baby, I would not give it up. I would love it. That's my biggest fear."

"Love is your biggest fear?"

"You know what I mean."

"Cindy, you know you already have this baby. This baby is a person. Do you believe that?"

"Yes, but—"

"My fear is you will make a decision that will haunt you for the rest of your life, and I don't want you to have to live with such regret. You have options that many of these other women don't have. Are you basing your decision on what Kevin wants?"

"Yes, I'll admit it. Abortion, right? Remember, those were the first words Kevin uttered, without any real consideration for what having an abortion means. He's not ready to have a baby either."

"Like you, he already has a baby. Can he come to terms with the two of you being pregnant?"

"He can come to terms with the idea of there already being a baby inside me, but he hasn't considered any possibility other than abortion. He doesn't know it, but he would love the baby too."

"Cindy, consider where you are, compared to most of the women at SAVE. You are a mature-minded woman, not too young to assume the responsibility. You and Kevin have good jobs, and together, you have excellent financial security. You don't have other children to consider. Women we counsel at SAVE are afraid, not for themselves, but afraid for the well-being of the child, should they give birth.

"Your biggest fear is not loving, but adjusting your life for the benefit of your child. Kevin's fear is no different. Being a parent is hard work, and I know it's fearful. I'll quote FDR here: 'You have nothing to fear but fear itself.'"

"I was afraid you would say that."

CHAPTER 9

For two decades, Jerry Phillips ran a successful law practice centered in Collierville, Tennessee, serving clients in East Memphis and Shelby County. Feeling a call to the ministry, he set his successful career aside to teach biblical doctrine full time. Speaking at seminaries and churches began early, with pro bono teaching of extracurricular classes at a local Bible college. He felt called as an instructor of the Sunday morning Bible study class at Open Door Church.

Personal financial investments offered Jerry an early retirement. To make up for lost time, he enrolled in Babcock Seminary's accelerated curriculum. He studied ferociously and researched every topic imaginable. Being a gifted writer, he wrote empirical articles for seminary publication, choosing words and images suitable for poetical essays. He graduated at the top of his class.

These days he leads an extracurricular Bible study group attended by friends, church leaders, and a few selected students in the modest conference room of his law office. The focus is apologetics, analyzing critical truths of the Christian faith, designed to provide believers with tools to express what they believe and why they believe it.

Kayla knew Jerry's law office well. Jammed with law books, crammed even tighter than usual to make room for Bibles, commentaries, and concordances, the office occupied the lower level of what Kayla saw as an ancient building on the town square. Kayla admired the value Jerry placed on preserving his multiple volumes, and she loved how he improved the old building, making it seem new again.

Kayla was not ready to resume class attendance with the Bible study group. Jerry recommended they meet Wednesday afternoon, a time he knew they would not be disturbed. They both agreed a follow up of the meeting with Pastor at Kayla's home would be of benefit.

Kayla sat at her usual spot. "Jerry, I can recognize and separate the difference between biblical truth and the court's truth. My truth, biblical truth, is considered by the court as no more than a belief. You and I believe the Bible is the truth. It doesn't just contain the truth. It is the truth. The court won't—can't—allow biblical truth, regardless of the evidence presented."

"Yes, you're correct. The presentation of facts contrary to the evidence is not allowed, even if true. The court sees truth in a relative sense, depending on the presented evidence. Nevertheless, while the prosecution and the defense may draw different conclusions from the evidence, the truth presented must adhere to that evidence. The system sees words spoken in an evidential context as truth. The judge will declare any truth presented contrary to the evidence as irrelevant. Biblical truth is irrelevant."

"Nothing personal, Dr. Phillips, but that is intellectual mumbo jumbo."

"Call it what you want. Many innocent lives have been saved by adhering to this principle. In legal discourse, it's a part of probative value."

"I can't relate to legal terms."

"The court evaluates the evidence presented—and the facts gleaned from that evidence—by the prosecution and the defense. In our current context, Mark Jones says a passenger in his car caused him to accelerate, which may be true. However, since no evidence exists to support this claim, his statement cannot be accepted by the court. The jury may believe it, but the judge will have instructed the jurors to base their decision on the evidence, not on what they think to be true. The jury will no doubt comply without argument, aligning themselves with the judge's order, and fulfill the law.

"This example favors the prosecution. But this principle can provide an even greater benefit for the defense. Consider a given jury is not conforming to this edict. The jury may believe a defendant is guilty without enough evidence for the required proof beyond a reasonable doubt, resulting in incarceration, or worse."

"I guess I can deal with that. It smacks of theatre, but seems fair."

"Given Frank Zingeralli's untethered imagination, the truth Frank sees will not be the truth the prosecutor sees. To your point, he will present his case in an award-winning fashion. You should do what's best for yourself—take whatever comes with patience and grace, recognizing the court does not seek the truth. Its one goal is to determine whether the defendant is guilty or not guilty based on the evidence presented."

"I can handle it, but I'm a little anxious about taking the stand. I'm finding my faith tested daily, and the idea of facing a cross-examination is hard to accept. To the judge and jury, Danny's death happened in the past. When I meet with Jack Williams at the DA's office, he is a little better, but he wants details, and he asks questions about the accident as if it happened in the remote past. No telling what tense Mark Jones's attorney will use. That's the toughest part—it's in the present for me."

Jerry slid the apologetics class syllabus across the table. "This may help. Check the outline for the upcoming class."

"'The Power of Faith.' It hits home."

"The Bible is filled with examples of those who lived for God and made life-threatening decisions that changed the world, based on their faith alone. In this session, we'll focus on Christians who are mercilessly rebuked in the world today. Yet, they hold fast to what they believe. We'll discuss how these Christians have been made stronger by the testing of their faith. They possess irrevocable inner security we can relate to in our own lives. I hope you will attend."

Kayla had an edgy tone in her voice she couldn't overcome. "I've got to work through the feelings I'm having right now about my faith and my life."

"Hold on, Kayla. As you know, your faith is based on what you consider truth and applying that truth to your life. Now it seems you may be despairing about spiritual truth. Five minutes ago, you were defending the truth."

"At times, I'm an exception to the truth. I know the truth. Whether I can apply it to myself is what bothers me. I know my life is blessed compared to others, people around the world who can't feed their children, or even get a drink of water while I bathe in drinking water. Megan and I visited this morning at St. Jude. St. Jude's parents live a lifetime of agony, dealing with the suffering of their children, who must deal with even more. Now I've got to deal with the loss of my son. I've not answered the 'why' question—why did God allow this to happen, but I've come to terms with it."

"Have you?"

"Well, I guess not. I've concluded I'm not going to find the answer. I've moved on to another *why* question. Why can't I accept what I believe?"

"You believe God has an answer even if he won't reveal it to you?"

"I believe God's sovereignty requires him to have answers, but I still can't apply this truth to my life."

"'Lord, I believe. Help my unbelief.'"

"Yes, I have said it over and over. It's like repentance. If you believe repentance comes with salvation, you should repent. If you don't repent, you don't have real faith, and you don't truly believe."

"Faith consists of two ingredients, Kayla. The first is believing in what you cannot explicitly prove, and the second is trusting what you believe as truth. It doesn't mean believing without evidence. If you're thrown overboard and don't want to drown, you cry for a life preserver ring. The first part of faith is believing visual evidence. You watch as the ring hits the water, and you believe it to be there. The second part is trust, grabbing ahold of the ring. Otherwise, you can't survive."

"Good analogy, Jerry. I'm not grabbing the ring. The question is not, why did I fall, but what do I have to do to survive, right? I know the answer but can't seem to swim toward the ring. Why?

"Because you haven't taken to heart the providence of God in his sovereignty."

"God's middle knowledge?"

"Yes. Did your son's death just happen as an unassociated event, like a leaf falling in autumn?"

"It's counterintuitive, but I believe it's a part of God's plan. At the same time, it's hard to believe he couldn't have created an alternative."

"Maybe, maybe not."

"I don't follow."

"How do you define God's middle knowledge?"

"I don't remember a book definition since you told us not to memorize but to apply. Apologetically, middle—"

"As I have stated, I don't want punditry. I want individual thinking. What does it mean to you?"

"God knows what will happen in every possible circumstance. He knows what people will do and say, of their own free will, if he places them in a certain situation."

"Give me an example."

"God knew what Paul would willfully write if he were in a jailhouse in Philippi."

"What do you mean by willfully?"

"Paul wrote advice to the Philippian church, writing a positive letter with pastoral advice, and told them he was content. He wrote to them with instructions God wanted them to receive. The Holy Spirit didn't dictate the words to Paul. He wasn't in a trance. He wrote from his heart."

"And God knew his heart?"

"Yes, and he knew what Paul would write from the Philippian jail versus what he would write in an alternative circumstance."

"What's the difference?"

"Well, God knew in what circumstance Paul would write from his own free will what God wanted to say."

"Couldn't God have determined a different place where Paul would freely write the same thing as he wrote from the Philippian jail?"

"Maybe, maybe not. I see what you mean."

"You've considered only the beginning of it. In the first place, how can God know what will happen in every situation every person can encounter in life?"

"He has foreknowledge. He is omniscient."

"Punditry."

"Okay, let me put it this way. God's power is all inclusive. He created our vast universe. He spoke, and it happened. God is powerful enough and intelligent enough to create some quadrillion planets circling trillions of stars in billions of galaxies. More than that, God requires that all those planets and stars are subject to the laws of physics. He shouldn't have a problem knowing what Paul would write in a given situation."

"You're off to a good start. You've applied your classroom training well. What else?"

"What do you mean, what else?"

"Does God put you in different circumstances, knowing how you will respond, what decisions you will make, and saying what he wants you to say using your free will? Sounds like puppetry, hands manipulating wires and ropes, for God's amusement."

"Yes, it does—to unbelievers, or to believers who've not considered it. God knew every condition surrounding the birth, life, and death of Jesus. He knew the incredible suffering Jesus would experience, but he allowed it. Even more, he foreordained it. Why would God foreordain the suffering and death of Christ? Why not find a time and place for Jesus's ministry where the people would accept his message, and make him king? Maybe God couldn't find such a time or place. That seems to be the key."

"Careful now."

"Right. We don't want to move from God being a puppeteer to God being the puppet, where he has no real control over the world. The activities of men acting out their free will can't dominate God. Still, it's contrary to reason to believe in this mysterious control God has over the free will actions of people. If he decides for us, we are not free."

"Now you're getting to the root of it."

"Okay, Jerry, I'm feeling like the puppet in this conversation. So, you tell me, where is—or better yet, what is—the root of it?

"We call it middle knowledge because it stands between God's natural knowledge and his free knowledge. Many scriptures deal with these three controversial topics together, and others address them individually. But that's not the root I want you to consider now, the basis of which will help you in the present."

"That's what I need."

"Although it's hotly debated, the first thing we have to accept is that middle knowledge is beyond God's control. God knows what will happen in a given situation, but he doesn't control what will happen. He chose to create the world he created after considering all the possibilities. If God's laying aside of this power were not so, we are back to the contradiction of his controlling our free will."

Jerry's voice exuded genuine kindness and compassion. "Second, we should also accept the true meaning of God's omniscience. He foreknew and considered every possible condition in your life, in all possible worlds he could create. He also knew every possible way you might react to those multiple conditions. He developed his plan for your life, foreknowing all decisions you would freely make in every possible circumstance. He perfectly performs his will through those circumstances without, in any way, diminishing your free will to act."

"Okay, so God can't control, or maybe it's better to say he has decided not to overrule my free will in a given situation. He can choose my every circumstance, to exercise my free will based on his will. Coming to terms with God's ability to know every possible scenario in the lives of all people, past and future, requires intense thinking. Even with an infinite number of possible situations from which to choose, there may not be one that, in our view, would be considered a good one. It's heartbreaking."

"Perhaps he created those quadrillions of planets around those trillions of stars in those billions of galaxies to demonstrate his ability to superintend close to an infinity of different situations in which people make free will decisions."

"I don't follow. Why would there not be an infinite number of possible scenarios from which to choose?"

"Consider what the word *infinite* entails. With an infinite number of possibilities, there would inevitably be a good one available. As we have already determined, such is not the case. The possibilities, therefore, cannot be infinite."

"I follow you. It gives an expanded view of the Bible when it says God chose us before the foundation of the world. He foresaw a circumstance in which I would freely accept Christ, and, out of all possible worlds, he created one in which that circumstance occurred."

"I love the way you have personalized it. You're getting close to the taproot."

"Could there have been a world in which I would have freely chosen not to accept Christ?"

"Maybe, maybe not. It may not be that simple—or that complex? A loving God wants everyone to accept Christ. Perhaps no possible world can exist in which every person accepts Christ. In the words of William E. Rankin, 'God could not have created a world in which square circles exist. He could not create a world in which Peter would not deny Christ if placed in precisely the same circumstance.'"

"Okay, are we ready to reveal the root buried in my condition?"

"Yes, we have arrived. Let me first set the stage again for what we have learned about middle knowledge. God knows all the possible worlds he could have created and what every free creature would do in all the various circumstances of those possible worlds."

"Yes, so far, so good."

"Consider Paul in another location. He and Barnabas preached at Lystra. One minute the crowd hailed them as gods. Shortly after proclaiming him a god, the townspeople stoned Paul, dragged him out of town, and left him for dead. God knew his placing Paul in Lystra meant being stoned. God, through his middle knowledge, knew the world he chose to create included Paul being stoned and left for dead, yet he created that world."

"I'm with you. We are back to where we started."

"Now, we are ready for the key to God's providence. There exists a reconciliation, a working together, of divine sovereignty and human freedom. An omniscient God can achieve his will through decisions freely made by all people in the world, whether good or bad. Situations we encounter today are the result of earlier free decisions made by other people, decisions which God had to bring about, to achieve his will."

Kayla looked left and right, searching both sides of her mind for an answer. "You're saying all circumstances created by the independent decisions of all people, good and bad, are combined to cause an unrelated situation—let's say the act of George Washington crossing the Delaware. All circumstances of world history can be accounted for by God achieving his purposes."

"Yes, you've hit the nail on its head. The apparent contradiction between God's sovereignty, unfathomable to us, and human freedom, which endeavors to work against his sovereignty, come together. God achieves his will by all human beings acting freely—a wondrous miracle."

"What about the bad stuff? How is God then not responsible for evil?"

"Simply put, God wills the good stuff, and he allows the bad stuff. He wants us to do well, but he permits suffering, and he allows creatures to do the sinful acts he knew they would do since he wills our freedom to choose. But in his providence, God so arranges things that, in the end, even the sinful acts of people and the suffering those acts can cause will serve to achieve his purpose. And we know his purpose, his will, is good.

"One of my favorite parts of the Bible is the telling of the story of Joseph in Genesis, and it points to God's middle knowledge. As you know, after his brothers considered killing Joseph, they decided to sell him into slavery, where he suffered for years. In the end, though, his success gave him a position second to the Pharaoh, and he saved countless people from starving, including his brothers and his father. When the truth came out, Joseph said to his brothers, 'You meant evil against me, but God meant it for good, to bring about this present result.'"

"You've given me a lot to consider, Jerry. These ideas provide an answer that will strengthen my belief. It still hurts, but accepting these ideas as truth helps to ease the pain."

CHAPTER 10

Megan strolled down Monroe Avenue, from the old Cossitt Library at Front Street, toward the cobblestone landing along the river. The upstairs conference room in the library added a studied atmosphere to the weekly SAVE meetings. She stepped out to allow members to congregate.

For February in Memphis, the day was unseasonably bright and mild, with a hint of the humid summer conditions only a few months away. Out on the river, the gusty wind blew in a chilly reminder that it was still winter. Megan turned up her collar with a shrug.

She grinned as a tugboat lashed to a group of barges slipped down the river toward the bridge, southbound for Vicksburg and New Orleans. The *Memphis Queen* paddled out toward the mouth of Wolf River, with passengers gathered on her second deck, out of the wind. It must be a private party, strangers creating memories of a city they don't know. I'm sure they had to pay big bucks for an outing in the dead of winter.

Megan usually arrived early, allowing time for a memorable walk along the ancient cobblestones that studded the slope. During the 1800s, steamboats could anchor in the firm footing year-round, and Memphis grew into a world leader in cotton, hardwood, and other commodities of the time.

Stepping stone to stone along the landing brought a flurry of memories. She thought of her dad taking her hand as they walked along the river bluff to board the *Memphis Queen* for an excursion toward President's Island. She listened with wonder as her dad told poetic stories of his youth, when he and his brother played along the riverbank as kids, just he and Uncle Jim. They cable-walked a barge and dropped onto Mud Island's muggy lair. They caked their hands and shirts with rusty mud and learned that time is short, then comes the flood.

For Dad, a kid who grew up in Hurt Village in the fifties, Mud Island was a vast wilderness where wompus cats prowled. Few families lived on the island in those days. The Bates brothers lived there, Albert and Nuby. They came to school wearing coon fingers attached to long chains that hung from their necks. Everyone marveled at their primitive lifestyle— no electricity, no gas, no running water. They exhaled a foul, undiluted odor that penetrated their clothes, their books, even their lunch pails.

As a kid, Megan's dad had a morning paper route covering Seventh Street to Front Street between Chelsea and Auction. He and Uncle Jim dropped their paper bags and ran through an opening in the concrete seawall to the edge of Wolf River. A network of barges and mooring dolphins made an ideal bridge to the island. They tight-walked across the cable of an abandoned barge to watch the Bates brothers row their little jon boat across Wolf River and drag the boat over to a cast iron bollard on the bank. With practiced precision, they turned the boat over to conceal its oars, chained it to the bollard, collected their books and their lunch pails, and scampered up the levy, headed for school.

Old Bill Padgett lived on Mud Island too. Dad said nobody ever knew where he came from or why he lived on the island. A cantankerous old coot, his bushy white eyebrows crashed into a bulbous nose. His mouth was little more than a hole in the bottom of his face from which he screamed profanities garbled by a rattling chain of deep-lodged phlegm. One could find no wompus cats at the end of the island where Padgett lived—nobody knew why, but none were surprised.

For Megan's dad, Mud Island created a world of danger, an enigmatic ecstasy of adventure, where lurked the constant threat and the joy of narrow escapes. Aside from the possibility of being shot by old man Padgett, wild people were hiding there, men who lived in the woods without having a home, derelicts—skywegians, Uncle Jim called them. No telling what they would do to a boy of ten or eleven.

Megan smiled at happy times she remembered before the tragedy of 2002 when November stole her youth. The memory of her dad's spirit of adventure and the loving times they shared, reliving those adventures along Wolf River, helped her through those difficult times.

To Megan, the college freshman, the horror of rape, coupled with the dread and guilt of abortion, seemed an insurmountable obstacle. The extreme remorse following the loss of her baby's life turned what seemed a reasonable act into the biggest mistake of her life.

Her parents were not in favor of abortion, but her dad agreed they would support her in whatever decision she made. Megan knew why her parents didn't stop her or refuse to accept her course of action. The decision was hers to make, using her best judgment. She had earned her dad's trust, and he would stand by her right or wrong. That's the way he operated. The best counsel in the world has little value if you can't make your own decisions. *Dad believed it was not my life if I didn't live it.* Megan often delivered that message to others.

So, here I am, hiking back to Cossitt Library for a SAVE meeting. Megan leaned her head and smiled at the poster taped to the door of the library, with SAVE printed in bold green letters at the top. SHARE ANTI-ABORTION VALUES EVERYWHERE circled the bottom of the poster, under the picture of a mom holding her baby in the center. It was a legitimate indication of Dad's idea of restraint.

Some outsiders asked why the group used such a weak byline to create SAVE as the acronym. It seemed closer to a gospel witness handing out tracts than a group trying to eliminate abortion. Megan responded that SAVE is a backronym for Share Anti-abortion Values Everywhere. Yes, the group's idea is to spread the gospel of giving birth and providing life. Screaming at potential moms about the rights of unborn children adds no value. SAVE doesn't offer hellfire and brimstone preaching but honest and accurate information. People can decide for themselves.

"Hi, Dad, how's everything?" Megan hugged her dad, who had posted himself inside the door to greet all comers. "How is Mom doing? Is she already upstairs?"

"Yes, she's helping Eliza set up. We are expecting a large group tonight, and I'm glad you're here, Megan. I hoped you would arrive early and have a chance to speak with Eliza before a bunch of people demanded her attention. How are things at St. Jude?"

"Going well, indeed. We got the best news today—you remember Carla and her mom from Argentina?"

"Oh yes, she has had a prolonged battle with ALL, bless her heart."

"Yes, well, her prognosis is excellent, and she had her last chemo treatment today. I'm hoping to be with her family this weekend before they head back to Rio Colorado. Carla's dad, Julio, will come on Friday to take them back. I've had so many good talks with Carla's mom, Sofia, and I love Carla to death. She has been a brave little girl, facing her cancer head-on. Like most of the kids at St. Jude, her attitude had a lot to do with her remission."

"All the kids at St. Jude are heroes. So are the doctors. So are you."

"Okay, enough of that, Dad. You're making me blush. It's true about the kids, though. Since they don't give up, they're never defeated."

Megan's dad greeted a couple who came in the door as her mom descended the staircase near the library's front door. "Megan, hello, sweetheart," her mom said, pulling her close with a kiss on her cheek. "I've missed you, honey. I know you're busy at St. Jude, but you don't come around much these days."

"Mom, you know I come as often as I can. The new office addition at St. Jude keeps me busy. Several of the supporting activities for proton emission are moving into the new office tower, and I'm part of the team to make sure everything goes without a hitch."

"I know, dear, you're doing everything possible under the circumstances. I hope things will settle down once you complete this phase of your operation."

"It's unlikely, Mom." Megan wondered what her mom meant by a phase of operation. *She's trying to visualize my relationship with St. Jude.* "You could say I'm in a lifelong phase of a lifelong operation."

"I know how valuable you are to St. Jude—and to the company that I'm thankful I don't have to know anything about," her mom replied joyfully. "Your dad and I are proud of the job you're doing. Keep doing it. We'll fit in wherever we can."

Megan was already up a couple of stairs. She turned around with a smile. "Thanks, Mom."

Megan staged the meeting room for a group of fifty or less, sufficient for most meetings. Eliza Stokes guaranteed excellent attendance at events where she presented. Megan made arrangements for additional foldup chairs to be used if the group exceeded the expected number.

She checked the stacks of current literature used to describe the long-term effects of abortion on the parents of the aborted child, and SAVE's drive to deliver their doctrine in a nonviolent, unthreatening way. If the message is authentic, people will listen and take it to heart.

No one was more authentic than Eliza Stokes. Born in Memphis and raised in a happy family, Eliza nevertheless dealt with the guilt of surviving a sibling at an early age. Her mother became pregnant after Eliza's fourth birthday but lost the baby late in her second trimester. Her parents believed it improper to explain the details of a miscarriage to a four-year-old. They told Eliza her brother or sister would not be born, without including the details. She remembered being confused and afraid, filled with anxiety. Her confusion led to guilt and a fear that she might be next. Family talks seemed to focus on the fact that Eliza was there while her brother or sister was not.

Megan welcomed Eliza to the meeting and thanked her for bringing her message detailing the effects of unplanned parenthood's death by abortion on those left behind.

"I'm thankful you were able to come, Eliza. I can't wait to hear your message tonight. I respect your story-telling ability, and your gift of making complicated arguments seem to have simple solutions."

"Thanks for your enthusiasm, Megan. Sometimes folks accuse me of making the simple and obvious more complex. How have you been?" Eliza wore a smile and offered a fervent shake of her head as she took Megan's hand. "One complex issue is the unaborted child we leave behind, a problem for which I have no simple solution."

"That's often a problem, but it's also often not a problem," Megan said, as she thought, *Duh, what a dumb way to put it.* The expression on Eliza's face seemed to be saying Megan had a knack for expressing simplicity differently. "Abortion is often chosen for reasons other than the woman's health or the inability of the potential mother to care for the child. People save lives when they understand the consequences and care enough to do what's right?"

"Yes, using abortion as a convenience, a way of avoiding responsibility, or as a means of after-the-fact birth control is a separate issue and should be prevented. Still, regardless of why, if we prevent abortion, many unwanted inner-city children are born into abject poverty, and they often suffer severe neglect."

"If I didn't know the truth, I would say you take a pro-abortion stance in certain cases."

"You've pointed to a reason so many people accuse me of making the simple more complex. Putting other issues aside, we can't deny the needs of unaborted babies abandoned by the people who advocated their birth. It's a dereliction of the responsibility we create for ourselves by preaching against abortion."

Megan's dad came up the stairs with Rochelle and her sister, Cindy. He seemed agitated. Rochelle had his arm in hers in a consoling posture, with Megan's mom following behind.

"What's happened, Dad? Is there a problem?"

"Oh, nothing we haven't seen a dozen times before. A young man came through the door with an obvious attitude of hostility. When I greeted him, he blurted out the usual angry accusations of sexism and racism heard from members of his group. I welcomed him to our meeting if he wouldn't cause any trouble. Still, he continued his thoughtless condemnation of our motive and seemed too ready for violence. When he directed profanity toward your mother, I escorted him out the door physically."

"So, you threw him out? I'm glad you did, but I'll bet he'll be back."

"He can join us if he remains peaceful and without volatile expressions of anger and cursing. I won't tolerate profanity."

Greetings ensued as the room filled with likeminded supporters and newcomers to the group, who came to meet and hear Eliza Stokes convey sympathy and compassion for causes that lead to an abortion decision.

Eliza's speech presented the historical context of the current abortion environment, maintaining that Planned Parenthood's process and overall goals mirror the history of poverty and welfare in this country.

"Lyndon Johnson's Great Society did not envision a permanent class of welfare recipients. Welfare intended to provide a temporary program, reflecting the intent of a sympathetic and compassionate government that recognized the need to assist individual citizens.

"Welfare gave enough to allow one to get by but not enough to provide the means to become independent and responsible. Welfare provided no education in living your life or taking care of your family, nor any incentive to find employment. Getting a job meant losing most, if not all, of your welfare benefits.

"It's a matter of controlling your life or having the government control your life. With welfare as a temporary means to allow a family to get on its feet, it should also provide training on how to live an independent life and take care of a family. The recipient then becomes responsible for his or her life.

"The welfare system soon became another way for politics to control people's lives. Provide enough so people don't have to work but not enough to enable receivers to take responsibility for their lives. It became a way to control people and influence their motives. The more people one can keep on welfare, the more one can count on their votes.

"Abortion rights developed in much the same way. Forget the eugenics argument about motives for the origin of Planned Parenthood. Think about where we are now. As the mouth of Planned Parenthood, the feminist movement has told indigent women that they can make their own decision regarding abortion. The child's father is not around anyway. Welfare has seen to that.

"'This is not a family decision. It's your decision alone to make.' Under the guise of health care, these women hear, 'It's your body; it's your life. You don't need any men around telling you what to do. You should take control of your own body.'

"The family is the basic element in our great republic. Abortion has done much to dismantle the family structure in this country, destroying this element."

Megan's dad saw the man he earlier escorted out the door to come in and take a seat. He leaned over to identify the man to Megan and whispered he was keeping an eye on him.

Eliza continued her presentation with stories of her childhood, the sibling she never knew, and the trauma she suffered. She expanded on the arguments for and against abortion and ended by returning to the historical American family context from which she began.

"As a black woman, I'm compelled to quote Dr. Mildred Jefferson, the first black woman to graduate from Harvard Medical School and a person grounded in what's referred to as the anti-abortion effort. She led much of the early efforts of the National Right to Life Committee. Dr. Jefferson said, 'Our great republic works because everyone respects the covenant of an organized society. We have choices that can be allowed, other choices that must be refused, and anybody who demands the right to do whatever one wants to do because one chooses to do so, demands social anarchy. But it means the collapse of the structure that maintains our society and maintains the country. And, of course, the most critical of that is the family structure. The family is the primary covenant because it is there to learn to participate and determine what part you are in the overall covenant.'"

Eliza opened the floor for questions. She dismissed those that focused primarily on Planned Parenthood. "We are not here to argue about the mission of Planned Parenthood in providing health care. We want to find ways to prevent unplanned pregnancy and the abortion that the pregnant woman sees as the only answer."

Megan asked about adoption. "Do you recognize adoption as an alternative to abortion? About 140,000 adoptions take place in the US annually, less than 400 per day, and a large percentage of those are international adoptions. With over 2,000 abortions performed daily, adoption isn't a viable alternative. Can you elaborate on the adoption issue?"

Megan and Cindy made eye contact, and Megan smiled. Cindy's look revealed her belief that Megan was thinking of her pregnancy, and Cindy seemed to believe Megan was communicating with her.

"Thank you, Megan. Adoption can be an alternative to abortion, but adoption is a limited recourse when you consider—"

"You people are a bunch of hypocrites." The angry man, who had returned after his confrontation with Megan's dad, stood. With a finger pointed as a gesture of affirmation toward no one in particular, he shouted, "Nobody's gonna want to adopt a fatherless kid from an uneducated, inner-city mother who can't even make ends meet. It's a kid that may be born already addicted to drugs caused by its mother. Abortion is the answer. What you people want to do is bring a child into the world who will suffer his entire life, and probably die in prison. He's in prison even if he's not in prison. He is never—"

"Excuse me, sir," interrupted Eliza. "This is the time in our meeting we reserve for questions. Do you have a question?"

"Why are you doing this?"

"If, by doing this, you mean trying to prevent abortion, the answer is at the same time simple and complex. The simple answer is, we believe abortion is murder, and we haven't found a legitimate reason to commit murder. The complexity of available means to prevent these murders is what we're here to discuss. You stated no one cares enough to adopt one of these unaborted kids. You are wrong—the people in this room care. And a great many people in other parts of the country and the world, people from all walks of life, rich and poor, highly educated and undereducated, care, and people of every race care. But caring doesn't mean we are all able, or willing, to line up for the adoption of every baby who would otherwise suffer death by the legalization of murder. We are seeking solutions. Adoption is one of a multitude of solutions. Many are complex, but some are relatively simple. My question is, what's your solution?"

"My solution is to allow what the Supreme Court has declared to be a fundamental right guaranteed by the Constitution."

"Your solution to the problem of abortion is more abortion? What liberal political office are you seeking? Sir, uttering another pro-choice euphemism doesn't address the real issue and is the oldest and weakest argument ever offered for any societal problem. It's the law. Do you not have a legitimate proposal, anything with substance?"

"People like you don't practice what you preach."

"From what you have spoken here tonight, you have shown you don't have anything to preach. We don't know what you practice," Eliza responded. "Let's move on to Megan's question."

"You people don't want a solution. You just want to cause trouble. Its politics, causing problems for people you see as inferior."

"Sir, we are trying to have a serious and legitimate meeting here tonight," Megan's dad said. "You don't seem to want to be a part of this discussion. We have let you have your say. Now I'm asking you to leave."

"I'm leaving, but let me tell you this. As long as abortion is legal, you don't have a chance. All your disgusting speeches about morality won't change a thing. I'm out of here." The man bolted down the stairs and through the door.

"Sorry for the distraction. Meaningful discourse is time-consuming," Megan's dad said, motioning two-fingered quotation marks around the word *discourse*. "But one thing he said is true. A woman's right to have an abortion is indeed the law and is the current context under which we must work. One day a different law may apply. Until then, let's concentrate on effective measures to provide real solutions, not just protests. Eliza, please continue. The question addressed, to coin a phrase, is the adoption option as an alternative to abortion."

Eliza continued, "Adoption is good. Adoption offers a viable alternative to women who don't want a child and don't want an abortion, based on religion, moral compass, or any other personal principle. But adoption is *a* solution, not *the* solution. Consider this: Adoption requires carrying a pregnancy to full term. That's a good thing, you say. That's why we're here. We want to stop abortions from happening.

"But consider this too: Adoption does not address the need behind abortion. Many—I should say most—inner-city or impoverished women with unintended pregnancies see abortion as their only choice. It provides an immediate solution. For them, abortion is a way to become unpregnant, motivated by misinformation from abortion providers. Facing an unwanted pregnancy, they are not interested in enduring the misery of taking their pregnancy to full term and creating a baby. Adoption is not an alternative."

Eliza saw a couple of hands go up. "Yes, Mr. Alladee?"

"You point to the founding principle of SAVE. Our goal is to address the needs that lead to abortion in the first place. We hear again and again, 'Abortion doesn't make a woman unpregnant. It makes her the mother of a dead child.' Eliminate the need, and you eliminate abortion. Our focus is to counteract the false, inaccurate, and unreliable messages delivered by abortion providers."

"Respectfully, eliminating the abortion is not enough," responded Eliza. "It's not just a moral issue. Many, many of these pregnancies are forced upon these women through rape, household abuse, lack of preventive measures, or decisions not capable of being made by the woman. The pregnancy is forced on her and is unwanted. In the same way, abortion is forced on her.

"History has shown that legislating morality is a fruitless endeavor. Reversing *Roe v. Wade* is not a solution. Making abortion illegal is not the answer. In general terms, no form of legislation is the answer. Government solutions equate to throwing money at the problem. The more money thrown, the worse the problem becomes. Ronald Reagan said it best. 'Government is not the solution to our problem; government *is* the problem.' The need is to prevent unwanted pregnancy."

"Contraception?" asked Megan's dad.

"If you believe life begins at conception, contraception may become an early-stage abortion. For others, contraception is like adoption—*one* solution, but not *the* solution. Adoption won't prevent or even diminish the rate of abortion; advocating for contraception won't either. Preventing conception is not altogether what I mean by preventing unwanted pregnancy. As with many problems in our society, solutions become complex indeed.

"Let me introduce another issue related to adoption. If you convince a woman to carry her pregnancy to full term, by presenting adoption as a viable option, you may create a problem that would not otherwise exist.

"Part of the abortion decision early on is to prevent the problem of attachment. Yes, once the abortion is over, you may have to deal with the reality of a dead baby, but abortion is a final act. There may be remorse, and lifelong doubts occur from time to time, but, again, with abortion, it's over.

"With adoption, a baby must be given up. Many of these potential mothers convince themselves, on the high end, a possible baby exists, and, on the low end, it's a mass of cells or a parasitic growth inside to be cast away.

"Once delivered, a real baby becomes a physical, lifelong reminder of the choice the mother made. Many of those potential mothers who can deal with abortion cannot deal with adoption. For them, adoption may be more of a problem than a solution.

"The solution is to prevent her unplanned pregnancy."

CHAPTER 11

The February sun was invisible. Megan drove through the neighborhood toward her parents' home, flooding her mind with thoughts of her many sunshine days growing up here. She steered around the winding streets to Kesswood Court, known for its wondrous stand of ornamental redbud trees in front of an imposing wall of lemony Southern magnolias. In early spring, red buds emblazon even their trunks in deep magenta.

Faded wisteria vines squeezed lamp posts, the creek's bridge, and pergolas along the way. Wisteria was a family favorite. Megan could barely wait for the glorious vine to bloom, twining around the white picket fence rails. Blooms hung like bunches of grapes, a waterfall of blossoms, on both sides of most streets in the neighborhood. Her dad faithfully pruned the vines on their property twice a year to keep them treelike and manageable. He considered his pruning a semiannual gift to their love of the vine.

Megan turned into the narrow, curved driveway leading to the home where she learned to love and be loved. She parked just inside the entry and walked through a thin veil of red twig dogwoods growing on either side of the driveway. They still had a light color, even in February but were a little smaller than they appeared in the summer. *Dad's pruning.*

Mounds of evergreen azaleas grew in strategic locations around the property. Megan helped her dad cover the smaller, eye-popping red and white azaleas with burlap. He said the burlap should not weigh directly onto the azaleas. He supported the burlap with little stakes arranged in a way to prevent the burlap cover from even coming in contact with the plant. Large rhododendrons don't require winter covering. Today they presented shades of grey and brown, mixed with a tinge of green. It was toward the end of a long winter's nap. They would be back.

Megan, the child, loved to spend time on the spacious front porch, where ten-inch round columns supported a roof projection of at least fifteen feet beyond the face of the house. As a little girl, she begged her dad to screen the front porch to keep the bugs out so she could spend the whole night there. Her dad said the screening would be okay for the back but wouldn't work on the front. Visitors might see it as a barrier and feel unwelcomed.

She rubbed her hand along one of the columns, remembering the times she had spun around them. *I love this place. I'm secure here like nowhere else.*

"Why did you park at the end of the driveway?"

The voice interrupting her thoughts startled her. "Oh, yeah, I parked out a good bit. I wanted to stroll along the driveway. It's peaceful without the wind blowing, even though it's close to freezing today."

Her mom grinned. "The yard is beautiful year round. I was around the side of the house, getting ready to spray the crabgrass pre-emergent and heard you drive up. Will you stay for dinner?"

"Yes, I had planned to stay 'till this evening. I wanted to talk with you and Dad about the upcoming trial. Wish we could sit out here and talk."

"Seems a little chilly to stay out. A pot of that maple cider you love is brewing, and we'll have potato soup at dinner."

"Yummy! Is Dad still working on the homework assignment Eliza gave him after the SAVE meeting?"

"Let's go inside. Dad wants to discuss that assignment with you."

The two of them walked toward the kitchen. Megan got a glimpse of her dad sitting in his office near the little library that he conjured up after settling into this new house just before Megan was born. There had been several other moves between the time her dad first moved from the Section 8 housing project called Hurt Village, and when he and her mom were married and moved into this house.

Each new move was a step up. The biotechnical equipment company that Megan's great-great-uncle in England founded in the late 1950s planned to expand its operation with a sales program in the United States. Megan's dad played an influential role in their effort, establishing good business relations in Memphis, which opened doors to success. He had no medical background, mastering the technical side of the business from scratch, but his effort paid off well.

To Megan, Dad understood that welfare was never more than a heartbeat away, and he repeated that principle aloud many times. In one way, she could envision his moving from an impoverished neighborhood to the lifestyle he had created for them and the life she had known throughout her childhood. Still, she could not picture him failing at anything. Her dad had wisdom and strength, a single-minded ability to make the right call, whether business, finance, moral principle, or leadership. Insecurity and doubt were foreign to him.

"Mom, are you and Dad doing okay?"

"Oh, yes. I don't know in what way you mean, financial, physical, or marital. But the answer is a wholehearted yes in every category. Your dad has worked smart, and he's worked hard for what we have achieved. All that talk about men not knowing their way without their women telling them what to do doesn't relate here. He has done it on his own."

"It doesn't work that way," Megan's dad said as he entered the kitchen. "I doubt I could have achieved much success without your mother, but even if I could have, I wouldn't have. She has had a more active role than she will ever take credit for." He gave her a hug and a quick peck on the cheek as he moved to the stovetop.

"You mean like Eve helping Adam?" questioned her mom. "She thought Adam didn't know what he wanted until she told him." There followed an elongated "Oooooh!" from Megan as her mother frowned a smile toward her with a raised eyebrow.

"Don't forget, it was Adam's sin, not Eve's."

"Riiight. Okay, Dad, what are you working on in there?" asked Megan.

Her dad sat his cup of cider onto the counter. "Remember when the angry guy came into the meeting the other night, and I asked him to leave?"

"Yeah."

"I got an email from Peggy, the events coordinator at the library, saying we are not allowed to distribute our literature within the library. I responded that we knew the rules and have been careful to display our literature in the meeting room and nowhere else. If removed, the literature is taken off the premises by one of our members. Peggy said someone left a handful of flyers on a couple of tables downstairs. It seems our angered visitor took a stack of literature and placed it on those tables. Now the library admin says we will have to find another place for our meetings. I've been dealing with them most of the day."

"So unfair," Megan said. "It must have been him. He knew it would create a problem, and he did it intentionally; otherwise, it would have been one table. We have a problem. We can't keep outsiders from attending—we want them to attend, but we should do a better job of surveying the space after our meetups."

"Well, dealing with literature misplacement used the valuable time I needed to address Eliza's question. How do we prevent unplanned pregnancies? Preventing pregnancy is an intriguing concept, considering, from the beginning, government officials and their legislation have worked against us."

"Eliza focused on the idea of stopping unplanned pregnancies. Stopping abortions took a back seat," Megan said. "It's difficult, but I'm trying to comprehend her full meaning in those terms. As usual, Eliza expressed a fundamental principle in clear and precise terms. What she advocates will lead to complicated issues. Contraception and abstinence are issues to deal with but are not relevant in this context."

Megan's mom gathered lettuce and other ingredients to mix enough salad for the dinner meal. She looked up from her cutting board with a frown. "I don't follow. How else does one prevent an unplanned pregnancy? We're not advocating tubal ligation and vasectomy. I don't get it."

"Those too," Megan's dad said, "but not against anyone's will. Preventing pregnancy is important, but no, that's not the issue. The operative word here is *unplanned*. As Eliza sees it, the answer is to make the unwanted pregnancy wanted."

"Shouldn't the goal be to prevent the unwanted pregnancy in the first place?" asked Megan's mom. "At first, I thought 'eliminate the unwanted pregnancy,' but that reminded me of Cobel Clinic, so I used the word *prevent*."

"They're not eliminating the pregnancy; they're eliminating the child." Megan saw the look on her dad's face caused by his concern for her feelings when the topic of abortion struck close to home. "Don't be concerned, Dad. You and Mom know I dealt with those issues long ago. Yes, I'll admit I have regrets, and I've expressed them to you. If I had it to do again, I would not choose abortion, but, as you taught me—what's done is done. I'm okay with this discussion."

"No better place to talk than at home with those you love and who love you," said her dad. "So, tell us—how do you view Eliza's position?"

"I can't visualize the issue completely, but I can see the problem as Eliza expressed it. If the focus is on the life of the child, then, to use Mom's words, eliminating the unwanted pregnancy doesn't mean getting an abortion, and it doesn't mean wanting the pregnancy. It means wanting the child to live. I've heard many people say their parents didn't want to become pregnant, but once they did, they didn't even consider an abortion. Once they became pregnant, they wanted the child. If I had it to do again, I would not have an abortion. I would have a baby. I would give birth.

"I'm not saying I would want to be pregnant, but I would want the baby's life. It's not the baby's fault. Who knows how many of those single, impressionable women got an abortion even though they wanted to give birth? They are better than me. I didn't want the pregnancy, and, at the time, I didn't want the baby, a mistake I've had to live with.

"That's Eliza's point. Whatever its cause, these women must decide their fate, but circumstances leave them power-less. They're stuck in a dependent environment, and they can't imagine any recourse. It may be rape, unprotected sex from a partner, or just having to deal with a poor financial condition—regardless, they are dependent. They contact Cobel Clinic, where they hear they have a right to eliminate an unwanted pregnancy."

Megan's dad raised his head. "What I hear you saying, at least what I hear as your interpretation of Eliza's position, is that a way is needed to make those women independent. With that, they will make the same decisions that other parents, men as well as women, make every day.

"Many pregnancies are unplanned and unwanted until they happen. Once the pregnancy is there, the focus transfers to the child. They don't even consider abortion as an alternative. It makes perfect sense, except for one thing. How?"

"That's one I can help you with, dear," Megan's mom said, with a wink toward Megan. "You must put them in a middle-class environment, a project that's been in the works forever, the welfare promise unlikely to be fulfilled. The American Dream seems not to be available to everyone. Shall I continue?"

"Your mom is right, Megan; people have tried everything under the sun, but, except for a few minor exceptions, none have provided a real solution. Increasing welfare checks, meaning more government control, is not the answer. I agree with Eliza. Reversing *Roe* will make things worse. I'll admit, I'm at a loss to envision a workable solution."

"What did you do?" asked Megan.

"What do you mean?"

"Well, you were on welfare, living in subsidized housing for, how long—years?"

"The truth is I was born into it. Your grandfather became physically unable to work, and he was bedridden over half his life. Your grandmother, my mom, worked at minimum wage for most of those years, raising a family and caring for your grandfather. Before his illness, Dad had farmed. They lost everything and had to move to the city where at least some help could be made available."

"So, what got you through it?"

"A multitude of things. It may seem trite, but there was a work ethic. We had family in England we didn't even know, and we didn't know if they were successful. That possibility encouraged us—like a roots thing. We heard rumors about that extended family in England, but, at the time, we had no idea how to connect with them.

"We believed we were just down on our luck, but we didn't understand how lucky we were. We had good schools, a roof over our heads, financial assistance from the government, and, best of all, we had a chance to work our way out of it."

"What you're saying is you were lucky because you were white," Megan responded.

"Yes, Megan, very perceptive and, if we will admit it, also true. Being white meant we had a chance to work our way out of it. Not everyone had the chance we had. Remember, those were the days of separate but equal."

"Separate and unequal, and wrong even if it had been equal," declared Megan.

"Perceptive again, Megan. It's a story that should be remembered and retold."

"That may be the key," Megan said. "Eliza may have the answer, but she wants it discovered by others, by us."

Megan's mom dished up the dinner salad and placed bowls of salad around the countertop. "White people?" The scent of her homemade raspberry dressing filled the air.

"No, by *us,* I mean we who have it within our power to help, white or black. Dad is right. It cannot be accomplished through legislation, although the government can help if they choose to help. It's not the church either, but they could help too. People who are financially, culturally, physically, and emotionally independent must do it. Those who can make the call to carry an unwanted pregnancy to full term, to the birth of a person, must do it. That's us."

"Again," Megan's dad said with his head down this time, "my question is how?"

"Adoption," Megan said.

CHAPTER 12

A great blue heron swept across Hyde Lake, one of his wings making tiny waves on top of the water with each swoop. He landed near the steel-framed swings where Megan and Rochelle sat. Megan took a gentle swing. "This is my second favorite place in the city. I love the light maiden grass and yellow foxtail planted around the lake. The fresh air blowing across the lake is enchanting. I know of nothing like it anywhere else in Shelby County. It's beautiful even in the dead of winter."

"Second favorite place? Oh, I get it. Your mom's house is your favorite, right?"

"Why wouldn't it be? The winter garden is pretty decent there too, and love is there, with a lifetime of loving memories. I'm lucky to have been able to grow up in the environment Mom and Dad created for me."

"We have both been lucky," Rochelle said. "Like two close-growing trees, our branches have been entwined most of our lives. We escaped *what-could-have-been.*"

Megan felt a twinge in her gut. She and Rochelle had been close, yet, in one way, they were far apart. The one could-have-been that should have been built a wall between them. Rochelle helped Megan climb over her wall of doubt. Now Rochelle wanted Megan to return the favor by pulling her sister Cindy over her wall of despair.

Megan sidetracked the issue for the moment. "Yes, if my mom and dad hadn't taken advantage of the opportunities offered, I might have grown up in a housing project like my dad."

Rochelle provided an artificial grin. "I haven't had to face any possibility of poverty. My parents were middle class all the way, and they had help from our large family. Don't forget. We are Jewish, so my family controls the world, right?"

"Right, you are God's chosen. How could any of you fail? Oh, look, here comes Cindy now."

Cindy walked a fast pace down the hill from the welcome center. "I was told you guys were at the Kitchen but figured I would try your favorite spot first. And here you are."

"Yeah, Megan is immune to the cold, so we're sitting here, and one of us is freezing. We should walk over to the Kitchen for lunch so we can warm up."

Megan led the way. "I can use a hike. Want to burn a few calories to justify ordering their key lime pie."

"So, Cindy," Rochelle asked, "have you and Kevin had a chance to discuss your options?"

"Kevin's a hard sell. I guess I am too. My life is a mess right now. It's too much to deal with."

"I can only imagine what you're going through, Cindy," Rochelle said. "How are you holding up? Does Kevin still have the same reservations about keeping the baby?"

"He won't talk in those terms. He's like, 'If you don't call it a baby, it's not a decision we have to make about a baby's life.' We each live in unreal worlds. I've tried to preach to myself the same message we present to pregnant women at SAVE— how abortion is wrong. Then we ask them to consider the benefit of the child involved. I've taken it for granted, believing these women would see our side of the issue. I've been kidding myself. Eliza is right. To these women, abortion provides their only escape. In one way, I gave lip service to our position without ever considering how it would apply to me. Now, I'm in the same predicament, and I'm no different. I don't have another way out."

Rochelle shook her head. "Cindy, we should talk this through. What you're saying is not reasonable."

"What's reasonable can change, Rochelle. I may not completely understand what is meant by extenuating circumstances, but—"

"It makes a bad action seem better," Rochelle interrupted.

"That's it exactly. It doesn't seem too bad when it applies to me."

Rochelle could see she wasn't getting through. "I'll quote, maybe misquote, Hamlet. It doesn't matter how it seems. What matters is how it is. And it's bad, no matter how it seems. Problems we encounter at St. Jude, for example—they may not seem too bad at first sight, but the truth is, these problems are worse than bad. And we all—parents, patients, doctors—sometimes have to face incredible adversity. Now you have to face adversity of your own."

Megan pushed open the door to the Kitchen Cafe, and they sat at a table near the fireplace.

"I know what you're saying, Rochelle. But you don't know what I'm going through. How else am I going to be free from this ever-present anxiety?"

Megan had remained silent since they left the swings and walked toward the Kitchen. She wanted to keep her ammo dry, hoping for a more reasonable approach. "Cindy, I know this issue changes its perspective when it becomes personal. And I know you well enough to believe that Kevin is influencing a part of your reasoning, but you are wrong in what you are thinking, feeling, and saying."

"Goodness, Megan, is this your way of contributing, or is this just judgment?"

"This is my way of preventing a decision you will regret for the rest of your life. Have you considered where you will be ten years from now if you do this? Cindy, you know abortion doesn't make anyone free, including you. You're already free, free to choose what you want to do. The women at SAVE are not free. They lack the freedom to choose. They don't have the freedom to choose not to have an abortion. Most of those women didn't freely choose to become pregnant, and they can't freely choose to have a baby. They are not free to make a decision either way. You are. Those women can't afford to become mothers. You can. Those women don't have the means to raise a child. You do. Many suffer abuse; some are on the verge of starvation, severely oppressed. Not you."

"Why are you scolding me like this, Megan? Of all people, you should understand where I'm coming from."

"You should listen, Cindy," Rochelle said. "I'm your sister, and I love you, but I can't support the position you're taking. Megan is right. You had better think this through."

"I don't know where I'll be in a month, forget ten years. I know where I am right now. And I know I'm not ready. I don't want to be a mother. I still need a mother."

Megan saw Rochelle's look of expectancy when their eyes met, indicating Rochelle considered this a good time for Megan to reveal her story. Megan was not ready. Lashing out in a fit of anger is retribution. She had extenuating circumstances of her own. "I want to speak to Kevin. He has as much responsibility in this as anyone, even more."

"He dropped me off at the welcome center and drove over to Bass Pro. I told him I would call when we were ready to leave."

"Good. Will he be open to talking with us? Do you have a problem asking him to meet us here?"

"I don't have a problem, but you know Kevin. He's not going to talk freely with a group of girls. He doesn't see an alternative either, and he'll say it's my idea anyway."

"Maybe he will consider a one-on-one with me? Rochelle, if you drive Cindy home, Kevin and I could visit."

"He'll treat this as a setup."

"We are not planning to trick him into anything. He should be willing to deal with this . . . this . . . miserable decision affecting both of your lives right now."

"He thinks the world of you, Megan. He should be willing. Let me call him now. If he agrees, he can be here in fifteen minutes."

***

Kevin hung his jacket over the back of his chair. "Crazy, it's snowing a couple of miles from here. Pretty light—nothing will stick, but enough to get my jacket wet. How's it going, Megan?"

"I'm doing well, thank you. Cindy told you she and Rochelle are together, so it's just you and me, kid."

"Yeah, Cindy said you wanted to talk to me alone. I didn't have to ask why. I haven't spoken to anyone. My parents don't even know."

"When will you tell your parents?"

"After it's over."

"Why wait?"

"I don't want them to talk us out of it."

"Why would they do that?"

"Because they believe it's wrong."

"What do you believe? Is it wrong?"

"In a way, I guess it's wrong. It's not illegal. It's not like we're breaking the law. It's wrong from a moral perspective, but right now, Cindy being pregnant is wrong. Does that make any sense?"

"No. Do you see where you're going with this argument?

"Look, Megan. Cindy and I aren't ready to raise a kid. I know I'm responsible for this. It's not Cindy's fault. But I can't be responsible for the life of a child. I'll take responsibility for having the abortion."

"Man up, Kevin. You're talking like a kid. Abortion is not simply deciding to do away with a problem. It's doing away with a part of Cindy's life. It's doing away with a part of your life too. From a partnership perspective, you're pregnant too, and you'll have an abortion too. Have you honestly come to terms with what you are doing? Kevin, you and Cindy already have a baby. Forget how or why it happened. A baby is alive, your baby is alive, inside Cindy."

"What would you do?"

"I can tell you what I would not do. I would not have an abortion."

"How can you be sure? It's not happening to you. You might not see it the way you see it now."

"How old are you, Kevin?'

"I'm twenty-six."

"My God, you're thinking like a sixteen-year-old. And you're talking nonsense. If I had an abortion, I'd be no less wrong than you are. Would my having an abortion make it okay? What I would do doesn't matter, Kevin. What you do is what matters now."

"I'm not convinced this is so wrong."

"When would it be wrong?"

"What do you mean?"

"When is it wrong to kill a baby? The third month, the sixth month, the ninth month, at birth? When is it wrong?

"After the baby is born."

"Because after it's born, it's a person, right?"

"Yes. It's illegal to kill a baby after it's born, because it's a person, and killing a person is murder."

"Bingo. So, the baby Cindy is carrying is not a person?"

"Well, most people say it's only a fetus, and it can't live on its own, and it's okay to do away with it."

"To hell with what other people think. What do you think?"

"I don't know what I think."

"Now you're telling the truth. Let me ask you this, Kevin. If Cindy carried the baby to term and delivered it as a person, do you believe the baby would have a childhood, become an adult, and do all those things a real person would do?"

"Yes."

"At what point is it okay to deprive your baby of the right to do those things, to have a life you agree it would have? Cindy is already over four months along. You say you will accept responsibility for the abortion. Are you willing to accept responsibility for taking away all the things your baby can do with its life from this point forward?"

"I never thought of it that way. Why are you crying, Megan? This is not your problem."

"Forgive me, Kevin. I'm not usually this emotional, but I can't bear the thought of depriving any baby of life. The baby has done nothing to deserve this. Do you see that?"

"Yes, I guess I do, when you put it that way."

"Okay, so what are you going to do about it?"

"I don't know."

CHAPTER 13

J ack Williams shuffled a stack of papers, straightened them by knocking each end on the desk a couple of times, and put the stack into the file folder. He placed his pen into its holder.

"Remember, you two are not on trial, and what will happen in court tomorrow will happen without your involvement. Now that the jury is selected, the trial will move at a steady pace. You two should just relax and try not to show any response to anything you might hear."

ADA Gingrich entered the room. "Kayla, you remember Assistant DA Gingrich. He wanted to meet Daniel before the trial."

"Good morning, Daniel; hello, Kayla; glad the two of you were able to come in this morning."

"Yes sir, good morning, Mr. Gingrich. Guess we'll be seeing you regularly for a while. Kayla and I are expecting good results from the trial."

"I will see you in court tomorrow. If you arrive early, we can walk in together. There will likely be media present that will ask you for a statement. You should have no comment. Let me know if I can help in any way."

"We should do okay. I don't want excessive attention in this. We will see you in the morning." Daniel and Kayla respectfully offered their hands.

Gingrich excused himself and left the office.

"Do either of you have any questions? Okay, good, we are done for today." Jack motioned for an officer to come into the room and gather the documents. As he offered his hand, he saw Megan sitting in the outer office. He leaned his head back, offered a friendly wave to Megan, and held up his index finger, asking her to wait a minute.

"Megan is waiting for us to finish," Kayla said. "We are planning a quick lunch today to catch up, and she wanted to meet Daniel before he heads back to his office." The three of them walked out of Jack's office together.

"Hello, Megan," Jack said. "What a pleasant surprise. You look great today. How've you been these last few days?"

"Doing well, thanks, Jack." Megan smiled in Jack's direction. "Hello, you must be Daniel." Megan presented both hands to greet Kayla's husband.

"Yes, I'm happy to meet you, Megan. Kayla has told me about the good work you are doing at St. Jude. I'm truly interested in the hospital's treatment of kids, and I'm embarrassed to say I don't know how things work there. I wish we had met you at an earlier time. Kayla and I have wanted to become more acquainted with the hospital and see some of the kids. It's one of those things we have intended to do, but—anyway, I'm glad for the time you and Kayla have had together, and I'm thankful for your willingness to participate in the trial."

"Thanks, Daniel. I'm happy to do what I can. I'm sorry for your loss and what you and Kayla are going through. I sincerely hope the trial goes the way we want it to."

"Megan, can you give me a minute with Daniel before he leaves? We will be brief."

"Sure, whatever you need, Kayla. I'll be right here."

Kayla and Daniel huddled near the doorway to speak with a little privacy. Jack patted the side of Megan's shoulder. "Megan, you've been an asset to Kayla's team. Thanks for your effort.

And Kayla has told me how much she appreciates having you in her corner as well."

"I haven't done much. Kayla and I have hit it off pretty well, and I'm impressed with how brave she is. She has held up well."

"Yes, she has. Listen, I hope this trial goes well and doesn't drag out too much. And I hope we can continue to be friends after the trial."

"Jack, are you asking me out? I don't mean right now, but later. After the fact?"

"Yes, yes. I like you, Megan. I would love to go out with you, whenever we agree the time is right. What do you say?"

Kayla walked over as Daniel left the room. "I'm ready to go whenever you are, Megan."

"We'll talk, Jack. I'm ready, Kayla. Heading to the Pinch District, right?"

"Yes, we can order a good sandwich and have plenty of time to visit. Goodbye, Jack. See you tomorrow."

Jack turned back into his office. "See you guys later. Have a good lunch."

"We should drive over," Megan said. They took the Front Street exit. "It's a little too far to walk."

"Yes, please, let's drive. Did I hear what I think I heard in your conversation with Jack? He has had his eye on you from the day the two of you met. You two make a great couple."

"I don't know. Jack's okay. He operates like a professional. But I'm not sure I'm ready to team up with anyone. Don't know if I ever will be."

They walked to the car for the three-minute drive to the Pinch District, a few blocks away.

"I'm surprised at what you say about teaming up, Megan. I'll bet a long line of doctors at St. Jude is waiting for a chance to team up with you."

"I haven't dated for a couple of years."

"The strong relationship you have with your parents made me think you would want a family of your own. I'm surprised to hear you're still single. Have you been married before?"

"No, I haven't even been much interested in dating. It goes back a long way."

"Oh, no. Sorry for the question. It's none of my business. I didn't mean to pry."

"No, it's okay. Let's just say I've steered my life in another direction. Who knows? Maybe one day that will change. My parents and the kids at St. Jude are my family, and I long for a close connection with those unaborted kids I've seen. I haven't been able to keep in touch with them, so no direct relationship is there. But I feel a strong connection."

"I'm proud of what you're doing there and your deep feelings for the kids you've saved. God is in that. The Bible says if God begins a good work in you, he will perform it until the day of Jesus Christ."

"I don't know what that means—until the day of Jesus Christ?"

"It means a good work God puts his hand on will last till the end of time."

"I've not heard it expressed that way before. It would mean a lot to me if God is involved in stopping abortion."

"God hates abortion. He is glad you are trying to prevent it."

Megan parked on the side street at the restaurant to avoid the parking meters in front. "We are trying to prevent what causes those abortions. If people got pregnant only when they wanted to have a baby, there would be no reason for abortion. Does God hate people who have abortions?"

"God doesn't hate people. He hates sin. He hates the sin that leads to abortion, the sin that causes the need for abortion. But God forgives sin, and he forgives people who sin when they ask for forgiveness. Sorry, Megan, I don't mean to preach. The Bible says we are all sinners, and I have to ask God each day, every day, to forgive my sin." Kayla picked up menus, and they chose a two-seat table near the wall.

"I don't see you as much of a sinner, Kayla. The way you believe has made you strong in the face of what you and Daniel are suffering. I don't see strength as sin."

"Thanks, Megan, but I have not been what anyone should categorize as strong. Daniel is the strong one. He knows the truth of scripture, and that makes him strong. What I have are nightmares, and I cry on the inside every waking minute."

"What's wrong with that? That's how we deal with our lives. The whole world is crying on the inside, Kayla. Funny thing though, it's the people who cry on the outside who get all the attention. So who are the strong ones after all?"

"The strong ones are those who do something about it, like you, Megan. You're the driving force behind your group, called SAVE, right? "

"Right."

"And I've witnessed firsthand the work you're doing at St. Jude. I couldn't function under such stress."

"It's my job."

"You know what I mean. I'm talking about who you call your family—how you treat the patients and their parents. They are not under your care, but you treat them as if they are." Kayla wanted to move the subject away from St. Jude. Talking about the reality of childhood suffering accelerated her heart-beat. "Tell me what's happening with SAVE. What led you to begin as a nonprofit?"

"My dad put it together in the beginning. He and Mom knew of my interest in stopping abortion, and we had many discussions. They saw SAVE as a way to channel my frustration into the satisfaction of taking positive action to stop it. At least that's how we saw it at the time."

"What has changed? The goal is the prevention of abortion, isn't it?"

"Yes, but several things happened to set us on the course we took from the beginning. The first thing is the scope. We met with groups of three or four and positioned ourselves on the immorality of abortion. Looking back, we were a little naïve, not recognizing how complex the issues are. Those early meetings mushroomed into what became an atomic explosion of unique cases dealing with needs we had not even considered. We began to see abortion as a symptom of a greater problem. *Roe versus Wade* gave us insight into the real issue."

"I'm not sure we are on the same page. Abortion is what kills the child. It's what prevents birth."

"Yes, it is. But let me ask you this. If you had a pill that you could take to prevent obesity, would that be a good thing? Weight gain is no longer a problem. Just take a pill—no action is necessary—no need to count calories or modify your diet. Exercise might be okay if that's what you want to do. But you don't have to exercise if you don't want to. On the other hand, you could gain a little weight if you wanted to. No problem. If you gain too much, take a pill. Abortion is the pill that makes pregnancy okay. Abortion takes the focus away from the cause of the pregnancy. Everyone knows gluttony is not a good thing. But it's not too bad, as long as you have a pill."

"That's a little hard to swallow. To a Christian, gluttony is a sin. You know, seeing this menu, I'm feeling a little temptation."

"I'm going to have a BLT and chips. Yes, I know. My weight gain example oversimplifies it a bit. But what I'm saying is not too rhetorical. It puts the finger on the truth of it. Even if you had a pill, you should refrain from gluttony on the morality of it."

"Okay, you're saying not to use abortion as an excuse to become pregnant?"

"Not using abortion as a contraceptive misses the point. I hear people say, 'My parents didn't plan on having me. I just happened. But they would not even consider having an abortion. Once Mom got pregnant, they made plans to have me as their child.'"

"I wasn't planned."

"You too? Okay, but after discovering the pregnancy, your parents planned every detail of your birth, and, by definition, you were not the result of an unplanned pregnancy."

Kayla agreed. "Most people can see the difference. Pregnancy forced on a girl through rape or incest, or for whatever reason, and the girl doesn't have the means to give birth, what you have is an unplanned pregnancy. And the remedy is abortion. Am I correct?"

"We are getting close, but we still don't have a complete picture. The difference is most of the pregnant women we counsel at SAVE don't have the freedom to choose for themselves how to deal with an unplanned pregnancy. Their culture chooses for them. Their poor economic condition chooses for them. If the pregnancy is the result of abuse, even rape, their abusers choose for them, and the choice made by others is usually abortion."

"So, what's the answer?"

"That's the sixty-four-thousand-dollar question. That may be the million-dollar question. Abortion has become a symptom of the real problem. In the same way, pregnancy, in and of itself, is not the problem. The problem is unplanned pregnancy, which we define as a pregnancy in which the potential mother cannot make her own decision about giving birth. The only choice she has, forced upon her or not, is abortion."

"Same question, what's the answer?"

"Stop unplanned pregnancy."

"How?"

"In the current state of affairs, no one is a hundred per-cent sure."

"Now, I'm depressed. I'm gonna lose my appetite."

"Even though we don't see a clear path, we should believe it exists; there must be a solution to the problem. Don't lose any sleep over it, Kayla. Many well-intentioned people are working on it. We should order."

"Yes. Two BLT's and chips please," Kayla said to the waiter. "Easy on the mayo."

CHAPTER 14

C indy worked late hours in her tiny, cubbyhole of a shop, little more than an extension of the two-car garage attached to her home. Kevin regularly helped her prepare meals for the next day's catering events. Cindy usually needed Tuesday night assistance preparing for the St. Jude team meeting.

Cindy lined the St. Jude bags for tomorrow's gathering around the table, and Kevin brought in boxes of nonperishables he had picked up at St. Jude earlier in the day. "Did the guys at St. Jude have everything we need?"

"Yes, you know they'll come through. Those folks are determined to make every detail count and prepare everything exactly as you have planned. Kay Kafe should be called Cindy Cafe."

"Very funny. The chefs know how important Megan's Wednesday meeting is, not only for the staff but also for the patients. Count on them to check the tiniest detail."

"They also know how tough Megan can be if anyone is disappointed in what they expect from the meeting."

"You know it. She and Rochelle can put the hammer down when they need to."

"Tell me about it. I told you how Megan raked me over the coals when we met at the Kitchen on Saturday."

"My coals were hotter, but we both know she's right. Like we agreed yesterday, we made our decision without considering long-term results. Line up the rest of the bags on the counter. I want to be sure we have each of them identified and no one gets left out."

"It's crazy how much you spend on these bags and the special, item-by-item containers, just to present a box lunch. How can you make any money with all these extras?"

"You have to spend money to make money. Rochelle reviews everything with the board for their approval. No conflict of interest exists, and she lets them know what they're paying for and the cost. She makes sure the business shows a small profit, but not too much. Their mantra of operation is top-of-the-line but not overboard."

"Sometimes, I wonder. You know, I'm tired of arguing about this abortion thing. Yesterday when we spoke with Mom and Dad, I knew how they would respond. Yeah, we made a big mistake, and we're making a bigger one. They sounded like Megan and Rochelle—like we are not able to decide for ourselves."

"I know, but they are right too. Here, these little packs of jellies are for everyone. Put one in each bag. I guess we waited this long to move forward with the abortion because we were not sure it's the right thing."

"It's true. Megan said I was acting like a sixteen-year-old, pretty childish. In one way, I know she's right. But when she said it, I wanted to tell her, if I were sixteen, I would run away."

"Have you considered running away? Don't open that bag. Those are for the guests tomorrow. Talk about childish. Let's get this done. I want the bags loaded tonight. That way, Tommy can lay out his part while I pick up the food tomorrow morning."

"Sorry. Yes, I want to run away now. But where am I going to go? Like the man says, wherever I go, there I am."

"I get it. You know, we are more alike than we might want to admit. Here, put the boxes at the top of the bag after you put in all the other stuff. The containers go just under the boxes to prevent any trouble loading the food. My relationship with

SAVE came to mind—letting those people down and not practicing what I preach."

"It's called guilt. I feel guilty too."

"How do you mean?"

"Well, like Megan said, deep inside, we both know it's wrong. If I agree to go along with having an abortion, I'm doing you wrong. And I'm doing the baby wrong. I don't have any responsibility toward the SAVE people, but you do. There I am again, doing you wrong and making you do them wrong."

"Wow, Kevin. You don't sound like any sixteen-year-old I know. I don't want you to think it's just my relationship with SAVE. If I'm right and they're wrong, I could just walk away—and I would, but I consider walking away without good reason as just saving face."

"Saving face can be important. It's showing that your life is not BS."

"I agree, but it's not the main thing. It's relatively unimportant. What's important is acting out our principles. We must do what we believe is right, whether it suits us at the time or not."

"I guess it's harder for me to make a decision based on my convictions. Everything happens for a reason, even if I don't know the reason."

"My goodness, Kevin. Who are you? You're a different person, a new man."

"After we talked this weekend, and since we told our parents everything, I can see things a lot clearer. I want to use reason to decide what to do. We should do the right thing, do what is smart, but I want to know why we are doing it."

"I'm with you a hundred percent. At first, you were dead set against my being pregnant, and you wouldn't stop until we ended it."

"I called myself going along with what you wanted to do."

"Maybe we don't know each other that well, after all."

"I want your happiness, Cindy, and you don't need someone who can't live up to his principles."

"Let's not forget about the baby. Are we doing this for him too, or for her, or for them—oh my God, I hope it's not them."

"Yeah, it's for the baby too. We've got a lot to consider, and a lot more to plan for. It's funny how we decided we were right when we both know it's wrong."

"Like Rochelle says, 'The first to plead his case seems right until another comes and examines him.'"

"I don't know where she got that, but I can see what she means. Each of us pled our case, and now each of us is cross-examining the other."

"I love you, Kevin, and I'm proud of you for helping me see the truth."

"I love you. We have an announcement to make."

"We'll have several announcements to make soon."

CHAPTER 15

M egan was surprised to see a packed house for the third consecutive SAVE meeting. Kayla's arriving early surprised Megan. "I'm glad you came, Kayla. We have snacks and soft drinks at the bar. Can I bring you anything?"

"No, thanks, Megan. I hoped I could help in some way. I don't know what to expect from the meeting, but I'm available to assist if you need help."

Megan put her arm around Kayla's shoulder to guide her toward the people she wanted Kayla to meet. "Thanks for your offer, Kayla. These meetings are informal, and we have everything in order. I wanted to introduce you to Rochelle and her sister Cindy."

"Yes, those are the two who work with you at St. Jude? Hello, I'm Kayla. You must be Dr. Meyers," Kayla said, looking toward Rochelle, the older of the two.

"Yes, I'm happy to meet you, Kayla, and please, it's Rochelle. That word *doctor* is beginning to make me look older."

"It also causes people to ask questions when they want a little pro bono medical advice," Megan said.

"Yes, that happens. Kayla, this is Cindy, who I'm proud to introduce as my sister," Rochelle said, with a wink directed at Megan.

"I'm glad to meet the two of you. I have a lot of St. Jude questions, but tonight, I'm impressed with the way you three have teamed up to work with SAVE. How do you have the time to do all you do?"

"We follow behind Megan," Rochelle said. "She is the one who does most of the work, with her dad, of course. We simply follow behind in support. Megan takes the one-on-one philosophy to heart. Megan, tell Kayla about your work with Lady O that has taken a chunk of your time the last couple of months. She is not a typical case."

"Like there is such a thing," Cindy said.

"Lady O?" asked Kayla.

"We don't use real names when we discuss our clients openly. It has proven better to speak in general terms. It keeps people with questionable intent at bay. She's an exceptional lady with enormous potential, trapped in her low-rent life. She is one of those people Eliza talks about, abused not only by her circumstance but also by the doctors and nurses she looks to for answers and recommendations. I've been with her at her last two meetings with Cobel Women's Health Clinic. The head nurse there, Suzan Winders, is impersonal, and offers little, if any, help to those she sees as her clients. Lady O feels torn between wanting to carry her baby to term and doubting whether she could deal with raising another child. She's trapped."

"What does the doctor say?"

"He told Lady O that everyone has to deal with the issue she is facing. Everyone struggles with having to make a choice. He's right, but he goes on to say everyone eventually comes around to see abortion as the better solution. It's not a baby anyway. He says it matter-of-factly, like telling your child eating a cookie before dinner will ruin his appetite. It's the standard operating procedure. She is little more than a number to them. Their job is to perform abortions, and they do whatever is required to make it happen, without compassion or empathy."

"You've seen a lot of inappropriate behavior, haven't you?"

"Yes, but I can understand their position in some ways. Still, they are way over the line with their lack of empathy. I don't have answers for Lady O, either. She asks for my advice, and, of course, I tell her we are not in favor of abortion, but what alternative do I have for her? I've spoken with her boyfriend, the father of the child. He won't allow the possibility of having a child, even if he wanted to. He tells me to mind my own business and let them get on with their lives. Discussing an alternative is forbidden. It breaks my heart. Lady O is going forward with the abortion, and there's nothing else we can do."

"We should take our seats," Rochelle said. "Your dad is ready to begin. Kayla, sit with us if you'd like. We would love to hear your take on what goes on here."

"This meeting of Share Anti-abortion Values Everywhere will come to order," declared Megan's dad. "We are happy to announce we will continue to meet in this hall, after a misunderstanding with the library administration from last week's meeting.

"Those of you who were in attendance last week will recall a visitor who created a bit of an uproar during Eliza's presentation. After that meeting, the library authority suspected we violated library rules concerning the distribution of our literature.

"We were able to resolve the misunderstanding with library management. Operating under the strict guidelines required by the library is now more critical than ever, without which we would lose the economy and convenience of meeting here.

"I'm happy to report that Eliza Stokes has requested to make an announcement I believe you will be glad to hear. She has also agreed to take any questions or address issues remaining after last week's meeting. I never tire of hearing Eliza express answers emanating from her captivating story and her fight against the complex state of affairs in the abortion battle, both in the US and throughout the world. Ladies and gentlemen, Eliza Stokes."

Eliza made her way to the front from behind the SAVE banner. "Thank you, Mr. Alladee. I'm happy to hear of your good job in dealing with the literature issue. We all know how the brochures and other documents SAVE distributes are a means to open the door for further contact. At the same time, they barely scratch the surface of the problems we encounter with abortion. Our message depends on nothing less than verbal one-on-one with our clients. We should take whatever action is required to make a face-to-face connection possible. The literature serves to open doors for direct communication.

"I use the term *client* to refer to those with whom we speak because the word connotes needing the services of a professional. We should take a professional approach, dealing with facts and expressing truth—real reasons abortions happen.

"I don't want to spend my time presenting statistics. We already know the numbers, the millions of lives lost, the millions of families, mothers, fathers, aunts, uncles, millions of brothers and sisters affected by abortion decisions. I want to take a different approach. I want to focus on what is considered a misplaced notion.

"I saw a reporter's interview of a young girl who argued women shouldn't be forced against their will to complete a pregnancy. She spoke at length about a woman's right to her own body and the need for government to guarantee that right. I didn't hear one word from the girl, the reporter, or anyone else, questioning the right of a woman to choose not to have an abortion. They all tell us, again and again, abortion is their only choice, even if they want to give birth. I'm as interested— more interested—in a woman's right to deliver a child and her unborn child's right not to be aborted.

"I grew up in the New Chicago neighborhood in North Memphis. My parents were poor, but they were together.

"My mother was a great woman who understood the requirements of a black person who expected to succeed. Mom didn't teach me that white people are racist or that black people are mistreated, either culturally or legally—regardless of whether either or both of those are true. The word *prejudice* was unspoken in our house. The world was the way it was, and we had to deal with it.

"My youth became complicated by my mother's miscarriage of a potential sibling, and the guilt I associated with that loss drove a desire in me to do more than anyone expected. I did well in school and graduated a year early, which offers both benefits and problems. If you enroll in college a year early, you graduate a year early, but you're a year younger than everyone else. You're considered a kid who doesn't understand how the world works, while you wonder how your classmates can be so dumb when they have a year on you.

"I'm telling you this because most of you know I've been at the forefront of Right to Life activities and associations. I fought social and political battles in the so-called anti-abortion movement most of my adult life. But you may not be aware of my being a proud Memphian, born and raised in the city. I am pleased to announce that my husband, Benny, and I are making immediate plans to return to Memphis for the duration. Benny is not a Memphis guy—he's from up north, but he is excited that, together, we're moving into a new phase of our lives as citizens of Memphis.

"Benny and I are thankful for the role that SAVE continues to play in fighting for the rights of unborn children and their parents everywhere. We want to assist in helping SAVE to strengthen its mission.

"Thanks for your approval of our participation. I'm open to discussing any questions or issues, as Mr. Alladee suggested." Hands went up. Eliza pointed to a raised hand. "Yes, miss?"

"Hello Ms. Stokes, I'm Cindy Meyers. Congratulations on your decision to come back home to Memphis. You will be a welcome addition of leadership.

"I didn't have a chance to meet you last week. I'm Rochelle Meyers's sister. I know the two of you have met. I wrote down a quote you presented last week from Dr. Mildred Jefferson. The quote seems reasonable; it's logical. Dr. Jefferson said certain choices should be allowed, but others refused. I'm reading this, 'Anybody who demands the right to do whatever one wants to do because one chooses to do so, demands social anarchy.' You indicated reversing *Roe v. Wade* and making abortion illegal is not the answer. Those seem to be opposing statements. Can you clarify how these two positions work together? Wouldn't the reversal of *Roe* accomplish this refusal?"

"Thank you, Cindy, for your astute observation, and I'm getting a whiff of sarcasm in your question. Let me begin by expanding on the quote. Dr. Jefferson went on to indicate that some choices, even legal ones, if made inappropriately, can lead to the collapse of the family structure as the key element of our culture.

"*Roe v. Wade* passed in 1973. Before 1973 abortion was illegal in the United States. After 1973 abortion became legal. How does *Roe v. Wade* affect the question of right or wrong? Was abortion wrong before 1973, and is it right today?

"At whatever date you choose, abortion is the killing of a life growing in a mother's womb, and killing a life is wrong. Yes, the choice is there for a woman to make. But the decision is wrong even if a majority vote dictates a right to make that choice.

"Reversing *Roe* is seen by people called pro-choice as legislating morality, and it is, but the passing of *Roe* is no different.

You cannot leave morality at the door when passing legislation. Call it natural law, the law of nature, God's law, God's will, or whatever you want; morality is changeless. Killing a baby is always wrong, and it's a choice a woman should not allow herself to make. Anything else?

Eliza pointed to one of many hands raised. "Thank you, Doctor. My question deals with the issue you just raised. Killing a baby is always wrong. Is it always right to carry a pregnancy to term? Giving birth to a child who will grow up in an atmosphere of violence, abuse, addiction, and lawlessness is much of what we see in many SAVE neighborhoods."

"Unequivocally, yes. The problem is not the birth of a child. The problem is the deranged environment in which the parents of the child live. Let me ask you this question. Visualize a family with three young children. One of these children, let's say a six-month-old baby, becomes ill or is abused by a family member or a neighbor. Maybe he or she is undernourished by the lack of food on the table. Should the six-month-old child just be killed, putting it out of its misery?"

"Of course not."

"Why?"

"Because the child is a baby, a human being, a person."

"What if the law allowed the killing of a six-month-old baby? Would killing the baby then be okay?"

"There will likely never be a law allowing the killing of a baby."

"Forget likelihood. If it was legal, would it be okay to kill a six-month-old?"

"No, killing a six-month-old would never be okay. It would always be murder."

"You have your answer."

CHAPTER 16

K im closed the Bible storybook her mom and dad read aloud to her during their devotional time. The tattered pages were evidence of her six-year-old intensity. She could recite most of the stories by heart. The great fun she had with her little brother when her mom read the stories strengthened her enthusiasm. She stared out the car window and counted the last few houses leading to her grandmother's house, where she would have to spend another day without her mom. "Mommy, how long will I be with Gramma Dean today? Will you be back in time for lunch?"

Kayla's throat tightened. "I'm not sure, honey. I know you don't understand why Mommy must be away, but you and Gramma will have a great time together today." The answer hung in the air like the excuse it was.

"Gramma doesn't play with me very much. Why do you have to go?"

"I'll explain it to you later, okay? I don't have a choice."

Kim's heart broke a little. "I know," she said, looking down, holding her book between her knees.

"Gramma is at the door," Kayla said. "Just park in front of the garage, and I'll take Kim to her."

Daniel waved to his mom. "Bye, sweetheart. I'm proud of you. I know you'll do good with Gramma today. I love you."

Kim leaned over to the front seat to kiss her dad goodbye. "I love you, Daddy, bye."

Kayla smiled as she took Kim by the hand and walked her to Gramma's door.

They both waved as Daniel backed down the driveway. Kayla touched a tissue to the corner of her eye. "I hate doing this. Kim's separation anxiety is normal, but we've hardly ever been apart. I want to work on some short-term separation to help her."

"You've had no reason to be apart. I'm thankful we don't have to worry about babysitters since Mom is available. Daycare would be out of the question. Thank God we're not faced with daycare."

"Kim is responding to my anxiety. I wasn't able to read with her this morning. I didn't want to upset her schedule. She needs a full night's rest. This trial hasn't even begun, and already we're having problems."

"I know." Daniel's voice fell. "The trial won't take too long. In the meantime, the minutes seem like hours. Hang in there, Kayla. God will help us through this. Remember what Pastor told us. We have to put this on the Lord and ask him to strengthen us."

"I know, but it's hard for me. Jerry, of course, says the same thing. I'm feeling a little sheepish. I wonder if he and Pastor ever have problems trusting in the Lord. I guess I wonder the same thing about you."

"Every Christian struggles with unbelief in some way. It's how you handle it that counts. You have to trust, even when you don't think you can."

"They stoned Paul at Lystra," Kayla whispered to herself.

"The Lystra story is a good example of trusting. The people of Lystra left Paul for dead, but he regained consciousness and continued preaching. What made you think of Paul?"

"Remember, I told you I met with Jerry in his office last week? He said God's foreknowledge of events doesn't prevent his letting events happen, even when those events seem bad or create disastrous results. I immediately thought of Paul. God allowed Paul's stoning."

"It's a part of what keeps us in the center of God's will."

"My heart knows it, but my head creates doubt."

"Paul had doubts too."

"He did? Where does it say he had doubts?"

"The Bible doesn't specifically say it, but he was a man who required salvation, just like every other man, and, as a man, he would have struggled much like the rest of us. As I said, it's not the doubt or problems with trust, but how you handle it that counts. Paul showed himself as a good example of handling it properly."

"Opposite of how I'm handling it. Daniel, I'm not sure I can do this. I don't believe God just took our beautiful little Danny from us, but is God willing this trial to happen and the pain it's causing? I don't want to have to deal with a trial."

"We don't have a choice, Kayla. God knows this trial is a temptation for us. He has it worked out if we trust him."

"God knows what's going to happen, and we can't change it."

"I'm concerned for you—the way you're talking. An unbeliever might put it that way."

"I know, Daniel. I'm just frustrated. I know things don't happen because God foreknows them. Just the opposite. God has foreknowledge because of what happens."

"Don't forget—all things work together for good. God doesn't compromise himself. He uses everything to bring about those good ends."

Daniel drove into the parking lot across from the courthouse. Local reporters stood by to question both sides. "I imagined there would be media again today," Daniel said, "but not this many. I see why Gingrich suggested we arrive early."

"I can't do this, Daniel. I know they want to ask me about Danny. All they want is their story. It's not fair."

"Honey, just stick close to me, and I'll move them like bowling pins if they don't let us through. We'll have no comment."

Alan Gingrich watched from a window above as Daniel put his arm around Kayla and bent forward to stiff-arm cameras and microphones coming at them. Questions whizzed by them like arrows. Kayla thought of Daniel's college football days where he zig-zagged between tacklers, stiff-arming toward a touchdown.

Inside the courtroom, Gingrich arranged the documents he would use to address the court. "You were lucky. Zingeralli uses the media. He made a statement and took a few questions. Jones didn't make it through for over ten minutes. I didn't expect this level of media. The loss of your baby has created quite a story. I regret your having to experience this added stress."

Daniel patted Gingrich's shoulder, acknowledging a prosecutor's demanding job, having to deal with legal issues continually. "Thanks for caring. We were praying to God for deliverance. I've discovered that the greater the need, the shorter the prayer. We simply prayed, 'God, help,' and he delivered."

They sat in the first row of the gallery behind the prosecutor's table, less than twenty feet from where Mark Jones and his attorney sat. Kayla looked over at Frank Zingeralli, making sure she made no eye contact with Mark Jones. She had had no contact with Jones since the accident and no real conversation with him that day. *What does he feel at this moment?* She caught a glimpse of Mark's face as he turned to speak to his attorney.

"Is this justice?" Kayla asked Daniel.

Daniel believed the ADA had probably met victims of every offense known to man. Some must have demanded death for whoever caused their affliction, while others just wanted everything to go away. "I know you don't like this, Kayla, but it has to work this way. This is not God's court. We're all just human beings, people trying to do what is right—yes, trying to provide justice. Don't be too harsh."

"I would accept an apology. I don't see where this will accomplish anything." Her eyes unavoidably met those of the defendant, and neither of them looked away.

Kayla read the look on Mark Jones's face as mournful and apologetic, in need of forgiveness, to which Kayla responded, as best she could, with a look of sensitivity. She didn't want to appear too forgiving. The current setting was inappropriate, and, knowing ADA Gingrich would not approve, she didn't want to risk it.

Kayla turned her head as the bailiff announced, "All rise. The Court of the Second Judicial Circuit, Criminal Division, is now in session, the Honorable Judge Ruth McCain presiding."

Judge McCain walked queenly to the bench, elevated but not lofty, like a good boss. She instructed everyone but the jury to be seated, and the bailiff read the charges.

Kayla remembered the one time she and Daniel sprang for the cost of attending an expensive dinner theatre, as she heard the bailiff swear in the jury. She saw two differences between this setting and the mock trial play enacted at the dinner theater—today, no meal is planned, and this is the real thing.

Judge McCain stared at length around the courtroom with a focus on no one in particular. With the slightest hint of a smile, her long pause seemed inappropriate, like a talent show host who quickly announces the winner after a long, awkward stare.

The courtroom fell laughably silent. Kayla leaned forward in anticipation of what the judge would say. She leaned for the eternity it took the judge to speak and nearly fell out of her seat once the judge broke her silence.

CHAPTER 17

J udge McCain spoke. "I regret we did not have enough time yesterday to call the first witness. By the time we got the jury seated, it was close to five o'clock, and everyone agreed not to push the schedule. Thank you all for your patience.

"The Defense has opted to reserve their opening remarks for the beginning of the defense case. The People did not object. Is the Prosecution ready to present its case?"

"Yes, Your Honor, the People are ready."

"Call your first witness."

"The People call Martin Diaz."

Officer Diaz moved to the stand.

"Raise your right hand. Do you promise that the testimony you shall give in the case before this court shall be the truth, the whole truth, and nothing but the truth, so help you God?"

"I do."

"Please state your first and last name for the record."

"Martin Diaz"

ADA Gingrich stood between the table and his chair. "Mr. Diaz, where do you work?"

"I'm an officer with the Memphis Police Department."

"You made the original report on the traffic accident of December 1, 2018, that is the subject of this proceeding. Is that correct?"

"Yes, I was the first officer on the scene and made the report."

"Would you relate the events that happened at the scene of the accident that day?"

"I received a call that a three-car accident had occurred on Poplar Avenue west of Central Library. When I arrived at the scene, I saw that one car was severely damaged."

"Can you identify whose car had severe damage?"

"The car that was driven by Kayla Dean."

"Tell us what happened to cause the damage to Ms. Dean's vehicle."

"She lost control, crossed into the oncoming lane on Poplar, and slammed sideways into a large steel light pole."

"What events led to the Dean car becoming out of control."

"The car driven by Mr. Jones—"

"The defendant."

"Yes, Mr. Jones pulled into traffic and caught the rear finder of the Dean car, causing the car to turn sideways. The driver, Ms. Dean, couldn't maintain control and swerved into the oncoming lane. The car traveled a couple of hundred feet and slid sideways into a steel light pole on the south side of the street."

"You refer to a three-car accident. What additional car was involved?"

"After the Dean car lost control and swerved into the oncoming lanes of traffic, it came into contact with a car that had stopped, waiting to pull into traffic. That car showed no real damage. The Dean car just brushed the front of the third car."

"Did you interview the driver of the car that caused the crash in the first place?"

"Objection, Your Honor. May we approach the bench?"

"Okay, come on up."

"Your Honor," Frank Zingeralli said, "Mr. Gingrich is asking for a legal conclusion. There has been no legal conclusion as to who caused the accident. I have no problem with asking questions based on facts. But this type of legal conclusion admits responsibility, and I don't see that as fair."

"Well, Mr. Gingrich," said the judge, "why don't you rephrase the question to allow the jury to hear the answer you want without claiming responsibility on anyone's part."

"I'll do my best, Your Honor."

"Officer Diaz, did you interview the driver of the car that made contact with the Dean car in the first place?"

"Yes, the car that was driven by Mr. Mark Jones. Mr. Jones stated that he was waiting to pull onto Poplar Avenue when the traffic cleared. The actions of a passenger in his car caused him to accelerate inadvertently, and his car moved forward, hitting the side of the Dean car."

"Did you speak with the passenger in his car who Mr. Jones claims caused him to accelerate?"

"Mr. Jones said the passenger had left the scene. There was no one to interview."

"Is that right? So, where did the passenger go?"

"Mr. Jones said he didn't know. She just walked off."

"She? So the passenger was a female. What was her name?"

"He didn't know. Said he picked her up just minutes before the accident. Said she was a homeless girl and needed help."

"A homeless girl? So, you were not able to determine the identity of this person?"

"No. Mr. Jones said he was traveling west on Poplar when this girl flagged him down. He said he doesn't usually pick up strangers or hitchhikers, and he was late for a meeting, but she looked like she needed some help. He wanted to give her a few dollars to help her out, so he pulled in the strip center there and stopped. She asked him if she could get in the car. He told her he was in a big hurry but said he would give her some cash, and she could ride with him until she got warm. Said he would let her out further down the road, closer to his meeting."

Jack Williams had a quizzical look on his face. He put the detective files into his computer bag and left the courtroom.

"Did the defendant tell you what happened next?"

"Yes, he told me this girl said some crazy things that scared him, so—"

"What crazy things?"

"He said she talked gibberish, not making any sense. He thought she was on drugs. He wanted her out of his car."

"So, he let her out?"

"Well, he said when he pulled into the strip center, he turned around. He stopped his car and offered her some money, but she grabbed all the money he had in his hand and tried to open the car door."

"That's when the accident happened?"

"Yes. Said he tried to pull her back into the car. When he grabbed for her, his foot hit the accelerator, and he went into the traffic and hit Ms. Dean's car."

"Did you write a ticket as a result of the accident?"

"Yes, I wrote the ticket to Mr. Jones."

"No further questions, Your Honor."

"Does the Defense have any questions for this witness?"

"Yes, Your Honor. Officer Diaz, you say that Mr. Jones told you his passenger had left the scene after the accident, is that correct?"

"Yes. Said he returned to his car after viewing Ms. Dean's car, and she was gone."

"Did you try to find the passenger?"

"What do you mean?"

"Did you look around for her? Maybe she was in a crowd of witnesses."

"No, there weren't many people around. I took the defendant's word for it."

"Did you speak with any witnesses at the scene?"

"No, the paramedics arrived, and I spoke with them. Ms. Dean's little boy was injured, and they took him to the hospital. Other officers on the scene spoke with a few individuals that were there."

"Has there been any attempt to locate this passenger for questioning since the date of the accident?"

"I don't know if there has or not. You would have to ask the detective division."

"Has any detective in the division asked you about the disappearance of this passenger?"

"No, I haven't spoken to anyone."

"No detective has approached you with a follow up regarding where this person might be or in what direction she might have traveled when leaving the scene?"

"Objection, Your Honor, asked, and answered."

"Sustained."

"No further questions, Your Honor."

***

Jack Williams was on a quick mission. He checked his watch. "Ten-fifteen," he said to himself. "That should give me enough time. How did I miss this?" He wanted to recheck his notes while driving but decided he knew enough. He hoped he could make it to Mark Jones's office before eleven, and to his second stop before noon.

Jack knew from his earlier visits that activity at the Jones office was rigorous, like an engineering office with more intensity. They were producing software, not hardware, so it was more office and production than manufacturing.

No foyer or reception area existed inside the building. Jack presented his ID to the person at a desk close to the front door. "I'm here to see Sally Ferguson."

"Oh, she's working heuristics," the man said, pointing to a group of people focused on laptops circling what looked like a drafting table.

Jack recognized Sally among the group. "Please, excuse me. I'm Detective Jack Williams with the Memphis Police Department. We spoke before. Could I ask you a few follow-up questions from our last meeting?"

"I guess so. What questions?"

"Last time we met, one thing you said got me to thinking. You said Mark Jones is a busy man, especially with this new software program you're introducing."

"Manufacts."

"Right. Mr. Jones stays busy, but when we talked before, you said he told you he had plenty of time, and that's why he was able to help this homeless person."

"I don't know about that. Mark's got a lot on his plate. He just said he had the time, so he stopped to help her. He may have had a meeting at Bass Pro. I don't know. Mark spends a lot of his time involved with fishing stuff."

"Being such a busy man, with all he has going on here, how does he have a lot of free time to spend at Bass Pro?"

"He delegates. He's got top-of-the-line, dedicated people here, and he knows the job moves faster when he doesn't attend to every detail. He spends a lot of time networking, meeting with people, and getting the word out."

"Thanks, that answers my question." Jack checked the time—ten-fifty. "That's all I need right now. Thank you."

Jack was greeted at the reception desk at Cobel Women's Health Clinic at eleven o'clock. He presented his ID. "Hello, I'm here to see Edith Watkins."

***

The courtroom was abuzz. No one could miss Jack Williams as he entered and moved with quick steps to the prosecutor's table. He passed a note to ADA Gingrich and whispered in his ear. Gingrich looked up at Jack, looked back at the note, and glanced toward Mark Jones. He rose to address the judge.

"Your Honor, the People ask for a brief recess."

"Approach."

Gingrich and Zingeralli approached the bench.

"What's this about, State?"

"Your Honor, we may have found the missing passenger from the Jones car. The State requests a recess until Thursday morning, to ascertain the facts and to call and prepare any witnesses."

"Counselor, what is your take on this?"

"Your Honor, I don't know about any of this. If new evidence is forthcoming, the Defense needs time to review and prepare. Also, I can appreciate the State's position in this matter. Since this is new information to me, I can use the additional day to prepare for the best way to move forward to protect my client's interest."

"I'm not going to agree to a lengthy recess, but I see both sides agree this is a necessary action. No one needs to hear anything until the facts are known. I will recess for the rest of the day. We'll move forward tomorrow. Step back, please."

"This is the right thing to do, Your Honor."

"Thank you, Your Honor."

"Ladies and gentlemen, it is necessary that the Court stand in recess until tomorrow morning, at which time we will reconvene. The Court believes this recess, though lengthy, is necessary. The jury is excused. See you tomorrow."

CHAPTER 18

"It just happened, Frank. I'm not sure anything else I could have done would have been much better."

"What you could have done better is tell me the truth." Frank stood his computer case on the meeting room table between the two of them, like the first block set in a stone wall.

"It had a simple beginning and started innocent enough. It wasn't a problem until they charged me."

"Mark, this may lead to additional charges. You lied from the beginning. Thank God you were not under oath. That's perjury. What in heaven's name were you thinking? You must tell me everything that happened—this time truthfully."

"The events in the story I told you are the truth, but it happened with a different person. How did Williams figure it out?"

"Your story, as you told it to different people, changed. You told the police you were late for a meeting and didn't have time to deal with this person you referred to as homeless. From his notes, the detective saw that you told others that you tried to help this person because you were in no rush. Being a good detective, Mr. Williams knows from experience that when a person's story is not consistent, it usually means they're not telling the truth. That made him focus on the one thing everyone already thought you were lying about—the homeless passenger.

He couldn't fathom why you stopped in the parking lot, and he decided to ask a different question. It wasn't a question of why you were in the strip center, but who was with you in the car. Digging deeper, he found that you were not the only one who didn't tell the truth that day. From his notes, the detective saw that your sister was late for work on the day of the accident. She told her assistant that her car was in the shop, and she caught a ride with another employee. When the detective interviewed that employee, he found she had not given your sister a ride to work that day. That was too much coincidence; he could only conclude your sister, Suzan, was your passenger. The question is, why did she leave the scene of the accident?"

"Again, it was innocent enough. She was already upset because we had been arguing. That's why I pulled into the strip center. She was screaming at me, and it made me nervous. I pulled into the parking lot to calm her down."

"What were you arguing about?"

"That's not important right now. It's been an ongoing thing for years. Suzan settled down some but got a little depressed, saying she was broke and couldn't even buy lunch. I offered her a little cash to make it through the day. That's when she grabbed the money out of my hand and caused me to hit the gas—so stupid. I moved forward only four or five feet, but it turned out to be just enough."

"Why didn't you tell me this in the first place? Why did she leave the scene?"

"When Suzan saw that Megan Alladee was involved in the accident, she didn't want to have to deal with Megan. She knows Megan from the health center where Suzan works. They battle regularly, so she took off and walked the rest of the way to work. It's less than a mile from where the accident happened."

"Why didn't you tell the cops Suzan was your passenger?"

"Well, at the time, it was just an accident. I made up the homeless girl story to protect Suzan's identity. Kayla Dean's baby was injured, and they took him to the hospital as a precaution.

When they arrested me after the baby died, I didn't want to tell the cops I had lied to them, so I kept the story as it was."

"You made a mountain out of a molehill. Your action proves how important being forthcoming with me and telling the truth is. I could have made this of minimal importance. Now the possibility of your story being true no longer exists. Now you're a proven liar. This changes everything."

"Especially for Suzan. She made a quick, thoughtless decision to avoid having contact with Megan Alladee, and now this. What's going to happen? Will she be charged?"

"I don't know, Mark. Right now, my concern is what's going to happen to you. The DA is going to want something to come of this. At this point, you haven't lied under oath, and he will consider that. I'll speak with him today. From this moment forward, you must tell the truth and the whole truth. Don't hold anything back."

"I would not lie after being sworn in. I decided I would tell you after that officer took the stand."

Frank got a text message signal on his phone. "The DA is preparing a warrant for Suzan's arrest. He's asking me to come to his office, which must mean he wants a deal. I have to tell you, Mark, this is going to drive a wedge between you and Suzan. Are you ready for that?"

"Telling the truth will implicate her in the accident."

"That has already happened, and that's as it should be. It's your car, and you are ultimately responsible for what happens in your car when you are driving. The truth is the accident would not have happened if Suzan had not done what she did. Jack Williams will want her statement before they decide what they are going to do."

"Once this gets out, and the press does their thing, this will not help my business," Mark said. "I may have to delay the go live date for Manufacts."

"Do what you think is best, Mark, but I would advise against that. It will feed whatever doubts any of your potential customers have. Separate this from the business and continue with the planned date. You should portray this as not affecting your business."

"How can I separate this from my business? The business and I are one."

"Life goes on, Mark. Are you going to present this new software program as functional only if you are doing okay? No, delay creates doubt, and dominos will fall. It's better to show strength. You were trying to protect your sister, and you can continue to help her if you have strength."

"Of course you're right, Frank. I'm just not thinking clearly. I'll deal with this in a way that's best for everybody, including Suzan. When will we know what the DA is going to do—with Suzan and with me?"

"Today."

CHAPTER 19

J udge McCain's adjournment for the day offered a reasonable excuse for Cindy, Megan, and Kayla to visit Wolfchase
Galleria mall. Megan and Cindy invited Kayla to tag along
on their shopping excursion as an excuse for Kayla to visit St.
Jude. She wanted a better view inside the campus without the
restrictions of a guided tour. Heading to the food court for a
snack before driving to St. Jude to deliver the cake plates and
dessert servers they purchased, they stopped for a look at the
carousel near the mall entrance.

The renovated carousel became the focal point of the mall
for Kayla. It reminded her of the day she first met Daniel. He
approached the carousel and waved at who Kayla guessed
would be his son or daughter. She couldn't determine to which
kid he waved. He waved to one after another. So much waving,
he must have been with a group, or he had an enormous family.
"You wave a lot," she said to him. "Are you here with a group?"

"No, I just like to see how many I can get to wave back. The
kids love to see everything passing by. I see it as a way to add
to their excitement. A bit silly, I guess, isn't it?"

"It's attractive. Like you need that." She embarrassed herself by being forward.

"Thank you. Which kid is yours?"

"I don't have one. I love the carousel and seeing how much
the kids love it."

"Goodness, already we have much in common. Hi, I'm
Daniel. And you are the beautiful—"

"Hello, I'm Kayla. Please, don't be bashful." Their relationship developed from there.

"Every carousel is beautiful," Megan said. "It's an axiom of personal memory. Who doesn't have a good life story about a carousel?"

"Daniel and I met at this one eight years ago. He was a handsome rock, and spirited, and he hit me up without hesitation. Of course, I encouraged him," Kayla said.

"That's so romantic," Cindy said. "Kevin and I met at a rock concert on Mud Island. He was pretty forward too, and I can tell you, I didn't have to encourage him."

"You've created a carousel of your own, Cindy," Megan said. "My story is about the Grand Carousel in the Children's Museum at Hollywood and Central. It opened a little over a year ago. It's a classic, originally located at the fairgrounds, and officially upgraded when the fairgrounds became Libertyland. It ran at Libertyland for over thirty years. The components of the carousel were crafted by hand with incredible care. I rode it many times with my mom and dad over the years. It remained in storage for over ten years after Libertyland closed. I haven't been to see it since it opened last year.

"We should plan a visit. It could be a great fundraising attraction for St. Jude if we could develop a program featuring St. Jude kids. They can't come for a ride, of course, but we might consider having pictures of some of the kids posted around. That would keep the focus on St. Jude and attract people who want to support the cause."

Kayla felt a bit of guilt about leaving Kim with her Gramma. The trial proceeding would have taken most of the day, and the trip to the mall wouldn't add any time. She decided it would be okay. "That's what I love about you, Megan—always thinking of the kids, and what will help them. I'm sure you will say it's just your job, but I know better. Right now, I'm thinking about how much I want to ride the Grand Carousel with Kim. She needs those childhood memories with her parents now more than ever."

"You need it too, Kayla," Megan said. "Maybe more than Kim does. It's fair to say you both need it. You and Daniel need it, together with Kim, but I know I don't have to tell you that."

"Granted. This trial is a lot to bear, but we are getting there, thanks to Daniel and his ability to remain strong spiritually. I couldn't make it without him."

They walked toward the food court. "You guys have a relationship most people only dream about," Cindy said.

"Daniel is a mature-minded person. He sees everything in a biblical context. Everything happens under God's will, although I'm having a hard time applying God's will to my life right now. Megan and I have discussed spiritual things and how I can't see my life in any other context. Cindy, you and I haven't talked. Megan told me a little about you and Rochelle, but I'm curious: how do you and Kevin view spiritual things?"

"We don't discuss it. You know my family is Jewish, and Kevin is not. In our culture, we will be unequally yoked, but my family doesn't practice what's called Orthodox Judaism. My dad talks a lot, but talking's not much without doing. After we're married, a question may come up about how we plan to raise our kids. Kevin won't want to practice anything Jewish, because he is not in favor of religion in general. To me, it's not a problem either way."

"I can't identify with what you're saying. It's likely to be a major problem. You guys should decide how you'll handle this issue before you tie the knot."

"You and Rochelle could have a good debate, Kayla," Megan said. "Rochelle is more Jewish than anyone else in her family. She doesn't practice Judaism either, but she has definite views about what Jews see as right and wrong, especially when they deal with raising kids."

"I'd like to discuss it with her. Managing what your kids believe is the highest level of importance."

Megan grinned and rocked back. "Rochelle detests the official Jewish position on pregnancy and abortion. She says interpretations of the Torah are equal to the number of rabbis available, and she's quick to point out that not one of them has ever been pregnant. She can't accept their first premise—for the first forty days, the fetus is only water."

Kayla frowned. "I can see how the Jewish tradition is in opposition to the first principles of SAVE. The question of when life begins is at the root of arguments on all sides of the issue. Every action we take should support the preservation of life, and we believe life begins at conception."

Cindy smiled. "The idea of life at conception convinced Kevin and me. My baby is alive, and abortion amounts to murder."

"I'm proud of you, Cindy, but I want you to expand on the point you and Kayla just described as the basis of our mission at SAVE. You should dismiss romance and emotion in what I'm asking you to consider. Consider the facts and nothing more. Put yourself in the place of many of the women we call our clients at SAVE. You're an intelligent, talented woman with good judgment, but financially destitute, possibly without even a roof over your head, and without a husband or partner. You're pregnant but have inadequate means of providing food, clothing, and shelter—without recourse, depending on the government for nearly every need. You're influenced by illegal drugs and physical abuse, with no way out—no light at the end of the tunnel— not even a tunnel. Would those circumstances affect your thinking?"

"Thanks for cheering me up, Megan. You come across a little like Eliza. Her arguments sometimes seem to encourage abortion. Given my inability to see myself in such a predicament, I don't know what I might do."

"A reasonable answer, Cindy, and it brings to mind what Eliza is saying. The woman I described can't envision herself being in your position either. Imagine if she could trade places with you. Would she decide to become a mom?"

"Yes, she would," Kayla said.

"I guess she would too," Cindy said. "So, where does swapping places leave us?"

"Eliza has told us abortion is not the issue. Unplanned pregnancy is the issue. Do you want your pregnancy to end, Cindy?"

"I want my baby to be born. I suppose you could define my pregnancy as no longer unplanned."

"Can you see how this woman may no longer have an unplanned pregnancy if she were able to trade places with you? It's not the pregnancy, but the predicament that's the problem, the environment in which the pregnancy is taking place. Eliminate that problem, and you may no longer have an unplanned pregnancy, not for all, but for many who act out of desperation. You eliminate abortion for those people."

"I see what you're saying," Kayla said. "But you're over-simplifying it. We've seen that eliminating poverty and the culture that feeds on it—pardon the expression—have been proven to be unachievable. Even if possible, I don't see how eliminating poverty stops unplanned pregnancy. Many people, rich and poor, have unwanted—and therefore unplanned—pregnancies. It's a matter of inconvenience, and abortion is still the solution for those women."

"One issue at a time, Kayla. Abortion for convenience, or using it as a contraceptive, is especially egregious, and it eliminates an unwanted pregnancy. Cancel the unwanted pregnancy, and you cancel the abortion, but these two abortions are not the same. It's a matter of motive. The indigent woman's motive may be pure. The contraceptive woman's motive needs work, but that work demands a different approach. Let's consider the destitute woman's solution first."

Kayla had to admit she was on foreign soil. She had not considered abortion issues as in any way related to her life. "Fair enough, but, again, we are talking about government welfare, which we have seen over and over, is no solution."

"Yes, the government, a la Ronald Reagan, is not a solution, it's a problem. The government's motive is not to prevent abortion. The government's motive is to provide abortion on demand."

Cindy was resolute. "So, I keep asking, what is the answer?"

Megan stopped walking and pushed her hands back against Kayla and Cindy. "If either of you were wearing a hat, I would say 'Hold onto your hat.' The answer is adoption."

Kayla sensed Megan's point, knowing it instinctively before she said it as if Megan wasn't speaking anything new. "I'm not sure I see how far this would go. You can't mean the adoption of unaborted kids, because we have concluded the adoption of unaborted kids is not the answer."

"I may not comprehend the meaning of adoption," Cindy said.

"No, I'm not advocating the adoption of kids, but let's start there. Adopting a kid is for a lifetime, right? You would provide parenting and leadership—rules of the road, so to speak—to help your adopted child grow to maturity. You would provide what he or she needs to lead a happy, healthy, and successful life. You would raise your adopted child in a loving home, with lifelong family relationships. The goal is autonomy and creating a legacy. Now, consider those elements in the context of adopting the pregnant mother and potentially the father, the whole family."

"This can't be legal adoption," Cindy said. "It doesn't seem possible. Are you planning to mentor these clients? I don't see how even mentoring a large group is possible. One or two maybe, but any form of adoption is out of the question. Imagine the personal involvement required, not to mention the expense."

Kayla could see the possibilities. "Megan is not talking one-on-one, Cindy. Consider the opposite. Planned Parenthood provides their services, for lack of a more accurate term, to millions of clients. And they don't take the initiative to do it one-on-one. The clients come to them. Am I on track, Megan?"

"Yes, you're getting the picture, although I don't see it completely. If we had a foundation to provide a real solution to unplanned pregnancy, think of what we could do. This foundation would not be a clinic, with any form of medically associated programs. Call it what you want, but the foundation would adopt pregnant families. And the adoptees would be subject to rules and regulations of the foundation."

"Sounds like the government and welfare," Cindy said. "Are people going to accept being governed by an alternative government?"

"It is not welfare," Kayla said. "Going back to Megan's original idea, if you legally adopt a child, you don't consider that adoption as welfare. You're not giving a handout. You're providing a lifelong commitment to raise a child. And the child is subject to your family's rules of the road, as Megan puts it."

In a broader, spiritual, doctrinal sense, Kayla knew about adoption and silently repeated her position. *I was born into the family of God when I became a born-again believer. God adopted me as an adult member of the family with the rights and privileges of all other members of the family.* "Adoption is the correct term for what we are considering here, but we should redefine the word. We are adopting adults."

"Slow down a little, Kayla. These ideas require intense discussion and hard decision making, not to mention enormous planning, depending on the decisions made. I want to talk with my parents, and I want to bring Rochelle into this. Cindy, what are your first thoughts?"

"You're both crazy to even consider this. So, we're talking about a new world consisting of a family of families whose only identity is unwanted—that is to say, unplanned—pregnancy, and they see no way out of their predicament but abortion. And we are considering adopting these families as a way of turning their unplanned pregnancies into planned pregnancies to eliminate their need for abortion? Crazy. Okay, I'm in. Could you guys adopt me?"

"Sorry, Cindy," Kayla said. "You would have qualified, but your pregnancy is no longer unplanned."

CHAPTER 20

M egan took the last bite of her pizza. "I know you asked in jest, Cindy, but your asking for adoption makes Kayla's point. We should redefine the word. It means the adoption of adults, but it should describe that adoption in newly defined detail. It's not a question of finance, but a question of how to bring these women to a place where they can make real, autonomous decisions. How can we bring them into the middle class?"

"I see what you mean. It's not just a handout; it's bringing them to a new level of—"

"Wait, Cindy, see that lady standing in the order line? That's Alice Beale, who works at Cobel Clinic. She's not a nurse, but she's involved in tech and record keeping at the clinic. I want to see if she will talk with me about Rachel's abortion. Kayla, Rachel is the one we called Lady O when we referred to her in the SAVE context."

"Oh, yes, you told her story at the meeting. Did she have the abortion?"

"I'm sorry to say, but I don't know. I haven't spoken to Rachel since the first of last week, and I don't know if she made it back to the clinic. Can you and Cindy drive together to St. Jude? I'll follow you shortly if Alice speaks to me."

"Yes, we'll pay the bill and head out."

Megan walked close enough to rouse Alice's attention. "You're in the right line, headed for great Chinese."

"Megan! Hi. You startled me a little. Didn't see you come up. Yes, I've grown to love Chinese. I ordered their orange chicken. It's exceptional. Have you ordered? Will you join me?"

"Thanks, I had lunch with a couple of friends, but I would like to join you for a minute or two. I wanted to ask you about Rachel Owens. Do you remember her? She and I were at the clinic last week. Rachel had planned to schedule an abortion, but she's still a little unsure of what she should do."

"Yes, I know her. She hasn't been back or contacted us since the two of you were there last week. Do you know if she still plans to have the abortion?"

"No, I haven't been in touch with her either."

"I know you want her to dismiss the abortion, but I'm not sure she can carry her pregnancy to term, or, worse yet, what she would do when faced with raising a child."

"She's like the majority of women at the clinic. She needs help and professional advice based on her particular problem. Have you spoken with her?"

"That's not in my area of responsibility. Nurses and doctors at the clinic counsel these women."

"Who?"

"Several people—the nurses, the doctors. Counseling is a requirement before any decision for abortion. I'll admit, we may have some preconceived notions, but, if it's what the woman wants, who are we to say she shouldn't exercise her rights?"

"Alice, I know you are supposed to speak the company line, but, between you and me, do you buy into such a weak argument?"

"Rachel has said abortion is what she wants."

"She has been told abortion is what she wants. She has been told abortion is what's best for her. She has been told she can't afford to have a baby. She has been told she doesn't want to be pregnant."

"She doesn't want to be pregnant."

"Why?"

"Megan, I'm sorry, but I'm not ready for this. I'm not prepared to argue these points with you."

"Fair enough, Alice, but let me ask you this. What if Rachel came to you and said she didn't want an abortion? What would you say to her?"

"I would advise her to tell her counselor."

"Nurse Winders?"

"Yes."

"What would Nurse Winders say to her?"

"You know the answer without my telling you. I'm not saying I agree with Suzan, necessarily, but this is a regular event. Most clients have doubts, but most of them come around to understanding abortion as a way for them to get on with their lives, and that's what they do."

"I don't want to argue with you either, Alice, but none of you know if any of these women who pass through your abortion factory are getting on with their lives. Once they go out of your door, they are on their own. No one knows what happens with any of them."

"I'll admit it. It's true. I sometimes wonder what happens to these folks after they leave the clinic. Some come to the clinic more than once. They must be okay, or they wouldn't come back."

"Rachel already has a son. He's four years old and is doing okay."

"I didn't know she's already a mom."

"She is an intelligent and gifted person who loves her son with all her heart. She is trapped in a world of physical and mental abuse, dependent on the government, at least financially—and drugs—she does not do drugs. It's an accident of birth. Had she been born in another environment, I think she would have flourished. Countless other women in this country, women of many cultures and races—men too, for that matter—have not been given a chance. They are born into a world without hope. Some may have squandered their opportunity, but the reality is these people can't see beyond their immediate circumstances because their world expects failure. Society demands it.

"My apologies, Alice. I'm ranting, but a lot of people, Rachel included, need more than financial help; they need assurance. They want to believe there's hope, and they need help in figuring out how to turn hope into reality. Nothing personal, Alice, but places like Cobel Clinic squander hope by lining women up for abortions, no different from lining up cattle headed for the slaughterhouse."

"I don't disagree with most of what you are saying, Megan. I'm a little trapped too, and reticent. I've had my share of disagreements with people at the clinic. Remember, I work with Suzan Winders, who sees abortion as the answer almost always. Scratch almost. Her goal is to increase the number of abortions done by the clinic, and her arguments supersede my ability for rebuttal. If I were to articulate my views, even close to the way you have done in this conversation, Suzan would fire me. I'm just trying to get by."

"I didn't know you had any disagreement with the clinic's policy, and I'm encouraged that you do. I can visualize you as an advocate for a higher cause."

"I wouldn't go that far. Remember, I want to keep my job. Suzan would not look favorably on the conversation we are having now."

"Anything we discuss is in confidence, Suzan, or no Suzan. Will you have any more involvement with nurse Winders regarding Rachel, if I can arrange for Rachel to revisit the clinic? I would like her to discuss not having an abortion, at least not immediately. Could a meeting happen tomorrow?"

"Suzan will be out tomorrow. She is involved in an ongoing trial her brother is having."

"Oh, I didn't even know she has a brother. Is he from Memphis?"

"Yes, his trial is happening now. Suzan had planned to be with me this afternoon, but she texted me saying the judge adjourned the hearing early today. She is with her brother this afternoon and will be involved with the trial tomorrow. "

A trial, adjournment today? There's at least a chance of a connection here. "What's her brother's name? Her brother is on trial?"

"Yes, he is on trial for a type of vehicular homicide from an accident he had a few months ago where a little boy died. His name is Mark Jones. Why do you ask?"

"I had no idea, Alice, but I'm a witness in that trial. I was involved in the accident. We shouldn't be talking about it."

"We shouldn't be talking at all. Suzan would kill me if she knew I have a connection, and here I am having lunch with you."

"I don't see any problem with our having lunch together and discussing a mutual client. Association between a friend of a defendant's sister and a witness in the trial shouldn't create a legal issue, so long as we don't discuss the trial."

"I don't see a problem either, but Suzan will. She sees any-thing outside her control as a problem. Sorry, Megan, I want to finish my lunch. You should leave."

"I'm with you, Alice, but what response will Suzan have when we meet with a mutual client at the clinic, knowing of a connection between her brother and me? I'm going to have to make her aware of the connection."

CHAPTER 21

E liza Stokes took a long-awaited view of the newly restored house she and Benny had clandestinely leased before their official declaration of a move to Memphis. With the relocation now official, Eliza began, in earnest, to work on the permanence of their new home. She invited Megan into her home office, a place Eliza simply calls her document room, an area packed wall to wall, nearly to ceiling height, with a lifetime of artifacts, awards, and certificates. Stacks of published articles by Eliza and others lined the shelves, along with artwork collected from her distant travels—and books, books galore.

Megan saw in these details the biography of a life devoted to others. "Wow, Eliza, this is beautiful, a testament to a meaningful life. I would love to hear the stories I'll bet are behind everything in this room—the story of your life.

"I love the height of these ceilings too. You're lucky they are tall, right? What are they, twelve feet? Athena would be comfortable here."

"Only if she remained seated," Eliza said. "This place is from a time before a building's utility bill became an element of design. Nearly every room has a fireplace, but most of them seldom have had a fire. One just turned up the thermostat when the outside temperature dropped. Back in the day, temperature controls were left on around the clock, even when the family traveled, and the home would be vacant for several days. Owners wanted a spring-like ambiance the minute anyone walked into the home. Times do change."

"Yes, they do. My dad says the utility bill is top-of-the-line in most decisions he and Mom make about their home. Were he here, he would ask about your tonnage requirement and would want to view your heater and AC equipment."

"Speaking of change, I'm interested in hearing what changes you're advocating for the family planning community. You seemed anxious when you called last evening. Adoption?"

"I see it as a redefined form of adoption."

"I'm intrigued. What's your plan?"

"I don't have a plan yet, at least not a formal, written plan, nothing comprehensive. What I have is an idea. If planned and developed into implementation, this program will positively impact the abortion rate everywhere. It's an idea I got from you."

"Should I expect to take credit or to accept blame?"

Megan smiled. "I appreciate the dialectic approach I've seen in your arguments at the SAVE meetings, and I've read enough to expect no less from you in talking one-to-one. Answer my question after you hear my argument. We should prepare for both fame and shame." She repeated from memory, "Abortion in the lowest socioeconomic classes of America results from, and is proportional to, the failure of government-funded social programs designed to bring an end to poverty. The number of abortions performed will increase with the funding of additional programs."

"You've practiced your statement well. Should we stop funding social programs altogether—food stamps, welfare, TANF, to name a few?"

"Yes, at some point. In the meantime, we should focus on removing the need for government programs that contribute to the problem. Requiring one to search for work to obtain assistance, when no work is available, defies logic."

"That argument is not new. What makes yours different?

"In my plan, the government is not involved. They are the problem, remember?"

"Yes, I remember."

"We have an opportunity to counter simultaneously those problems that additional government programs create. We don't demand that our people look for jobs that don't exist, or jobs these people wouldn't qualify to hold anyway, even if the jobs were available. We help them to succeed, by training them to create the availability of jobs, and we train them in managing the new life those jobs will make available. The government is neither capable of providing nor motivated to offer training of life skills."

"Is this your reformed adoption? You said you're adopting the parents, rather than the unaborted children?"

"Yes, but it's complicated because we are focused on unplanned pregnancy and abortion."

"Can I offer some immediate advice?"

"I hoped you would."

"Whatever else you do, don't call it adoption. Adoption brands you as racist, and no matter how you seek to redefine it, the majority of people are going to see it in financial terms. I can point to a multitude of insurmountable obstacles associated with the idea of adoption you neither want nor should have to overcome."

"What should we call it?"

"Use an acronym that won't raise any governmental eyebrows and won't be seen as racist from the outset."

"We have no racist motive whatsoever."

"You and I know that, but few people outside our group and no people in any political camp will recognize that. They will assume a racist intent."

"I don't understand what you're saying, Eliza. We want to provide a means to allow all women to make decisions without being influenced by their negative culture or motivated by a dire financial predicament. How is that racist?"

"This is the stereotypical reality of perception, Megan. Why are members of this lowest socioeconomic class of our society poor? Why don't they have jobs? Why are they getting food stamps? Why are they on drugs? Why are they destitute? Why do they make questionable judgments? The stereotypical answer is because they are lazy, they don't want to work, they want a hand-out, and they don't value their health, their environment, or their kids."

"Those stereotypes are what we want to eliminate. The government and society as a whole should be motivated to discount those ideas. Success will follow a moral motive and intent of our own."

Eliza pulled a large photograph from the credenza behind her desk. "Do you recognize this building, Megan?

"No, I don't. It looks like an Elizabethan mansion. What is it?"

"You are close to being correct. Let me tell you the story. You know I grew up in the New Chicago neighborhood in North Memphis. Both of my parents worked. My father worked at the Firestone plant less than a mile from our house. Thank God, he had that job. It provided a steady income for our family and great thankfulness, a combination of pride and humility, on the part of my father.

"My mother worked as a maid in the house shown in this picture. She awoke early enough each day, even weekends, to ride a city bus downtown and catch a transfer to arrive at this house before eight o'clock. She cleaned the entire house, washed dishes, and did the laundry, all the jobs one can imagine a maid would do in such an upscale home.

"I accompanied her to this home many times during school holidays or when no one was available to care for me. My mom and I loved that house. The people who lived there, of course, were white, and, in our eyes, they were rich people. Their daughter, Jane, and I became friends. Not much older than me, I was amazed by the way the girl lived, but, you may be surprised, I don't recall any racism or prejudice on the part of those white people. I don't know if they were racist or not. That's not the issue.

"I had no sense these people were, in any way, better than me, or that they had a life I should have or even consider having. They resembled my picture of the people at Disneyland. Disneyland had castles and kings and queens. Everything at Disneyland seemed perfect and unattainable, but that was the way it should be. No one ever expected to live a Disneyland life. It was a fantasy world, and everyone loved it.

"This house was Disneyland to me. I couldn't tell if the people who lived there were acting a part, like those people at Disneyland, or if they lived there in reality. It didn't matter."

"I'm not sure I see how your story applies."

"One day I told my mom how I couldn't understand the life those people lived, and I wondered if Jane, who had become my friend, could understand the life we lived in New Chicago. As I told Mom, half the time, I couldn't follow what the girl was saying. She talked about things I couldn't fathom in my wildest dreams.

"I will never forget my mom's response. It says more about my mom and dad than anything else. My mom said, 'Jane can't help it, Eliza. It's not her fault that she's rich.' From that moment on, I've seen everyone I've met in a new context. No one can decide where they are born."

"You hit the nail on the head, Eliza. It's the first premise of our idea. Poverty is not necessarily the poor person's fault. If given a chance for success, a permanent job, and a way to leave poverty behind, few people will refuse to latch onto it. Welfare and food stamps diminish the possibility of freedom. The solution comes through training, not just training for a job, but training about how to manage your new life. It's one thing to train for an available job, but how to deal with a new, reliable, and sustainable income is essential training."

"Be careful, though, Megan. Remember, to whom much is given, much is required. As a child, Jane couldn't help being rich, but as an adult, she can determine what she will do with her riches. With wealth comes control, the ability to make decisions, not only in the rich person's life but also in the lives of those less fortunate. As you've pointed out, poor people lack autonomy. Decisions are made for them, either by circumstance, by the government, or by other people in their environment.

"With the newfound autonomy that you expect for these people, you may find the pace of decision-making ability will exceed the judgment needed to live within the wage. We can only hope to have problems associated with the temptation to create debt. But living beyond one's means and the self-defeating expectation of more government hand-outs are problems you should expect to encounter.

"These are middle-class issues that may not lead to poverty. They just strengthen its chains. It will take an ironclad contract to guard against a political machine working to that end. Adoption won't do it."

"We can use your leadership to reinforce that doctrine. You have the potential, and—"

"Wait, wait, Megan. You're moving much too fast for me. This idea is not a 100-meter dash. It's a marathon, and a marathon runs at a slower pace. You have a world of planning and programming ahead of you."

"Sorry, my apologies, Eliza, I'm with you. I've maintained this need for planning and promoting too. I'm just getting a little pumped. We made the mistake of sprinting during the startup of SAVE, a mistake I don't want to see made again. I want your involvement using this approach. For my part, should this idea be implemented, I will take a behind-the-scenes role as well."

"Working in that role won't be easy for you, but I've seen its benefit in my career. You should set the pace for others to follow."

CHAPTER 22

Assistant DA Gingrich entered the office where Frank Zingeralli was waiting. "Hello, Frank. This is an unusual case. We're barely an hour into the trial, and this new evidence surfaces. I'm assuming you knew nothing of this?"

"You know me better than that, Alan. Besides, this helps my client, and it would have been at the top of the list to identify first. He's been trying to protect his sister at his expense."

"She has already confessed to being the passenger in your client's car during the accident. She's in the box now."

"Is she telling the same story?"

"She admits to grabbing the money, but points out that her brother is the one who accelerated."

"But he wouldn't have done that had she not grabbed the money. Mark admits he should have told the truth from the beginning, but no one had a clue this would come to prosecution for homicide. At the time, it was just an accident, and Mark wanted to protect Suzan from being discovered by the third party, Megan Alladee."

"What does that have to do with anything?'

"Ms. Alladee and Suzan have had an ongoing pro-life, pro-choice rivalry for many years. Alladee runs an anti-abortion movement that protests the activities of Cobel Clinic, where Suzan works. Suzan didn't want Megan to know of Suzan's involvement in the accident."

"So that's why she left the scene. As far as I know, she hasn't offered that."

THEN COMES THE FLOOD

"My client's motive was innocent enough. And he planned to tell the truth when under oath. He and Suzan were arguing. Mark pulled out of traffic and into the parking lot because it was unsafe to be in traffic with his sister yelling at him. He was protecting her, the same as he tried to protect her with his homeless girl story. Mark lied to protect her, not himself. Granted, he was wrong in both cases, but his intent was good. Now his sister is trying to make him guilty of everything."

"She's doing exactly that. She agrees with your client's version of events, but, in her view, she did nothing wrong."

"How can she believe that? A kid died as a result of what she did."

"She says she didn't kill anybody. It's odd, but she says your client didn't kill anybody either. She has strange ideas about a lot of things. She seems intelligent enough but says things that make one wonder. She comes across as defensive and angry and shows no remorse. It's just not her fault."

***

Suzan answered questions not only from the detective but also from an officer sitting at the end of the table with a note pad. The officer asked what seemed to Suzan as random questions—personal stuff, her correct address, and who they might contact in case of an emergency.

"How long have you lived at your current address?"

"Seven years."

"Do you own the home?"

Jack Williams interrupted. "Back off, Joe. We're talking about important facts here. Ms. Winders, you acknowledge you and your brother were involved in a heated argument before the accident, isn't that right?"

"Yes."

"You also agree that you grabbed money from your brother's hand, right?"

"Yes."

The officer quickly asked, "Do you own the home?"

"No. I pay a mortgage." Suzan saw this as a good cop, bad cop routine.

"Joe! Cool it. Ms. Winders, your grabbing of the money caused your brother to accelerate into oncoming traffic, isn't that right?"

"I took the money. My brother accelerated into oncoming traffic, not me."

"Why did he accelerate? What caused him to do that?"

"You'll have to take that up with my brother."

"I'll do that. Now, what was behind this argument with your brother that meant having to pull off the street for safety? Was he violent towards you?"

"No, Mark is not a violent man. We have our disagreements, but we're usually able to work it out."

"But this time you couldn't work it out? Again, why were you arguing?"

"I don't believe the subject of our conversation is in any way relevant to the accident. I've told you everything I know. I've decided I should speak with an attorney before I answer anything else."

The detective rubbed the back of his neck. "Okay, we're done here. You got everything you need, Joe?"

"I guess so."

"One last thing Ms. Winders. You don't seem to be in any way aggrieved that the accident caused the death of a child. Why is that?"

Suzan offered no response.

The detective left Suzan sitting in the interrogation room and spoke with the sergeant on duty. Other officers stood around, waiting to hear what they had to say. "She's not going to give us anything. Her action led Jones to accelerate, causing the accident and the death of the child. Now it's up to the DA."

***

Gingrich tapped the eraser end of his pencil onto the table. "Tell you what, Frank. Your client lied to the police, and I can understand the context. At the time, it was only an accident. Although it didn't turn out to be the case, he pulled into the parking lot as a safety measure."

"He lied to protect his sister, not himself. He seems filled with remorse."

"Granted, but he continued to perpetuate the lie after being charged. Lying is lying. He had no business carrying a lie forward."

"He felt trapped. He feared the additional charges brought against him would create even greater problems for his sister, so he kept it going without considering the real consequences."

"That's enough, Frank. Don't make me change my mind. I'll offer him probation, and the judge will want a fine for a guilty plea to a Class E felony involuntary manslaughter charge. I can't reduce it any further."

"What about a nolo plea? His business is entering a critical phase, and civil action can ruin him."

"He is going to have to face the truth. That includes taking the stand to testify to what happened. In the meantime, he'll have to seal his lips—no public expression in defense of his sister, and no talk with the media whatsoever."

"I'll present that to him, including the nolo plea. Is that agreeable?"

"One slip, and he's finished. The deal's off. Make sure he fully understands that."

CHAPTER 23

"Thanks for coming in early," ADA Gingrich said to Kayla and Daniel. He motioned for them to be seated. "I know you're wondering what is going on with the court."

Daniel took the lead. "We're confused, and why wouldn't we be. We haven't heard anything about what happened yesterday or what we can expect today. All we've heard is there may be some new evidence. What, exactly, does that mean?"

"It's called new evidence because it answers questions not previously answered."

"What questions?" Daniel asked.

"Two questions are fundamentally related to moving the proceedings forward. The first is whether there was a passenger in Jones's car, and the second is if there was a passenger, who was it? Answers to both these questions came before the court yesterday. Not having a hundred percent certainty of identification led to the confusion. There was probable cause, but a court announcement requires a warrant."

"Why not allow testimony that would identify this passenger and issue the warrant outside the proceedings?"

"If any delay caused the word to get out, the subject might flee, so the judge called a recess to keep the information under wraps until a warrant could be issued and the suspect taken into custody."

Kayla leaned forward. She stared at the ADA. "Okay, who in the world is this person?"

"It's the defendant's sister, Suzan Winders. Since she fled the scene, the DA feared she would flee again if she heard we were after her."

"This isn't making much sense," Kayla said. "Megan called me last evening saying she discovered Mark Jones is the brother of Suzan Winders. Suzan manages the women's health clinic, where Megan spends her time protesting. She will die when she finds out Suzan was the passenger in Mark Jones's car during the accident. It makes no sense."

"Jones made up the homeless girl story to protect his sister's identity."

"So now we are supposed to accept this sister of Mark Jones as being responsible for our son's death?" She turned to Daniel. "Daniel, why is this happening? Why is God allowing all this?"

"I don't know Kayla. I don't understand this either. Maybe it will come to us later. For now, we have to accept it and try to deal with it." He took Kayla's hand.

"There's more," Gingrich said without any change in temperament.

"What?"

"Suzan Winders will be prosecuted to the fullest extent the law allows. Jones has agreed to plead to a reduced charge, effectively ending this trial. We will go through those proceedings this morning. The charge is still homicide, reduced to a Class E felony that could allow his release on probation without requiring any jail time. He will also pay a fine. I'm sure this is not what you wanted to hear."

Daniel put his arm around Kayla and pulled her to himself. "No," Kayla said. "In one way, this is a relief. I came to believe Mark Jones did not directly cause any of this. I believed he told the truth about a passenger causing him to move into the traffic.

He didn't do it on his own. I understand why the law cannot see it that way, but I'm glad the judge saw it to some degree."

"I see it that way too," Daniel said. "We have forgiven him for whatever role he played, I guess his lack of judgment, in causing the accident."

Gingrich laid the new case folder in front of Kayla and Daniel. "Now, we will begin a new prosecution—Suzan Winders."

***

"My client has no comment," Frank Zingeralli said. "He cannot speak. It's an ongoing investigation."

The press closed in as Frank and Mark moved arm in arm down the steps of the courthouse.

"Why did you lie about your sister being in the car with you? Is she the one who caused the accident? Is she responsible for the death of Kayla Dean's little boy?"

"Don't respond in any way, Mark. They're trying to make you say something you don't want to say." Frank pushed Mark into the back seat of the car, waiting at the curb, and they sped off.

"I'm glad you took the deal, Mark. I'm still a little surprised the DA offered it. I think we had a chance, going forward, with a mystery girl as the cause, but once they discovered Suzan was involved, that changed everything. I'm glad it's over."

"It's not over. It's just beginning."

"I see where you're going, and I agree. It's the beginning of a nightmare for Suzan, but at least you got through it without any jail time. Thankfully that part is over. Judge McCain is another factor. Gingrich convinced her Suzan was the one to go after, and he saw you as a victim of her action. They made it look like Suzan ran away to keep from being charged. Since she is a nurse who didn't render aid, it makes her leaving the scene even more appalling. She might have been able to help a dying child. She left because the accident was her fault."

"Another lie. The facts don't bear that out. I told them why she left the scene. It was innocent enough. They are not willing to consider why she didn't want to hang around because it weakens their argument."

"That's how the system works, Mark. I hope Suzan has a good lawyer."

"She doesn't want a lawyer, and she will plead not guilty."

"Is she crazy? She can plead anything she wants, but she is in far more trouble without an attorney. She will be in jail until her arraignment. With her attitude, if she shows up in court without someone to speak on her behalf, there's no telling what her bail will be. Someone should talk some sense into her."

"If she remains in jail, I won't see her until after the arraignment. Can you speak to her?"

"No, I can't, Mark. Conflict of interest, you know. But I can arrange for an associate to try. It's Roy Ingram. I'll ask him to contact you. You should keep this between you and me."

The car turned the corner and pulled alongside Mark's office. "You've got to help make her see the light, Frank."

CHAPTER 24

W ith most of its lights turned on, and people scattered around periodicals and research computers, Cossitt Library looked different during business hours. Megan suddenly realized she didn't use the library as a library, but only as a meeting space. It was a different place altogether.

Megan, Rochelle, and Cindy set up for the meeting. When Kayla entered, she set her handbag on the floor near a stack of folding chairs. "I wanted to get here a little early to help out. I'm glad you're all here. I know you heard what happened today at the trial."

"Yes, Megan filled us in," Rochelle said.

"I know what happened, but I don't get it. Why did the DA let this guy off?" Cindy asked.

"It's a little unclear, Cindy. They're going after Jones's sister. They decided the case was a little tainted by the discovery of his sister, and no one, including the judge, believed Jones truly fit a case for the charge. He became somewhat of a victim because of his sister."

"I guess I can see a little of that. It's hard not to feel for the guy; he seems so overcome with guilt. Anyway, Kayla, Megan said you might want to speak with us before the meeting. We have a little time."

"Can we sit?" A little unsure of where to start, Kaya tried to settle her mind. *These are some of the brightest people I know,* she thought. *They have experienced unsheltered lives unfamiliar to me.* "I need help in settling this trial in my mind and

heart. My husband, Daniel, is uncommonly supportive. He's with Kim now so I could be here. Thank God, he helps me physically and spiritually. I have others in my church and my family who I look to for guidance. But I need some one-on-one with you guys, who I have come to respect. We've known one another for such a brief period, but our time together has been different. For me, we have only the events surrounding this trial and my son's death in common, and I guess that's the point. I need some perspective."

"Enough said, Kayla. I know where you're coming from," Megan said. "It reminds me of Lady O. Remember her? She made it back to the clinic and had an abortion. I don't know if I could have had any influence at the end, but the point is, I wasn't there, and they rushed her through. If I had been there, who knows?" Megan shifted her chair a little closer to the table. "It was hard for me to accept such a close relationship of events and people, a series of things that didn't happen. In your case, it was a series of coincidences that did happen."

"My pastor says a coincidence is God's way of remaining anonymous."

"I believe that's a quote from Einstein," Rochelle said.

"You would know," Cindy said.

Kayla wanted to be sure they knew her motive. "Listen, girls. I believe that everything in our lives happens for a reason. God is in control, and he directs the world, the universe, following his great plan. I sincerely believe it with all my heart, and I couldn't live peacefully without that belief. Right now, I'm having trouble living peacefully with it."

"Gosh," Cindy said. "Doesn't your life center on the study of why things happen the way they do—why you believe the way you believe? I never dreamed you would have doubts."

"Apologetics," Kayla said. "Yes, you're correct. I should not have this problem."

"Back off a little, Cindy," Rochelle said. "None of us has all the answers. None of us lives free of doubt. Living our lives despite those doubts says who we are."

"My apologies. I meant it as a compliment. If even the strongest people around can show a little weakness, it gives me hope for my life. Sorry, Kayla, I meant no offense."

"That's okay, Cindy. I know what you meant. I don't mean to imply that I'm struggling with what I believe. I'm struggling with what I don't believe. Does that make any sense?"

"Kayla, there are four people at this table," Rochelle said, "and I would venture to guess we have four divergent views about life.

"Why do things happen the way they do? Is it coincidence, luck, sometimes being unlucky, maybe fate, or does life include a divine element? Is God responsible for the good? Easy to say yes to that. Is God also responsible for the bad? Not so easy."

"Is God involved at all?" questioned Cindy.

"See what I mean? Two varying views within the same family. And you make three, Kayla. I know you believe in a very personal God who directs and controls." Rochelle turned to Megan. "What about you, Megan?"

Megan looked up. "Kayla and I have discussed what we believe about the meaning of life. She knows I'm open to more than one explanation of what happens, in general, and specifically."

Cindy shook her head. "That's a good answer, Megan. No commitment either way." Rochelle leaned toward Cindy with a frown, and Cindy moved her head back. "Don't look at me that way, Rochelle. Megan can take care of herself. I see her do it every day. Care to expand on what you're saying, Megan?"

"I need some help too. Kayla has helped me better understand the spiritual side of things. I learned a long time ago that I don't have all the answers. Kayla strongly believes what I struggle to even consider—her Christian belief, for example."

"Thanks for that, Megan."

"It's true," continued Megan. "Without a deep, spiritual belief like yours, one needs a higher than average pain threshold to work at a place like St. Jude, especially as a doctor, like Rochelle. We have fewer answers, even though we have more questions, but we've learned so much from all those families with suffering kids. We've learned to accept what we don't understand.

"What I believe is irrelevant. Action is what counts. My answer to those ugly questions is to try to do something good, even without having answers to important questions. All I need to know about God is he wants me to do good, to do something worthwhile, not for a reward in heaven, or a reward in this life, for that matter. God wants me to do good because it's the right thing to do."

Kayla was again surprised at Megan's bringing God into the picture and knew Megan was not directing anything at her. *She's directing it at herself.* "Thanks, Megan. I admire you for that. I wish I could have your outlook, knowing what I know. Having your outlook, I wish you could know what I know."

"So why the level of anxiety over this trial? Are you doing the right thing?"

"Well, I'm not the one who's doing it. With no intent on Jones's part, I would accept an apology, but the court can't do that. The court has to proceed with judiciary action, and courtroom justice is not unscriptural. It's a biblical requirement. In this case, it's a requirement of the people. It's not a requirement of mine. Demanding individual justice through the court is vengeance, and vengeance is not scriptural. The state is not giving me any choice. I'm being swept along with it and required to endorse it, but I can't do that. My baby boy is dead. Nothing is going to change that. This trial, portrayed as justice served, seems to be justice carried out to placate the people."

"I agree with you, Kayla," Rochelle said, "with a caveat. You refer to scripture. I know you study the scripture from a historical, as well as a spiritual viewpoint. The Old Testament portion of your Bible, especially what you refer to as the Pentateuch, includes the history of Cindy's and my ancestry, the nation of Israel. You and I share a belief in that text."

"Yes, I believe in the verbal inspiration of the Bible."

Rochelle continued. "The first book of the Bible is Genesis, and the first chapter of that first book proclaims the creation of the universe. The account portrays God as making all things. He made the beasts of the earth, the birds of the air, and the fishes in the sea. He made all these groups of things, but he didn't make a group of people. He made one man and one woman. He looked to them to create the people, the culture, all of humanity. In the first chapter of the first book, we see the indication of a personal God, a God who deals with individuals."

"And those first two individuals are who got us all into trouble," Cindy said.

Kayla felt Rochelle made a good point, one on which she could expound, but she wasn't there to preach. She directed her response specifically to Cindy. "Yes, I believe that's true, and a way out of our trouble also began with those two individuals." Then to Rochelle, "I'm sure you have a larger context, Rochelle."

"Yes. In the Pentateuch, one sees a progression of God's dealing on a personal level until the era of Israel as a nation. In that context, one can see God begin to deal with the nation as a whole. I can't go much into specifics here. The point is, while God deals with you and me on a personal level, we can see a history of God's dealing with people on a national level as one. No doubt, many in the nation of Israel resented being swept away with God's demands for the nation as a whole."

"These days, it's the world," Megan said. "It's not just a nation. All humanity acts like one. With the internet, we have instant communication. People have common needs—regardless of nationality or race, regardless of culture."

"You're right, Megan," Rochelle said. "I used my example because I recognized a shared belief between Kayla and me and how we see God's direction in our lives. St. Jude is a good example of what you are saying. It's a worldwide community with a common need. Race relations sometimes get in the way, but shouldn't. In this country, racism is primarily light skin versus dark skin. In other places, it's some other identity, but the reality is, it shouldn't matter."

"If there is a God," Megan said, "He is dealing with the whole world on an individual basis. And he's dealing with individuals in the world as a whole. That probably doesn't make much sense to you spiritual scribes, but it makes sense to me."

Kayla could sense how firmly Megan's statement expressed what Kayla saw as the truth. "Is God letting it all happen by chance, Megan? If there is a God, is he working to control any of it?"

"I don't know Kayla. You've hit on one of those questions I quit asking."

Megan's response left Kayla conflicted—reluctantly accepting Megan with no answer but thankful that, for herself, she had no reason to ask. "This little discussion has helped me. I can celebrate knowing our beliefs are not so far apart, and everything is open for discussion. Cindy, I want to speak with you further."

"Why would you want to do that?"

"Well, don't in any way take this as demeaning, but it seems you haven't drawn all your conclusions about some of the issues we've touched on here. You have a different slant on things, and I'd like to hear your position as it develops."

"You're in for a boring discussion," Cindy said.

"We'll see."

"Hello ladies," Megan's dad said, as he and Eliza entered the room together from the top of the stairs.

"Hi, Dad. Hello, Eliza. Glad you could come."

"It worked out well," Eliza said. "Your dad told me your mom couldn't come, and I would be traveling alone, so he offered to pick me up. I'm open to not driving," she winked.

"I get it," Megan said. "We're working our setup for the meeting. Cindy brought snacks and a little fruit. They're in the fridge. We've been talking about Kayla's trial. She's in for a new one since they threw out the first one. I'm sure Dad told you what's happening."

Eliza unzipped her computer bag without looking up. "It may be for the best, Kayla."

"How so?"

"God is watching out for you. A new trial may be his way of getting you some relief. From what I saw, you weren't ready for the first one."

"I guess you're right. At least with a delay, before the new trial begins, maybe I'll be better prepared."

"Every good and perfect gift is from above," Eliza said.

CHAPTER 25

Megan's dad called the meeting to order. Attendance was down. Eliza suggested SAVE meetings should be held once a month or at least extended to biweekly. Megan's dad agreed, especially with preparation for the new nonprofit, in which they were all becoming involved.

A motion passed to extend SAVE meetings to a biweekly event, moving to monthly at a later date. A few attendees stayed back after the meeting for a quick snack, but within minutes, the room held only the group Cindy called the founders, who now included Eliza and Kayla.

"Rochelle," Megan said, "I've never heard you speak candidly about your religious beliefs or spiritual beliefs or sacred beliefs. I don't know what term to use."

"The Talmud," Rochelle said. "I've studied much of what Kayla would hesitate to call the dogma of Jewish belief. You're right. It's difficult to know how to refer to Judaism. It's not a religion, and it's not a race. On the other hand, it's both. It depends on who is defining what it means to be a Jew. It can be highly convoluted, and most of us have learned to be tolerant."

"It seems odd. In all this time, we've had almost no religious communication, not the least of which is what being Jewish means to you," Megan said.

"What does being Caucasian mean to you? It's one of those unspoken things people accept without much discussion. With Kayla, the context is usually spiritual, hence the discussion."

"That's true. Kayla comes across as spiritual without being religious, if you follow what I mean."

"Yes, I follow," Rochelle said.

Cindy and Kayla completed the kitchen cleaning and helped Megan and Rochelle fold and stack chairs. "Let's check around for any wayward literature or anything else related to the meeting. We can't be too careful."

Megan asked herself what she would do were she in Kayla's shoes. She admired Kayla's dedication to her beliefs but felt Kayla shouldn't wear emotions on her sleeve. *Not sure I would do that. I can't say how I would walk where she walks. She has faith, which answers some questions and creates others.* "Kayla, does your faith ever waver?"

"Tough question, Megan. The answer depends on who is asking because who is asking determines the definition of faith. It's not fair to ask, 'What do you mean by faith?' That would be answering a question with a question. It's laughable. A person gets asked, 'Do you believe in God?' 'Yes.' 'Do you have a belief in God?' 'No.'"

"Sorry, Kayla, I didn't mean to light a fuse."

"No, you didn't. Please, this is important. Let me finish. Webster says faith believes in something for which there is no proof. The Bible says faith is the evidence of things not seen. People have come to define faith as something you believe without evidence, but that misses the point. Without faith, belief is unbelief. Again, 'Do you believe in God?' 'Yes.' 'Are you a believer?' 'No.'"

"I guess I see what you mean. So, does your faith ever waver?"

"No. Faith is given to me from God for conviction—to believe the truth. And true faith can't be shaken. Faith is not based on *what* I believe, but on *who* I believe."

Megan seemed surprised to see Rochelle's approval of Kayla's position. "Rochelle, how do you interpret what Kayla is saying?"

"I agree with her position. Kayla's beliefs are rooted in Judaism. She and I both see the Old Testament, the Hebrew text, as scripture. We may understand its meaning and its message differently. But our historical views of Judaism and Christianity, for the most part, coincide. It's at the beginning of the New Testament where everything begins to separate, historically and spiritually."

"Why is that?" Megan asked, believing she knew the answer.

"I'll answer first, Kayla, and you can counter with anything I misstate. Christians see the Old Testament as preparing for the story told in the New Testament. Christians see Jesus in the Old Testament. Some of the stories in the Hebrew text showing God intervening in the lives of the people of Israel—quote, his chosen people—are seen by Christians as preincarnate appearances of Jesus Christ. Christians see Jesus as the seed of the woman promised in the Garden of Eden."

"That's accurate, Rochelle," Kayla said. You have described the 'who I believe' versus the 'what I believe.' I'm impressed with your insight, which comes from hard study."

"Rochelle practically invented study, at least in our family," Cindy said.

"I'm interested in how you see the relationship of Judaism and Christianity, Cindy," Kayla said. "Care to contribute?"

"I wouldn't presume to add anything to what the doctor says. I haven't considered much about being Jewish or studying the Torah the way Rochelle has. Maybe I will, but I like the way she expressed her view of that relationship."

Megan placed the last chair on her stack. She paused to consider the idea of a new trial for Suzan Winders. She dreaded the negative impact another prosecution would likely have on Kayla. "I'm not sure how anything we've covered today will help your mindset in this new trial, Kayla. This one will be a challenge. I could meet with you and Daniel to help prepare for what I believe you will encounter in dealing with Suzan Winders."

"Thanks, Megan. I've never even seen her, so I don't know what to expect. You think it will be tough?"

"Believe me, any stress you have now will increase by a factor of ten with Suzan involved. I've known her for many years, and I can at least help you prepare."

"I'd like that. Let me talk with Daniel. He will hesitate because he won't want to put you out, but he is also reasonable. He'll come around, especially if he thinks it will help me."

"Megan has told me Daniel wants to visit St. Jude," Rochelle said. "I wouldn't presume to offer St. Jude as a place to discuss ongoing legal matters, but a visit from you and Daniel may be a good place to begin. The three of you could at least have a post-campus tour meeting and see where it leads."

CHAPTER 26

T he front door to Mark's home opened. "I'm here." Suzan threw her scarf and windbreaker over the sofa and sat at the kitchen bar.

"How is your Sunday afternoon going?" asked Mark. "I'm having a drink. How about you?"

"Yeah, whatever. You don't drink, so when you say you're having a drink, I know no alcohol is involved. Don't do that to me. Alcohol, please."

"At your service," Mark said, as he served what he had prepared for her with faux politeness.

"Wow, a French 75. How did you make it so quickly?"

"I knew you'd want something. I got it started and finished it when I saw you pull in the driveway. Mine is a lot easier."

"You call that a drink? What is it, a Virgin Mary?"

"Well, its Bloody Mary mix with lime. It's so good, it needs no alcohol. Besides, yours has double alcohol, gin, and wine, to make up for mine."

"Alice and I have these when we are traveling. The 75 refers to the caliber of a weapon, so it just takes one."

"Okay, now you're cut off." Mark ringed his glass with the lime and took a sip. "I'm glad you worked with the attorney Frank brought in, or you'd still be in jail. That would have served no purpose at all."

"Thanks for bailing me out. I didn't figure you'd ever want to speak to me after the problems you've had."

"You know better. I don't blame you. It just happened. It's not anyone's fault. Had we known the consequences, neither of us would have made the decisions we made."

"I don't know. If that bitch Megan Alladee hadn't been there, none of this would have happened."

"That's harsh," Mark said. "It's not her fault. Without her being there, you would not have had a reason to leave the scene, but the homicide charge would still exist. Who knows where we would be had it happened any other way?" Mark dropped an ice cube into his glass. "I knew you had problems with her before the accident, but I didn't know the extent. What problems are there?"

"You know she works with that anti-abortion group called SAVE. They have the same hypocritical views all the others have. You know how they work. They want to take away the rights of women. The worst part is, they don't care what happens to those babies after they're born or the mothers of those babies. How can they sleep at night?"

"Okay, settle down. Don't get so riled up."

"Megan Alladee manages the group. She hates any woman who gets an abortion, herself excluded. She is especially hostile toward me. I've never done her any harm."

"She had an abortion?"

"Years ago, when she was eighteen or nineteen; I don't remember exactly."

"You handled her abortion?" Suzan took another sip and affirmed she assisted at Megan's abortion. "I can see why you didn't want to confront her at the accident." He twirled his glass. "The problem now is she will likely be a witness in your trial. How are you going to handle that?"

"I doubt she will be hostile in court. If she is, at least she'll be cross-examined. The DA should charge her as well.

"Her car wasn't moving and was struck by Kayla Dean's car. I don't see how Megan contributed to the accident in any way."

"So, now you're on a first-name basis? Even so, she is a part of it."

"When are you meeting with your attorney—Roy Ingram, right? If you plead not guilty, what's his plan for your defense?"

"I don't know. I'm not even considering those charges right now. All I know is I didn't do anything wrong, and I'm not going to admit anything. I hope you'll stand behind me."

"They won't let me."

"Why, what do you mean?"

"A part of my plea deal prevents me from taking part in any defense on your behalf."

"That's crazy. What if you get called as a witness? What are you going to tell them?"

"The truth. What would you have me tell them?"

"Telling the truth is one thing. Testifying against me is another. If my attorney calls you as a witness, it will be in my defense."

"The DA is not going to let that happen. The state will have me on their witness list. And they have prevented me from speaking with any reporters or talking in public at all concerning their case."

"My God, they've set up my brother to be a hostile witness."

"My guess is I'm in violation now with this conversation we're having. It seems a little odd, but, for whatever reason, the DA's restrictions didn't prevent me from posting your bail. I guess booking doesn't carry as much weight as charges in an arraignment."

"I guess I should vacate this place before I make any statements you can use against me."

"That's not fair, Suzan. I'm not doing any of this by choice. It just happened. Neither of us made choices. We just reacted to events." Mark hesitated before saying anything further. He poured another glass of Bloody Mary mix and twisted a lime into the glass. "You know I didn't ask you to stop by today to debate any of this. If they ask, I want to be able to tell them we didn't discuss it. However, they can't prevent us from hashing out anything not related to the trial."

"I know what you want to say, Mark, and I don't want to hear it. You've gotta put this out of your mind. I'm tired of arguing. I'm not up to it, especially today. I just got out of the clink, remember?"

Discussion of what Mark referred to as brother-and-sister stuff seemed improbable, but he believed they had to have a plan. "I'm concerned something may come up before or during the trial, and we should be prepared for it, how we're going to handle it."

"I thought we weren't supposed to talk about the trial. You and I are the only ones who could bring anything up. Are you going to bring it up?"

"Of course not." Mark hated the idea of assuming a problem not dealt with would work itself out. "Let me tell you, Suzan, that detective, Williams—Jack Williams—doesn't know how to stop. He keeps digging until he finds something. If you plead not guilty, he will dig deep, and I don't want any part of it."

"The prosecution is going to be busy with what I bring to the table and won't have time for anything else."

"Suzan, that's crazy talk. They've got a slam dunk. You don't have anything to bring to the table. If you fight this, anything you bring to the table will make it worse, and you'll lose."

"Maybe so, but I'm going to fight anyway."

"No judge is going to allow some radical nonperson defense. I know how you see this. But it won't hold up. They're not going to listen to any of it."

"They have to listen to reason. Besides, I'm not the one who pulled into traffic. You are. It wasn't my fault."

"What they won't listen to is anything unreasonable. There is a precedent for the charges they will bring against you. You're not required to be the driver to be seen as the cause of an accident. Then you left the scene—a nurse leaving a scene when a baby was injured. Regardless of the real reason you left, they will say you were trying to avoid any charges. Everybody will see, as I do, you have no remorse for the death of that baby. You're stacking the deck against yourself."

"You're discussing the trial again, Mark."

"I'm trying to make you see the thin line you're walking. I'm trying to keep you from doing something you will regret for the rest of your life. If they uncover what happened, you'll face additional charges. You may be in jail for the rest of your life."

"It was ten years ago, with no adjudication."

"That's because you lied and got away with it, and knowing the few facts I know makes me a party to it."

"I didn't lie, Mark. I just didn't tell the whole truth, so you don't know the whole story."

"I don't want to know anything. You should try to make a deal with the DA. Failing that, you should plead guilty, and it would help if you showed a little remorse."

"You're talking about the trial again, Mark."

CHAPTER 27

Kayla was mad at March if anger was possible for her. Daniel says Kayla being angry is like Tinkerbell pounding her fists on a tree stump. It doesn't make any noise.

March now saved an hour of daylight to provide additional time for more work. But an extra hour only expands existing work to fill the additional time available. She remembered that fact expressed as somebody's law, probably a mom with a five-year-old child.

Irritated by the March wind pushing the umbrella she had unfolded over their heads, Kayla carried Kim high in her arms. That kept their heads as close under the umbrella as possible, since the rain was light but seemed stronger with the chilly wind.

She felt frustrated for not checking the forecast before scheduling a drive downtown to visit with Cindy, knowing that only metered spaces were available for parking. She fished for coins to cover at least an hour and hurried up the Court Avenue hill next to the Fourth Bluff.

Kayla resigned herself to the idea that anger was difficult for her. She acknowledged the fruits of the Spirit included gentleness, meekness, and self-control. Anger is a harmful plant growing in the spiritual garden and must be rooted out as soon as possible. She better described her irritation as sadness, another weed that usually doesn't grow as tall but can be harder to dig up—sadness sometimes mixed with gladness. This March was a mixture of both.

Jerry had convinced her to attend the Bible study sessions again. She was glad but sad—glad to be back in fellowship with the group. The class expressed how off track the discussions had been without her input. Glad, with a genuine sense of relief, that now things could get back to normal—sad to consider, at least for her, it will never be normal. March, a year ago, she felt her little Danny's second trimester kicks during class. She mused he was offering his amen to her views.

Kayla wondered what Cindy was feeling at this point in her pregnancy. It was a little too early for any kicks or movement. She had barely begun to show. Today's get-together followed up the discussion the four girls had three weeks ago. She and Cindy talked off and on, but nothing either of them would call a sit-down conversation.

She and Kim entered the building where Cindy worked a box lunch for a group of architectural tenants. Kim ran to the group of elevator doors as one opened. "Kim, honey, be careful. Don't enter any of the elevators, okay?" Kayla said. "We are waiting on Cindy here in the lobby. She should be here soon."

"Okay, Mommy, I just want to watch. Take the elevator up, take the elevator down, take the elevator up, take the elevator down, take the elevator up, take the elevator down—then we spin around." Kayla smiled as she watched Kim sing and act out the elevator song. She's beautiful. Life goes on.

Cindy was the last to come out of one of the elevator doors. She exited the door sideways, with large, insulated lunch bags strapped over her shoulders. She dumped the bags against the wall across from the elevators. "Hi, sweetheart, you must be Kim," Cindy said to the little girl standing next to the door. They had not met, but Cindy guessed no other little girl would be there to greet her.

"Yes, ma'am. I'm Kim."

Cindy hugged Kim. "Hi, Kayla. Hope you haven't been waiting long. I'm going to leave these bags here on the floor. Tommy is coming down behind me, and he'll move them out. We can go over to the snack bar if you want. I'm sure they'll have something Kim will like."

"That's fine," Kayla said. "Kim will be okay. Honey, are you ready for a snack. They've got some good stuff here."

"Okay, Mommy. I'll be good."

Cindy was impressed with how well-behaved Kim was. They walked toward the lobby snack bar—Kim skipping along without Kayla so much as holding her hand. "She is beautiful, Kayla, so sweet and restrained. I hope I'm going to have one like her."

"God did that," Kayla said.

"You had something to do with it too."

"Same thing. I trust the Lord to provide for everything." Kayla wanted to tell Cindy what she believed, regardless of how she felt. Even in sadness, God provides.

"That's why I wanted to talk with you, Kayla. You said you wanted to hear my views. I want to hear yours."

"My views concerning what?" Kayla ordered an applesauce cup for Kim and a latte for herself.

"I should have held a box lunch back from the meeting," Cindy said. "Then again, it's too much. I'll have a latte as well." They walked back to the main lobby.

Kayla handed Kim a little book from her purse. "You can read this after you finish your snack. So, Cindy, what can I address today to help me hear your views?"

"Since we talked at the SAVE meeting, I've been considering my faith—or better said, my lack of faith. I don't seem to have faith. Yes, I know, I have faith the elevator will take me up and down, but I'm talking spiritual faith here."

"The elevator goes up, the elevator does down," Kim sang.

"Careful," Kayla said. "She hears everything."

"Right, I'll remember that. You explained to me what Christians call the gospel, and I heard some things I've not heard before. It's different from anything anyone in my family believes."

"It's told in a Jewish context."

"I never considered any relation of Jews to the New Testament. Rochelle says the New Testament was written by Jews, to Jews, about Jews."

Kayla understood why Cindy came to her with questions about faith. She knew Cindy had spoken with Rochelle but likely hid some significant feelings as siblings sometimes do. "That's not 100 percent true, but I get what you're saying. Yeshua came as Messiah to the Jews. The Hebrew scripture, the Old Testament, presents a Jewish Messiah. Christians believe the Jewish Messiah is Yeshua." She was sure Rochelle had covered belief in a Jewish Messiah with Cindy. "However," Kayla continued, "Christianity is not Jewish. The first Christians were Jewish believers who had been preached to by Jewish believers. Many of them believed a Gentile should become a Jew if he or she wanted to be a Christian. The Jewish question was set aside in the early church, whose members were mostly Jews."

Cindy put her hand to her forehead like she had a headache. "This is a conversation for you and Rochelle. I'm not knowledgeable enough to discuss theology. What I want you to share is faith, your faith."

"Tell me what you mean."

"You say your faith is unshakable. I'm not surprised by that, but I don't fully understand it. I'm stuck on an age-old question that asks, 'How can I have faith in a God who allows the world to suffer?'" Kim handed her little storybook to her mom.

Kayla fished through her carryall to retrieve a substitute. Cindy put a hand on Kayla's arm. "Are we okay for Kim to hear this?"

"It's fine." Kayla smiled. "We won't say anything I can't explain later."

"Well, that is the one hang-up I can't seem to overcome. I see it everywhere, especially with kids, who don't have anything to do with causes. Yet you seem to have no problem with it."

"This calls for a double negative, Cindy. I don't have no problem with it. I struggle with it, too, maybe more than you do."

"Now, I don't follow. How can that be?"

"Since I'm a believer, I'm required to believe those answers the Bible provides, accepting those answers by faith, even if I can't readily apply them to my life. Being a Christian is not always easy."

"That's confusing to me. Megan says she can't get answers. If the Bible gives you the answer, where's the problem?"

"Good question. Let me ask you this. If the Bible could answer the suffering question for you, would you be able to accept it?"

"I guess it depends on how reasonable the answer seemed to be. I don't mean to be offensive, but most of the answers people give using the Bible don't seem reasonable. Do those answers seem reasonable to you?"

"I can be blunt about it. Many of those answers the Bible provides lead to other questions. If I'm questioning tragedy in my life, the answer is, 'All things work together for good to those who love God.' It's an answer I'm thankful for, and the one I believe. But it's a difficult thing to accept without asking a follow-up question—what specific good results from the tragedy in my life?"

"I see what you mean. So what's the answer to the follow-up question?"

"Notice how the first answer included the phrase, 'to those who love God'? What would you consider a reasonable answer to *your* question regarding the suffering of people who not only don't love God but also blame him for all that suffering?"

"I don't see a reasonable answer. What's your answer?"

"God has a plan, and he's in control."

"I've heard that unreasonable answer before. It means he lets suffering happen, or he causes it."

"Looks like we need a follow-up question to your first answer too. If a loving God has a plan for the world, would it necessarily be a good plan?"

"Yes."

"If God's plan is good, and God is in control, then God is in control of a good plan, correct?"

"Sure."

"The follow-up question may be the same in both cases— what specific good results from the tragedy in my life, in your life, or the suffering in everyone's life?"

Kim interrupted. "Mommy, is this the story you and Daddy were telling me?"

"Yes, it is honey, but Ms. Cindy and I are going to talk about some things you may not understand. You and I can talk later, okay?"

"Okay, I'll keep reading."

Cindy hugged Kim. "Thanks, Kim. You're such a sweetheart." She watched Kim begin to read another book. "The answer?"

"Okay, Cindy, if we searched through the scripture, both Old Testament and New Testament, would we find that the Bible portrays God as a good and loving God?"

"Yes, I know enough to agree the Bible shows God to be good and loving. I also see times when the Bible shows God to be angry and frightening."

"Much like a typical dad can be?"

Cindy leaned her head. "Not my dad, but some dads, I guess."

"Then we have resolved that God is a good and loving God in control of a good plan. The Bible also says no person can comprehend the mind of God. All things are of him, through him and to him, and it speaks of the glory due him. Only a God of all-knowing capacity can see his plan from beginning to end. God's providence allows him to see what tragedy may have to happen to bring a free-willed people together to carry out his plan. Only an all-knowing God can have good reasons for allowing bad things to happen."

"I can't wrap my mind around that."

"Our finite minds can't expect to have an understanding of what only God can comprehend. He must see whatever evil he allows to take place in such a grand plan as necessary. We have to trust a loving God not to let these things happen unless they were required to accomplish a good that might take years and years to materialize. We can believe an all-powerful, all-knowing God can create a glorious outcome from an inglorious event.

"The Bible tells us God made the world and everything in it. A good and loving God will allow only the evil necessary to accomplish the good of his plan. When God does not prevent an evil event, it's because he has a divine reason for allowing it. He works all according to the counsel of his own will. His will is the perfect plan."

"I'm having a hard time with that. Surely an all-powerful God could find a way around allowing evil."

"If God is a perfect God, one is required to consider the idea of a world without evil as being possible, but not attainable. The idea is that God can bring about only an attainable world. If a world without evil were attainable, a good, loving, all-knowing, all-powerful God would have actuated it. Since he didn't, it means a world without evil is not attainable."

"That seems to be arguing in circles."

"Well, if you believe a good God is always going to do what is good, you'll end with a reasonable explanation. Sometimes what God knows is good seems bad to us because he sees the end from the beginning, and, in our finite minds, we can't. I have faith that God will use what seems bad to me now as a means to accomplish the goodness of his plan. That's what it means to me when the Bible says all things work together for good."

"You've put your heart in this, Kayla. I'm going to talk with Rochelle again. I don't know if she has considered her experience in this way. I'm amazed at how she can deal with the suffering at St. Jude with such a straightforward, positive attitude. The same with Megan. Now I see that in you."

"Don't misunderstand me, Cindy. I don't take any of this lightly or without concern. I grieve over the tragedy I'm dealing with in my life. Like I told Megan, I'm crying on the inside, and I walk a narrow emotional path. I believe God is okay with that. He doesn't require us to be stupid about it. He knows what we are going through."

"That's good to hear. Rochelle spoke about your ability to meet stress with contentment."

"She could have been referring to herself."

"I see it in Megan too. I admire them both for what they have had to overcome. They see things from different perspectives— you know, Jew and Gentile. They support one another at St.

Jude, and I can only imagine how Megan leaned on Rochelle through those years of working together at SAVE and St. Jude."

"Megan has acknowledged Rochelle's undying support."

"I was just a kid, but I remember how hard they worked all through college."

"Iron sharpens iron, so one person sharpens another. I've drawn a lot of strength from Rochelle and Megan, and from you too. You've had to deal with your tragedy. I believe God wants us to work together to strengthen one another. You guys help me grow spiritually, and I hope I can, in some way, return the favor. I believe the good and loving God we've been talking about brings people into our lives to help bridge the gap between success and failure."

"Mommy, God is good all the time. All the time, God is good," said Kim.

CHAPTER 28

T he metal building reminded Kayla of the warehouses built along the street near Daniel's office. Pockmarked and graveled pavement made parking as precarious as a NASA Mars landing. She remembered this warehouse-of-a-building when it was new, built as a top-of-the-line health club catering to more affluent types. Although a metal building structure, the complex was constructed using an architectural brick and mortar design for the porte-cochere. The entrance gave rise to an enchanting atmosphere, which included beautiful and inspirational artwork from local artists.

The current owners demolished the glass-covered atrium to make room for additional parking right up to the new front door. After being converted to a kids' trampoline park, the only identifying marker was a well-lit sign at the entrance identifying its name as Jumping Around. Kayla could see a slight irony. Real estate has a way of jumping around. Plans are made, developed, and funded, usually followed by construction. Dreams become a reality. Those dreams often become nightmares.

Real estate exists in life, and, in life, change occurs, at times better, sometimes worse. New plans are made, developed, and funded. Kayla believed the changes in this bit of real estate reflected entropy, a subject Jerry often included in his classes. Since creation, the universe tends toward entropy—disorder. To reverse that disorder requires the input of energy.

Can the disorder ever be overcome? It seems doubtful. Kayla knew the style this place once represented. She was a little sad, seeing it now and thinking about what it would likely become.

Once inside, Daniel got in line to register Kim and her little friend Jennifer.

Kayla looked past the crowd of kids toward the manager's office. "Are you okay, staying with Kim and Jennifer? I'll try to grab a table near where they will be jumping. I see Megan is already here. She's in the front office talking with the manager."

"Yeah, I'm fine," Daniel said. "Can you believe Jennifer is going through the Ninja Warrior course? She's six. Kim isn't ready for that. She doesn't even know what a warrior is. I'll catch up with you and Megan shortly."

"You know Kim's going to want to do her own thing. Keep a close eye on Jennifer. We want her to play safe."

"They'll be fine. You go ahead."

Kayla caught Megan's attention and motioned toward the kindergarten balloon slide. Megan waved and signaled she would meet her within five minutes.

A light Saturday crowd at the park surprised Kayla. She found a group setting near some bouncy slides and a little climbing gym where Daniel and the kids would come as they made the rounds.

Megan pulled a little bench over to give them a place to talk. "Hi, Kayla, you guys got here earlier than I thought you would."

"Yeah, we didn't know what to expect since we've not been here before. I'm glad you suggested we come. Kim will love it. She told us her friend Jennifer is a member, so we asked her parents if she could join us. I see you had your meeting with the manager."

"Yes, the Jumping Around folks have sponsored several fundraising events for St. Jude, and they've generated significant contributions over the last few years. I wanted to thank them for their effort. Some of the kids who entered the events have visited the hospital and become more involved. That makes it even more special."

Daniel showed Kim how she could use the bouncy slide to crash into the sponge pit. She showed no hesitancy after watching Jennifer swing from a rope into all the sponges. "You're lookin' good, kids. You guys play here for a bit, and we'll move over to the trampolines near the Ninja Warrior gym."

"Looks like they will have a blast," Megan said. "How are you, Daniel?"

"Great. Good to see you, Megan. Did you have a good meeting?"

"Yes. This place has been helpful over the last couple of years. I'm glad you decided to come today."

"It's amazing, isn't it?" Daniel said. "I remember when this place was top-of-the-line real estate. It's changed dramatically—close to a dump these days—but it provides good revenue for someone's business and great fun for the kids, which I love. I guess it's a matter of how one looks at it."

"And who's looking," Kayla said. "They say the eye is a window to the soul. To us, it's a dump. To the kids, it's paradise."

"I don't understand what that means," Daniel said. "Is it a window *to* the soul or a window *of* the soul? One looks in, the other looks out. The Bible says the eye is the lamp of the body. If you look at the good stuff, your body is full of light. If you look at the bad, your body is full of darkness."

"Sorry, Megan," Kayla said. "Daniel puts everything in a biblical context. That's what I love about him."

Megan smiled. "It's not a problem. What Daniel is saying seems positive, and it makes sense. I don't know how the people who owned this place when it was top-of-the-line saw it, but the people who own it as a dump are pretty charitable. I guess God works in mysterious ways, right?"

"His wonders to perform," Kayla concluded, with a wink toward Daniel.

Daniel raised both hands with a forlorn look. "Okay, let's look at the kids. They're having a great time. I'm going to take them over to the trampolines. Megan, don't forget, I still want to have that St. Jude tour sooner than later. I know you and Kayla want to talk, so I'll see you guys shortly."

"Okay, have a good time," Kayla said. "We'll be here. So, Megan, can we get something to drink, a cup of coffee, maybe?"

"Sure, let me run over to the counter and pick it up. If you hang here, we won't lose our place. Okay?"

"I'm good." Kayla wondered about her demeanor when talking with Megan. She was sure Megan didn't want to gossip, or speak negatively, or be hateful. Megan was concerned they couldn't deal with what Suzan might bring to the table. It seemed reasonable to expect Megan to help them.

Daniel appreciated Megan's offer to help. He wanted to act in fairness toward someone neither he nor Kayla had ever met. They had prayed together, not knowing what they might have to face in this new trial, and they prayed for Suzan. Kayla had no animosity toward a person for whom she prayed.

"I don't know how you take your coffee, so I brought some of everything."

"Thanks, Megan. I take it black. So, how are things going with the nonprofit?"

"My dad is a bulldozer when moving things forward. I'd be in trouble were it not for him. No one can better deal with the red tape of nonprofit issues when filing with the IRS."

"It sounds frightful."

"I was intimidated by the process scope during our SAVE startup. The business plan, charter, bylaws of the organization, selecting board members, corporate documents dealing with tax laws, articles of incorporation—it sounds like a step-by-step process. I guess it is, but it can be terrifying without qualified people to make it happen. The documents required are difficult to complete. I'm amazed at the incredible number of people who make it through. It takes intense people like my dad, with the help of numerous volunteers and people like Eliza Stokes, people with excellent judgment. Sorry, Kayla, I'm ranting."

"I couldn't have done it."

"Neither could I. In my lack of understanding during the SAVE startup, I pushed too hard to move the process forward, and I made mistakes. Of course, my mom and dad let me make those mistakes so I could learn something, and, quicker than you might think, I did. In my ignorance, I argued incorrectly for a mission statement emphasizing a need to stop abortion. Dad understood how we needed to work on the underlying cause of abortion. As I said before, I eventually learned the impossibility of preventing it legally."

"A law against abortion doesn't stop abortion, but you weren't working for the passage of legislation against abortion, were you?"

"No, but I naïvely expected our SAVE activity to reduce abortion by making it socially unacceptable."

"I can see why that mission wouldn't work. Abortion has steadily become more socially acceptable."

"As they say, you catch on quick. I want this new startup to focus on moving families into a position that minimizes the need for abortion—unplanned pregnancy. I believe reducing abortion can be a byproduct of giving women the power to make choices they are currently unable to make."

"Well put," Kayla said. "I want to be a part of it." Kayla stood and hollered "You go, girl" to Kim, as Daniel gave Kim a high five after a double jump into the sponge pit. "Daniel seems more excited than Kim. That little Jennifer is used to getting a high five for everything she does. She's a physical little girl."

"Kim is coming along well," Megan said. "She's one of the most positive and best-behaved little girls I know."

Kayla sensed the emotion Megan couldn't hide as she spoke. "I know you're picturing your kids at St. Jude. Megan, and I'm proud of you for that."

"And I know you're watching your beautiful Kim while thinking of your little Danny. Our lives are such a mixture of feelings."

They smiled and hugged.

Kayla made a motion to wave away the slight blur in her eyes. "We're just a couple of broken birds. Let's fly away from this."

"I'm with you. Sorry for my emotion—you're saying you want to be a part of the startup?"

"Yes. I'll admit, providing a way for fewer babies to be aborted appeals to me. Daniel and I have discussed the idea of my becoming involved, and, as I knew he would, he encouraged me to do what I think is best. Where could you use my help?"

"What might be best for you is to have a conversation with Cindy. She wants to be involved. I can see where the two of you working together could accomplish some good results. Whatever you and Cindy discuss should be brought to my dad's attention. He's the authority on every foundation activity and will guide the complete process. I'm sure he can help with the best first steps to take. Can you talk with Cindy?"

"Yes, I'd love to. I look forward to partnering with Cindy. She is a resourceful lady. I'm sure Rochelle wants to be involved too."

"I believe she will," Megan said, "but for now, just work with Cindy, and you guys talk with my dad. I can set up communication where we can work together under his leadership.

"We considered what might happen in this new trial. Do you want to have Daniel bring the girls over to play with the balloons so we can talk about Suzan? Sorry, that sounds bad. I don't mean it the way it sounded. I meant to talk in the context of things involving Suzan."

"I knew what you meant. I mean it in the same way. We can talk, and I can fill Daniel in later."

"What I want you to come to terms with is Suzan's inflexible demeanor. She seems to be arguing continually, and her attitude comes across as negative. Her passion for a cause is often mistaken for anger."

"Is this the result of a personality disorder?"

"I doubt it, but who doesn't have a disorder of one kind or another? Let's just say she will be continually on the defensive."

"Okay, what else?"

"Well, some of the positions she has regarding children are dreadful."

"She hates kids?"

"I don't know how she feels about kids generally, but her stance on abortion is as extreme as any I've seen. Most abortion proponents say an unborn child is in no way a person. But she extends her position to post-birth."

"She believes in partial-birth abortion? That's not much of an issue these days, is it? I regard people who advocate partial-birth abortion as dishonorable."

"I'm not talking partial-birth abortion, Kayla. I'm not talking abortion at all. I'm talking about babies who have been born, not subject to any form of abortion. Suzan doesn't believe a newborn baby is a person. A newborn has no rights as a person until months after birth."

"I guess I didn't know anyone honestly believed anything like that."

"In her mind, that's her defense. I'm not saying she will make that her defense in court. But she won't hesitate to make you aware that, in her view, you didn't lose a child in the accident. Danny was not a person. I don't know what term she would use, but she will say Danny was less than a person."

"Goodness, Megan. I don't know what to say. I guess it's better to know in advance in case something like this comes up."

The girls came running over with Daniel close behind. "This turned out to be a good place for the girls. They're having a blast."

"Mommy, can you come with us to the ninja place? Jennifer wants to show me what she does. Will you come with us?"

"Sure, honey, I want to see what you do, too," Kayla said.

"I hope none of these issues surface during the trial," Megan said. "But I don't want you to be surprised by hearing it for the first time in the context of the trial."

Daniel took Kim into his arms. "Megan, can you stay for a while and join us for warrior trials? It sounds challenging."

"Yes," Megan said. "I wouldn't want to miss any kind of warrior trial."

CHAPTER 29

M egan reminded herself of the season as she drove into her parents' driveway. *Those April showers are ready to pierce the root. The buds will soon upshoot.* She decided today was one of those thankful days where the positive overtake the negative.

Her mind was a marvelous mix of anticipation: *Bountiful spring is ready to open its door. The nonprofit startup is a tiny light at the end of a long tunnel, and Kayla and Cindy are making inroads toward a lasting relationship. All's right with the world. At least this evening seems okay.*

Megan was surprised at her clear and active mind, working rapidly today. *Wow, Chaucer and Browning, two of my favorites. How do these memories come to mind? I owe it to my parents.* She remembered how they used Dad's ever-growing library daily, reading books together before she could understand on her own. A positive attitude naturally produced mental images of her fondness for the literature.

Late-March winds blew up a brewing storm and a longing for the milder climate ahead. *With this March weather, how can April be the cruelest month?* She grabbed her folded umbrella from the back seat. *My banker might want this back tomorrow. There I go again. All these memories—this will be a good day to talk.*

Her dad was, of course, at his desk, surrounded by his books. Megan scanned a few as she walked into the room, opening *Jack of Dover*, a book they read together when she was five or six. She remembered how her mom repeatedly asked her dad not to read too fast. "Give her time to absorb the feeling of what you're reading," she would say. "Bandits and talking horses need some time."

We can experience comfort in remembering the past. We can think of what might have been, but it's more like reading a book for the second time—we know how it's going to turn out. "We know we will make it through. We're here, after all," Dad would say. "We know of others who had some of the same troubles, and how they turned out. We seem greater than the sum of our experiences."

Megan closed the book and scanned a few others that brought back memories.

"I know what you're thinking," her dad said.

"Do you now?"

"You're thinking what a great job your mom and I did raising you."

"Well—"

"And I'm thinking what a great job you did teaching us how to raise you. You were supremely successful."

"Thanks, Dad. You have a way of providing a compliment all around."

"So do you. Now, how are we going to untangle this ball of yarn? What do we mean by adoption?"

Megan booted up her notebook. "I've created a list of benefits I believe this idea of adoption provides, followed by problems we could encounter along the way. I've combined these positives and negatives to show our top five destinations, what planners call critical success factors. Viewing obstacles is a good place to begin. We can take these to the team as it develops for their input and response."

Megan's dad reviewed the scaled list Megan had worked up. "You've combined related destinations, I guess, to narrow the mix. I like that. Number one—provide a way for adoptees, now called members, to earn a living wage. You've pointed to the cornerstone of the nonprofit mission."

"It's the cornerstone of the American Dream, Dad. I see this as an entrepreneurial opportunity unavailable to a specific group of people. Parents see the American Dream as a way to make life better for their children. The next generation should do better than the current generation—work hard, save a little, and provide an excellent education for your children so they will do better.

"This group is less concerned with their children, having been told to murder their children before they're born. They can't choose. Working hard is not a choice if you don't have a job. Upward mobility is meaningless if you have no income. I see politicians getting rich by working for corporate profit any way they can. They help companies outsource jobs, and our people are left unemployed. Then the government steps in.

"'Don't have a job? Don't worry. The government will support you.' Call it what you want; it's welfare. You'll barely get enough to eke out a meager living by picking from the government garden.

"Votes are the harvest in this garden, and there's a constant threat. 'Vote for me, and you'll be secure. Vote for the other guys, and they'll take away your welfare, your food stamps, and your Section 8 housing.' This threat leaves a member of this group with only one real choice—perpetuate her, or his, substandard life."

"You're advocating a way to eliminate welfare, food stamps, and subsidized housing. That is an expensive prospect. How do we create a living wage for this group?"

"Dad, I know you are aware of the means and methods I'm proposing. You just want to be sure I'm fully aware. I'll state it for you.

"The operative word is *temporary*. At one time, you were on welfare. I don't think you received food stamps, but you accepted Section 8 housing."

"There was commodity distribution in those days," her dad said, "and we were grateful for that. But my family never participated in what would become known as a food stamp program."

"Whatever you call it, any help available to your family was temporary. I'm in favor of temporary assistance. The government's role is to provide this temporary assistance until these people can be trained—not just to do a job, but how to live as a result. We can cover this in number three on the list.

"You taught me to require that grants and other funds we receive don't restrict our activities regarding training. We are not training these folks to create resumes and successfully interview for jobs. SAVE could prepare them for that. We are teaching them how to create jobs for themselves, using skills and talents they sometimes don't even know they have.

"We are offering a physical, technical environment in their neighborhood that they've never had before. These folks will have a place where they can come to receive training to develop their businesses and how to deal with their success. They will learn how good choices will benefit their lives. As wages grow, welfare begins to end." Megan tapped the side of the screen next to the bullet point that referred to the government's assistance as being available only temporarily.

"It's unlikely everyone in this group will have a marketable skill or talent. What happens with these people?"

"We can't accept failures in this area. Look at number two. It's FAMILY. We can create partnerships within the family.

We may also be able to find existing jobs for these members, and the life skills training is also needed and available to these members."

"I'm glad to see you've included those members. No one is left out, and referring to it as a family strengthens that point. It's about creating a family."

"That's right. I'm not referring to a community. I'm calling it a family—it's adoption, remember? The term *community* has some negative connotations in this context. It doesn't take a community. It takes an individual as part of a family. We'll see in number five on the list where the family member moves out after reaching a level of maturity, which is a typical event in the life of a family."

"Your mom and I have worked diligently to keep our large family in contact. You've collected some of the genealogical data we trusted to draw the family tree accurately."

"Yeah," Megan said, "I had a blast doing the research when I could devote the time. That time is no longer available."

"What you're doing here is different," said her dad. "No lineal descent exists with only one generation from the day we begin. I've searched for a way to keep track of the data we will accumulate. This group resembles a club more than a family."

Megan worried about referring to members without including the "family" modifier. "Members of a club can drop out, and the club writes them off as former members. We see members of SAVE as a family, but if a member chooses to leave, we drop them from the roles. Adopted family members may drop out, or one may even get disowned. Still, disqualification as a member of the family never comes to pass.

"Check out the bullet points I've included here. Family relatives are grouped by quantifiable skillsets rather than by blood. We will need a way to provide instant linkage with future generations. In a practical sense, without speaking too meta-phorically, if we are unable to build a traceable family tree from the beginning, we will suffer dramatically."

"Yes, it boggles the mind more than a little bit. Genealogy is a bridge we are not ready to cross. We're not even ready to build it yet. I'll work on it."

Megan struggled with the idea of the bridge building required to create what amounts to collateral descent. "I know you will. So will I. We should have more heads involved. Do we have any board member commitments? I've spoken with a couple of members of the board at St. Jude—no takers."

"I've presented some ideas to several competent candidates. The truth is, we need a better definition of our specific mission and intent before we can generate sufficient interest. I've had a good response to the ideas we present, but any real candidate wants to see it in writing."

"I want Rochelle involved in this discussion. Her ability to come up with ideas for debate is phenomenal."

"That's a good plan. All qualified people we can bring together in this dialogue will help. We want to include legal and financial people as well. Let's see, number three deals with living an orderly life. You're including classroom instruction on how to budget, set priorities, and respect the law."

"Yes, this is number three but is as important as anything on the list. Most of the people we adopt will have little expe-rience in managing their financial and legal lives, not to men-tion moral issues when dealing with the law. Some of it relates to fear—the law represents a group set up to take something from you."

"Yes, I've seen that. When called in to deal with violence, the police may arrest the person causing the violence, who will later be released, return to the scene, and cause more violence than before. Getting the police involved again will only make it worse. It's a tradeoff."

"More like a catch-22," Megan said. "When the police are around, everyone is under suspicion, and everyone stands to lose. I can see the position this puts the authorities in, but it doesn't make much difference. The more effort everyone applies, the worse it gets. No one is ever there to intercede before the violence occurs. No one is ever there to prevent an argument from escalating into violence. That's where we come in. It's part of our training."

Megan's dad scratched his head. "I see the danger there. I believe the best way to deal with what leads to violence is training in how to deal with the financial side. New sources of income provide opportunities for a different view of a given state of affairs."

"It's complex," Megan said. "To some extent, income creates a part of the stereotypical issues we face. I've seen some of the ladies at SAVE, who have jobs with a good income, nothing great, but in some cases adequate. They get paid on Friday, and they're broke on Monday."

"What causes that?"

"I don't have a simple explanation. It's true that some just don't know how to manage money. *Budget* is a four-letter word. Another side of it has to do with that fear I referred to. Money is seen as a temporary thing at best. It won't last. You have to get rid of it before someone takes it away. We don't just imagine that. It happens nearly every day. Having a job does not create a steady income—another four-letter word to some extent. The job is seen as temporary—here today, but gone tomorrow—and most are blameless. It's the reality of existence for many people."

"I'm sorry, Megan. I know how much this troubles you. Without question, we need training, but can it be adequately provided? What qualified person will be acceptable to provide this training?"

"A member of the family. Someone who will be there when they could be somewhere else. Someone with skin in the game. Someone who cares, who can offer hope. I don't see this as a utopia, Dad. It's a pragmatic solution to a problem made worse by other unrealistic solutions that have been tried by plenty of well-intended people."

"I'm with you, Megan. It won't be easy, but, as the man said, we're not doing it because it's easy. We're doing it because it's hard. Next on the list is the pride of ownership."

"This is the emotional part for me. Imagine a person with relatively low self-esteem, a person who has practically no ownership of her life, much less ownership of any tangible property. We're talking about a person who believes she has no right to choose—not many rights of any kind—suddenly being told to take charge of her destiny.

"Using talent and capability that these women already possess to create sustainable income is our goal. They own the jobs they create. The men in their lives hear the same story. We will market their trainable skills to local businesses on an individual basis. It's a way for companies to improve their corporate and personal lives, and it helps to manage their workload. We will train our family members in every way possible. These businesses want someone reliable to do those tasks they don't have time to do or don't want to do.

"Last on the current list is moving out at maturity. It's more moving up than moving out. Maturity means these members no longer require the basic training those new members need.

Many will become mentors of those who come after them. They become the parents and grandparents of new family members."

"This is good work, Megan. What you've presented here has been the basis for articulating the details of our mission statement. I've spoken with several attorneys, but we haven't been dealing with specifics. Our charter and bylaws will contain specific statutory requirements that support a sustainable process, but broad enough to ramp up future requirements not on the drawing board today."

CHAPTER 30

" **S** ocial traditions can generate a feeling of kinship, a sense of connection." Kayla remembered Jerry making that positive statement, followed by ensuring everyone that the tradition of man nullifies the gospel. Jerry had a knack for using contrast to make a point—in this case, contrasting the value of secular family tradition with the detriment of religious tradition. Kayla believed she knew the difference.

Sunday morning service, with its new emphasis on nontraditional hymns and contemporary singing, was hard for seniors to like. Pastor reluctantly replaced the organ with unconventional musical instruments to accompany those hymns. A set of drums encased in a Plexiglas shield created a beat that rocked the floor, accompanied by a bass guitar, rhythm guitars, and saxophones.

These Wednesday evening services are a little nontraditional too. Formerly referred to as *Prayer Meeting*, these days, it's called *Fun Fellowship*. It consists of a combination of youth and choir activities at one end of the building and a junior minister delivering a topical sermon in the sanctuary. Tonight's message included a brief appeal to newer members concerning complaints from long-term members troubled by changes in Sunday services. "The early church didn't sing those old hymns," declared the young music minister. "They didn't listen to rock music either," responded a church elder.

Kayla saw the benefit contemporary music offers in reaching a younger group, and a larger congregation allowed two Sunday services, one contemporary and the other traditional. It's a good thing, she concluded. It expands the congregation, reaching the younger group who didn't grow up listening to hymns written early in the eighteenth century.

Kayla saw another break with tradition tonight. Pastor didn't attend the service. Earlier, she emailed Pastor and Jerry, asking if they could spend a little time with her after the service. Jerry participated in the service, and Pastor came in toward the end. A couple of interested parties stayed back. Are they just being nosy?

"Hi, Jerry. Hello, Pastor. Glad the two of you have time to talk this evening. The service was good, but I miss the singing we once had on Wednesday nights. I miss the hymns, but I doubt many would attend a traditional Wednesday service. So, the choir director reduced the Wednesday night music to zero. This session is for fervent believers only."

Pastor held his Bible up to his chest. "I thank God for all who continue to come faithfully. The righteous are not shaken. Their hearts are steadfast."

"There may be a false dichotomy here," Jerry said. "I love some of those ancient hymns, filled with doctrine, but I'm also blessed by the new—what we call Christian Contemporary Music or CCM. My youth included no church attendance, so I don't have much of a history with either form."

Kayla was a little defensive. "Some of the new stuff is sentimentality, but much of it is not, and when you use the word *ancient*—remember, one can love old hymns without being old. But contemporary music helps to extend the gospel into unknown places."

"It's like praying for the souls of dead people," Jerry said.

Pastor looked up, as the two lingerers walked away. Kayla frowned. "Okay, Jerry, I have not done that, but I'm curious—what doctrine supports this view?"

"I'm not addressing doctrine, Kayla. Think it through. The Bible teaches no second chance is possible after death."

"After that, the judgment," said Pastor.

"Yes, and no future event can cause something in the present to happen—reverse causation. Correct?

"Correct."

Jerry continued, "God answers prayer. In his divine foreknowledge, he knows in advance your every prayer, past and future. In the same way, he chose which prayers he would answer before you prayed them."

"Okay."

"Let's say God foreknew that you would pray for the dead person in question, and, as a part of his plan, he decided in advance to answer your prayer. Is it possible he could have brought that person to salvation without your knowledge of it?"

"So, he would have answered my prayer in advance."

"Yes. Is it possible, then, that God, foreknowing it would take contemporary music to bring this generation to the gospel, is answering a multitude of prayers not yet prayed?"

Kayla's mind wrestled with the idea of answered prayer and unanswered prayer—more to the point, unanswerable prayer. There's no use in praying for a soul who died without Christ.

I'm not praying for a second chance, she said to herself. "I'm praying God would have called this person into the blessed hope before he died," she said aloud. "Many will say that's a wish, not a prayer."

Pastor bowed his head slightly, which Kayla took as offering assent.

"Think in these terms, Kayla," Jerry said. "Prayer involves communication with God. Wishing lacks communication. If you never communicate, God can't answer, and our subject is without hope."

"God works the tiniest details of our lives into his plan," Kayla said. "Some of those tiny details can carry the greatest weight. That's a good lead-in to my email."

"You indicated some concern for the nonprofit Megan and her dad have been working," Jerry said. "Are you troubled in some way by their intent? I know you have been in detailed discussion with Megan."

"I've met and talked with Cindy, Rochelle Meyer's sister, over the last couple of weeks. Neither of you has met Cindy. She runs a small catering business primarily serving Midtown. She caters Megan's weekly meeting with people involved in the proton therapy system at St. Jude. I met Cindy at a SAVE meeting, and we've connected well."

"You will be a good witness for her," Pastor said.

"That will work both ways. Cindy's interest in the non-profit has given her a key role in the startup. My concern is the significant interest I've developed in being involved with the program."

"My guess is, you're a bit unsettled and questioning whether you want to commit to an active role this soon after such a tragedy has occurred in your life."

"Active commitment explains it exactly. I'm not ready for such a commitment right now. But I can sense God moving in my heart for these people—the people creating the program and the people to whom they are ministering. I believe God caused our paths to cross, and I'm trying to determine what he intends for me. At the same time, I want to be sure that I've overcome those doubts that have kept me out of fellowship—maybe it's guilt, I don't know. Daniel says it will just take time. I don't know if it's too early or not."

"We should begin with a word of prayer," Pastor said. Jerry, would you lead us?"

"I'd be happy to, Pastor." Jerry prayed, "Heavenly Father, thank you for your perfect will for our lives. Thank you for the Bible, your word, teaching us to think the choices in our lives through. We ask you to give our sister Kayla and our brother Daniel the wisdom to make good and right decisions as they face these difficulties. They continue to follow you; they want to honor your will and need your heavenly touch right now. Thank you for all you have done and will do for us, and we pray that we may pass your truth to the next generation. We pray in the name of Jesus, our Lord. Amen."

"Thank you, Jerry. Kayla, don't lose heart. Though outwardly, we are wasting away, yet inwardly we are renewed day by day. Your troubles are achieving for you an eternal glory that far outweighs your difficulties. We look not on the seen, but the unseen, since the seen is temporary, but the unseen is eternal."

"I'm questioning where I am right now, Pastor. I've lost my little Danny. That's real, and I can see it. Then I look at Megan, and I marvel at her strength. She has devoted her life to the kids at St. Jude, while she works tirelessly defending babies who aren't even born yet, some of whom, if they're born, may end up in St. Jude themselves. Megan has lost a number of the kids she deals with at St. Jude, and I can see the emptiness in her when she loses one to abortion. I believe God is using her in a specific way."

"Yes, I see Megan is a strong person, and I can see how God is strengthening you, Kayla. I believe you are on the verge of a new beginning for yourself, but I know you don't want this to focus on you. With that in mind, I'm not telling you to go for it. But I want to encourage you to move forward in faith. You know how to do that."

"Thanks, Jerry. Cindy and I have scheduled a meeting with Megan and her dad to determine our next steps. I'm confident the Lord wants me in this. I can count on Daniel's support and his help going forward. Thank God for him."

"I'm happy to hear it, Kayla," Jerry said. "Tell me, how far have they progressed toward founding the nonprofit? I doubt they are far enough along for a startup date."

"No, they're far from that milestone. The current issues are corporate documents, a business plan, charter—things like that. Megan's dad says the charter and bylaws must be specific enough to complete the nonprofit application accurately. Once they are ready to file, the articles of incorporation will include the name of the nonprofit as My Free Choice Foundation."

"As I understand it, articulating their intent, and defining their mission, is their most difficult task. It's a unique approach to dealing with abortion—I guess I should say dealing with the needs of folks faced with such a difficult decision. How do they—"

"They can use all the help they can get. I should say *we* can use all the help we can get. Yes, there is another reason for my email, Jerry. I hope you will become involved. Megan asked about your legal expertise—whether you would be available for discussion."

"You know I am no longer practicing. I can work with you to provide some counseling as you move forward. Still, I'm not in a position to accept fiduciary responsibilities."

"I understand your position. Everything is moving toward the final stages, and I would love to know I can keep you in the loop. Who knows what's around the corner?"

"Tell you what. I'll contact Megan's dad after you've had a chance to meet with him to offer what help I can in the context I presented. Deal?"

"That sounds like a good deal to me. Thanks, Jerry. And thank you, Pastor. Now, let's talk a little about that Sunday service music."

CHAPTER 31

Megan didn't waver from her commitment to honor the value of a workday, and her Wednesday meetings held to a tight schedule. She arranged for Cindy and Rochelle to remain in the meeting room with her, undisturbed, for a twenty-minute session.

"Your biggest threat is political," Rochelle said. "Your stated mission is strictly apolitical, but you must face the reality of decisions having a direct bearing on your success made by a fierce political community."

"I follow you," Megan said, "but I don't see any threat as worthy of changing our mission. We will not endorse any political views or policies."

"Yes, I agree," Rochelle said, "It's right to stay true to your mission, but virtue is no defense against the political process. In your effort to remain fair to all comers, excluding no one, you become stereotyped with the stigma of being against stereotyping. You may be labeled as racist because you don't focus on a particular group. There can be a gap between what you are and what you appear to be. That's the politics of it, and the government will do everything it can to correct your position."

Megan indicated her agreement. "We have to find a way to convince the government to view these people as individuals who want to work their way out of a community of dependency. We need an exemption from some of the rules of the game."

Megan, and especially Rochelle, began to recognize Cindy's newfound commitment to an active role in the nonprofit.

"Imagine I'm assisting with the management of the nonprofit," Cindy said. "Why do I have to convince the government of anything? The government doesn't want people to remain in poverty. Of what, exactly, am I convincing them?"

"You're convincing them of your need for temporary assistance, not a long-term partnership. That's a foreign concept to lawmakers. In its interest to help, the government is interested in your compliance with their rules, in perpetuity, more than how you benefit from their help," Rochelle said.

"I don't follow what you mean."

"I do," Megan said. "She's referring to their regulatory standards. Dad and I have worked on documents required for the startup of the corporation that will become the nonprofit—our mission statement, charter, and articles of incorporation. Our mission is unique. We don't fit the mold. We've looked at other unusual startups who have submitted those documents to the IRS. We also checked samples of the government's response, how they question a typical company's core purpose. Our goal is to submit an accurate and exact statement of our vision—where we want to go, and our mission—the process that will take us there. Sounds simple, but it's a complex preparation, wading through a marsh."

"That's as it should be," Rochelle said. "If those regulations weren't in place, fake nonprofits would eventually become the majority."

"I'm not advocating the elimination of regulations. I'm saying it goes too far. I believe they want to help, but I don't have much faith in their understanding of what their help sometimes means. That's also the politics of it."

"You're a quick learner," Rochelle said with a smile.

"Kayla says belief without faith is unbelief," Cindy said.

"She's talking religion."

"Well, we were discussing her taking the stand in court and swearing to tell the truth. Kayla believes the court wants to help her see justice, but she has no faith in the court's ability to accept real truth. That's her way of saying belief without faith is unbelief. It gets complicated."

Megan pointed toward Cindy. "In one way, Cindy, what you're saying gets right to the heart of it."

"Wow."

"Follow me on this," Megan continued. "Members of this adopted family of ours see the police department as people who don't act in their best interest, but most don't see cops as enemies. Some do, of course, but most don't. Even if individual cops have the best intent, experience has shown, when police are involved, things get worse. Right or wrong, this family has no faith in the police department, the courts, or the legal system as a whole."

Rochelle and Cindy shrugged. "Not much new there, Megan. Anyone who has ever lost a case in court believes that. There has to be more."

"Much more. My dad tells stories about his family's time on welfare when they lived in subsidized housing. An office managed the projects, a central location that housed inspectors, people who kept a close watch on all tenants. Inspectors made sure those who had jobs earned no more than what would be considered minimum wage. They held tenant assets to bare necessities, and even the slightest increase in salary could jeopardize their benefits.

"All the project apartments had big parking lots, but most were empty since owning a car was suspect. Dad tells of a meeting with inspectors at the office where his mom proposed acquiring a used pickup truck to start a small business that would benefit everyone. The idea was to carry loads of food she bought at the farmer's market on the edge of town for resale to the tenant community at competitive prices. Most of the families had no way to travel to the farmer's market. People would benefit from fresh food delivered to their apartments, available for a price no higher than they would pay at the grocery store. Never mind it's a store they had to walk to, then carry their groceries back home.

"The inspectors were not against an idea of obvious benefit to the tenants. There would be enough income to pay for the truck and operation of the business. Once calculated, the additional income, along with the value of the truck and the company itself, pushed the family's asset value above their current level of benefits. 'Please allow an exception since this is a prospect of such benefit to all involved,' my grandmother pleaded. The inspectors were baffled, but rules are rules. No exception was allowed.

"The business wouldn't have generated enough to pay for nonsubsidized housing, much less the expenses needed for my disabled grandfather. My grandmother abandoned the venture, but one can imagine how this little business could have provided significant income, even jobs for a few of the other tenant families. A tiny little business could have been a means to free Dad's family from their miserable financial condition—but rules are rules."

"It's easy to see how circumstances could trap people in poverty, or even lead to homelessness, should a catastrophic event occur. It's different today," Cindy said.

"Today is worse, Cindy," Megan said. "You should consider what's at stake here for you.

"Today, poverty is not just being poor. It now includes an environment of drugs and violence. That means an escalation of rape, random shootings, altercations with police, more hunger, more homelessness, and more one-on-one violence. The simple act of venturing outside can be life-threatening.

"Today, we're dealing with a group trapped like never before. Welfare forces them to look for unavailable jobs, and job training doesn't help. Government assistance doesn't train these people to develop any level of self-reliance. It trains them in consumption, with almost no possibility of escape. That's our family."

Megan expected the new level of doubt she read in Cindy's demeanor. She didn't want to scare her away. Still, Megan owed Cindy help in coming to terms with what this commitment meant for her, physically and emotionally. Now entering her second trimester, she would be in full swing with the nonprofit at the time of her delivery.

"How can we expect to change anything, Megan?" Cindy seemed out of breath. "I guess I've been too naïve to consider the danger we may have to face. I love being energized by the challenge, because I want to help these ladies at SAVE. I want to help them to see how they can have a better future. Now I'm scared."

"Cindy, this is why I wanted the three of us to get together after the meeting today," Megan said. "I wish Kayla could have been with us. I know how close the two of you have become, especially about being involved with the nonprofit. I want you to dig deep, to be sure this is right for you. You should also make Kayla aware of your feelings. I want your involvement, and I appreciate the willingness you've shown to move forward, but you've got to be sure."

"Megan, thanks for dealing with this early on," Rochelle said. "Cindy, I'll support whatever action you choose. I know you want to play as significant a role as you can. Whatever you decide, I'll help you deal with the issues you'll face. I can't commit to daily activity with the nonprofit, but I'll pledge to become involved every way I can."

"Goodness, thank you, Rochelle. That means everything to me."

"It means a great deal to me, too," Megan said. "I can envision some intense board membership conversation on the horizon, Rochelle."

"I don't know. I see a *902 meeting* coming up," Rochelle said candidly.

"I'm sure I don't know what the two of you are contriving," Cindy said, "but I'm not surprised. Let me just say how much I appreciate your not pressuring me in any way. I have to deal with something I didn't anticipate, but I'll make the best of it."

"I know you will, Cindy. You should speak with Kayla to make her aware of this discussion and your current mindset. She has these same decisions to make. I believe Kayla is planning to talk with my dad. I recommend you join them. Dad will have more of the specifics required for physical setup and the safety of our daily activities once we roll out the process."

"I'll set up a time he and I can meet. I need whatever insight I can get about what will be needed, I guess, to work around the legal requirements. That may not be the best way to put it, but that's how I see it now."

"Dad may surprise you with his political clout. He doesn't want to admit it, but he has a wide circle of friends and acquaintances. He knows how to play the game."

"Yeah, I've seen him in action a time or two, and he was ready and honest. The toughest part is being upfront and keeping your cool when playing with all comers, good and bad.

"That's the politics of it," Megan said.

CHAPTER 32

K ayla rubbed her hand across the smooth, polished top of the sixteen-seat table. Jerry's conference room was a safe place. Glad to be back in fellowship with the Bible study group, she believed her doubts would diminish by the truth of the word being delivered and taught. The last several weeks had strengthened her, and her classmates brought comfort as well.

She watched Megan underline a couple of sentences in the handout Jerry provided for the class. Kayla invited Megan to attend this morning as a way to offer Megan a look at a challenging view of life and to give her a chance to present the latest needs of the startup to Jerry.

Kayla removed the last few handouts from the table. "Megan, I hope you found today's class worthwhile. I know this is not your bailiwick, but with your level of comprehension, I hoped you would get a lot out of hearing how our class members express their beliefs."

"Oh yeah, it was enjoyable," Megan said, "and I appreciate an expression of sincere views, especially when an outsider like me is present. The honesty was unmistakable. It's refreshing. Of course, I have a million questions."

"I knew you would. I don't have all the answers, but I'd love to hear your questions. Who knows where that could lead us?"

Jerry said goodbye to the last couple of students to leave and turned to Kayla and Megan.

"I'm thankful to have you back with us these last several weeks, Kayla, and I'm glad you could also join us this morning,

Megan." Jerry knew how much the Bible study meant for Kayla's spiritual growth and how much her insights meant to the class. He was a bit unsure of how much Megan got from it.

"Thanks, professor. I learned more than I expected," Megan said.

"Please, call me Jerry. We're a family, so everyone's on a first-name basis. I know how much you appreciate the idea of family.

"Kayla, the class debated when things would get back to normal after your return. This morning was about as normal as it gets."

"God has provided clarity," Kayla said. "I prayed not to be bewildered. Daniel has been so good. He's shown the strength of controlling those feelings he keeps below the surface. I've let it all out. Pastor advised me to throw it all on God, and he was right. He has opened doors I didn't know existed. I'm thankful for all he has done, and thank you, Jerry, for standing with me."

"You and Daniel have been good witnesses for the Lord, and your presence has been a great value to the class.

"We are covering some deep issues related to God's working in our lives, and our obligation to exercise our free will responsibly. What's your impression of what you heard here today, Megan?"

"You presented the class discussion well—the little bit of time we had together after class was good. Everyone welcomed me with open arms. I expected a little brimstone that I'm glad didn't happen."

"You are always welcome here," Jerry said. "You are a child of the universe."

"I felt welcomed. Everyone referred to Compatibilism as if they grew up with the concept. I've not heard of it."

"Funny how students can come to grips with, what to them, are new ideas when they see the Bible supports those ideas," Jerry said. "It's not easy to reconcile divine sovereignty and human responsibility. How can a decision I make today affect a predetermined future? How can Judas be responsible for what God intended before the foundation of the world?"

"I don't have any of those answers, but I'm impressed with people who have firm beliefs, and your students seem confident. I'll have to research Compatibilism, but I have to admit, I don't like -*isms*," Megan said, "especially capitalized words ending in -ism. Practically everything we deal with at St. Jude is an -ism.

"Not long ago, I read a blog about Christianism. Had I missed something? After reading the discussion, I realized that Christianism is nothing more than a philosophy whose believers are Christianists. Now we have Compatibilism, believed by Compatibilists."

"Believed by Christians," Jerry said. "Place the word in mid-sentence and use a lower case *c*. Does that help?"

"Not much. How can I overplay it if it's just another lower case word?"

"That's funny." Jerry smiled, "I'll keep your derision between the two of us."

"Thanks. Speaking of mockery, what's your assessment of my dad's latest debate with our 501c3 attorneys about our non-profit process?"

"I know they are having trouble with the family adoption concept. I'm glad you guys chose Dewitt Childers to represent the foundation. They are a top-notch nonprofit legal and consulting firm. Don't dismiss their position out of hand."

"It's difficult to convince people that anything new is worth-while," Kayla said. "All you hear is 'We don't do it that way' or 'we have never been asked that before.'"

"Being attorneys, they like to deal with facts rather than con-cepts," Jerry said. "The idea of individual startup companies housed under a 501c3 umbrella termed as 'adoption for life' is not easy to assimilate. Their job is to identify the difficulties you will encounter in dealing with the IRS and ways to deal with those difficulties while holding to your mission. I believe they will make it happen."

"I trust Dad's ability to keep everything on track. How did your discussion with Dad go this week? I know he told you we are naming the foundation My Free Choice."

"The name suits your family-of-companies intent. The com-munication you and your dad have had with local businesses about potential outsourcing to qualified and trainable members is a good beginning. With no ability to demonstrate any proven history, convincing those companies of MFC's ability to pro-vide their service is tough. It's a common problem with new operations, one for which your business plan must provide a solution."

"Yes, we see what Dad refers to as our puerility as a major constraint. These folks are newly adopted, but we can't allow them to perform like children. Dad has solicited companies who see the benefit and will commit to the cause. We want a partnership with these companies to sponsor the enterprise, and we will announce them publicly. We'll offer pro bono services in exchange for their investment of the time it takes to bring our members up to speed. We hope to qualify for grants to get us over the initial training hump to help establish our qualifi-cations in the shortest time possible."

"Government grants became the chief topic of discussion," Kayla said, "when Cindy and I met with your dad. Grant funding occupies an important place on the action item list, but it's at the top of the difficult-to-achieve list. Your dad says qualifying for government money indicates enterprise credibility and attracts private funding. It's a difficult process that will likely require an outside consultant not currently in place. From what I've seen, we may need a grant-writing grant."

"Dad has a history with SAVE's grant proposal process. SAVE depends more on private donations, but we've had our share of dealing with the difficulty of government funding."

"We also discussed enterprise resource planning software, ERP," Kayla said. "My lack of experience and insight made for a limited discussion. Cindy was better able to handle the subject of software."

"We also discussed ERP," Jerry said. "My advice is not to move too quickly. I don't see the need for even considering a sophisticated software system early in the game. Developing an easy-to-manage process-driven sales cycle is the first goal. Time and resources won't allow the implementation of difficult-to-manage system integration. Just keep the process flowing without redundancy and use software needed to manage volume rather than the complexity of data."

"That sounds more complex than Compatibilism to me, Jerry," Megan said. "Are you available to help us, using the expertise you so obviously have?"

"I'll do what I can. I would bet your experience with SAVE has taught you that less is more in the business process."

"I've seen some of that, but we use what one would refer to as application software—spreadsheets, an accounting application, a web browser, and a few others. In the case of My Free

Choice, I believe we will need more than has been required at SAVE. It may be difficult to apply less when you need more."

"Amen to that," Jerry said. "The key is not how much or how little, but what is right for our particular situation. I can help determine the best fit."

Kayla could see progress. "Megan, given my limited experience with any business process, what can I do to help in the immediate future?"

"You'll pick up as much as you need in the business cycle by simply being involved, and you'll be a big help in the hands-on working of what will become the operational process. I've asked Cindy to work with Eliza Stokes to glean her incredible experience. Eliza can bring together what I would call the necessary elements of the human resources side of things. She has the marketing skills we need to get the word out. Eliza has also helped Dad work with leaders in the businesses he contacted and community leaders. Some of these people are activists on both sides of the political system, and Eliza is beginning to communicate with family members who qualify for adoption. You and Cindy can team up to help Eliza."

"I can do that. I'll have Kim with me much of the time. I don't want her to suffer from my absence—if you know what I mean."

"I don't see a problem with Kim. She could benefit from seeing you in action. Jerry, I don't believe you've met Eliza Stokes. Would you be open to meeting with her? I believe the two of you would do well, and she would benefit from your legal expertise. The two of you together could create something special without any fiduciary requirement."

"Thanks, Megan. I'm open to any possibility, so long as nothing qualifies as legal practice. We haven't met, but I've heard about Eliza. And I've read some of her works. I would welcome a chance to meet her and work with her in any way I can. Please bear in mind, though, time is a limited resource in my current calling, but I'll do what I can."

"Thank you, Jerry. I know it's presumptuous to come as a visitor to your office and classroom and hit you up for participation in our startup. I may seem pushy at times, but I've learned I don't have the luxury of being timid. I believe you want to help in any way you can. I understand time constraints too, and I'm not offended by the limitation those constraints can cause. We are grateful for every minute volunteers can devote to us."

"I'm with you, Megan. No one ever got anywhere in my line of work as a lawyer or Bible teacher by being faint-hearted."

"I see that in you. Okay, from a team perspective, I believe the most effective branching of duties and activities will come from a group meeting with all parties involved. We should set up a time when all current players can meet to discuss the first steps. I want to include Dad, Eliza, you Jerry, Kayla, Cindy, Rochelle, board member candidates, and me. We don't want the attorneys present for this one.

"Kayla, if you would, please be the contact person for this group meeting. Dad can email everyone to announce the meeting and indicate you as the point person for response. We must use a time when the whole team can participate, no exceptions. Kayla, can you also coordinate the meeting location? The Cossitt Library would be good but might not suit all participants. Dad will work with you."

"I can do that," Kayla said.

"Jerry, are you in favor of a group meeting to act as a kickoff to make the game official?"

"Yes, enough preliminary work has been done with the corporate charter and articles of incorporation to answer current questions and provide issues to consider and discuss. We can move forward with individual and subgroup activities. We have much to discuss. I'll do some preliminary work with my contacts to offer valuable input for additional topics that won't stall the process."

CHAPTER 33

S uzan sat her clipboard on top of the file folder she had already tossed onto the table and thumbed through the medical documents it held. She wore a knitted sweater over a collared scrub top and cargo pants, which she considered appropriate attire for her meeting with her attorney. The file folder and clipboard held a sampling of irrelevant order forms for medical supplies and abortion literature. It was all for show. Suzan knew that, but Roy Ingram didn't. Suzan wanted to portray an air of professionalism.

"So, let's sort this out." Roy placed his file between them. "Before we begin, Suzan, I want to impress upon you how important it is that you be truthful with me. I must know everything you know. I can't protect your interests unless I have all available facts, every available detail, with nothing held back. Do you understand what I'm saying to you?"

"Goodness Roy, it was an accident. I didn't do anything wrong. I'm being charged with something my brother did. The DA cut a deal with Mark so he would help them come after me. If Mark—"

"Suzan, stop. I don't want to hear it. Here are the facts. These charges are for a felony that could cost you a significant part of your life. Add the charge of failing to render aid, and what's unimportant to you is meaningless. It's time to deal with these facts. Now, let me begin by asking you some questions, and I want straight answers. Okay?"

"Okay."

"The first question is, why did you leave the scene?"

"Mark's car was hardly damaged, just a fender bender. The fact is, we figured he would get a ticket, and that would be the end of it."

"So, you left before you knew whether there were any injuries?"

"I didn't want to be late for work, and it happened less than a mile from my office, so I took off. I knew Mark could contact me if he needed to."

"Did you and your brother discuss whether you should leave?"

"No, I left while he went to look at the other car."

"So, you left without talking with your brother?"

"Yes."

"As I understand it, the accident was caused by Mark accidentally hitting the accelerator after you grabbed money from his hand."

"That's what he says."

"What do you say?"

"I just wanted to get out of the car. We had been arguing."

"What were you arguing about?"

"What does that have to do with it?'

"Suzan, please, I want to know everything."

"It's been going on for years. Mark got ahold of some money I had when I was having some legal problems, and I never got any of the money back."

"What legal problems?"

"I don't want to get into that. It was a long time ago, and nothing came of it. Everything was dropped—nothing ever adjudicated."

"Dr. Joyner was involved?"

"You know about this?"

"I did my homework as any good attorney would do."

"So now you're after me too."

"I'm trying to protect you. I know the DA is looking into a case involving Dr. Michael Joyner, a case in which you were, in some way, involved. I haven't been able to review it in much detail. It sounds like they didn't have everything they needed to bring charges against Joyner. Still, an investigation of events in which you were ever involved is not good for you. First things first—let's get back to the question at hand: what were you arguing about? You say it involved money. In what way?"

"While I was involved with the Dr. Joyner thing, legal bills were accumulating. Mark and I had inherited a little money from my mother, who had recently passed, not much, but we tried a little investing. Mark had a deal with one of his business associates, and we agreed to do it together. Mark says things didn't go well, and the legal bills kept piling up. Mark told me he had to settle the deal for a loss—we lost it all. I never saw a dime of my money. Mark made a mistake, and I paid for it. Sound familiar? As it turned out, we would be better off had we stayed in the deal. That's our perpetual argument."

"What was your connection to Dr. Joyner? He relocated to Boston when no charges resulted, right?"

"Yeah, I believe he took a job involving research for one of the universities there. The DA accused him of using an illegal abortion procedure to extract intact body parts for sale. The body parts market is big."

"Did you assist the doctor's use of illegal methods?"

"He didn't use any illegal methods. That's why they brought no charges."

"Joyner took so much care to preserve intact body parts that investigators believed some babies survived the abortion. Supposedly they were left to die after the abortion. It's difficult to believe a doctor could allow anything so gruesome."

THEN COMES THE FLOOD

"The evidence presented showed the doctor designed the procedure for the mother's safety."

"More evidence is forthcoming—we can cover that later, but let's get back to the business at hand. Your brother said he pulled into the parking lot at the strip center because driving while the two of you were arguing was unsafe. He says you needed some cash, and when he tried to give you a few dollars, you grabbed the money from his hand, causing him to accelerate. Is that what happened?"

"Yes, but he should have kept his foot on the brake. If he had put the car in park in the first place, none of this would have happened."

"If you hadn't grabbed for the money, it wouldn't have happened. If you hadn't been arguing, none of this would have happened. If you hadn't gone together on the investment, none of this would have happened. Do you see why none of those earlier events is relevant to what is happening now?"

"I see them all as relevant."

"What you see as relevant has no consequence. We have to deal with what is in front of us now."

"I understand."

"Okay, back to my first question. Why did you leave the scene? You say you didn't want to be late for work. Come on, Suzan. You know there's more to it than that."

"There's Megan Alladee."

"Megan Alladee? She's the driver of the third car involved in the accident. What does she have to do with your leaving the scene?"

"The DA should be going after her. She has as much to do with this as I do."

"The third car was stationary and not even in the street. Megan Alladee's only involvement in the accident was being there. She didn't contribute in any way. What's your connection with her?"

"She's an anti-abortion activist and leads a group called SAVE, a group she and her father founded. Her people maliciously protest nearly every activity performed by Cobel Clinic, where I work as a nurse. They corner our patients at the clinic and continually scream at them when they leave, calling them murderers. Megan Alladee has called me a murderer and worse. She hates women who have abortions and believes the doctors who work at clinics like Cobel are evil."

"So, you just didn't want to face her at the accident?"

"It's more than that. I have no fear of Megan Alladee, and I've confronted her on many occasions. If she knew Mark was in any way related to me, she would do whatever she could to go after him, accusing him of everything under the sun. I left to keep her from knowing Mark has a connection with me."

"So, you left the scene to protect your brother from being assaulted by Megan Alladee?"

"As I said, this Megan Alladee person will take any action she can to make life miserable for me and anyone related to me. She's a hypocrite. She wants to make abortion illegal and will stop at nothing to prevent the clinic's patients from exercising their rights. No one stopped her when she wanted an abortion."

"She has had an abortion? It seems you would approve of that."

"I assisted with her abortion at Cobel Clinic when she was around eighteen. Not long after she aborted, she and her father started the anti-abortion group. I think it was a way to deal with her guilt."

"This is not much to go on, Suzan. You claim to have done nothing wrong and blame your brother for the accident. You left the scene and lied to investigators, saying you had no involvement in the accident. The DA will portray you as an angry, cold

241

person, without remorse. Is that how the jury will see you, or will they see someone who believes she made a mistake and is sorry for what happened?"

"If they want an apology for something I didn't do, they're not going to get it."

Roy placed his pen on top of the file folder and pushed his chair back. "Have you had any communication with the family whose child died as a result of the accident?"

"Why would I communicate with them? They've accused me of killing their baby."

"For weeks, only your brother, Mark, was being charged. In all those weeks, did you ever reach out to the Dean family to express sorrow for their loss?"

"No, I don't do that sort of thing. Listen, Roy, I know where you're going with this. I'm sure you've heard people protest my crazy views on abortion and what they call infanticide. I base my position on scientific fact. What they call crazy are medical and scientific facts. What I call crazy is the religion on which they base their beliefs. The science of abortion nullifies religious dogma."

"I don't care about your ideas regarding science or religion or abortion for that matter. What I care about is how the jury perceives you. Perception becomes reality in a trial like this. No one's going to believe you intended to do any harm. But the prosecutor says it's an accident you caused, and your poor judgment caused the baby's death. Add to that your lack of regret, sorrow, and remorse, and the jury is likely to agree."

"I want to take the stand to tell my side of it."

"Unquestionably no."

"The truth will be stated directly to the jury only through my testimony."

"Direct testimony will create a no-win proposition. Your direct testimony will open the door for the prosecution to persuade the jury of your guilt."

"The way to convince the jury of my innocence is to have the last word."

"That's the worst thing you could have said."

CHAPTER 34

J ack Williams was in agony. He read his last email sent to arrange a meeting with Megan and Kayla together. Megan's response seemed to indicate Jack had asked her out—again. Kayla responded, "Okay, see you there." Megan's response was "Confirming a meeting in your office." Jack read Kayla as saying, "Okay, see you there." He read Megan as saying, "I'm not going to meet with you anywhere but your office."

Jack thought about his telling Megan he wanted to go out with her when the time was right, meaning after completion of the trial. Jack decided the timing was right once the Mark Jones trial ended, but Megan didn't see it that way. When he called, she had a reason not to accept, but with each refusal came the assurance that she would see him when the time was right.

Jack decided not to push the issue in any way during today's meeting. He planned to include no hint of his deep desire to spend some nonjudicial time with Megan.

Kayla and Megan walked in. Jack was thankful they came together. He feared his inability to self-control should Megan arrive ahead of Kayla.

"Good morning, you guys. Thank you for coming. We have a few issues to discuss."

"Hello, Jack," Kayla said. "We're glad you decided to meet with us together. I guess we're past the point of needing to keep our stories separated? Now we can make the drive downtown together."

"I've asked to meet at a different location several times." Jack immediately regretted that statement. He had lost control within the first two minutes.

"You've never asked me to meet anywhere else," Kayla said.

"You're happily married, Kayla," Megan said.

"Yes, I am."

Jack bit his lip, bowed his head, and looked at the floor as if he were inspecting it for unevenness.

"Don't take it to heart, Jack. I didn't intend to embarrass you. I truly would like to meet with you one-on-one at another location. I promise we will do that. Between my duties at St. Jude and the time this new startup is demanding, I'm as busy as anyone could be. I guess I've been too ambitious, maybe a little egocentric—guilty as charged."

Jack took her response to heart. He felt ransomed. "I've been busy, too," he lied. "We'll make it happen."

"I'll be patient," Megan said.

Jack aligned a few objects on his desk. "So, you'll see some changes in this new trial. We can't discuss any details of the trial this morning. However, some new developments could result in a drastic change of events."

"What developments?" Kayla asked.

"I'm sorry, Kayla. I can't discuss the developments either, but I spoke to ADA Gingrich, and we owe it to you to let you know as much as we can. These developments will affect your trial."

"This isn't making much sense to me, Jack. You want to tell me how these developments will affect my trial, without telling me the developments? What does that mean?"

"It means new charges will be filed," Megan said.

"What makes you say that Megan?" asked Jack.

"Listen, I've known Suzan Winders for many years. We go way back. She and I have been at odds the whole time. Some years ago, a lot of scuttlebutt got started about investigations involving a gynecological surgeon who managed Cobel Clinic. Rumors spread about Suzan Winders's involvement in some illegal activities at the clinic. I don't know what happened to the doctor, but the authorities brought no charges against anyone at the clinic. Is that what this is about?"

"I can't discuss it, Megan. What I want to do this morning, Kayla, is to assure you the DA's office wants justice for you and the person or people who caused the death of your son. Whatever happens in this trial will not preclude your receiving justice. It's often difficult to see the big picture in judicial proceedings, but, rest assured, we take everything into account."

"Am I right in believing this upcoming trial is not about Danny or me? Is it going to be about these other developments?"

"I didn't say that. The trial is the *State versus Suzan Winders* for—excuse me for having to repeat it this way—vehicular homicide, the killing of your son Danny. A second count includes leaving the scene and failing to render aid. I want to let you know this in advance. After the trial begins, you may feel left behind. I wish I could offer more, but I can't."

"Kayla," Megan said, "I know what Jack means. I don't necessarily agree with it, but I can understand why it's happening. The media will go after what they portray as the big story, and there's no way the court, the DA, or anyone else can stop it."

"I appreciate your trying to soften the blow, Jack," Kayla said. "I came to accept long ago that, in reality, we don't control anything. God is the one in control. He has already worked it out—we just don't know how. It's what we talked about in the Bible study class you attended with me," Kayla said to Megan.

"Future events are there as if they have already happened. I can take solace from that."

"I'm relieved to hear you put it that way, Kayla," Jack said. "You could say God is just using the court, and me, to carry out whatever those events may be."

"That's good, Jack," Kayla said. "You said it correctly. I didn't know you're a believer."

"Yes, I'm a Christian, but, as my mother would say, you can't be much of a Christian if it's a secret."

"Wow," Megan said, "I'm in a Bible study this morning. Pretty deep thinking, Jack. I didn't know a prosecutor would allow himself to see it that way."

"I was troubled about how you would respond to this news, Kayla. I should have known better."

"Megan, I think Jack wanted you here this morning to help me in case I had trouble dealing with this, and I know you will. I'm thankful to have you on my side. I guess I should ask, are you okay? I know this hits close to home with you also, given your history with Suzan Winders."

"I guess I've come to expect worst-case scenario any time Suzan is involved. If you're okay with it, how can I not be? I'm anxious to see what's on this predetermined horizon."

"God has provided, and he will continue to provide, but be careful, Megan. Remember, even if we believe the future is pre-determined, there is never a reason to believe we don't affect what the future holds."

"I hear you, Kayla. I'm doing the best I can, but I'm still struggling with how it all works."

"The worst thing we can do is nothing," Jack said.

"My pastor relates a shipwreck story about a Christian and an atheist stranded on an island. The Christian, who believed God would provide for them, prayed continually, but the atheist said prayer wouldn't help. Days later, a boat came to the island, and the atheist got on board, but the Christian decided to stay behind, believing the Lord would provide. An unfruitful year passed, and another boat showed up, but the Christian stayed on the island, saying God didn't want him to give up and would provide for him. He later starved to death. In heaven, he asked God why he didn't provide. God said, 'I sent two boats.'"

"I've heard that one. It's a good story," Jack said. "It reminds me that, when faced with a multitude of decisions, we have to trust God to lead us into making the right call."

"The man had no reason not to get on the second boat. Why didn't he leave the island?" Megan asked.

"That's what God wanted to know," Kayla declared.

Megan continued, "What if God intended the man to stay on the island? How does the man know what God wants him to do?"

"God is not a playwright," Kayla said. "We're not actors in God's eternal script. He expects us to make decisions, to use our free will to make those choices he has already determined how to use in future events. God can also overcome some of the decisions we make, like leaving the island if he wanted the man to remain there."

"You're saying the man in your story decided not to escape the island. If the man decided to escape when God wanted him to stay on the island, God could have prevented him, in some way, from getting onboard."

"Or he might not have sent the two boats," Jack said.

"Well, God wanted the atheist to escape," Kayla said. "That accounts for the first boat. The Bible shows numerous examples where God intervenes when someone makes a bad decision. The apostle Paul was in the region of Galatia. God had told him to go into all the world and preach the Gospel, so, when he got to Phrygia, Paul decided to preach in Asia. God prevented him from going to Asia. Paul then decided to go to Bithynia, but God prevented that also. In this way, God directed Paul to preach at Philippi. If you read the story, it's easy to see why going to Philippi was the right thing to do."

The position Kayla and Jack were portraying seemed reasonable to Megan, even if she could not accept the theology. She wanted to be agreeable and directed her question to Kayla. "What's the right thing to do concerning this trial?"

"I believe God will have his hand in whatever happens. I'm praying for strength to keep my emotions in check, and, as my husband does, I'll try to accept what I don't understand."

"I'm proud of you, Kayla," Megan said. "In February, you seemed to be at a low point, dealing with so many emotional difficulties. Completely understandable. I can't imagine what I would have done if I were in your shoes. Now, here you are, solid as a rock. It's amazing how much you've changed."

"God did that," Kayla said.

Megan understood how Kayla's faith means more than facts or feelings, not just Bible beliefs or theology, and it gave her pause. Kayla's conviction was the guiding principle in every facet of her existence. *What faith do I have in my life?*

"Sorry for the two of you having to drive downtown for this brief meeting," Jack said. "This may become a significant chain of events, and I wanted you to hear it from me, Kayla. Thanks for your coming also, Megan."

Megan smiled. "Thanks, Jack. Hope we can get together soon."

CHAPTER 35

Her phone rang with the tone Megan had set for an unknown caller.

"This is Megan . . .

"Yes, I can talk . . .

"That was so long ago. I don't want to have anything to do with it . . .

"That's not my problem. I don't want to hear it. I have to go. Please, just leave me alone. It's not any concern of mine . . .

"I don't care. I'm through talking. Goodbye."

Megan disconnected the call. A slight tinge of guilt bothered her. *It's unlike me to be so apathetic. I don't want to allow harm to come to anyone, but that's not me anymore. Why now? Why didn't they deal with this all those years ago?*

She sent a text to Rochelle. MEET ME AT 902 TODAY. Megan considered Rochelle would sense her insistent tone as if the text needed an exclamation point rather than a period. They had been together less than an hour ago.

Rochelle responded. WHEN?

WITHIN THE HOUR.

Rochelle came back immediately. 30 MINUTES FROM NOW. SEE YOU THERE.

***

They met in room 902.

"Megan, what's happened? You look pale."

Megan nervously dabbed her eye with a tissue. "My God Rochelle. I never dreamed this would happen. I got a call from the police station. They caught the guy who raped me. God, I shouldn't have to deal with this now."

"Slow down, Megan. How did they make the connection? Come to think of it, how would they not make a connection, with the technology available these days? What do they want you to do?"

"I'm not sure. I don't even know where the guy is. Ron, remember that name? Ron Hicks. I killed him in my mind years ago. Now he's back. He's alive. And they want me involved with him."

"Megan, I'm so sorry. Is he being charged? Do they want you to testify? What are they planning to do?"

"I don't know for sure. The last thing I heard was at least five years ago. The state had a push to investigate rape kits that had been sitting, untouched, on the shelf for years. No one realized how rape kits all around the country had not been investigated or connected in any way. Busy investigators put kits into storage and destroyed some, I guess, to make room for more. I got a call saying they were reopening my case.

"It didn't mean much to me at the time. Like hundreds of other women, I believed the evidence of my assault was on the shelf. It turns out I was right. With a push to reopen cases, I read where the authorities were communicating among different states to tie evidence from different cases together. Most rapists don't do it only one time. I guess they found where this guy, Ron, had raped someone else—who knows, maybe more than one."

"You need some time. I know you will come up with a plan. It's a shock right now that's taken you by surprise. You'll get through it."

"I wish I could be sure of that. Think of it, Rochelle. I've kept this undercover all these years. Now I'm faced with a public release. My reasons for keeping it secret, my right to privacy, won't mean a thing. This time it will be a media rape."

"We should take the initiative to confront this without hesitation. We will try to protect your privacy and prevent a public release."

"Thanks, Rochelle. I need some time. I'll develop a plan, but I've got to relieve this pain I'm feeling. The police are going to say I should do my part, so this guy doesn't get away with this and continue to be a threat to others. They're right, of course. But I'm not ready for that. It goes against everything I've worked for. I don't know what to do."

"I know you don't, but you will. The first thing you should do is hire a lawyer. You need legal protection, the best we can find, someone able to work in this arena."

"What arena *is* this? I just want them to consider my right to privacy. I want to help, but I shouldn't have to sacrifice my life."

"You want someone who can speak for you and act to prohibit any authority from taking advantage of your predicament."

"That makes sense. I don't know where to start."

"Let me speak with some people I know who have had to deal with privacy issues in their lives, and we'll go from there. In the meantime, we should determine where this guy is and what the police intend to do."

"If his arrest is made public, rape kit investigators will come out of the woodwork. They'll want interviews. They will detail everything. Forget about what it means to me, or other women like me who don't want their lives to become a media focus. Rochelle, we've got to stop this, no matter what it takes."

"Let's make certain that actions we take don't create suspicion. We don't want any preventive measures to be the cause of this getting out. Megan, you should remain calm, maintain business as usual, and not discuss this with anyone."

"I've been trying to do business as usual for the last sixteen years, and I've gotten pretty good at it. One reason is that I have been in control. I've been able to make the decisions. That is no longer true. Whether it's the cops, the court system, or the media, someone else is going to make these decisions for me, with no concern for what I want to do."

CHAPTER 36

T he laid-back atmosphere of the café with no menu matched its confusing, hyphenated name, Good Memphis-Eats Cafe. Servers came to one's table and announced what they were serving today. Megan and her dad loved the idea of getting a home-cooked, surprise meal.

As usual, her dad had arrived early, got seated at their regular table, and ordered two peach Bellini Mocktails. Megan knew her dad didn't care much for the drink, but, knowing it to be a Megan favorite, he usually drank one too.

"Hi, honey, thanks for taking my call and meeting with me. This place brings back a lot of good memories, doesn't it? I've got some good info to go over with you—" he stopped in midstream. "What's wrong, honey? I can tell when something's amiss. What is it?"

"I've got a problem, Dad."

"Is it the trial? I heard Suzan Winders is making a spectacle."

"How do you know about that? It happened only a couple of hours ago."

"I got an email. Don't know much. I'm not sure I know what her position is. Sounds like they are trying to keep a lid on it."

"Kayla called me. She didn't have much detail. I'm surprised the judge is letting the defendant rant. ADA Gingrich sees her as trying to cover up her shady past. He brings up things from her past to refute some of her claims. I don't see where it has much to do with what caused the accident. That's not the problem, Dad."

"Is it a problem at St. Jude?"

"No, Dad. They found the rapist. My rapist." Megan covered her face with both hands, then brushed them aside with a pronouncement. "I can't let this get to me." Her hands went back over her face.

Her dad leaned over the table and put his hand on her shoulder. "Goodness, Megan. That seems incredible. What happened?"

"I'm not sure. The police called yesterday and said they arrested this guy and discovered a connection that linked him to me. It must be a DNA connection."

"I'm glad they caught the guy, but I recognize the significance for you. After so much time, I had hoped this would never happen. It's a score for the authorities, and they will want to reap the benefit."

"That's my problem. They will release this to the public and will contact the media if they haven't already done so."

"Megan, excuse me a minute. I'm going to step outside to make a call. Order now if you want. Whatever they have is fine with me."

"Dad, you know I don't want this to get out. Who are you going to call?"

"Don't worry, honey. It will remain confidential. Be right back."

A server came to the table to announce the café's offering today. Megan let her speak, knowing servers get as much credit for presenting as for serving. "Thanks, Gertrude," Megan said. "Please give us some time. I'll motion for you when we are ready."

"That's fine, Ms. Alladee. Just let me know."

Megan considered the possibilities if her life story went public. Most people who knew her well would be sympathetic.

Some would likely blame her in some way. She let this guy off the hook for so long. Why didn't she come forward sooner? Does she have something to hide?

She hadn't thought about Ron Hicks for years. Her parents never asked for any details. They didn't care much about what motivated her to keep everything quiet. Rochelle had never been first to mention the abortion, or why Megan didn't give birth. Rochelle knew how much Megan had been against abortion before any of this ever happened, yet she never asked about it.

She searched her mind. *How could anyone know what I was going through? Being naïve in many ways, I remember having these intense fears. I feared what might happen. In retrospect, that fear seems nonsensical, but at the time, it was real. What if this guy Ron came back and wanted to have a part in the baby's life? What if he wanted to be a part of my life, become part of the family? He would say I wanted to have sex, or I wouldn't have gone into his room. He would have rights.*

Abortion was the only way to keep him out of my life. And it worked, until now. It won't be the way I feared, but he will soon become involved in my life.

"Okay," her dad interrupted her thoughts. "I contacted Commissioner Beatrus. He and I go way back. He will intervene. Don't worry, Megan, this is on the level. Commissioner Beatrus and I have been friends since we were kids. No one's going to disregard his position on anything having to do with the legal process in this city."

"Does he know it's about me?"

"No, all he sees is a criminal arrested in some other state. We're doing nothing improper here. We're buying time."

"I don't know, Dad. This special treatment doesn't seem fair. How do you even know how to make this happen? Who are you?"

"Forgive me, Megan, but I'm only asking for a little time so we can decide what's best. I'm not asking for anything unfair. I'm only asking that they treat you fairly."

"Rochelle says I need an attorney. Should I hire one?"

"Well, you've done nothing wrong. You don't need anyone to act legally on your behalf, at least not at this point. But you could use someone connected with the system who can make good decisions on your behalf. An attorney is the best fit, but unless something extremely unusual happens, we both know this is eventually going to come out. I don't see any way around that."

"I keep saying I need more time. Should I beat the media to the punch and tell everyone? Most of the people at St. Jude will get it. Of course, some won't, and most will see me differently. I guess this is one consequence of the decisions I've made over the last decade."

"You're an expert at dealing with consequences, Megan."

"I'm more concerned with the people at SAVE. 'Hey, ladies, you know how I've preached about how wrong abortion is? Well, I forgot to mention, I've had one. My bad.' A tough row to hoe, Dad."

"You'll be surprised how receptive those people can be. They've seen everything, including being blamed for what they couldn't control in their lives. I can see where this could strengthen that bond. Remember, we are dealing one-on-one with those folks. You've now delivered a personal message to them. They will now see, more than ever, you do know what they are going through."

"Yeah, Dad, in some ways, I know you're right. But our critics won't see it that way. The pro-death group will see hypocrisy."

"Possibly, but who cares what they see? They invariably use whatever excuse they have at a given time—let's not discuss the foundation details today. You've got enough to deal with right now."

"No, Dad, bring me up to date, but be brief. I believe in what we are doing, but I'm going to look to you to move things forward until I'm able to deal with my personal life."

"I know, Megan. I'm with you a hundred percent. And your mother and I want to be with you each step of the way.

"I'll just mention a couple of things. Work continues on the 501c3 application, and it will take a good bit of time to complete it correctly. The charter has been drafted and is ready for review. We've contacted potential board members, and we're meeting face-to-face with critical partners. Several have suggested specific bylaws for the organization. It can be a complicated process and difficult to bring to a conclusion. It must be comprehensive and understandable.

"I won't finalize anything without your input and approval. I hope hearing a little progress will help."

"Thanks, Dad. That helps, and you're right. We can't afford to lose sight of our goals for this nonprofit. I'm thankful to have you at the helm. Whatever else happens, we've got to provide a way to give these women the ability to make decisions about their lives."

CHAPTER 37

The trial of Suzan Winders began much like the trial of her brother, with the jury sworn in and opening statements made. The prosecutor called Officer Martin Diaz, who gave the same testimony he presented at the Mark Jones trial. The second day of the trial began with the judge's summary of trial events, and the trial proceeded.

"Does the Prosecution have any additional witnesses?"

"Yes, Your Honor, the Prosecution calls Megan Alladee to the stand."

"Megan Alladee, please come forward and be sworn."

The courtroom deputy raised his arm. "Please raise your right hand. Do you swear or affirm that you will tell the truth, the whole truth and nothing but the truth, so help you God?"

"I do," Megan questioned to herself, *what is the truth?*

"Megan, please state for the record your name."

"Megan Alladee."

"What do you do for a living?"

"I'm a site manager for Proton Beam Transportation Systems."

"Do you live in Memphis?"

"Yes."

"How long have you been a resident of Memphis?"

"I've lived here all my life."

"Please tell the Court what happened on December first last year."

"I stopped at an ATM near the library where I had planned to scan some research documents for a project involved with my job. I placed the money in my handbag and put it in front of the passenger seat. I had coffee—"

"Objection, Your Honor, narration."

"Sustained. Mr. Gingrich, ask another question."

"What happened next?"

"Before I pulled into the street, I felt a little jolt to my car. I looked up and saw a car moving in the wrong direction, out of control."

"What happened next?"

"The out of control car crashed into a light pole. I ran to see if anybody was hurt. I called 911."

"Then what happened?"

"The police and paramedics came. I spoke to the police officer, who asked me what had happened."

"Thank you, Megan. Do you know the defendant, Suzan Winders?"

"Yes."

"How do you know Suzan Winders?"

"I'm part of a nonprofit group called SAVE, which works with abortion clients of Cobel Clinic where Ms. Winders is a nurse. I know her from the clinic."

"On that December first, did you see the defendant at the scene of the accident?"

"No, I did not see her at the accident."

"Thank you. No further questions at this time, Your Honor."

"Does the Defense want to cross-examine the witness?"

"Yes, Your Honor. Ms. Alladee, how long have you known Suzan Winders?"

"Many years."

"How many."

"Over fifteen years."

"Is it correct to say you and Ms. Winders are on opposite sides of the abortion debate?"

"Yes, Ms. Winders performs abortions, and my group tries to prevent abortions."

"Would you characterize the relationship between you and Ms. Winders as positive?"

"Well, we're on opposite sides of the abortion issue. In that sense, the relationship is negative, I guess."

"Would you classify that negativity as extreme?"

"Objection, Your Honor. Leading the witness."

"Sustained."

"Ms. Alladee, have you ever had an abortion?"

"Objection, Your Honor. Relevance."

"Counsel?"

"It goes to the defendant's motive, Your Honor."

"Objection overruled. The witness may answer the question."

Megan looked at her mom and dad. They had a help-less look in their eyes, and Megan knew she had no way of avoiding an answer. She looked at Kayla, whose facial expression seemed surprised and informed, yet sympathetic. ADA Gingrich looked startled.

"Your Honor?"

"The witness will answer the question."

"Yes."

"How old were you when you had the abortion?"

"Twenty."

"Was the abortion done at Cobel Clinic, where Ms. Winders works?"

"Yes"

"Did Ms. Winders, as a nurse, assist with the abortion?"

"Yes."

"The truth is, having an abortion is how you first met Ms. Winders. Is that correct."

"Yes."

"And your animosity toward Ms. Winders has grown continually. Is that correct?"

"Objection, Your Honor. Badgering the witness. Ms. Alladee is not on trial here."

"Sustained. Counselor, what's your point?"

"Your Honor, I want to establish that Ms. Winders left the scene to prevent being accosted by the witness. I have no further questions for this witness."

"Redirect Your Honor," said ADA Gingrich. "Ms. Alladee, Do you blame the defendant for your having an abortion?"

"No, it was my choice. Suzan Winders sells abortions to the public. I don't blame her for doing her job."

"No further questions, Your Honor."

"The witness is excused."

"Does the State have any additional witnesses?"

"The State rests, Your Honor."

***

Reporters were outside the courtroom door and shouted abortion-related questions. An officer whisked Megan and her mom and dad into a holding room opposite the courtroom and shut the door. "Remain in this room as long as you want," the officer said.

"Thank you," Megan's dad said. "We'll stay here until the reporters decide to leave."

"Megan, I know how hurtful this is for you," Megan's mom said, as the three of them hugged. "I'm so sorry, dear."

"Thanks, Mom. Well, Dad, I guess this answers it for us. Everything's going to come out now. I see the irony here. If this trial weren't already a media event, no one would care. Tonight's news has its leading story." Megan looked into nothingness, as tears flowed down her cheeks. "How can this be happening? What explanation can I offer all those people who depend on me for the truth, for the facts?"

"Megan, don't even think of it in those terms. All those people will see it how they see it, regardless of whether they hear it from you or the media. It won't matter to people who care."

"I'll be seen as a different person."

"You'll be seen as the hero you are, Megan."

The door opened, and Kayla and Daniel came in.

"The judge declared a fifteen-minute recess right after you guys left. The deputy told us you were here," Daniel said. "I hope you don't mind our coming in like this."

"Not at all," Megan's mom said. "We're glad you came."

"I love you, Megan," Kayla said. "I'm responsible for the pain I know you are feeling right now. She kissed Megan's cheek and embraced Megan's mom and dad."

"I wish I could have told you about this sooner, Kayla. Other than my parents, only Rochelle has known—and Suzan Winders. It's been in cold storage. I dread how it's going to look after it thaws out. I'm sorry you had to hear it this way, Kayla. When I was nineteen—"

"Hush, Megan," Kayla said. "It makes me love you more. When you answered yes on the stand, it reminded me how God has seen you through this, and he will continue to do so. He has known about it too. You may not see much importance in that right now, but it means everything. And I pray you will see his hand in all you have done through these years."

"I've been kidding myself," Megan said through her tears. "God hasn't had any part of my life during this time. It's not that I blame God. I'm the one to blame."

Megan could not decide what she should do. Her mind was a painter's pallet of mixed thoughts. *How am I going to face the people at work, or SAVE? Will they see me as a liar, someone who covered up the truth?*

"I've got to go. Kayla, you should go back to the courtroom. Dad, can you and Mom help get me to my car?"

Her dad felt unusually helpless. "What are you going to do? Do you want to come to our house? We can drive you there and come back for your car later."

"No, Dad. I want some time alone to get through this. How can I get to my car?"

Kayla wanted Megan to escape. "Daniel and I can lead the reporters aside, and maybe the three of you can get out unnoticed. Will that work?"

"Yes," Megan said. "We can talk later, Kayla. I don't blame you for any of this, okay?"

"Sure, Megan, call me when you can. Let's go, Daniel."

The reporters followed Kayla and Daniel away from the front door, while Megan and her parents fled to the parking lot and Megan's car.

Megan drove east, with no destination in mind. She had no way to escape. *Now I have to deal with the media. Once they make a connection with Ron Hicks, they will make him the story. They will put the two of us together like we were lovers or something. These sixteen years have only postponed my nightmare. I'm the tramp that let this guy take advantage of me. I murdered my child to keep him out of my life, to deprive him of having a child. It was my doing.*

"Wait, Megan," she said to herself. "This is what they want you to do. Snap out of it. You know better."

She texted Rochelle, in case she had not heard.

I TOOK THE STAND TODAY. IT CAME OUT THAT I HAD AN ABORTION.
SO SORRY, MEGAN. WHERE ARE YOU NOW?
I'M DRIVING.
COME TO MY HOUSE TONIGHT.
I NEED TO BE ALONE.
THAT'S THE LAST THING YOU NEED.
I'LL BE OK. TALK LATER.

Megan drove by the high school where she and Rochelle graduated. *Was high school more than a week ago? Einstein was right; time is relative. How long will this take? Probably forever. I should have come clean long ago. Sight is as relative as time, how you see things. As they say, hindsight is the best—20-20. Can't change anything now.*

As if programmed, she drove to Hyde Lake and parked uphill from her corner of the lake near the swing set. *It's beautiful here—no need to get out. I'll sit here for a bit to clear my mind.*

She pictured her dad's face. *Bless his heart. He doesn't know what to do either. This is the first time I've seen him speechless. Hope he can figure something out.*

A lake surrounded by jonquils, a beautiful picture. They don't know what it means either. New beginnings, love, and friendship. "Even told the golden daffodil," she sang in a low voice. *What do any of them know?*

***

Megan's body jolted. She froze, like trying to keep herself from falling off a cliff. She realized she had been napping. *How could I have fallen asleep? I guess that's what happens when your mind goes blank—when no real thinking is involved. How long have I been here?* She looked at her phone. *Nearly an hour—that seems impossible. I've got to move on this.*

Megan remembered she needed some food for lunch for the rest of the week. She stopped by the grocery and went straight to the produce area, then to pick up lunch meat and bread.

"Megan, is that you?" a voice interrupted.

Megan turned around. "Mr. Jones, right?"

"Yes, but it's Mark. I haven't seen you in a while. How are you? I wasn't at the trial today, but I heard what happened. I'm sorry you got dragged into this."

"So am I. It shouldn't be a big deal, but no one has ever known I had an abortion."

"I know it's a major concern for you. Suzan told me a couple of weeks ago that she had assisted with it, but I didn't know you had kept it under wraps. Things tend to get complicated."

"I don't want to talk about this right now."

"Of course, I understand, my apologies. It's none of my business."

"Okay. I'll see you at the trial if you're planning to attend. See you then."

"I should be there before it's over. Take care. By the way, I don't know if you are aware, but I've been talking with your father concerning your new nonprofit. He and I are planning to meet one day this week."

"No, I wasn't aware of that. What have you been talking about?"

"Your dad wants to know if the new software package I'm promoting might be useful in dealing with people you will serve in the nonprofit. I think he had planned to speak to you today. Guess that got postponed."

"We were not in a position to talk software today. Got to go. See you somewhere."

"Okay, bye."

Megan left the grocery with only two bags, which she tossed into the back seat as if she were throwing them into the garbage. She looked at herself in the rearview mirror, not sure she recognized the person she saw there. "You're being led around—a dog on a leash. Suzan's brother's software? Dad, what are you doing? Is Suzan the administrator? Will she have access? No, of course not. It doesn't work that way. Still." She realigned the mirror, cleared her eyes, and drove out of the parking area.

CHAPTER 38

"Is the Defense ready to proceed?"

"Yes, Your Honor. The Defense calls Suzan Winders to the stand." Roy Ingram had to force those words out of his mouth. He was unconditionally against Suzan testifying, but she demanded her constitutional right. Roy reminded Suzan she had a more beneficial right not to testify. She never wavered from her intent to take the stand.

He knew the prosecutor decided against calling Mark Jones, fearing the jury would see his testimony as prejudiced and create grounds for an appeal. Roy wanted to call no witnesses, believing their best defense would be his closing argument.

He would restate the case already made. Suzan left the scene to avoid contact with Megan Alladee. He would convince the jury the charges brought against her were unfounded—the driver of the car accelerated and caused the accident.

Suzan didn't see it that way. She insisted that she testify.

"Suzan Winders, please come forward and be sworn."

"Please raise your right hand. Do you swear or affirm that you will tell the truth, the whole truth and nothing but the truth, so help you God?"

"I do."

"Please state your name for the record," said Roy Ingram.

"Suzan Winders."

"What do you do for a living?"

"I'm a registered nurse on the staff at Cobel Women's Health Clinic."

"Suzan, can you relate the facts of your involvement in the accident of December first last year?"

"My car was in the shop, so my brother drove me to work. My brother and I got into an argument along the way, and he began to yell at me, as he often does. He says I can never do anything right. We decided to pull into a parking lot to get out of traffic."

"Who decided to pull into the parking lot?"

"Well, we both know it's unsafe to be distracted when driving. I told Mark we should pull over, and he agreed."

"You were less than a mile from the clinic where you work. You couldn't have driven another mile?"

"I didn't want any of the people I work with to see us arguing. I wanted it settled before we got there."

"Testimony has shown that your brother wanted to give you some money. When he took money from his pocket, tell us what happened."

"That's what we had been arguing about—money. My brother had turned around in the parking lot and drove up to the street. I wanted him to stay in the parking lot and turn the engine off, but he pulled up to the driveway, left the motor running and didn't even put the car in park. The money he has is mine, so when he took it out, I reached for it. Since he didn't have the car in park, I guess he took his foot off the brake, and the car went forward."

"The accident happened, and you left the scene. Why?"

"I needed to get to work, and, as you said, we were less than a mile from the clinic, so I walked the rest of the way."

"Didn't you want to stay around to make sure everything was okay?"

"Well, my brother's car had little damage, and the second car across the street from my brother's car had no damage. I couldn't see the third car, so I didn't know if it was damaged. It sort of looked like a minor accident, so I decided to walk on to work."

"But the third car was badly damaged, and there were injuries. Had you stayed around, you would have seen that."

"Yes, but I didn't know it at the time. I figured my brother would just get a ticket, and I knew he could call me if he needed to. It's not like I ran away or tried to avoid anything. If my brother had called me, I could have been back there within a matter of minutes."

"After the accident, you told investigators you were not involved. Why did you tell them that?"

"Well, my brother told the police he had picked up a homeless person, and the homeless person was in the car when the accident happened. I was afraid if I said something contrary to my brother's story, it would get him into a lot of trouble, so I went along with his story."

"So, you lied to protect your brother?"

"I took action that would cause less harm. At the time, it seemed like a simple accident my brother had to deal with."

"But that's not how it turned out. A baby died as a result of the accident. How do you feel about that?"

"People make decisions with the information they have at the time. I'm truly sorry if any decisions I made caused harm to anybody."

"Nothing further, Your Honor."

"Does the Prosecution have any questions?"

"Yes, Your Honor. Ms. Winders, your brother testified that he lied about the homeless person to protect you from being charged with leaving the scene or failing to render aid. Rather than you lying for him, he lied for you, right?"

"He acted on the information he had at the time.

"He lied to protect you, right?

"That's what he said."

"When your brother tried to give you enough money for the day, you shouted, 'I'll take it all. It's mine anyway' and grabbed all the money from his hand, right?

"All the money Mark has is mine."

"Did you holler the words, 'I'll take it all'?"

"Yes."

"You grabbed the money out of his hand, right?

"I took it."

"And you tried to get out of the car, right?"

"I was afraid of what my brother was going to do."

"You were afraid he would become physical with you?"

"No, I knew he would continue yelling at me, and that would cause confusion, so I left. He could call me back if he needed to."

"He wouldn't call you back because he knew you caused the accident, and he didn't want any trouble for you. That's correct, isn't it?

"No, at the time, he didn't know of any serious injuries, nothing that would cause us to be here today."

"He knew everyone would blame you for the accident, didn't he?"

"No, one of the reasons I went on to work is because I saw Megan Alladee in the second car. I knew she would cause trouble for my brother if she knew we were related."

"How could she cause trouble for your brother?"

"By lying about what had happened."

"So, let me get this straight. You caused an accident, left the scene, lied to your coworkers about the accident, and then lied to investigators about your involvement—all to keep Megan

Alladee from lying about what happened? Is that what I'm hearing, Ms. Winders?"

"Objection, Your Honor, badgering the witness."

"Sustained, move on."

"Yes, Your Honor. You told coworkers someone other than your brother drove you to work. Having no details of the accident, you told your assistant, Alice Beal, you rode with Edith Watkins that morning—no reason to lie about it, right?"

"It looked like I had walked to work. I didn't want to explain any details, so I told Alice I rode with Edith."

"You misrepresented what happened that morning. The truth is you have misrepresented yourself in everything you've said here today, haven't you?"

"I don't misrepresent myself. I deal with facts. As a nurse, I deal with scientific and medical facts. As a person, I try to tell it like it is. I don't misrepresent the facts."

"Do you know the facts about Dr. Michael Joyner, who, at one time, ran the Cobel Clinic where you work?"

"Objection, Your Honor. What happened with Dr. Joyner has no bearing on this case whatsoever."

"Mr. Gingrich, where are you going with this?"

"Sidebar, Your Honor?" Gingrich and Roy Ingram moved to the bench.

"Your Honor," Gingrich said, "the defendant has made a blanket statement in saying she doesn't misrepresent the facts or herself. She opened the door to the impeachment of her testimony. I want to demonstrate her history of misrepresentation of facts, a condition she denies."

"I will allow you to proceed. But remember, your questioning has no bearing on whether the defendant is guilty of the charges brought against her. I'll inform the jury."

"Yes, Your Honor."

The judge addressed the jury. "The objection is overruled, with this qualification. The defendant has made claims of character the Prosecution seeks to contradict. You cannot consider anything said in this line of questioning as evidence in weighing the defendant's guilt or innocence. You must consider it only in the context of whether the defendant has or has not misrepresented herself. Mr. Gingrich, you may proceed."

"Again, Ms. Winders, you just told the Court you deal only in facts. I ask again, do you know the facts about Dr. Michael Joyner, who, at one time, ran the Cobel Clinic where you work?"

"No charges were ever filed against Dr. Joyner."

"That's not what I asked. It's a yes or no question. Do you know the facts about Dr. Joyner?"

"Answering yes or no is misleading. I don't know all the facts."

"As facts accumulated, you repeatedly told investigators you knew nothing of Dr. Joyner's abortion procedure, right?"

"He did everything necessary to protect body parts for recovery of the cost of providing the abortion. I had nothing to do with it."

"Are you saying you did not know of his procedure?"

"I knew the doctor took some extreme measures to protect the clinic in its effort to recover the cost, as I said. But, I had other duties that required my time in the clinic."

"Did you assist Dr. Joyner in the performance of surgical abortions at the clinic?"

"I was one of three assistants at the time."

"Dr. Joyner, however, repeatedly referred to you as his most valued assistant, right?"

"Objection, leading the witness."

"Sustained."

"I have no further questions for this witness, Your Honor."

"Does the Defense want to redirect?

"No, Your Honor"

"The witness may be excused."

"Does the Defense have any additional witnesses?"

"No, Your Honor. The Defense rests."

CHAPTER 39

C indy was proud of her bit of clairvoyance. Today's regularly scheduled St. Jude meeting had been canceled, and Megan took the day off. No one knew where Megan had gone, including Rochelle. With such a beautiful day, Cindy guessed Megan would find her favorite spot at Shelby Farms.

"You're not answering your phone or responding to texts." Cindy sat her shoulder bag against the swing-set frame. "I've been trying to reach you. The meeting Kayla and I had with your dad yesterday evening is important. Rochelle told me what happened in court Monday, and said she hadn't been able to reach you either." Cindy moved to the swing beside the one where Megan sat motionless, staring across the lake. "I thought, of all places you could be, this is the most likely, and I took a chance. Are you okay?"

"I'm fine, Cindy." Megan pursed her lips. "My life is being ripped apart. The court revealed the privacy of my past, and my future life is in jeopardy." She feigned a smile. "Other than that, everything is fine,"

"Megan, I'm so sorry about all this. I wish I could do something to help make things right. I don't know what I could do."

Megan pushed her swing back. "Thanks, Cindy. There's nothing anyone can do. I'm just having a hard time dealing with the latest turn of events. That's all there is to it." She came back to a sitting position.

"I know you are, Megan, and I don't blame you." Cindy was unsure of how forthright she could be in expressing empathy with the Megan she knew as a rock. "I was shocked to hear what happened in court. I don't know any of the details, of course. It's none of my business, but, Megan, I want you to know, you are still my hero, more now than ever. I don't know how you've dealt with it all this time."

Megan understood and appreciated Cindy's concern. *I might as well tell her what I couldn't bring myself to say to her before.* "You don't know the half of it."

"I know I don't, and as I said, it's not my place to know."

"Here's what everyone's going to know in a couple of days. I fell for a smooth-talking guy Rochelle and I met at a Veteran's Day event when I was nineteen. Like the idiot I was, I went into his motel room, and he raped me. I got pregnant."

"Gosh, Megan, I had no idea. Did they ever catch the guy?"

"Yes and no—he got away. We didn't have a clue where he came from or where he went. At the time, I was sure everyone would blame me since I voluntarily went into his room. That's what led to the abortion decision. I thought the guy might come back and want to be a part of the baby's life."

"You say yes and no. Was he eventually caught?"

"That's the problem I'm dealing with now." *My God, I can't believe I'm saying this.* "The humiliation, the anguish, the feeling of torture is impossible to describe. I wanted this person out of my life without revealing what had happened. Otherwise, I'd be seen as a rape victim by some people and as a slut by others, so I decided to keep it private.

"Last week the police said they caught someone accused of another rape, and they believe he is the one who raped me. I don't know the details, but if it's true, this animal is now back in my life. I was trying to deal with this guy's capture, and before I can even determine if it's the same person, the abortion gets announced in court. Now everything that happens will be filtered through whatever people think, without me saying anything."

"It's hard to believe this could escalate so quickly. What are you going to do?"

"I don't know. Right now, I'm trying not to go crazy. I misjudged what would happen if I kept everything to myself. At the time, it seemed like the right thing to do. How wrong could anyone be? I've got a decision to make."

"It's personal. What you do in your life is your business."

"I should have considered the effect my decisions would have on other people."

"I don't see how that matters. People have no right to expect you to modify your life for their benefit."

"It's not that simple, Cindy. What seems right at the time can have disastrous results. Look at yourself. You can't imagine what your future would hold if you and Kevin had an abortion. Over time, a good solution can create hopelessness, not just for you and Kevin, but for your parents, your sister, for many others, not to mention for your baby. If you don't believe it, look at me."

"I don't see it that way, Megan. I am looking at you, and I admire your unselfish devotion to others, particularly unborn others. What motivates your unselfishness? Is it the passing on of a big heart from your parents? Did they teach you it is better to give than to receive in some incredible way? Is it the legacy of your grandparents' poverty? Is it your principled character? It's all those things, but now I see it from a different perspective."

"You don't see it for what it is. At the time, I thought only of myself. I was just a kid, looking for protection, blinded by pain, with no real view of the consequences."

"You did what was right for you."

"I was selfish."

"Rochelle says it's never wrong to do what you think is right. Okay, let's say you did it for yourself, for your protection. You say having the abortion was selfish, but look at the result. So much good has come from what you call a selfish decision."

"It's a stretch to make a direct connection."

"A decision you made as a teenager led to the creation of SAVE, resulting in the birth of children. Those children will create families—generations of people who would otherwise never exist. Without the history of SAVE, there would be no My Free Choice, which I believe will lead to the prevention of many more abortions and the success of just as many families."

"You could attribute that to guilt rather than altruism."

"I don't believe that, but, even if true, it doesn't change the result."

"You're saying I should be grateful for being raped? Should we give this guy a trophy?"

"I'm sorry, Megan, I didn't mean that at all. I just want to help you deal with it." Cindy saw a faraway expression on Megan's face. "Are you okay?"

"Yes, I'm sorry. I just realized what I said. It shows the negative mindset that excessive stress can cause. My life has changed forever, and it's difficult to maintain a rational thought process. Every person I deal with for the rest of my life will either know or have the ability to know the details of this private part of my life, and I won't know what they know or what they believe." Megan looked at Cindy's face. *Does she consider herself to be the first?*

"I can't comprehend what you're dealing with, Megan. I believe most people will see this for what it is. Your friends, your coworkers, the people who know you for who you are, will have sympathy for what you're going through, not as a victim, but as someone who can overcome. They already know you that way."

Megan moved from sitting motionless in the swing to a wooden recliner near the water's edge. "Thanks, Cindy. Sometimes it takes getting through my little pity party before I can decide on a plan of action. I'll get through this. I just don't yet know how. Enough of this for now. So, you wanted to tell me about your meeting with Dad?"

"Yes, Kayla and I were gathering written instructions from your dad. He suggested we research data from other compa- nies that have organized the required documents—purposes and powers of the organization, things like that. My tote bag is full of documents he assigned to Kayla and me. Kayla's com- puter case poked out when we left. Megan, your dad is such a wealth of knowledge. He comes up with the tiniest details; he considers every possibility."

"I know. Dad's not bashful with details. The key is separating busywork from what has value. He's as good as they come. I'm glad you and Kayla are willing to be such an important part of the foundation. But you didn't find me to discuss documents. What's going on?"

"Kayla and I were busy sorting our assignments, and were ready to leave when the doorbell rang, and in walked this guy Mark Jones. I didn't know what to do. I had not met the guy, and I felt bad for Kayla. She left the courtroom yesterday, picked up Kim, and drove to your parents' house. Suddenly, holding Kim close, she's standing there in front of this guy who killed her son."

Megan's blood was about to boil. *Why is this happening? Kayla doesn't deserve this. Is God trying to test her? What's going on?* "Dad would never intentionally let that happen. What did he say?"

"He seemed more shocked than we were—and upset. He told Jones to leave immediately, and he apologized to Kayla for letting it happen. He said he and Jones had planned to have dinner somewhere—I guess your mom is out. Anyway, Jones arrived over an hour early, and your dad told Jones he should have called to ask if being early was okay."

"This is bad," Megan said. She took a few steps toward the lake, then stepped back. "My God, this puts Kayla in a terrible fix. I'm sure she was scared, not expecting anything like that. Did Jones leave?"

"He was so apologetic. He's a fairly large person, but I thought he was going to cry, like a little boy. He asked Kayla to please forgive his being so inconsiderate and said he had no idea anything like this could have happened. He didn't even know of a connection between Kayla and your dad. He immediately headed for the door, and your dad told him to come back at the time they scheduled."

"Poor Kayla. I'm responsible for this. I ran into Mark Jones at the grocery on Monday, and he told me he and Dad had planned to meet at some point this week. I intended to speak with Dad, but of course, I put it off. What happened?"

"Jones headed for the door. Kayla stopped him. She asked him not to leave and looked at your dad for his approval. He didn't say anything—just looked at her with surprise. You know how Kayla operates. She's so forgiving and always wants to consider what others are feeling. She was the calmest person in the room."

"I can't believe what I'm hearing. What did she do?"

"Well, if you can believe it, she said she didn't mean to pry, but asked if he and your dad were conducting business together."

"That makes sense. She was asking Dad whether she will be exposed to him later."

"I don't think that's it. Your dad said they were looking at software for the startup. I think Kayla had already put two and two together and had a sense why they were meeting."

"That's incredible. What did Kayla say?"

"She said you guys met with her Bible study professor a couple of weeks ago. You discussed the level of server and software needed for the startup. She knew Jones was in the software business and figured he and your dad reviewed his program."

"I attended one of Kayla's classes, and we met with her teacher, Jerry. We talked about several issues, especially Jerry's expertise in working with software. He probably set up the meeting between Dad and Jones."

"Your dad had mentioned Jerry calling him before Kayla and I left."

"Kayla never fails to surprise me. So Jones shows up unexpectedly, creating what could have been a shootout, and it ends with a discussion about how to use his software?"

"Well, it wasn't the discussion you might imagine. The main thing Kayla wanted your dad—and Jones too, I guess—to know is that she was okay with whatever was considered best for the startup."

"How did you leave it?"

"Everyone was satisfied, especially Jones. He couldn't believe Kayla would want to ever be in the same room with him again. He was so grateful for her attitude toward him."

"So Kayla sacrificed her needs and feelings for the good of everyone else. Amazing!"

"You said it. We were all so emotional. I was afraid Kayla was going to ask that we all pray together. Thankfully, she didn't do that, although, if she had asked, we would have agreed to do it."

CHAPTER 40

The judge called for ADA Gingrich to present his closing argument. Rather than provide evidence for the state's position, Gingrich reviewed and summarized the facts and testimony given in the case. He was brief. His borderline nonchalance seemed to indicate an open-and-shut case.

He closed with a standard admonition. "I'll stop here, but I'll submit this: If you look at the evidence and you regard the poor judgment used in the actions taken by the defendant, you will conclude, on that December day, the defendant's negligence was deadly, and she is guilty as charged. Thank you, ladies and gentlemen."

"Does the Defense wish to give a closing argument?"

Roy Ingram was not as brief. "Yes, Your Honor. May it please the Court, ladies and gentlemen of the jury, this is the last thing I'm going to say. This is the last chance I'll have to speak to you about Suzan Winders. The way the justice system works, the State gets the last word, and I won't have a chance to answer anything he says if he gets the last word."

Roy paused and looked directly at several jurors, those he had been watching and who he felt were leaning toward the defendant's argument. He continued. "I'm going to ask you, please, consider what I would say in answer to whatever he has to say. If you do that, I believe you will be fair.

"After everything is said and done, we are left with three tough questions. Answering these questions will help you see that Ms. Winders is not guilty of the charges of which she is accused.

"The first question to answer is this. According to the evidence presented, was Ms. Winders negligent in her act of taking money from her brother's hand before the accident? To answer that question, you must consider three things." Roy took one step to the side of where he stood in the direction of the table where Suzan sat. He stood perfectly still, allowing the jurors to question what their first consideration should be. He continued without moving or gesturing in any way. "First, consider this: The car in which she was a passenger was not in traffic, but in a parking lot off the street."

One juror showed a slight change in her facial expression, which Roy read as a positive sign. "Second, consider that the car in which she was a passenger was not moving. It was at a standstill in the parking lot." He could read no body language in response to the second consideration.

"Third, consider that she was not driving the car in which she was a passenger. She was not the driver. She was a passenger who had no control over the operation of a car that was not moving and not in traffic. She was confident her brother would have control of the car once it moved." Three jurors turned their heads slightly, which Roy took as a sign they were thinking things through.

Roy moved back to his original position behind the podium in the center in the courtroom. "The second question to answer is this: Why did Ms. Winders leave the scene of the accident? Was it to prevent being accused, or to avoid being arrested? Did she leave to avoid being charged? Think about those three elements, one at a time, to answer why she left the scene. Was she afraid of being accused, arrested, and charged?

"She had planned to stay until her brother, the driver of the car in which she was a passenger, got his ticket, and they could be on their way. Then she saw a third party, a woman who she testified had caused much distress in her life over many years. I don't want to be confronted by that woman, Ms. Winders thought to herself, and when she connects my brother with me, she will lash out at him too. She decided to just walk to work. It's within walking distance. My brother won't have to deal with this crazy woman's rantings." Roy looked at the judge as a way to give the jurors a moment to consider what he said.

"The third question to answer has to do with doubt. We went through the evidence in this proceeding in a couple of days. We've watched, as each of you listened attentively to the evidence presented, to faithfully discharge your obligation as a juror to the best of your ability. Now it's time for you to decide whether the Prosecution has presented its case in a way that proves, beyond a reasonable doubt, that Ms. Winders committed any crime.

"We hear a lot about the principle of proving beyond a reasonable doubt, and how the prosecutor has the burden of responsibility. Ask yourself, what does the prosecutor's burden require? It requires the exclusion of all reasonable doubt in the mind of a reasonable person. You must go into that jury room and answer the question a reasonable person would ask. Has the Prosecution left you with no reasonable doubt?

"That's a technical question. The real question to answer is this. Did the prosecutor present any evidence that eliminates the fear of convicting an innocent woman? That's the last question you must answer.

"To sum up—was she negligent? Why did she leave the scene? Is there any doubt? If you take those questions to heart and reasonably consider the evidence, you must return a verdict of not guilty. Thank you, ladies and gentlemen."

The judge allowed Roy to be seated. "Mr. Gingrich?"

"Thank you, Your Honor. Ladies and gentlemen, I'm allowed a brief rebuttal to what amounts to a misinterpretation of the evidence just presented by the Defense counsel's closing statement. I bring to your attention the same three questions he asked.

"Number one: Was the defendant negligent? The facts show the defendant was in the front seat of a south-facing car less than eight feet from westbound traffic flowing at the posted speed limit. She disregarded the fact that when she grabbed the money from her brother's hand, her action created disorder and chaos, which included a substantial risk of death or serious bodily injury. She is a highly educated adult person, a registered nurse, who knew the risk associated with her angry and childish action.

"Number two: Why did she leave the scene? Knowing her action of grabbing the money caused the car to move into the traffic lane less than eight feet away and run into the vehicle driven by Kayla Dean, which caused Ms. Dean to lose control and crash into a utility pole, the defendant, rather than taking responsibility for the accident and, as a nurse, making sure she was there to help in case of injuries, decided to leave the scene and, in doing so, to leave her responsibility behind. She was at fault and knew it. She was afraid of facing charges as the cause of the accident. So she took off.

"Number three: Is there any doubt? It is improper for me to try to do the judge's job. I won't at this time try to define what the judge will define for you, or try to answer what Defense counsel calls a technical question. I will just remind you, as jurors who are reasonable people, you can determine for yourselves, with no reasonable doubt, the defendant is guilty of each count in this indictment, her actions caused the death of Kayla Dean's little boy, and you have to find the defendant guilty. Thank you, ladies and gentlemen."

The judge spoke to the jury. "Now, ladies and gentlemen, it is my duty to instruct you on the law as it applies in this case."

***

The brief closing statements by both the defense and the prosecution surprised Kayla. A bigger surprise was Judge McCain using over forty-five minutes to instruct the jury. She believed the judge was duty bound to reduce any misunderstanding by the jurors of their mission. It seemed the judge did the opposite.

"Why is she so vague?" Kayla whispered to Daniel as the judge spoke.

"I guess it's just legalese," Daniel said.

"More like legal unease. She is confusing the jury."

The judge went through an explanation of each count in the indictment—vehicular homicide, failing to render aid and leaving the scene of the accident. Kayla couldn't discern from the judge's explanation precisely what the charges were or how the jury should deliberate.

The judge instructed, "Do not speculate as to the answers to questions to which objections were sustained or the reasons for the objections."

Kayla passed a note to ADA Gingrich: *I don't understand any of this. How is the jury supposed to understand it?* Gingrich responded with a gesture indicating *we will talk later.*

The judge seemed to place particular emphasis on the state's burden of proof beyond a reasonable doubt. She further instructed the jurors: "If the evidence is so evenly balanced that you are unable to say that the evidence on either side of an issue preponderates, your finding on that issue must be against the party who had the burden of proving it."

The judge concluded, "It is your duty as jurors to discuss the case with one another in an effort to reach agreement if you can do so. Each of you must decide the case for yourself but only after full consideration of the evidence with other members of the jury. Don't hesitate to change your mind if you become convinced by reexamining your opinion that you were wrong."

The jury was dismissed and began deliberations at 10:45 A.M. The judge reminded all interested parties, should the jury not have a verdict by 4:45 P.M., everyone must be back in the courtroom by that time because she would let the jury go home at 5:00 P.M.

Kayla and Daniel camped out at the snack bar, where Daniel stayed on his phone for close to an hour. Within three hours, the jury had reached a verdict. They hurried back into the courtroom.

The judge explained the procedure she would use to call the jury back and how she would ask the foreman if they had reached a verdict. She would read the decision to be sure it had been signed and dated, and hand it back to the foreman. She reminded all present not to react to the verdict, no matter what it turned out to be.

"Okay, bring them in." The jury was seated, and the procedure began.

"In Count 1, the first defined offense, charging the Defendant with vehicular homicide, did the jury reach a verdict?"

"Yes, we did."

"What is your verdict on Count 1?"

"Not guilty.

"In Count 2, charging the defendant with failing to render aid and leaving the scene of the accident, did the jury reach a verdict?"

"We did."

"What is your verdict?"

"Guilty."

The judge thanked and dismissed the jury. She set a date for sentencing on the guilty verdict and adjourned the Court.

CHAPTER 41

The Thursday SAVE meeting at Cossitt Library seemed to be a cross between a haphazardly staged political event and an old movie debut, where patrons mingled in the lobby, waiting for the show to begin. Small groups of ladies gathered here and there, whose only subject of discussion seemed to be others in the room.

Some attendees came dressed in jeans and tank tops. Others wore business casual. A few men wore long-sleeve shirts and ties; their sports coats hung over their chairs. A young couple wondered about two men who were in deep discussion, wearing caps, each holding a punch glass in one hand and a cookie in the other.

This night's group represented the best example of Memphis diversity anyone could imagine. It appeared that a hodgepodge of the city's culture had come together to celebrate that diversity. Three members of the press showed up with assistants carrying portable cameras, asking for Megan Alladee, revealing they were there to film Megan rather than cover the meeting.

With standing room only, Megan's dad questioned whether the meeting violated the fire code. He didn't have a count but was sure the crowd exceeded the maximum number allowed.

"I'm happy you could come tonight, Jerry," Kayla said to Jerry Phillips, one of the few who wore a tie. Jerry rolled his sleeves up two folds, which, in his mind, portrayed him as dressed in leisure attire. Long ago, Jerry decided to better present his informality in language than in attire. He knew people recognize suits as authoritative, even if they detest what the people wearing them have to say. Jerry believed his acceptance came across when ordinary people heard what he had to say, coming across as one of the guys.

"I had to come," Jerry responded. "I now have an official connection with this group of founders, and I want to know more about the people who will come together to make it happen. More importantly, I want to show my support for Megan. She hasn't appeared since that dreadful announcement in your trial. I haven't seen her here tonight. I'm glad she wasn't at the trial yesterday to witness that unexpected verdict. Have you spoken with her?"

"No, I haven't," Kayla replied. "I texted her but got no response. Cindy was with Megan yesterday, and she said Megan seemed positive, considering what she's going through. I haven't seen or spoken with her since briefly meeting with her at the trial on Tuesday. Her dad says he hasn't heard from her either. That's unusual. They are usually in constant contact. Rochelle says—"

"Hello, Doctor Phillips, hi Kayla," Megan's dad said as he approached. Jerry took the emphasis on the word *doctor* in the spirit likely intended, focusing on the clear difference between Jerry and most of the crowd. "Good to see both of you. Have either of you heard from Megan?"

Both Jerry and Kayla shook their heads.

"I'm a little concerned, not having heard from her today. It's unlike her not to be the first one here. She wants to address, without delay, the concerns many in this particular group have with the current issue and answering their questions. Tonight's meeting is not the usual SAVE event. Megan wants tonight to focus on MFC, not on her."

"I spoke with Rochelle as I came in," Kayla said. "She said Megan was at St. Jude today, but she left before Rochelle had a chance to talk with her. Rochelle knows Megan better than anybody. Megan seemed intent on whatever she was dealing with today, and Rochelle says she's learned not to interfere when Megan is in action. Rochelle told us not to worry. She doesn't know what Megan is doing but has confidence it will serve her purpose and turn out to be good."

"I hope she's right. It's not like Megan to go off the deep end," said her dad. "It's also not like her to keep me in the dark. I have to hope for the best."

"She'll be okay, I'm sure," Jerry said. He raised his orange juice glass in salute to Megan's dad. "What a cross-cultural turnout this is tonight. Congratulations. Many have great anticipation to hear what's next, thanks to your steadfast dedication to the cause. 'The hand of the diligent will rule.'"

"Diligence is a great teacher," Megan's dad said. "I've generally learned what not to do—don't travel alone. This turnout is a response to the whole team's effort, especially yours and Cindy's," he said to Kayla. "Much thanks to you too, Jerry. Eliza has leaned on your recommendations when dealing with the paring of our family members with the companies we hope they will serve. Eliza does a magnificent job, doesn't she?"

"She's incredible," Jerry said. "Her insight and judgment are unsurpassed."

"Eliza brought four ladies tonight nominated as first adoptees," Kayla said, "and husbands of two of them also came."

"We are referring to these people as adoptees, but Eliza has asked us not to use that term in public," Megan's dad said. "Each of us is referred to as a family member, making all our family members the same. We don't want adopters and adoptees. That creates division. We are just members of the same family."

Kayla placed her hand over her mouth. "Duly warned," she said. "My vocabulary has been reduced. Oh, look. Eliza is moving to the dais, getting her six new family members seated near the front." She looked at Megan's dad with a slight smile. "I guess it's time to get started. I hope Megan comes in at some point."

Jerry and Kayla took seats in the back, near Cindy and Kevin.

"This meeting of Share Anti-abortion Values Everywhere will come to order. Tonight is a special meeting for SAVE. I'm sure most of you know, we have announced the creation of My Free Choice, a family of families, working to achieve what amounts to the demise of unplanned pregnancy. We plan to release the grip of poverty and welfare that seeks to control so many of our lives.

"I'd like to welcome members of the media who are with us tonight. I hope you will have a story to tell regarding SAVE and the My Free Choice family from what you hear in this meeting tonight. I predict this venue will host an expanded media presence in future sessions, reporting stories related to the people who will help us grow our family.

"It is also my honor and privilege to welcome and introduce to you a new member of the family, Dr. Jerry Phillips. We are happy to announce Jerry's participation in an active role, to accomplish the founding and continuing growth of My Free Choice. Thank you, Jerry, and welcome."

The media were perplexed. Why would the leadership begin this meeting when the primary player is absent? They reasoned that Megan is in hiding, refusing to accept and deal with her ongoing dilemma. She is unable to face public scrutiny.

"I'll spare you the details, but I want to announce we are nearing the official startup of My Free Choice. One of the toughest parts of beginning an organization like this is satisfying the government's mandate to guarantee that we serve a tangible and currently unfulfilled public need.

"One of the most challenging questions to answer is, at the same time, maybe the simplest one for the government, the IRS, to ask: What is it you're going to do? And they give plenty of advice to help answer that simple question. Here are a couple of suggestions they offer. Number one:

> The organization must fully describe the activities, in which it has engaged, currently engages or expects to engage, including the standards, criteria, procedures, or other means adopted or planned for carrying out the activities: percentage of total time and effort devoted to carrying out each activity: the anticipated sources of receipts and the nature of contemplated expenditures.

"Here's another:

> Provide a detailed description of your past, present, and future activities. Submit a list showing each activity you have conducted, currently conduct or plan to conduct. Beside each activity, indicate the percentage of the total time devoted to the activity. (Note: Total time should add to 100 %.) In addition, explain when, where and how each activity is conducted. For

whom are the activities conducted? By whom
are activities conducted?

"They've been so helpful." The crowd had a good laugh. "I
want to announce to you that we have satisfied all the requirements necessary to qualify as a nonprofit organization. Since
we are not what's called a successor organization, our next step
is for the board members to determine what interaction My
Free Choice will have, if any, with SAVE.

"Okay, enough of that. Now I want to turn the program over
to Eliza Stokes, whose unparalleled insight and unquestioned
fidelity to our cause are crucial. Eliza takes charge, and she
gets it done. She has made strong inroads with local sponsor
companies who will help formulate our initial, critical service
rendering. We are off to a tremendous start, and we are excited
to have Eliza share what she has experienced. Thank you, Eliza;
the floor is yours."

"Thank you . . . thank you so much," Eliza responded to the
enthusiastic and prolonged applause. "Thank you—my goodness—I hope I can be worthy of that intro. Much has happened
in not much time. I've been amazed by the business community's avid interest in how we can help these companies to center
their process. Process centering is made available by the service MFC offers."

The reporters motioned for the cameras to move toward
the stairway entrance. The audience followed the direction of
the cameras.

"These businesses will be—" Eliza stopped in mid-sen-
tence, surprised to see Megan at the top of the stairs. "Hello
Megan, I'm so glad you made it. Ladies and gentlemen, Megan
Alladee." There arose cautious applause by most of the group

along with a standing ovation by founders and other members of SAVE. "We were wondering—"

"My apologies for being so late. I couldn't prevent it," Megan said.

Megan's dad was happy and relieved to see Megan, but he hesitated. Looking toward Kayla, Kayla beamed, clapping her hands and smiling with a satisfied nod.

Cindy was mindful of the conversation she and Megan had at Hyde Park the day before. She struggled to hold back her emotion.

"You're never too late," Eliza said. "And please, tell us about this impressive gentleman you have with you?"

Megan looked at Kayla as if she were making the introduction directly to her. "I'd like to introduce Mark Jones. For those of you who don't know Mr. Jones, he is the leading local expert in customer relationship management. His company has developed a state-of-the-art customer relationship management system called Manufacts. I want to reveal the latest development with Manufacts as it relates to MFC when time allows. Again, my apologies for arriving late." Megan and Mark walked toward where the founders were seated.

"Mr. Alladee," Eliza said, "If it would not be out of line, I'd like to ask Megan if she is ready to tell us more right now."

"I don't see that as unacceptable," Megan's dad said.

"Megan, I don't intend to put you on the spot . . . well, in a way, that is what I intend to do." The audience chuckled at her playful tease. "Are you prepared to take the mic and tell us more?"

"I'm happy to if you will allow devoting a significant chunk of your time," Megan responded just as playfully.

Megan took the floor. Mark took a seat, conscious of the need not to appear trying to be too close or too far away from

Kayla. Kayla didn't seem to notice either way. Her attention focused on Megan.

"Let me begin by first thanking everyone for your love and support in these trying of times. It has been incredible and consistent, and unrequited on my part. The water has been rising against the dam—and not calmly."

Megan turned toward Eliza. "Eliza, I sincerely thank you for allowing me this breach of your time to cover this mixture of events. What you have to present tonight is of vital importance. Still, a moment or two will suffice to address some of the questions I know people have, especially members of the media, who I see are present at a SAVE meeting for the first time." Eliza raised her hand, acknowledging an answer to prayer.

"Yes, it's true. I had an abortion at the age of twenty, just two months after my birthday. It seemed the right thing to do at the time. I know that sounds hypocritical, given what I have preached to you—since shortly after that event and the founding of SAVE, to the present. With the realization that I came to after the abortion, and the knowledge I have gained, I now know I made an error in judgment. The abortion was unnecessary, unwanted, and unchangeable. I know many of you in this group can identify with what I'm saying.

"So, what happened? Why did I do it, and why are you just now hearing of it? Many years ago, at age nineteen, I was raped." Tears immediately streamed down Megan's cheeks. She had not intended to be so blunt. It just came out. Megan was amazed at the relief that came with uttering those three words. She had not considered how vital that utterance was to her.

"Forgive me. I'm not crying because I was raped. I'm crying because I've made the announcement official. Please, don't misunderstand. I'm nobody special. I'm no different from countless other girls facing this trauma. Outside the people in this room and a few others, I'm no more than a statistic. When I refer to an official announcement, I'm not suggesting it's an announcement to the world. I'm making it official to me. Yes, I was raped.

"I can't explain the details here, but I decided to keep it to my family and myself. I see that as a wrong decision too, one which I can't excuse, but I have to accept. So, please, let's move on to the business at hand—My Free Choice Foundation and the important development leading to my bringing Mr. Mark Jones to the meeting."

"Excuse me, Ms. Alladee," one of the reporters said. "Can you answer a couple of questions?"

"Make it short."

"You said you consider keeping this to yourself was a mistake. Had you ever considered making this announcement earlier?"

"Yes, about a million times, but what I've said should be enough. Take it for what it's worth—announcing it publicly meant announcing it to myself."

The reporter didn't hesitate to ask a second question. "This was so long ago. Was anyone ever arrested for the assault?"

Megan knew this would be one of the first questions asked and had decided she would refuse to answer it. She understood there was no way to avoid a direct answer without arousing suspicion. "I can't discuss that. Even if I could, I wouldn't discuss it in this context. Enough said. Let's move on."

Megan's dad stood with his hand raised. "I have a question for you, Megan. What's this about a state of the art software system called Manufacts?"

"Thanks for the question, Dad. In answering, I must address my reason for being tardy tonight. Several members of the team have met with Mark Jones to research the benefit of using his CRM software for MFC. Some will ask, what's so unique about CRM? Not much, unless you talk with Mark Jones. He has developed Manufacts, which uses a process to create a new, proprietary meaning of the word *customer*. Sorry, but I can't cover the details here. I'm late because Mark has spent the entire day educating me on his concept, and I'm encouraging the founders to listen to what he has to say.

"Without taking more of Eliza's time, let me say that I asked Mark Jones to accompany me here tonight to impress two points. As a first point, his attendance will support the personal interest he is taking with the startup of MFC. He wants to become more involved.

"The second point is mine. His coming to the meeting tonight makes my recommendation more official. It's my job to officially introduce Manufacts to the team and to all who are here tonight. It had to come from me. Here's why.

"A group of SAVE members began a discussion at the beginning of this year to address the issue of unplanned pregnancy. How can we offer the degree of stability and freedom necessary for a minimum standard of living and working required for a woman, hopefully, a man and a woman, to make autonomous decisions about their pregnancy? Sustainability is an absolute requirement. By sustainability, I mean a program that meets the long-term needs of a growing family, a family of families, if you will.

"We can talk through the night and still not cover all the resources needed—human resources, financial, political, technological, management. It takes people with expertise and talent and volunteers of many different stripes. It takes people who want to sponsor, people who can decide what needs to be done and take steps to make it happen.

"With that said, my coming to the meeting tonight accompanied by Mark Jones draws attention to the most critical resource of all—belief. Believing in our ability to do what we decide to do is one thing, but believing it's the right thing to do is another.

"The reporters here tonight are following up on a revelation that surfaced in the testimony I gave in court and speculation that I have been hiding out as a result. Yes, I've been unavailable for the last couple of days, but I'm not hiding.

"I've taken to heart what Kayla Dean has been teaching me about belief. Kayla made a split-second decision about Mark Jones and his software concerning My Free Choice. She has every right to state her opposition, not only to the use of the Manufacts software but also to Mark Jones's involvement on the team. Kayla didn't exercise her right. Without hesitation, she said yes to Mark Jones and Manufacts. Kayla believed it to be the right decision, and she acted accordingly. She does what she believes is right without having to consider the consequences.

"Thank you, Kayla. Because of you, I'm learning how to believe and how to act on it. For you media folks, here's your story.

"My Free Choice Foundation is on a perilous journey we believe will lead to the solution of what seems an unsolvable problem—the elimination of unplanned pregnancy. We are doing it because we believe it's the right thing to do. With that, I'll yield to our scheduled speaker, Eliza Stokes. Please listen carefully and take to heart what she has to say. She believes."

CHAPTER 42

M egan spoke with the officer inside the police station lobby. "I'm Megan Alladee. I'm here to see ADA Gingrich. Am I in the right place?"

"Yes. Ms. Alladee, we've been expecting you. Would you wait here a moment, please?"

To Megan's surprise and slight displeasure, Jack Williams suddenly appeared, before the officer could dial his phone. "Hello, Megan. Thanks for coming. I know you didn't expect to see me this morning. Given the situation, the ADA asked me to help you with what we're asking of you today. I'm sorry for the way this surfaced in the courtroom. Had we known in advance, we could have prevented it from coming out the way it did. We wouldn't have put you on the stand."

"That's alright, Jack. I wasn't expecting anything to surface at the trial, but it did. What's done is done." Megan knew some questions had been answered in Jack's mind. "I would have told you eventually."

Jack held up his hand apologetically. "It's okay, Megan. I understand why you chose not to tell anyone, and I don't want you to feel embarrassed or uncomfortable in any way."

"I don't feel anything like that, Jack. I'm not embarrassed."

"Poor choice of words, Megan. That came out the wrong way. I didn't mean it the way it sounded. My apologies. Can we start over?"

"I'd like that. I've had some regrets, but I got over being embarrassed long ago. There's no opportunity in shame."

"Decisions we've made in the past are what make us who we are today."

"Kayla likes to say our lives are only a breath. I agree with her. We are here for a relative moment, but I believe the decisions we make in a moment can last forever."

"I see it every day. Those who come through the justice system come because of the choices they have made. The thing is, good or bad, we make some decisions of our own accord. Others we can't control. They're unavoidable."

"This guy, Ron—is that his real name?"

"Yes, Ronald Hicks."

"He assaulted me and forced me to make some decisions. I decided to have an abortion, and I decided not to tell anyone about it, or why I did it. Without even being aware, I made the decision not to go after this guy. Now I have to live with those decisions."

"Give yourself some credit. You were a teenager, but you did what you thought was right."

"Don't misunderstand me, Jack. I'm not motivated by guilt. I'm telling you what I've come to understand. Yes, I've brooded over those things that happened to me and the decisions I made as a result. None of those things can be changed, and, thankfully, I've tried to make the best of it. I've often wondered what I would have become had those things not happened, and I had made different decisions."

"I know a few good things that have happened, which wouldn't have happened."

"Yes, that's my point. A lot of good has come out of SAVE. My dad and I have worked hard to give those women a chance, and we have had some success. But I sometimes question my motivation. Have I tried to make a difference in other people's lives, or have I just been trying to change my life? Honestly,

I never had a sense of guilt. It wasn't my fault, so guilt is no motive. I know I can't change what happened to me. Saving those kids from abortion will not bring back my aborted child. I don't think that has influenced me. So what is it?"

"I know a little of what you mean," Jack said. "It's like tithing in church. Am I tithing so the church can do its job, or am I doing it to make me feel better about myself?"

"That's it exactly. I remember when I first met Kayla, and she talked about her faith. I considered faith as believing in something you couldn't be sure was true. Do I believe and therefore have faith, or do I have faith and therefore believe? Kayla showed me why it doesn't matter. Helping people makes me feel good. What's wrong with that?"

"I've always believed giving is the right thing to do. When I give, it makes me feel good. When I don't give, it makes me feel bad. I guess the motive doesn't matter."

"There's a thin line there. No one's forcing you to give, and no one's forcing me to work with SAVE. Choosing our actions pales in comparison to what others face. My kids at St. Jude—they make the most gut-wrenching decisions imaginable, sometimes daily, and they do it in what seems a cheerful way. That's my definition of heroics."

"I guess you could say we sometimes choose to do certain things we may not want to do and consider bad at the time to prevent being forced into choosing worse things later. Unfortunately, those kids don't have an option."

"Spoken like a true attorney, Jack, but I guess I see it in the same way. Kayla says everything is good, or, at least, everything works for good. It takes God to do that. So, what good thing are we doing today?"

"We're holding a bad person accountable. Are you ready for this? If you pick this creep out of a lineup, are you willing to testify in court?"

"I don't know. Has he done this to other girls in Memphis, or will he be charged for what he did to me?"

"You know he was charged with rape in Ohio a couple of months ago. The girl is in her late twenties. The Ohio authorities saw a potential DNA match and contacted us. It turned out this guy was last seen by someone in Ohio who told the authorities he was staying with relatives in Memphis. He wasn't hard to find. We will press charges here; then, he'll be extradited to Ohio to stand trial there."

"I figured there would be a statute of limitations. How can he be charged here? It was so long ago."

"Legislation was passed over ten years ago to allow prosecutors to indict a person's DNA profile even if the person's identity is unknown. The indictment keeps the statute of limitations from running out. When we arrest the suspect, prosecutors can move forward with the case. Your case got in under the wire. An indictment was issued against the DNA on record at the time. So, we can move forward."

"That doesn't stop the victim's statute of limitations. Mine expired long ago. I want this guy to pay, but I don't want to relive what happened." Megan put her hand on Jack's arm. "I know what you're going to say, Jack. I have a responsibility to put this guy away, to keep him from hurting other girls. But why put that responsibility on me? The cops didn't try to put my rapist away during that time. Who knows how many other unknown girls he's raped?"

"At least one."

"Is that my fault?"

"Of course not, Megan. Look, you have a right to be upset, to be angry. The authorities handled your case poorly."

"My case—the cops didn't even believe there was a rape. They thought it was my fault. There never was a case. I remember how they handled it and the questions they asked. I don't want to go through it again."

"The truth is, we won't be able to make much of a case without you."

"The truth sat on the shelf for five or six years before they claim the case was reopened."

"Okay, Megan. What do you want to do? I have a lineup scheduled for ten o'clock, less than fifteen minutes from now. If you are willing to pick this guy out, we can go from there. He won't be able to see you at all. You'll be protected."

"I'm not afraid of facing him, and I don't need any protection. I'll pick him out in person."

"Not necessary, Megan, but I'm a little confused. You're not afraid to face your rapist, but you're afraid to go to trial?"

"That's a dumb question, Jack. I'm not afraid to go to trial, but think of the questions they will ask. Why did I put myself in that position—did I want to have sex, or did I enjoy it? Just asking those questions will make the news, and people will think it was, in some way, consensual. That's not the story here. And what effect might some false narrative have on the startup of the foundation? It could create chaos. No, I don't need more confusion. My responsibility is to prevent it."

"I've been amazed at how little of this has been in the press. Your testimony in the courtroom came right after we captured Hicks. I said, 'Oh, no. This is all going to come out now.' But it didn't happen."

"I want to keep it that way. Again, another reason I don't want to testify. If Hicks is in the lineup, I'll pick him out, but that's the end of it. Let him go to court; the DNA you have should be enough. Tell them I named him in the lineup."

"That won't mean much. Your refusal to testify will weaken our case. Hicks will say it was consensual."

"I see how this works. Have you not heard a word I've been saying? You need this to go to court for you, not for me. 'Oh yeah, we captured this guy after many years of hunting him down. Justice can now be served.' That's BS, and you know it, Jack. That's not justice. That's public relations. The court gets a win, and I pay the price. The foundation pays the price, and those aborted babies we've been talking about—they pay the price."

"None of it is fair, Megan. I know how you see it, but I can't think in those terms. I have a job to do, and I have a responsibility to the DA. I work for him, and I have to do whatever I can to make things happen in the context of the justice system. Yes, things were left undone for a great deal of time. But it's evident. Laws were broken, and, from our perspective, as officers of the court, it's our job to see justice served, and it should be served here and now. If you refuse to testify in court, our hands are tied."

"Do I understand this correctly—if you don't try him here, then Hicks will be sent to Ohio to stand trial there?"

"Yes, the DA will have to decide if the case is strong enough without your testimony. They'll call other witnesses, Rochelle probably being one of them, and the DNA evidence is there. But the strongest case against the defense will be your testimony. It doesn't seem reasonable, and the DA won't like it, but I will stand behind your right to withdraw."

"Maybe we can still have hope for you, Jack."

"I care for you, Megan. It's your choice, and I'll hold firm, but I don't agree with what you're doing. You're letting your feelings override what reason says you should do."

"My head never knows what my heart is thinking. I'll do the lineup. That's reasonable, but that's all I can do. I'd say let him stand trial for raping someone a couple of months ago. Then he'll be in jail, where he belongs. That's the goal, isn't it?"

"That's the goal. The problem is we don't know what's going to happen in Ohio. If the victim refuses to testify there, Hicks could go free." Jack saw ADA Gingrich waiting for the lineup to begin. "We have to go. Do your best to identify this guy, Megan."

***

"He's the one on the right, number five," declared Megan.

"Are you sure he's the person who raped you?" asked ADA Gingrich. "This guy looks like a lot of other people you may know. He's an average looking person."

"Yes, I'm certain. He hasn't changed much. He looks like the same person he was in 2002." Megan was surprised at how easily she could identify this man she was with only half a day. But she had no doubt. Her real surprise was her immediate response to seeing him again. She had long thought, if she ever saw him, she would feel only hatred for what he did to her. Instead, she had a neutral response, like seeing a TV news report showing a man identified as raping someone she didn't know. "Why did you put him on the right?" she asked Gingrich. "I figured he would be in the middle. I visualized he would be number three. The last place I expected him to be is on the right."

The curtain closed, and the lineup walked out. "We do lineups in sort of a blind way. We don't line them up in any particular order, and the person conducting the lineup doesn't know who is in the lineup. We don't identify them in advance."

"Are you alright, Megan?" Jack placed his hand on her shoulder. "How do you feel?"

"I don't feel anything. Don't misunderstand. This creep should pay for what he did, but he is not someone currently in my life. He has never been, and I want to keep it that way."

"Thank you for doing this," Gingrich said to Megan, as he walked out the door.

Jack escorted Megan to the exit. "I'm glad you said what you said as we were leaving. ADA Gingrich heard for the first time that you don't want to testify, and it's good he heard it from you first."

"I wasn't directing anything at him. I was telling you how I feel."

"I know, but in that one statement, he heard everything he needed to hear. I'm sure I'll be in his office within ten minutes. Now it begins."

"Now it ends, at least for me. It's over."

CHAPTER 43

S aturday is a good team workday. It's natural to thwart personal plans on weekends, provided the planner is committed to the cause. Weekdays carry a commitment to one's job. Saturday requires a more significant commitment; work is without pay.

"Today is important. Thank you for coming." Megan spoke from her seat at the head of the table. "We've set up four zones for today's work. Dad, the library was kind enough to arrange for you, Jerry, and me to meet in the small conference room downstairs. We want to review the deal Jerry has presented for a permanent My Free Choice location. We've all seen the proposal. The building is in the community where many of our family members live and will offer easier access for them. I'll meet the two of you there in twenty-two minutes.

"Eliza, your idea of bringing first-generation family members today is good. Use our regular meeting room for plenty of laptop and notebook space. Spread them around to begin training."

"Thanks, Megan. These sisters of ours are anxious to dig into the flow chart mapping plan we've created, with two sponsor companies already in place. The ladies are excited, and I'm excited for them."

"Rochelle, a special thanks for your coming this morning. If you haven't heard the latest, Rochelle is meeting potential partners interested in getting their company leaders involved with our mission. How many do you expect?"

"Six are confirmed," Rochelle said. "I want them to meet each of you. They want to hear details about our most immediate needs. These folks bring future funding potential and can open doors for local grants to develop our training program."

Megan smiled at Mark and Kayla. "Mark, thank you for joining us. Kayla, you, Cindy, and Mark can work in this room after we break up. I want your focus on how Manufacts can help us beginning day one. Take all the time you want. I believe Mark's program is critical to analyze plan implementation in a real-time scenario. Will Kim be okay to stay in the little nursery we have set up? She has plenty to keep her occupied."

"She will be fine. If she needs anything, she knows how to find me."

"Okay, we're all set. Let's get to it. Oh, before we go, Dad, what's the latest on the political fallout from your city hall meeting?"

"We're looking at small potatoes. Several council members are concerned about a planned protest scheduled after we announced our possible home, and they'll rally outside our building during move-in. These days, anything people don't understand demands a demonstration.

"They think we simply want to defeat Cobel Clinic. It's a pro-choice thing motivated by a misconception of our intent. They don't understand why minimizing abortion is only a byproduct of our effort. Let these women choose for themselves what they want for their bodies and their lives. I don't think much will come of it."

The group moved to their meeting locations. "Dad, I'll see you and Jerry downstairs." Megan waited for the room to clear and spoke to Kayla. "I want to be sure you are okay with how we're grouping this meeting today."

"I'm good with it, Megan. We should forget those events behind us and reach for what is ahead. I believe I'm doing what God wants me to do, and nothing else matters to me."

"Cindy, are you ready to move forward?"

"Yes, completely ready. Kayla and I will do our best."

"Mark, anything you want to say before we begin?"

"Just one thing. I spoke with Suzan after she was released, and I want everybody to know, she has no interest in Manufacts. Of course, she won't support us either. Kayla, I like your idea of forgetting what's behind and moving forward. I don't have that ability. I can't forget, but I hope we can put anything involving Suzan behind us."

"I'm there," Kayla said.

"Me too," Cindy said.

"That's good. I'll leave it with you." Megan packed up her folders and headed for the door.

"Close the door on your way out," Kayla said. "Okay, we're ready. What's the shortest route to comprehension, Mark?"

"I have a few handouts for review later. I emailed a link to download a trial version of Manufacts we can use today. Did you look at the software?"

"Yes, I've reviewed enough to see it's user friendly. Access works well and without delay. I've had some experience with CRM at St. Jude. But I can see a different approach here, with flow charts that define different responsibilities."

"Navigation works well," Kayla said. "It's user friendly, but I need the basics."

"Let's begin with what we can expect at startup. Everything happens as part of a process. At the root of our training is what we call 'centering the process.' Process centering eliminates waste. Waste equals any error in the process."

"How is the process determined in the first place? We aren't carrying on a process already in place. Who knows how we will do what we will be required to do?"

"Good question," Mark said. "Self-examination, design, and redesign are three precepts we use at each step in fulfilling customer needs. We have customers, and we are customers. Change is the result of process redesign to eliminate waste. A complicated process amounts to a series of yes and no questions."

"Sounds complicated."

"Stepping through yes and no questions is surprisingly simple. We could send a rocket ship to the moon."

"Oh, no. It's rocket science."

"Funny. Plotting process steps is time-consuming, but all users of our system are involved. The goal is an error-free process. Training creates believers in the process flow."

"I'm a believer."

"The plan is in place once we formulate the process, and Manufacts operates within that context. Plan success happens when family members follow the process."

"We don't know our family members or our customers. How do users see transactions between members and customers— between members and members, for that matter?"

"The customer database is limitless. Other members, who Megan calls brothers and sisters, will also be your customers, and you will be theirs. Useable data develops at a rapid pace, with members providing a knowledge base by working within the program."

"This will be an exponential growth of data. How can we expect members to deal with what might become an excess of available data?"

"Statistically speaking, the software knows everything there is to know. Admin-level users will determine who has access to what data and to what extent. Not everybody needs to know everything. The key is to provide real-time access to what's needed."

"You're saying the data is up to the minute," Cindy said, "but a user will access nothing more than what process fulfillment requires. Is that correct?"

"Correct, but it's not just data. We don't do any process work outside the program. The result is instantaneous and accurate information reporting. Tasks accomplished between members and customers create useful information available on an as-needed basis."

"What guarantees complete availability of necessary data, but not more?" asked Kayla.

"Another perceptive question, at the heart of the plan. Users have up-to-the-minute, accurate information with clear visibility. Customers receive consistent service and hear the same accurate and timely information regardless of who delivers it. You will be able to accomplish what you set out to accomplish, provided you trust the software to deliver everything you need."

"I have faith in a process we have yet to define," Cindy said.

"On your screen is a ten-step sales process flow chart. Please understand—that word *sales* is a generic term. It's semantics. We can substitute any term we want to use in place of sales. The key is the process flow chart. Let's begin there. Click on the Process tab, and we can make changes."

***

Mark left Kayla and Cindy to work on the beginnings of a flow chart for the activities of MFC without his input. He walked next to Megan as she made her rounds.

"You've put a great team together, Megan. I'm amazed at the world you've created and allowed me to see and be a part of."

At Rochelle's group, they heard a message of benefit to companies that allow the foundation to further the company's mission and plan for success.

"I met Rochelle, but I've spoken to her on just one occasion. She seems to be all about using her impressive resume to convince people to listen. She speaks with authority and confidence without a hint of impropriety."

"She is a good person and a friend and mentor. She operates out of the goodness of her heart. I would lose most battles without her leadership at St. Jude."

"It's impressive. Cindy and Kayla are quick learners. I'm anxious to see the flow chart they are putting together. They caught on to the idea immediately."

"Having good software helps."

"Good software does help, but without determined users, not much can come of it. Cindy jokes around a lot, which I attribute to her general cheerfulness. I've heard her complain some, but her barbs are just comedy, a way to kid herself."

"She acts like she doesn't get it," Megan said, "but deep inside, she is diligent and insightful. I believe she will manage the foundation positively."

"Most would not have picked her as a manager. Some see her as a little short on experience and judgment. You see something in her many others don't."

"As you say, she is a quick learner. And she will be partnered with Kayla. God bless Kayla, she can do anything she sets her mind to."

"That's why I want to speak with you. As I said, I'm truly thankful—thrilled—that you and Kayla have allowed me to enter your world. You've tolerated the suffering I've had so much to do with causing the two of you. I admire how patiently you have turned a lifetime of pain into comfort for others."

"Thanks for saying that. I know you never intended to cause any grief, and I don't hold any animosity toward you. But your concern is not me, it's Kayla, right?"

"Yes, she may be too forgiving. When Suzan was released, Kayla showed no discomfort. It made me see how odd her reaction is. I'm afraid one day she may wake up and realize how badly she's hurting. Who knows what will happen then? I don't want to be the cause of more harm to you, her, or the foundation."

"You don't have a clear understanding of what motivates Kayla."

"No, I don't."

"Kayla is a person of faith. Her faithfulness transcends worldly events in her life. She and her husband, Daniel, believe in forgiveness. They would rather die than be unforgiving. There won't come a time when she wakes up. She is already awake. She forgives you, and she forgives Suzan. Even more, she forgives a system that doesn't seem to operate on her behalf. With the end of the trial, she forgave Suzan."

"That's difficult to comprehend. I hate to admit it, but Suzan is completely unsympathetic. She's mean-spirited and intolerant of everything Kayla believes. Her past is a series of shenanigans that would make Ma Barker blush. How can Kayla be sympathetic?"

"It's a sorrow based not on emotion but compassion for Suzan's spiritual unbelief."

"Suzan is amused by the idea of compassion. To her, compassion is a weakness."

"Yes, I know. Suzan and I have been going at it for a long time. Abortion is her solution to unplanned pregnancy 100 percent of the time. I've learned to deal with her mania. Still, her notion of the legal non-personhood of babies is inexcusable and lacks a hint of compassion."

"I have never been in favor of Suzan's role at the clinic, and especially during the time Dr. Joyner managed the clinic."

"Those were tough times."

"Yes, but that's a different discussion. What I see with this foundation and its plan makes me want to be involved. I'm donating my software and will guide the training of its use. I can be instrumental in the acceptance of your program with some of my client companies, which I'm sure Suzan will fight. I know you can see why my involvement will create some otherwise unknown difficulties."

"It becomes a personal problem between you and Suzan," Megan said.

"Yes, a problem I am willing to confront, but it's more than just a personal issue. When it becomes a public issue, I won't be able to deal with it publicly. Please understand. I won't make any public statements or be involved in any public discussion regarding Suzan. I believe she will agree to do the same."

"Kayla will be glad to hear that. She hasn't said she would not react to Suzan in a public forum, but I know she won't. We will positively present our case and move forward. Let Suzan and Cobel Clinic portray themselves however they choose.

"Let's see how Eliza is doing with the family. You know, most of these women never even hear a kind word, much less a presentation designed to help them. Eliza takes an empathetic approach in presenting to this group."

"The job requirement creates a long journey for all involved," Mark said. "I don't know how she can make it happen."

"We're asking this family of ours to accomplish a goal not many of them will even consider possible. Eliza is sensitive to that. She understands the lives they have to deal with, and her leadership offers hope. If anyone can do this, it's Eliza."

"Don't know what I can do outside training," Mark said, "but I will do anything I can to make this program a success."

"Thanks, Mark. Jerry contacted the real estate agents on the property, and I see they have arrived. I should also meet with them, but I want to check on Kayla and Cindy. Let's head back."

"Okay. I'm glad to see a permanent home on the horizon that will house a server. Jerry knows how beneficial that is to the effort. Jerry and I have done business for some years, and I can say you're lucky to have him. You have some tough times ahead, and he's one of the coolest and calmest people I know when there's a crisis. Jerry keeps his head and keeps everybody under control. He's usually the smartest guy in the room. Still, he operates with such restraint, nobody sees him as the intellectual he is."

"He sort of reminds me of my dad, always under control. Dad's leadership style lets him control his circumstances by controlling himself. He and Jerry make the best team imaginable."

"Mark tells me you guys have this thing down pat," Megan said to Kayla and Cindy.

"Oh yeah," Cindy said. "All we like is learning the details."

"Cindy's way ahead of me," Kayla said. "I'm going to need a lot of prayer."

"Great, that's one of the things you're in charge of," Megan said.

CHAPTER 44

Megan's dad secured the lease on the My Free Choice property with a rider to allow the contract to be transferred to MFC once the foundation setup was complete.

Megan believed announcing this milestone would help settle the minds of sponsors and potential investors of time and money. *It's official. This is who we are, and this is where we will be. Family members can make plans for a new job at a specific location, arranging for transportation to and from, familiarizing themselves with the neighborhood, businesses in the area, restaurants, shops, and suppliers.*

She gathered her dad, Jerry, Rochelle, Cindy, Kayla, and Mark to make an immediate announcement to Eliza and the family members at today's meeting. Rochelle's potential partner group, five men and three women, were eager to witness this event. Rochelle had aroused their interest in knowing more about MFC and wanting to meet the team.

Eliza's spirit was on fire. She raised her hand and thanked the Lord. A few high fives among the group showed their enthusiasm in believing this was going to happen.

Rochelle and Meagan hugged. "You're doing it again," Rochelle said. "And I'm proud of everything you're doing."

"My head is swimming a little," Megan said. "It's like we've been backed up in a long line of rush hour traffic trying to make a delivery on time. It seems the traffic is clearing a bit, but I can see even more traffic getting on the ramp."

"You're a good driver, Megan," Rochelle said. "We'll get there."

"Listen, folks," Eliza said to the family group. "This announcement means several things to each of you. It means you are the first generation of a new family. We are in this for the long haul, and you want to be in it the same way. You must invest in My Free Choice, not in dollars and cents, but an investment of your commitment to take advantage of an exceptional opportunity for your advancement.

"It means a lot of hard work to study and learn and to apply that learning toward making your life better for you. I want you to make good decisions for yourself and your family."

Three hands of the family group went up. Eliza pointed to one, as she held up a hand toward the other two. "Please state your name before you ask a question. I want you to become accustomed to identifying yourself as a participant in any discussion while you're here at the foundation."

"My name is Teresa. When will we start getting paid? I don't have any money."

"You get more money than I do. You don't have no money because you let your boyfriend drink it all up. Oh yeah, my name is Louisa. Will I be allowed to bring my kids to work? I can't afford to pay for no daycare."

"Wait, Louisa," said Eliza. "Rules apply here. The rule is we ask and answer one question at a time. We address one issue for discussion at a time. Do you understand?"

"Yes, ma'am."

"Teresa, the ability to manage income is one part of the training you will receive as a family member of the foundation. Studying is a part of your necessary investment I referred to before you asked your question. A part of your training will include one-on-one discussions on the issue of family members controlling funds. To answer your question, receiving foundation funds will depend upon how well you respond to training and contribute to the program. That may not be the answer you expected or one you fully understand. We can better address this answer together after the meeting today. Louisa, I'd like you to be a part of that discussion as well. Can the two of you stay?" Both agreed to meet for discussion.

"The answer to your question, Louisa, is easy to state but difficult to apply. Your children are family members. The foundation recognizes that any work you undertake outside the home requires your kids to be adequately supervised and protected while you're away. The new foundation home will include daycare so your kids can be near you while you work. Ideally, the long-term plan is for family members to work from their homes. That's the tough part. Implementation means all family members must be ready, willing, and able to do the work independently. Determining that level of ability will vary from member to member. Yes, Louisa, you can bring your kids to work."

Eliza pointed to the third member who had raised her hand for a question.

"My name is Sylvia. My question is about me, personally. Will I not be allowed to be a member of the family if I have an abortion?"

Mark Jones leaned over to ask Megan's dad discretely whether Eliza had set up these women to ask these particular questions.

"In one form or another," Megan's dad said, "these are questions these women must answer daily. No planning or setup is required."

Eliza knew the foundation rule concerning issues of personal life. Nevertheless, she decided an answer to this question would be more forceful coming from Megan. "As with all issues related to family members, foundation rules apply here as well. Megan, as a founder of MFC, are you in a position to address this question?"

"Yes, I'm prepared to answer anyone who asks for a reason. Let me first ask you a question, Sylvia. Are you in a position to carry your pregnancy to term?"

"I don't see how I can, even if I wanted to. My husband, Carl, says I've got to have an abortion. He says we don't have any choice. We can't get by as it is."

"One more question, Sylvia. Does becoming a member of the MFC family change any of that?"

"I don't see how it does," Sylvia said.

"Okay, let's start there," Megan said. "Less than five minutes ago, Eliza said she wanted you to make the right decisions for yourself and your family. Now, you may think abortion is the right decision, or you may not. The point is, you and your husband don't believe you have a choice. You can't choose not to have an abortion.

"As stated early on, the mission of MFC is to provide a means to allow women to make decisions, influenced only by what they believe is right, or what they want to do. We want a way to give women, and their men, the ability to make life choices, including abortion.

"If the foundation had a rule forbidding family members from getting an abortion, that's just someone else making your decision for you. We don't have any such rule.

"Our goal is to help you make a decision not to have an abortion if you so choose. You know how we want you to decide, but until you can make a free choice, it's not a decision at all.

"We believe the quicker you can make intelligent, rational decisions, either way, the better. In the meantime, we want you to be open to explore other possibilities."

"Thanks, Megan. Are there other questions—from anyone? Questions from Rochelle's group?"

One hand went up. "Yes, sir?"

"Hello, I'm Josh Davis from the Briley Automotive Group. I appreciate what I hear as a unique approach to the cause. I wanted to address the startup. Do you have an official date for the foundation to begin activities?

Megan's dad asked if he could respond. "We have our EIN and will complete the final documents next week. We can then move forward with bringing in members, the commencement of training, and putting the complete process in place. With a permanent location, we can set up our server for email and financial programming. Manufacts is on-demand, but we want everything to be associated with our location. Our attorneys have advised that we can take tax-free donations and apply for grants as if we were fully operational."

***

"We have a long way to go," Megan said to Kayla, "but it seems we have, at last, taken the first step."

"No pun intended," Kayla said.

"It's been a long first step, with many seemingly unrelated difficulties to overcome."

"What do you mean by unrelated difficulties?" asked Kayla. "Are not all areas of our lives related?"

"Well, I said seemingly unrelated. Yes, it's all related, but I'm amazed at how compartmentalized we tend to make our lives. It's supposed to be a good thing, but is it? Everything relates in some way, but we approach solutions as if they're unrelated."

"Have you done that?"

"Yes, I guess I have, without realizing it. I'm not the same person at work as I am at home. At work, I have to keep my defenses up. At home with Mom and Dad, I'm different. I'm uninhibited in every way. I'm a different person in public than I am in private."

"Most people are."

"Yes, but not to an extreme. I don't let my personal feelings interfere with anything socially."

"Do you see that as necessary? I know it's not pretense on your part."

"It's not a conscious thing. It's based more on regret than on rational thinking. I've had this feeling that any choice had to be immediate, or something bad would happen. The way to maintain control was to do it now. Any procrastination meant problems would keep backing up until eventually the dam would break. Even the wrong choice was better than no choice. So, I made some bad decisions."

"Contentment leads to solutions. Regret looks at causes, and creates confusion."

"In college, I wondered what it would be like to know what other girls know. My friends knew what it was like not to be pregnant, not to have an abortion."

"Not to be raped?"

"If only . . . if only I hadn't taken a particular action. If only this or that hadn't happened to me. Thankfully, I decided regret is just a way to feel sorry for myself. Who knows what all those girlfriends, who lived such pristine lives, had been through? So I had to cool it. But it didn't stop me from making decisions without thinking things through."

"You've overcome a lot, Megan. Many girls in your position would not have made it. You did, and you did it well."

"I owe it to a lot of people—my parents, Rochelle, and people like you. You've had many regrets to deal with, Kayla. How do you do it?"

"When the Bible talks about forgetting what's behind and reaching forward to what lies ahead, it includes a lot of waiting—waiting on the Lord."

"That's the difference. I couldn't wait. I had to act immediately, or I would lose any chance of making things right."

"Waiting on the Lord is not being idle. It's not just waiting on God to do something. The scripture says people who wait on the Lord will mount up with wings of eagles. They will run and not be weary, and they will walk and not be faint. You will be a busy person if you're waiting on the Lord."

"I've never heard that before. I guess I thought Christians were people who wouldn't accept what was going on in the real world."

"I remember a debate held in our church between Jerry and an atheist, where they argued about evolution. This guy said Christians deny evolution because it's easier to maintain a state of conformity when you reject large bodies of information that are difficult to assimilate. Jerry responded that he never met an evolutionist willing to assimilate the large body of information contained in the Bible."

"I've been guilty of that. I guess I never knew a true Christian until I met you. Eliza is a Christian, but we've not discussed her religious conviction. It's a shame more Christians don't associate with people outside their churches, at least with people who aren't practicing Christians."

"More do than you might think. Jerry is a good example. He works with all comers, and he's a professor of apologetics, one of the deepest Christian thinkers I know. So now you know at least two."

CHAPTER 45

Since the weekly SAVE meetings moved to biweekly, the last two meetings saw reduced attendance, and the agenda focused primarily on the discussion of My Free Choice and its potential startup. An MFC scheduling conflict canceled the previous session.

A month between sessions seemed an eternity, and most attendees believed tonight's meeting would morph into MFC. Their missions were nearly identical, the chief difference being the mode of operation. SAVE had no employment component, and MFC focused on free choice regarding abortion. The long term goal was eliminating unplanned pregnancy, thereby preventing abortion, but means and methods are critical.

Some new family members wanted to abandon SAVE altogether. Others thought it best to modify the SAVE mission statement in a way that would allow the groups to merge. SAVE members favored automatically becoming MFC family members. Unlike SAVE, jobs would be available at MFC, and jobs offered hope. The startup pointed out a problem with SAVE—it provided no promise of independence.

Megan and her dad had discussed the conflict, and Megan favored the idea of consolidation. Her dad cautioned that any changes require legal documentation. Mission statements could be legally modified, but the exempt purpose must remain intact. Donations and grants were used only for SAVE's original mission intent. He advised moving slowly, with complete documentation prepared only after hearing adequate legal advice.

Once the meeting was called to order and announcements were made, Megan's dad welcomed new attendees. New family members were introduced, along with several who already have SAVE membership. Some confusion developed concerning how these SAVE members would hold membership in two organizations. They were told not to consider it a problem in any way. They should focus on the new organization and the training required for a new job to be assigned.

Jack Williams sat between Megan and Kayla. He was welcomed as a first-time attendee; Megan was glad he had come and decided he wanted to bring her up to date on the Ron Hicks thing. On the other hand, Jack didn't have to attend a SAVE meeting for that. He must feel guilty about Suzan Winders getting off and wants to see if Kayla is okay. He didn't have to come for that either. His curiosity may have directed him to investigate SAVE and MFC. He had mentioned attending a couple of times during their meetings in his office.

Megan addressed the issue of how the SAVE organization would move forward, given everything happening with the new group. "Dad's right," she said to the group assembled. "We've dealt with a lot of issues. We should proceed with caution and, as Dad pointed out, the benefit of good legal counsel. We have more to consider. The two boards will meet for further discussion. In the meantime, our new headquarters on Crump Boulevard will host future meetings of SAVE."

"That should do it," Kayla said quietly to Jack.

"How do you mean?"

"Members of the founding team are all here tonight, and they want to talk about My Free Choice. Moving our meetings to the new headquarters will sideline SAVE, and that may be a good thing." She raised her hand.

"Yes, Kayla."

"Would it be proper for Cindy and me to attend the joint board of directors meeting?"

"Dad, what do you think? Do you see any problem with that? No? No one sees a problem, Kayla. We would welcome you.

"For those of you who may not have heard," Megan continued, "Kayla Dean and Cindy Meyers have agreed to be joint operating managers of MFC. They will run the day-to-day activities of the foundation. We don't know what their titles will be—director, associate director, VP. We haven't made it official yet, but they will be family members. Your meeting with the joint boards will be of tremendous value. Thank you.

"Dad will continue tonight's meeting, pointing to some SAVE member victories and how we can use the benefits gained through SAVE to support the new startup. And let's not forget how the new organization can benefit the program at SAVE. We have an opportunity for a team effort to strengthen both groups. Dad, you have the floor."

Jack rose as Megan moved from the dais to take her seat. "I don't see how you do it, Megan." He placed his hand on the side of his cheek as if reviewing a to-do list.

"What do you mean?"

"You have an overloaded work schedule at St. Jude and many years of managing a nonprofit where you worked tirelessly against abortion. Now you're starting a new and autonomous nonprofit group, not to mention all that's been going on in your personal life—how do you do it?"

"The better question might be why. I don't mean why do I try to direct SAVE and now MFC, but why do I try to direct all the details?"

"Delegate." They said the word simultaneously and laughed.

"I guess that's a jinx; you owe me a Coke," Jack said.

"At least a high five," Megan said as they high-fived.

Megan's dad looked in their direction, with a pause and a smile. Megan curled her arms under her chin and subdued a laugh. She nudged against Jack's arm. Both straightened up with a stern look as if they were paying close attention, each suppressing a smile.

The meeting continued with the usual routine of revealing abortion-related events over the last several weeks. Eliza spoke briefly about progress in the training program, and the advantage of being able to draw from the ongoing activities of SAVE. As he often did, Megan's dad had attendees break into groups for informal discussion related to recent events at SAVE.

Kayla left the room to find Daniel and Kim, who were working in the children's section of the library. They decided it best for Kim to miss the meeting. She and her dad used the time to experience the library. Jack spoke with Jerry as they waited for Rochelle and Megan. They discussed possible opportunities created by Rochelle's work with potential donor companies. Jerry and Rochelle moved aside with Megan's dad to review the next steps needed for grant applications.

"Still involved with the details, I see," Jack said to Megan.

"You got it," Megan said. "Why don't I let someone else run things? I'm working on it. When I see a need, I move forward without much thinking. I believe things will differ with MFC. I'll have two managers, after all. It's going to be Kayla and Cindy at the mic going forward."

"Kayla is an incredible choice," Jack said. "I don't know much about Cindy, but she seems capable."

"They make a mean team," Megan said. "We're blessed to have them, and you should note, no one chose them. They both volunteered from the start."

"With the two of them at the helm, I guess you'll have some time to work on other things."

"Oh, no, don't go there, Jack, please. I suspected you came tonight to tell me about the Ron Hicks trial. My available time has nothing to do with it."

"I wasn't going in that direction, Megan. I thought you might have some time for me."

Megan was puzzled. *Why is tonight a good time for this? He's persistent—I'll give him that.*

"There's no time like the present," Jack said as if reading Megan's mind.

"Okay, Jack. We can spend some time together. How about dinner this weekend?"

"I'm in love with you, Megan."

Megan froze, then turned her head toward Jack. "That's impossible, Jack. You don't know what you're saying. We don't even know one another."

"I know you. I know who you are. It's who you've been all along."

"You're scaring me a little, Jack. You found out who I've been only three weeks ago."

"That's not true. That's not who you've been. That's something that happened to the person you are and have always been. You are a strong, intelligent, resourceful, fearless, warm, and loving woman. That's the person I fell in love with before I heard what you've had to deal with all your life. That doesn't change the love I have for you."

"You say that, and you may mean it, but it matters. I've tried it before, with other guys I've dated, and it matters. It mattered every time. You know I care for you, Jack. But you're speaking a language I have forgotten how to speak. I used to know, but I guess it's been so long, I've forgotten the syntax."

"You will get it back, Megan, because you're who you are. When I heard what happened that day in court, I grieved."

"It would make you think twice."

"No, that's not it. I grieved because I realized I didn't know what to do. I still don't know, but I sincerely want to learn. You can count on that."

"I can't talk right now, Jack. This is not the time or the place. I'll have dinner with you. I can't promise anything else." Megan remembered her dating experience. She spent a lifetime of equating romance with trauma, stigmatizing her response to intimacy on her date's part. Because of her unwillingness to relate one detail of her life, she could sense her date was expecting what would be considered a normal response. While her date was asking himself if this is the girl he wanted to develop a relationship with, or at least date again, she was asking herself if this guy might be a rapist. Being normal required her to bear an emotional load her date didn't carry.

"It's a start," Jack said. "I'd say, let's go tonight, but I guess it's already too late."

"Tonight won't work. Kayla is due back in a few minutes, and she, Cindy, and I will meet. I want to get with Eliza too."

"Will tomorrow night work for you?"

"Okay."

"Great, I'll be patient. We've waited for the time to be right. I hope you see now as the right time."

"We agreed to wait until after the trial. Now we have two trials behind us. Guess we could wait on the third."

"We can't do that. The DA says there's going to be a third, but it won't be anytime soon. We're lucky the court has denied bail; otherwise, this guy would be in the wind. I'm sorry for how all this has worked out. It's unfair."

"Don't worry, Jack. I don't understand why, but I've come to believe things happen for a reason. And I don't blame the police department. Things were different way back when. A lot of it was protocol, or standard operating procedure, or whatever you want to call it. The police department has a tough job to do, and I support their effort. You're a part of that department too, and I support what you do."

"Thanks for that, Megan. Sometimes the toughest part involves how things turn out. Concerning these two trials we've completed, neither of them turned out the way we wanted. I can't convince myself that justice was served."

"Kayla doesn't see it that way. You should talk with her. She is happy with the result. She believes both trials concluded the way God wanted them to."

"I can see why she believes that. Seeing it from her perspective, I guess I believe it too. But it's hard to accept. I'm looking across the room, and there's the man who killed her baby. And she's working with him."

"Incredible, isn't it? What you don't know is that she requested that he be allowed to work with her. Some people believe the system took advantage of Kayla by letting Mark Jones off the hook. The truth of it is, she's the one in control. She didn't connive or manipulate anything in any way. She waited and let it happen."

"And the Suzan Winders trial? She got off too, you know. The judge put Suzan on probation as she did with her brother. She had to pay a significant fine, but got no more than a hand slap."

"Who knows? Kayla may have seen that coming too. I know she didn't have much interest in seeing Suzan go to jail. Kayla sees Suzan as an incentive, not just for herself, but to keep me going too. And she's right. I have to keep my guard up as long as Suzan can thwart our mission. According to Kayla, that's all good."

CHAPTER 46

After a month of appropriating equipment and furniture, along with some light remodeling, window repair, and in-depth cleaning, MFC had its new headquarters on Crump Boulevard. The building proved to be an ideal setup for the operation of the foundation. Two small offices occupied the ground floor of the two-story building. A conference room upstairs was adequate for meetings with up to fifteen attendees. The main floor activities area was an open square featuring full-length windows on the front elevation. Eggshell walls and hardwood floors offered a professional setting.

Jack Williams was helpful in the move. Megan was surprised but grateful that Jack was adept at odd jobs needed before moving in. She learned he worked with homeless shelters and rescue missions, using his free time to haul donated materials and furnishings. He coordinated minor building repairs, including roofing, gutter and downspout cleaning, and light plumbing. He had every tool imaginable and devoted the use of his pickup to make things happen when necessary for their continued service.

Today's activities included a final Saturday meeting of the startup team before officially opening on Monday. They planned a last-minute review of everything needed for completion of the process. Cindy sent invitations to city leaders, the media, donors, and known volunteers, listing the official first generation adoptee families—thirteen families designated as founding family members.

Workstations, which included a laptop computer, an electrical outlet, a chair, and a wastebasket, were set up around seven large tables that filled half the space. Some half-height filing cabinets were in line along the wall behind the workstations. Large whiteboards, intended for flow chart design and visibility, circled the room.

Megan, her dad, Jerry, Eliza, Rochelle, and Cindy relaxed in the upstairs meeting room for an informal meeting. After resolving conflict in her anticipated fall schedule at Liberty, Kayla planned to arrive before noon. Cindy and Rochelle brought in drinks and snacks provided by Cindy's Fit the Pace Catering service, left yesterday in the upstairs kitchen.

"Dad, we began SAVE with the smallest team imaginable," Megan said, "just you and Mom and me. Rochelle, I don't mean to leave you out. You were there for us too."

"My role was minimal. I had a full schedule in those days. I remember thinking I should have done more," Rochelle said.

"You did plenty. Can you imagine if we had the team we have now? What were we thinking?"

"We weren't as smart as we are now. We didn't do as much thinking then," Megan's dad said.

"That's true. We have so much to be thankful for. What a dynamic team we have here. Thank you all so much."

"We also have an exceptional plan for success," Eliza said. "When I see all these whiteboards around the center and consider what's in store for us, it fills me with pride and excitement. We will begin next week with these new family members creating and building their process."

"I know what you mean, Eliza. We have an incredible opportunity."

"It makes me nervous," Cindy said. "I agree with you, Megan. It doesn't even seem possible."

CHAPTER 46

"Not to worry, Cindy," Megan said. "Eliza's going to be right there with you, as will Kayla. It's a learning process for everyone. I want to be involved in that process-of-creating-a-process too."

"I can see everyone playing a part in the new beginning," Jerry said.

Cindy placed both hands on her belly. "I'm glad everyone wants to be involved. I'm less than a month away, and I want to do as much as I can before I have to take off. Kevin is going to be a busy man for the next couple of months."

"We already know the process," said Eliza, "but it must be created over the next several weeks before we can know it and learn it. How exciting—I'm glad we have Manufacts. It allows us to define our process properly. The software is far above anything I've seen before."

"If we didn't have Manufacts," Megan said, "we would have something else."

"I'm not sure how the whole thing works, or whether it will give us everything we need," Cindy said.

"If it doesn't give us what we need, something else out there will," Megan said.

Jerry moved his hands below his chin, the fingers of each hand touching the other. "That's a biblical concept Megan."

"I sort of understand what you mean, Jerry, but I wouldn't have made the connection," Eliza said.

"You lost me," Megan said. Her dad was silent.

"It refers to fatalism," Rochelle said. "He's going back to Eliza's statement. While we know the process, we must create it before we can know it. God foresees everything, yet he offers us free will. It embodies the incompatibility of foreknowledge and free will. If God has foreknowledge, then all events happen by necessity, and we have no free will. We can't create something God has already foreknown."

"That's certainly not my belief," Eliza said. "We have free will. We may not always be free to act—the very basis for My Free Choice—but we are free to believe or not believe."

"I doubt anyone in this room favors fatalism," Jerry said. "On the other hand, can we change the future? Is it determined beforehand what our process is going to be, or are we free to make it whatever we want it to be?'

"We can make it whatever we want it to be," Eliza said.

"Eliza," Jerry asked, "do you believe God has foreknowledge of all future events?"

"I most certainly do."

"Do you believe God's foreknowledge of our process means our process is already determined?"

"Yes, I believe that too."

"Do you see incompatibility between God's foreknowledge and our free will?"

"No, I don't."

"How do you reconcile the incompatibility?

"You can address that seeming incompatibility better than I can, Jerry. My faith doesn't require reconciliation."

"Good answer, Eliza. You call it a seeming incompatibility. I like that," Jerry said. "Many thinking people have argued about those incompatibilities for centuries. Have you seen those arguments in the Jewish community, Rochelle?"

"It's a divisive issue," Rochelle said, "but it's a contradiction that didn't seem to bother the writers of the Bible, so those writers didn't make an issue of it. Like them, I've accepted it without resolving the conflict."

"You make a good point, Rochelle," Jerry said. "I wish more evangelicals would take that approach to their doctrinal disputes."

"Okay, so how does this affect our business process at MFC?" asked Cindy.

"Let me put on my professor's hat to answer that, Cindy."

Megan could recognize a setup when she saw one. "I've noticed that about you, Jerry. You never pass up a chance to teach."

"It's what professors do. Cindy, can you see how Eliza's saying we know the process but must create the process before we know it creates a contradiction in logic?

"I took her meaning in another way," Cindy said. "We know it, but we have to see it completed so we can know it in full and learn it in depth. Is that not correct?"

"Yes, you're correct, but that doesn't relieve the contradiction. Let's consider it in counterfactual terms. A counterfactual is a statement contrary to a fact. It takes the form of a statement beginning with the word *if*. For example—if the contract is signed, the road will be built. Eliza said she's glad we have Manufacts, software that allows us to define our process properly. In other words, if the software is available, we will have our process."

"Okay, so what? I believe that's a true statement," Cindy said.

"Now consider Megan's statement. 'If it doesn't give us what we need, something else out there will.' Is that a true statement?"

"Probably."

"Probably, but not definitely. You see, that's often the problem with counterfactuals. One may be true in the indicative sense. If John Wilkes Booth didn't kill Lincoln, someone else did. It's easy to see the truth of that statement. When you consider a more subjunctive mood, that statement changes. If John Wilkes Booth had not killed Lincoln, someone else would have. You might conclude that statement to be probably true, or possibly true, but not necessarily true."

"I see what you mean," Cindy said.

Jerry continued. "As we move forward with the foundation, many business decisions will require this type of thinking. The questions contained in our flow chart will require our answering no to any question asked in the subjunctive mood. The process cannot move forward, absent an absolute yes answer."

"That's good instruction, Jerry," Eliza said. "Please address how our free choice answers to flow chart questions lead to a foreknown process."

"Thanks, Eliza. The answer debunks the idea of fatalism." Jerry sensed that Rochelle agreed with his approach. He believed she could express how to resolve the seeming incompatibility of God's foreknowledge and personal free will. "Rochelle, can you summarize this in one or two statements that address our foreknown process which we haven't determined yet?"

"Yes, I can. With all we've said here, it makes for a simple resolution. We don't create the process because God foreknows it. He foreknows the process because we create it."

"Amen," Jerry said. "Fatalism says God has foreknown the future, and the future must happen the way God has foreknown it will happen, and free will does not exist. Cindy, you are wearing a red sweater today, and God foreknew you would wear that sweater, which means you were fated to wear that red one. You couldn't have chosen another one. The truth is you could have chosen to wear a yellow sweater, assuming you have a yellow one. Had you made that different choice, God would have foreknown a yellow sweater instead.

"This reasoning affects how we choose to run the foundation's business, with our process being a good example. We should determine to do the best job we can to create the best process we can, with a little help from God, in my view. There's no '*que sera sera*, whatever will be, will be,' to it. Our process will result from using our free will, making it entirely up to us."

CHAPTER 47

Kayla felt a sense of urgency. Should her studies at Liberty take a back seat to the foundation? *Being Kim's mom requires my physical presence.* The role she had accepted at MFC Foundation would involve Kim in a way unavailable in her apologetics curriculum. *I can't accept a second-rate effort at Liberty. God doesn't want that, but I believe he wants me to take on these responsibilities—I just don't know how he intends for me to manage them.* She prayed God would settle her heart and mind to lead, guide, and direct her choices.

She entered the MFC headquarters building and marveled at the quality of preparedness completed in the available timeframe. Volunteers helped to spruce up the exterior of the building and reconditioning of the adjacent parking lot Megan's dad negotiated for MFC's use. The building was older but benefited from the owner's foresight in providing regularly scheduled preventive maintenance.

Major furnishings donated by local sponsors were of high quality. Kayla rubbed her hand along the back of an upholstered sofa as she walked toward the tiny office set near a side entrance. Everything at MFC demonstrated the hand of God at work as a testimony to his faithfulness.

"Hey, girl," Megan said. "How did it go at Liberty this morning? Everything okay?"

"It's all coming together. My job is to make myself ready for whatever comes. How did everything go here this morning?"

"We began with a brief discussion of what I would call 'best practice' advice. Jerry introduced a different view of our future based on how we operate in the present. It was difficult to digest at first."

"Sometimes, these professors can be a little incorrigible, and Jerry's one of them, bless his heart. But he's usually on target and makes a good point. You can't imagine how much I've learned by listening to Jerry. I wouldn't trade it for the world."

"This morning, he taught us about fatalism, at least why no such thing is possible. I've never considered the ideas he presented—how the smallest activities in our daily lives are undetermined in advance. He presents ideas like an artist painting a portrait. He starts with an outline of what he will include in the finished portrait, then applies light brushstrokes using multiple layers until a face appears."

"Wow, Megan, you're a bit of an artist yourself. That's an accurate explanation of how Jerry works. He presents multiple sides of each topic and demonstrates why people believe what they believe, allowing those ideas to marinate. He wants his students to arrive at their beliefs through independent thinking. If you listen closely, it's hard to disagree with his conclusions."

"I know what you mean," Megan said. "A complex argument presented in clear and simple language is hard to refute. It works like Mark's software. I've been a little hesitant to accept the software's value, for obvious reasons. Still, I've seen how his system can break down the most complicated issue into simple digital components. It's yes or no, on or off."

"As Mark said, 'We could send a rocket to the moon.'"

"Well, first, you've got to have a rocket."

"That's our process," Kayla said. "Thankfully, it's not as complicated as a rocket, which means fewer people will be required to step through it. But it's going to take a lot of folks."

"The good side is we don't need scientists, especially not rocket scientists. We want thinking people dedicated to getting it done. We have a number of those good people."

"That's the beauty of it. Our priority is to convince our family members they can do it, with our help, of course. In the beginning, they will see it as rocket science."

"I'll bet most people will be surprised at how adept our family members are when given a real chance. Remember Rachel Owens, our Lady O? She is a first-generation family member, and she is as sharp as they come. I predict she will become a leader of the pack. We'll have to run fast to keep up with her."

"I was delighted to hear she was one of the first candidates Eliza interviewed. I'm excited when I consider what I can learn from her. Will her boyfriend be willing to help her?"

"I don't know. We've talked, but I don't know much about the boyfriend. We'll bring him in and see what happens."

"Jerry and I have spoken with some members of our church. They are willing to help and have volunteered to offer some extracurricular activities, along with classes, to help bring some of our people forward. Rachel's boyfriend would be a wanted candidate for recruitment in a program like that.

"Jerry told them MFC is not a religion-based nonprofit. Therefore, we can't bring in Bible study or religious activities."

"I'm glad he explained that and glad he recognizes it as well. Jerry could lead those activities in a nonreligious way, and his teaching would be invaluable, as long as classes meet somewhere outside the church."

"Jerry would welcome that, but don't forget, Jerry is Jerry, and whatever he teaches will be put in the vein of truth. He will teach not only what is correct, but also why it's necessary. It won't involve religion but may lead to class members wanting to know more."

"Family members exposed to Jerry's teaching can only be a good thing. That makes sense, and I'm glad to hear Jerry would take advantage of the opportunity. I might attend those classes myself. I'm learning more and more from these two Christian friends I'm lucky to have."

"I'll tell you, Megan, I've learned as much from you. I've spent a good part of this year in a war between feelings of contentment and doubt. You know how much I struggled with the pragmatics of being a Christian witness after some unimaginable sadness in my life. I know—everyone has her cross to bear, so why am I complaining?"

"I'm an admirer, Kayla. How you played the hand that life dealt you has helped me more than you can imagine."

"That's how God works. He brings people together, sometimes in convoluted ways, to inspire one another. The Bible says two are better than one. If either of them falls, one can help the other up, but pity anyone who falls and has no one to help her up."

"That's what I've experienced in the time we've worked on My Free Choice," Megan said. "Every member of the team has, at some point, had a positive influence. Rochelle has been a lifelong friend who stood by me through thick and thin. Eliza has prevented more stumbling blocks than I can count. Cindy's progress has been an inspiration. And Jerry continues to be an authority I can trust. I don't even need to mention my mom and dad. They are everything."

"Now, you can add Jack to that list. I can see where the two of you are headed."

"I never gave Jack a chance. I guess I couldn't convince myself he would take a different approach. He's the first person

I've been comfortable with, although sometimes he goes a little overboard."

"In what way?"

"He's unselfish to a fault."

"So?"

"Don't get me wrong. I love it, but I don't know how long it will last."

"How long do you think it should last? It sounds like you want that part of him to fade."

"It's complicated. How can a person like Jack, who deals with the dregs of society every day, be so positive? He's worked on dozens of cases of abuse, neglect, violence—many of them cases of rape—being exposed to the worst side of humanity. Yet when we're together, he sometimes comes across as naïve."

"He reminds me a little of Daniel. The day I met Daniel, I envisioned him as a rock star. From that day forward, he's been a man of love, joy, and peace. He maintains control of everything he does with patience, gentleness, and goodness, without a trace of pride. His faith in God and faithfulness to me makes me a stronger person. I call it the humility of understanding. He doesn't always agree with me, but he supports my decisions because he understands they're mine to make."

"That's it exactly, Kayla, the humility of understanding. Jack freely admits he doesn't know what I need from him, but he is willing to do whatever it takes to learn. He understands he doesn't know what to do and just does the best he can. That's humility. I don't want that to stop."

"Jack is not naïve, Megan. He's usually the smartest guy around, smart enough to love you for who you are, without any pretense. He's an attorney who works for the DA. He knows some of our family members at MFC who've been through the legal system. As you've said, he's known plenty of women who've gone through disastrous experiences after becoming pregnant from being raped. He knows as much about our family as we do, maybe more. Yet he's outside clearing the parking lot while we're inside making decisions that affect those people's lives."

"Oh my, he's outside because I haven't asked him to come inside."

"He's trying to do the best he can."

"Poor Jack. The way you put it, I'm not sure I'm good enough for him."

"Jack's asking the same thing about you because he sees you for who you are. Think of it, Megan. You've had this terrifying rape that happened in your teens, which led to pregnancy. You struggled with the choice you made for abortion and the guilt associated with losing a child and being afraid of people finding out. Now you're a woman with a past of saving lives, of helping children deal with deadly diseases. You're on the way to saving countless others. You've faced the animal who raped you, and the nightmare of people knowing your innermost secrets. Now you have the victory of being loved for who you are."

"God did that," Megan said.